HOME SCENES

AND

HEART STUDIES.

BY

GRACE AGUILAR,

AUTHOR OF "THE WOMEN OF ISRAEL," "DAYS OF BRUCE," "THE MOTHER'S RECOMPENSE," "WOMAN'S FRIENDSHIP," "VALE OF CEDARS," ETC. ETC.

NEW-YORK:
D. APPLETON AND COMPANY,
200 BROADWAY.
MDCCCLIII.

PREFACE.

Having so recently published The Days of Bruce, I feel called upon to offer some explanation of my reasons for thus rapidly intruding another volume of the writings of Grace Aguilar upon the notice of the public.

"It is the last;" and if an apology be needed, the desire which I feel to see in a collected form the works of my beloved child must prove my excuse.

The principal story in this volume, "The Perez Family," was written and published so far back as the year 1843, but, from circumstances attending its publication, is comparatively unknown. Two other stories, "The Edict" and "The Escape," have also formed the subjects of a small volume.

As contributions to "The Book of Beauty," "The Keepsake," and "Friendship's Offering," while relatively under the editorship of the Countess of Blessington and Mr. Leitch Ritchie, many of the shorter pieces will be recognised, and some others owe their introduction to the literary world to Mrs. Newton Crosland

(Camilla Toulmin); to these kind and considerate friends my daughter had opportunities during life of expressing her grateful thanks.

The Works of Grace Aguilar are now before the public—the present volume being the conclusion of a series in which the delineation of the Character of Woman has been the chief design. The wishes of the author of "The Women of Israel" will be fulfilled, should the unceasing labours of a life, too early closed, awaken sentiments of pure affection, and illustrate by example the delights of Home.

SARAH AGUILAR.

October, 1852.

CONTENTS.

HOME SCENES AND HEART STUDIES.

The Perez Family.

CHAPTER I.

Leading out of one of those close, melancholy alleys in the environs of Liverpool was a small cottage, possessing little of comfort or beauty in outward appearance, but much in the interior in favour of its inhabitants; cleanliness and neatness were clearly visible, greatly in contradistinction to the neighbouring dwellings. There were no heaps of dirt and half-burnt ashes, no broken or even cracked panes in the brightly shining windows, not a grain of unseemly dust or stains either on door or ledge,—so that even poverty itself looked respectable. The cottage stood apart from the others, with a good piece of ground for a garden, which, stretching from the back, led through a narrow lane, to the banks of the Mersey, and thus permitted a fresher current of air. The garden was carefully and prettily laid out, and planted with the sweetest flowers; the small parlour and kitchen of the cottage opened into it, and so, greatly to the disappointment and vexation of the gossips of the alley, nothing could be gleaned of the sayings and doings of its inmates. Within the cottage the same refinement was visible; the furniture, though old and poor, was always clean and neatly arranged. The *Mezzuzot* (Deut. vi. 9, 20) were carefully secured to every door-post, and altogether there was an indescribable something pervading the dwelling, that in the very midst of present poverty seemed to tell of former and more prosperous days.

Simeon and Rachel Perez had married with every prospect of getting on well in the world. Neither were very young; for though they had been many years truly devoted to each other, they were prudent, and had waited till mutual industry had removed many of the difficulties and obstacles to their union. All which might have been irksome was persevered in through the strength of this honest, unchanging affection; and when the goal was gained, and they were married, all the period of their mutual labour seemed but as a watch in the night, compared to the happiness they then enjoyed.

Simeon had been for several years foreman to a watchmaker, and was remarkably skilful in the business. Rachel had been principal assistant to a mantua-maker, and all her leisure hours were employed in plaiting straw and various fancy works, which greatly increased her little store. Never forgetting the end they had in view, their mutual savings had so accumulated, that on their marriage, Perez was enabled to set up a small shop, which, conducted with honesty and economy, soon flourished, and every year brought in something to lay aside, besides amply providing for their fast-increasing family.

The precepts of their God were obeyed by this worthy couple, not only in word but in deed. They proved their love for their heavenly Father, not only in their social and domestic conduct, but in such acts of charity and kindness, that many wondered how they could do so much for others without wronging their own. Perez and his wife were, however, if possible, yet more industrious and economical after their marriage than before, and many a time preferred to sacrifice a personal indulgence for the purer pleasure of doing good to others; and never did they do so without feeling that God blessed them in the deed.

A painful event calling Perez to London was the first alloy to their happiness. A younger sister of his wife, less prudent because, perhaps, possessed of somewhat more personal attraction, had won the attentions of a young man who had come down to Liverpool, he said, for a week's pleasure. No one knew any thing about Isaac Levison. As a companion, Perez himself owned he was very entertaining, but that was not quite sufficient to make him a good husband. Assurances that he was well able to support a wife and family, with Perez and Rachel (they were not then married), went for nothing; they wanted proofs, and these he either could not or would not bring; but in vain they remonstrated. Leah had never liked their authority or good example, and in this point determined to have her own way.

They were married, and left Liverpool to reside in London, and Leah's communications were too few and far between to betray much concerning their circumstances. At length came a letter, stating that Leah was a mother, but telling also that poverty and privation had stolen upon them. Their substance in a few troubled years had made itself wings, and flown away when most needed; and Leah now applied for assistance to those very friends whose kindness and virtue she had so often treated with contempt. The fact was, Levison had embarked all his little capital (collected no one knew how) in an establishment dashing in appearance, but wanting the basis of honesty and religion. After seeming to flourish for a few years, it, of course, failed at last, exposing its proprietors to deserved odium and distrust, and their families to irretrievable distress.

For seven years Perez and his wife almost supported Leah and her child (secretly indeed, for no one in Liverpool imagined they had need to do so). Leah was still too dear, for the faults and follies of her husband, and perhaps her own imprudences, to form any subject of conversation with her relatives.

At length Leah wrote that she was ill, very ill. She thought the hand of death was on her; and she feared it for her child, her darling Sarah, whom she had striven to preserve pure amidst the scenes of misery and sin which she now confessed but too often neared her dwelling. What would become of her? Who would protect her? How dared she appeal to the God of the orphan, when her earthly father yet lived, seeming to forget there was a God? Perez and his wife perused that sad letter together; but ere it was completed, Rachel had sunk in bitter tears upon his bosom, seeking to speak the boon which was in her heart; but, though it found no words, Perez answered—

"You are right, dear wife; one more will make little difference in our household. Providence blessed us with four children, and has been pleased to deprive us of one. Sarah shall take her place: and in snatching her from the infection of vice and shame, may we not ask and hope a blessing? Do not weep then, my Rachel; Leah may not be so ill as she thinks. I will go and bring her and her child; and there may be happy days in store for them yet."

Perez departed that same night by the mail to London; but prompt as he was, poor Leah's sufferings were terminated before his arrival. Her death, though in itself a painful shock, was less a subject of misery and depression, to a mind almost rigid in its notions of integrity and honour as that of Perez, than the fearful state of wretchedness and shame into which Isaac Levison had fallen. Perez soon perceived that all hope of effecting a reformation was absolute folly. His poor child had been so repeatedly prevented attending school, by his intemperate or violent conduct, that she was at length excluded. Levison could give no good reason for depriving his little girl of these advantages, except that he hated the elders who were in office; that he did not see why some should be rich and some should be poor, and why the former should lord it over the latter. He was as good as they were any day, and his daughter should not be browbeaten or governed by any one, however she might call herself a lady. To reason with folly Perez felt was foolishness, and so he contented himself with entreating Levison to permit his taking the little Sarah, at least for a time, into his family. Levison imagined Perez was the same rank as himself, and, therefore, that his pride could not be injured by his consenting. Equal in *birth* perhaps they were, but as far removed in their present ranks as vice from virtue, dishonesty from truth.

Perez, however, glad and grateful for having gained his point, made no comment on the many muttered remarks of his brother-in-law, as to his *conferring*, not *receiving* an obligation, by giving his child to the care of her aunt, but hastened home, longing to offer the best comfort to his wife's sorrow by placing the rescued Sarah in her arms. And it was a comfort, for gradually Rachel traced a hand of love even in this affliction; the loss of her mother under such circumstances, proving perhaps, in the end, a blessing to the child, if her father would but leave her with them. She feared that he would not at first; but Perez smiled at the fear as foolishness, and it gradually dwindled away; for years passed, and the little Sarah grew from childhood into womanhood, still an inmate of her uncle's family, almost forgetting she had any father but himself.

But it is not to the unrighteous or the irreligious only that misfortunes come. Nay, *they* may flourish for a time, and give no evidence that there is a just and merciful God, who ruleth. But even those who have loved and served Him through long years of probity and justice, and who, according to frail human perceptions, would look for nothing but favour at His hand, are yet afflicted with many sorrows; and our feeble and insufficient wisdom would complain that such things are. If this world were all, then indeed we might murmur and rebel; but our God himself has assured us, "There will come a day when He will discern between the righteous and the wicked, between those who serve God and those who serve Him not." And it is our part to wait patiently for that day, and that better world where that word will be fulfilled.

Perez had now five children. Reuben, his eldest son, was full five years older than the rest, a circumstance of rejoicing to Perez, as he hoped his son would supply his place to his family, should he be called away before the threescore and ten years allotted as the age of man.

To do all he could towards obtaining this end, Perez early associated his son with him in his own business of watchmaking; but too soon, unhappily, the parents discovered that a heavy grief awaited them, from him to whom they had most fondly looked for joy. They had indeed striven and prayed to train up their child in the way he should go, but it seemed as if his after years would not confirm the sage monarch's concluding words. Wild, thoughtless, and headstrong, Reuben, after a very brief trial, determined that his father's business was not according to his taste, and he could not follow it. His father's authority indeed kept him steady for a few years, but it was continued rebellion and reproof; and often and often the father's hard-earned savings were sacrificed for the wild freaks and extravagance of the son. Perez trembled lest the other members of his family, equally dear, should suffer eventual loss; but there is something in the hearts of Jewish parents towards an eldest son, which calls imperatively for indulgence towards, and concealment of his failings. Again and again Perez expended sums much larger than he could conveniently afford, in endeavouring to fix his son in business according to his inclinations; but no sooner was he apparently settled and comfortable, and his really excellent abilities fairly drawn forth, than, by negligence or inattention, or some graver misdemeanour, he disgusted his employers, and, after a little longer trial, was returned on his father's hands.

Deeply and bitterly his parents grieved, using every affectionate argument to convince him of the evil of his ways, and bring him back again to the paths of joy. They did not desist, however their efforts and prayers seemed alike unanswered; they did not fail in faith, though often it was trembling and faint within them. One hope they had; Reuben was not hardened. Often he would repent in tears and agony of spirit, and deplore his own ill fate, that he was destined to bring misery to parents he so dearly loved. But he refused to believe that it only needed energy to rouse himself from his folly, for as yet it was scarcely more. He said he could not help himself, could not effect any change, and therefore made no effort to do so. But that which grieved his parents far more than all else, was his total indifference to the religion of his forefathers. His ears, even as his heart and mind, were closed to those divine truths his parents had so carefully inculcated. He knew his duty too well to betray infidelity and indifference in their presence, but they loved him too well to be blind to their existence.

"What is it to be a Jew," they heard him once say to a companion, "but to be cut off from every honourable and manly employment? To be bound, fettered to an obsolete belief, which does but cramp our energies, and bind us to detestable trade. No wonder we are looked upon with contempt, believed to be bowed, crushed to the very earth, as void of all spirit or energy, only because we have no opportunity of showing them."

Little did he know the bitter tears these words wrung from his poor mother, that no sleep visited his father's eyes that night. Was this an answer to their anxious prayer? Yet they trusted still.

Anxiety and grief did not prevent Perez attending to his business; but either from the many drains upon his little capital, or that trade was just at that time in a very low state, his prosperity had begun visibly to decrease. And not long afterwards a misfortune occurred productive of much more painful affliction than even the loss of property which it so seriously involved. A dreadful fire broke out in the neighbourhood, gaining such an alarming height ere it was discovered, that assistance was almost useless. Amongst the greatest sufferers were Perez and his family. Their happy home was entirely consumed, and all the little valuables it had contained completely destroyed. Perez gazed on ruin. For one brief moment he stood as thunderstricken, but then a terrible shriek aroused him. He looked around. He thought he had seen all whom he loved in safety, but at one glance he saw his little Ruth was not there. His wife had caught a glimpse of the child in a part of the building which the flames had not yet reached, and with that wild shriek had flown to save her. He saw her as she made her way through falling rafters and blazing walls; he made a rush forward to join and rescue, or die with her; but his children clung round him in speechless terror; his friends and neighbours seconded them, and before he could effectually break from them, a loud congratulatory shout proclaimed that the daring mother had reached her child. A dozen ladders were hurried forward, their bearers all eager to be the first to plant the means of effectual escape; and clasping her Ruth closely to her breast, regardless of her increasing weight (for terror had rendered the poor child utterly powerless), the mother's step was on the ladder, and a hush fell upon the assembled hundreds. There was no sound save the roar of the devouring element and the play of the engines. The flames were just nearing the beam on which the ladder leaned, but hope was strong that Rachel would reach the ground ere this frail support gave way; and numbers pressed round, regardless of the suffocating smoke and heat, in the vain hope of speeding her descent.

Perez had ceased his struggles the moment his wife appeared. With clasped hands, and cheeks and lips so blanched, as even in that lurid light to startle by their ghastliness, he remained, his eyes starting from their sockets in their intense and agonized gaze. He saw only his wife and child; but his children, with horror which froze their very blood, could look only on the fast-approaching flames. A wild cry of terror was bursting from young Joseph, Ruth's twin brother, but Sarah, with instinctive feeling, dreading lest that cry should reach his mother's ears, and awaken her to her danger, caught him in her arms, and soothed him into silence.

Carefully and slowly Rachel descended. She gave no look around her. No one knew if she were conscious of her danger, which was becoming more and more imminent. Then came a smothered groan from all, all save the husband and the father. The flame had reached the beam,—it cracked—caught—the top of the ladder was wreathed with smoke and fire. Was there faltering in her step, or did the frail support totter beneath her weight? The half was past, but one-third to the ground remained; fiercer and fiercer the flames roared and rose above her, but yet there was hope. It failed, the beam gave way, the ladder fell, and Rachel and her child were precipitated to the ground. A heavy groan mingled with the wild shriek of horror which burst around. Perez rushed like a maniac forward; but louder, shriller above it all a cry resounded, "Mother! mother! oh God, my mother! why was not I beside you, to save Ruth in your stead? Mother, speak; oh, speak to me again!" And the father and son, each unconscious of the other's presence, met beside what seemed the lifeless body of one to both so dear.

But Rachel was not dead, though fearfully injured; and it was in the long serious illness that followed, Reuben proved that, despite his many faults and follies, affection was not all extinguished; love for his mother remained in its full force, and in his devotion to her, his almost woman's tenderness, not only towards her but towards his little sister Ruth, whose eyes had been so injured by the heat and smoke as to occasion total blindness, he demonstrated qualities only too likely so to gain a woman's heart, as to shut her eyes to all other points of his character save them.

A subscription had indeed been made for the sufferers by the fire, but they were so numerous, that the portion of individuals was of course but small; and even this Perez's honest nature shrunk in suffering from accepting. Religious and energetic as he was, determined not to evince by word or sign how completely his spirit was crushed, and thus give the prejudiced of other faiths room to say, "the Jew has no resource, no comfort," he yet felt that he himself would never be enabled to hold up his head again; felt it at the very moment friends and neighbours were congratulating him on the equanimity, the cheerfulness with which he met and bore up against affliction.

Yet even now, when the skeptic and unbeliever would have said, surely the God he so faithfully served had deserted him, Perez felt he was not deserted,—that he had not laboured honestly and religiously so long in vain. The wild and wayward conduct of the son could not, in candid and liberal minds, tarnish the character of the father; and thus he was enabled easily and pleasantly to obtain advantageous situations for his two elder children.

The dwelling to which we originally introduced our reader was then to let; and from its miserably dilapidated condition (for when Perez first saw it, it was not as we described), at a remarkably low rent. An influential friend made it habitable, and thither, some three months after the fire, the family removed.

And where was Sarah Levison, in the midst of these changes and afflictions? In their heavy trial, did Rachel and Perez never regret they had made her as their own? nor permit the murmuring thought to enter, that, as the girl had a father, they had surely no need to support an additional burden? To such questions we think our readers will scarcely need an answer. As their own daughter Leah, they loved and cherished their niece, whose affection and gratitude towards them was yet stronger and more devoted than that of their own child, affectionate as she was. Leah had never known other than kind, untiring parents; never, even in dreams, imagined the misery in which her cousin's early years had passed. To Sarah, life had been a strange dark stream of grief and wrath, until she became an inmate of her uncle's house. Though only just seventeen when these heavy sorrows took place, her peculiarly quiet and reflective character and strong affections endowed her with the experience of more advanced age. She not only felt, but acted. Entering into the feelings alike of her uncle and aunt, she unconsciously soothed and strengthened both. She taught Leah's young, and, from its high and joyous temperament, somewhat rebellious spirit, submission and self-control. She strengthened in the young Simeon the ardent desire to work, and not only assist his father now, but to raise him again to his former station in life. She found time to impart to the little Joseph such instruction as she thought might aid in gaining him employment. Untiringly, caressingly, she nursed both her aunt and the poor little patient sufferer Ruth, telling such sweet tales of heaven, and its beautiful angels, and earth, and its pleasant places, and kind deeds, that the child would forget her sorrow as she listened, and fancy the sweet music of that gentle voice had never seemed so sweet before; and while it spoke, she could not forget to wish to look once more on the flowers, and trees, and sky. And Reuben, what was his cousin Sarah not to him in these months of remorseful agony, when he felt as if he could never more displease or grieve his parents; when again and again he cursed himself as the real cause of his father's ruin; for had not such large sums been wasted upon him, there might have been still capital enough to have set him afloat again. For several days and nights Sarah and Reuben had been joint watchers beside the beds of suffering; and the gentle voice of the former consoled, even while to the divine comfort and hope which she proffered, Reuben felt his heart was closed. He bade her speak on; he seemed, in those still, silent hours, to feel that, without her gentle influence, his very senses must have wandered; and that heart must have been colder and harsher than Sarah's, which could have done other than believe she was not indifferent to him. Sarah did not think of many little proofs of affection at the time; she was only conscious that, at the very period heavy affliction had entered her uncle's family, a new feeling, a new energy had awakened within her heart, and she was happy—oh, so happy!

It was to Sarah's exertions their new dwelling owed the comfort, cleanliness, and almost luxury of its interior arrangements; her example inspired Leah to throw aside the proud disdain with which she at first regarded their new home—to conquer the rebellious feeling which prompted her to entreat her father to apprentice her anywhere, so she need not live so differently at home; and not only to conquer that sinful pride, but use her every energy to rouse her natural spirits, and make her parents forget how their lot was changed: and the girl did so; for, in spite of youthful follies, there was good solid sense and warm feelings on which to work.

Sarah and Leah, then, worked in the interior, and Perez and Simeon improved the exterior of the house, so that when the little family assembled, there was comfort and peace around them, and thus their song of praise and thanksgiving mingled with and hallowed the customary prayer, with which the son of Israel ever sanctifies his newly-appointed dwelling.

Rachel could no longer work as she had done; her right arm had been so severely injured as to be nearly useless; but Sarah supplied her place so actively, so happily, that Rachel felt she had no right to murmur at her own uselessness: the poor motherless girl she had taken to her heart and home, returned tenfold all that had been bestowed. She could have entered into more than one lucrative situation, but she would not hear of leaving that home which she knew needed her presence and her services; and this was not the mere impulse of the moment: week after week, month after month, found her active, affectionate, persevering, as at first.

The most painful circumstance in their present dwelling was its low neighbourhood; and partially to remedy this evil, Sarah prevailed on her uncle to employ his leisure in cultivating the little garden behind the house, making their sitting-room and kitchen open into it, and contriving an entrance through them, so as scarcely to use the front, except for ingress and egress which necessity compelled. This arrangement was productive of a twofold good; it prevented all gossiping intercourse, which their neighbours had done all they could to introduce, and gave Perez an occupation which interested him, although he might never have thought of it himself. Both local and national disadvantages often unite to debar the Jews from agriculture, and therefore it is a branch in which they are seldom, if ever, employed. Their scattered state among the nations, the occupations which misery and persecution compel them to adopt, are alone to blame for those peculiar characteristics which cause them to herd in the most miserable alleys of crowded cities, rather than the pure air and cheaper living of the country. Perez found pleasure and a degree of health in his new employment: the delight which it was to his poor little blind Ruth to sit by his side while he worked, and inhale the reviving scent of the newly-turned earth or budding flowers, would of itself have inspired him, but his wife too shared the enjoyment. It was a pleasure to her to take the twins by her side, and teach them their God was a God of love, alike through his inspired Word, and through his works; and Joseph and Ruth learned to love their new house better than their last, because it had a garden and flowers, and they learned from that much more than they had ever learned before.

For nine months all was cheerfulness and joy in that lowly dwelling. The heavy sorrow and disquiet had partially subsided. Reuben was more often at home, and seemed more steadily and honourably employed. Twice in six months he had poured his earnings in his mother's lap; and while he lingered caressingly by her side, how might she doubt or fear for him? though when absent, his non-attendance at the synagogue, his too evident indifference to his faith, his visible impatience at all its enjoinments, caused many an anxious hour. Simeon and Leah gave satisfaction to their employers, and Sarah earned sufficient to make her aunt's compelled idleness of little consequence. Perez himself had been gladly received by his former master, as his principal journeyman, at excellent wages; and could he have felt less painfully the bitter change in his lot, all might have been well. Pride, however, was unhappily his heirloom, as well as that of Levison. With

Perez it had always acted as a good spirit—with Levison as a bad; inciting the former to all honourable deeds and thoughts, and acting as religion's best agent in guarding him from wrong. Now, however, it was to enact a different part. In vain his solid good sense argued misfortune was no shame, and that he was as high, in a moral point of view, as he had ever been. Equally vain was the milder, more consoling voice of religion, in assuring him a Father's hand had sent the affliction, and therefore it was love; that he failed in submission if he could not bear up against it. In vain conscience told him, while she was at rest and glad, all outward things should be the same; that while his wife and children had been so mercifully preserved, thankfulness, not grief, should be his portion. Pride, that dark failing which will cling to Judaism, bore all other argument away, and crushed him. Had he complained, or given way to temper, his health perhaps would not have been injured; but he was silent on his own griefs, even to his wife, for he knew their encouragement was wrong. There was no outward change in his appearance or physical power, and had he not been attacked by a cold and fever, occasioned by a very inclement winter, the wreck of his constitution might never have been discovered. But trifling as his ailments at first appeared, it was but too soon evident that he had no strength to rally from them. Gradually, yet surely, he sunk, and with a grief which, demonstrating itself in each according to their different characters, was equally violent in all, his afflicted family felt they dared not hope; the husband and the father was passing to his home above, and they would soon indeed be desolate.

It was verging towards the early spring, when one evening Perez lay on his lowly pallet, surrounded by his family; his hand was clasped in that of his wife, whose eyes were fixed on him with a look of such deep love, it was scarcely possible to gaze on her without tears; the other rested lightly on the beautiful curls of his little Ruth, who, resting on a wooden stool close beside his bed, sometimes lifted up her sightless orbs, as if, in listening to the dear, though now, alas! but too faint voice, she could see his beloved face once more. One alone was absent—one for whom the father yearned as the patriarch Jacob for his Joseph. Reuben had been sent by his employer to Manchester, and though it was more than time for him to return, and tidings of his father's illness had been faithfully transmitted, he was still away. No one spoke of him, yet he was thought of by all; so little had his conduct alienated the affections of his family, that not one would utter aloud the wish for his presence, lest it should seem reproach; but the eyes of his mother, when they could turn from her husband, ever sought the door; and once, as an eager step seemed to approach, she had risen hastily and descended breathlessly, but it passed on, and she returned to her husband's pallet with large tears stealing down her cheeks.

"Rachel, my own dear wife, do not weep thus; he will come yet," whispered Perez, clasping her hands in both his; "and if he do not, oh, may God bless him still! Tell him there was no thought of anger or reproach within me. My firstborn, first beloved, beloved through all—for wayward, indifferent as he is, he is still my son—perhaps if he tarry till too late, remorse may work upon him for good, may awaken him to better thoughts; and if our God in His mercy detain him for this, we must not grieve that he is absent."

For a moment he paused; then he added, mournfully, "I had hoped he would have supplied my place—would have been to you, my Rachel, to his brothers and sisters, all that a first-born should; but it may not be. God's will be done!"

"Oh, no, no; do not say it may not be, dear uncle! Think how young he is! Is there not hope still?" interposed Sarah, so earnestly, that the colour rose to her cheeks. "He will be here, I know he will, or the letter has not reached him. You cannot doubt his love; and whilst there is love, is there not, must there not be hope?"

The dying man looked on her with a faint, sad smile: "I do not doubt his love, my child; but oh, if he love not his God, his love for a mortal will not keep him from the evil path. His youth is but a vain plea, my Sarah; if he see not his duty as a son and brother in Israel now, when may we hope he will? but you are right in bidding me not despond. He is my heaviest care in death; but my God can lighten even that."

"Death," sobbed Leah, suddenly flinging herself on her knees beside the bed, and covering her father's hand with tears and kisses, "death! Father, dear, dear father, do not say that dreadful word! You will live, you must live—God will not take you from us!"

"My child, call not death a dreadful word; it is only such to the evil-doers, to the proud and wicked men, of whom David tells us, 'They shall not stand in the judgment, nor enter the congregation of the righteous, but shall be as chaff, which the wind driveth away.' For them death is fearful, for it is an end of all things; but not to me is it thus, my beloved ones. I have sought to love and serve my God in health and life, and His deep love and fathomless mercy is guiding me now, holding me up here through the dark shadows of death. His compassion is upon my soul, whispering my sins are all forgiven; that He has called me unto Him in love, and not in wrath. There was a time I feared and trembled at the bare dream of death; but now, oh, it seems but as the herald of joy, of bliss which will never, never change. My children, think that I go to God, and do not grieve for me."

"If not for you, my father, chide us not that we weep for ourselves," answered Simeon, struggling with the rising sob; "what have you not been to all of us? and how may we bear to feel that to us you are lost for ever; that the voice whose accents of love never failed to thrill our hearts with joy, and when in reproach ever brought the most obdurate in repentant sorrow to your feet, that dear, dear voice we may never—" he could not go on, for his own voice was choked.

"My boy, we shall all meet again; follow on in that path of good in which I have humbly sought to lead you; forget not your God, and the duties of your faith; obey those commands and behests which to Israel are enjoined; never forget that, as children of Israel, ye are the firstborn and beloved of the Lord; serve Him, trust in Him, wait for Him, and oh, believe the words of the dying! We shall meet again never more to part. I do but go before you, my beloved ones, and you will come to me; there are many homes in heaven where the loved of the Lord shall meet."

"And I and Ruth—father, dear father, how may we so love the Lord, as to be so loved by him?" tearfully inquired the young Joseph, drawing back the curtain at the head of the bed, which had before concealed him, for he did not like his father to see his tears. "Does He look upon us with the same love as upon you, who have served him so faithfully and well? Oh, what would I not do, that I may look upon death as you do, and feel that I may come to you in heaven, written amongst those He loves."

"And our God does love you, my little Joseph, child as you are, or you would not think and wish this; my works are not more in His sight than yours. Miserable indeed should

I now be, if I had trusted in them alone for my salvation and comfort now. No, my sweet boy, you must not look to deeds alone; study the word of your God to know and love Him, and then will you obey His commandments and statutes with rejoicing, and glory that He has given you tests by which you may prove the love you bear Him: and in death, though the imperfection and insufficiency of your best deeds be then revealed, you will feel and know you have not loved your God in vain. His infinite mercy will purify and pardon."

His voice sunk from exhaustion; and Rachel, bending over him to wipe the moisture from his brow, tenderly entreated him not to speak any more then, despite the comfort of his simplest word.

"It will not hurt me, love," he answered, fondly, after a pause. "I bless God that He permits me thus to speak, before I pass from earth for ever. When we meet again, there will be no need for me to bid my children to know and love the Lord; for we shall all know Him, from the smallest to the greatest of us. But to you, my own faithful wife, oh, what shall I say to you in this sad moment? I can but give you to His care, the God of the widow and the fatherless, and feel and know He will not leave you nor forsake you, but bless you with exceeding blessing. And in that heavy care—which, alas! I must leave you to bear alone—care for our precious Reuben, oh, my beloved wife, remember those treasured words, which were our mutual strength and comfort, when we laboured in our youth. How well do I remember that blessed evening, when we first spoke our love, and in our momentary despondence that long years must pass ere we could hope for our union, we opened the hallowed word of God, and could only see this verse: 'Commit thy ways unto the Lord, trust also in him and he will bring it to pass.' And did He not bring it to pass, dear wife? Did He not bless our efforts, and oh, will He not still? Yes, trust in Him; commit our Reuben unto Him, and all shall yet be well!"

"Yes, yes, I know it will; but oh, my husband, pray for me, that I may realize this blessed trust when you are gone. You have been my support, my aid, till now, cheering my despondence, soothing my fears; and now—"

"Rachel, my own wife, I have not been to you more than you have to me; it is our God who has been to us more—oh, how much more!—than we have been to each other, and He is with you still. He will heal the wound His love inflicts.

But for our erring, yet our much-loved boy, I need not bid you love him, forgive him to the end—and his brothers and sisters. Oh, listen to me, my children." He half raised himself in the energy of his supplication. "Promise me but this, throw him not off from your love, your kindness, however he may turn aside, however he may fall; even if that fearful indifference increase, and in faith he scarcely seems your brother, my children, my blessed children, oh, love him still. Seek by kindness and affection to bring him back to his deserted fold. Promise me to love him, to bear with him; forget not that he is your brother, even to the last. Many a wanderer would return if love welcomed him back, many a one who will not bear reproach. Do not cast him from your hearts, my children, for your dead father's sake."

"Father, father, can you doubt us?" burst at once from all, and rising from their varied postures, they joined hands around him. "Love him! yes. However he may forget and desert us, he is still our brother and your son. We will love him, bear with him. Oh, do not fear us, father. There needed not this promise, but we will give it. We will never cease to love him."

"Bless you, my children," murmured the exhausted man, as he sunk back. "Sarah, you have not spoken. Are you not our child?"

She flung down her work and darted to his side. She struggled to speak, but no words came, and throwing her arms round his neck, she fixed on his face one long, piercing look, and burst into passionate tears.

"It is enough, my child. I need not bid you love him," whispered Perez, so as to be heard only by her. "Would you were indeed our own; there would be less grief in store."

"And am I not your own?" she answered, disregarding his last words, which seemed, however, to have restored her to calmness. "Have you not been to me a true and tender father, and my aunt as kind a mother? Whose am I if I am not yours? Where shall I find another such home?"

"Yet you have a father, my gentle girl; one whom I have lately feared would claim you, because they told me he was once more a wealthy man. And if he should, if he would offer you the rest and comfort of competence, why should you labour throughout your young years for us? If he be rich, he surely will not forget he has a child, and therefore claim you."

"He has done so," replied Sarah, calmly, regardless of the various intonations of surprise in which her words were repeated. "My father did write for me to join him. He told me he was rich; would make me cease entirely from labour, and many similar kind offers."

"And you refused them! Sarah, my dear child, why have you done this?"

"Why," she repeated, pressing the trembling hand her aunt held out to her between both hers; "why, because now, only now, can I even in part return all you have done for me; because I cannot live apart from all whom I so love. I cannot exchange for short-lived riches all that makes life dear. Had my father sent for me in sickness or in woe, I should fly to him without an hour's pause. But it is he who is in affluence, in peace; and you, my best, kindest friends, in sorrow. No, no; my duty was to stay with you, to work for you, to love you; and I wrote to beseech his permission to remain, even if it were still to labour. I did not feel it labour when with you; and I have permission. I am still your child; he will not take me from you."

"God's blessing be upon him!" murmured Rachel, as she folded the weeping girl to her bosom.

A pause of deep emotion fell upon the group. Perez drew her faintly to him, and kissed her cheek; then saying he felt exhausted, and should wish to be left alone a brief while, Sarah led the twins away, and, followed by Leah, softly left the apartment. Simeon and his mother still remained beside his couch.

The night passed quietly. Sarah put the twins to bed, and persuaded Leah to follow their example, and, exhausted by sorrow, she was soon asleep, leaving Sarah to watch and pray alone; and the poor girl did pray, and think and weep, till it seemed strange the night could so soon pass, and morning smile again. She had not told that permission to remain with her aunt had been scornfully and painfully given; that her father had derided her, as mean-spirited and degraded; that as she had chosen to remain with her poor relations, she was no longer his daughter. Nor did she pray and weep for the dying, or for those around him. One alone was in that heart! Why was he not there at such a moment? and she shuddered as she pictured the violence of the self-accusing agony which would be upon him when he discovered he had lingered until too late. Hour after hour passed, and there was no footstep. She thought the chimes must have rung too near each other; for as one struck, she believed he must be at home ere it struck another, and yet he came not: she watched in vain.

Day dawned, and as light gleamed in upon the dying, there was a change upon his face. He had not suffered throughout the night, seeming to sleep at intervals, and then lay calmly without speaking; but as the day gradually brightened, he reopened his eyes and looked towards the richly glowing east.

"Another sun!" he said, in a changed and hollow voice. "Blessed be the God who sets him in the heavens, strong and rejoicing as a young man to run a race: my race is over—my light will pass before his. I prayed one night's delay, but still he does not come; and now it will soon be over. Rachel, my true wife, call the children; let me bless them each once more."

They were called, and, awe-struck even to silence at the fearful change in that loved face, they one by one drew near, and bowed down their bright heads before him. Faintly, yet distinctly, he spoke a blessing upon each; then murmured, "The God of my Fathers bless you all, all as you love Him and each other. Never deny Him: acknowledge Him as One! Hear, O Israel! the Lord our God, the Lord is one!"

The words were repeated in tears and sobs by all; he fell back, and they thought his spirit gone. Minutes rolled by, and then there was a rapid step without; it neared the door, one moment paused, and entered.

"My son, my son! O God, I thank thee! Reuben, my firstborn, in time, I bless, bless—" the words were lost in a fearful gurgling sound, but the father's arms were flung wildly, strongly round the son, who, with bitter tears, had thrown himself upon his neck—and there was silence.

"Father! oh, my father, speak—bless, forgive me!" at length Reuben wildly exclaimed, breaking from that convulsive hold to sink as a penitent upon the earth. He spoke in vain; the spirit had lingered to gaze once more upon the firstborn of his love, then fled from earth for ever.

CHAPTER II.

It is two years after the mournful event recorded in our last chapter that we recommence our simple narrative. When time and prayer had softened the first deep affliction, the widow and her family indeed proved the fulfilment of that blessed promise, "Leave thy fatherless children to me, and I will keep them alive, and let thy widows trust in me;" for they prospered and were happy. Affliction, either of failing health in those compelled to labour, or in want of employment, was kept far from them. The widow, indeed, herself often suffered; but she thanked God, in the midst even of pain, as she compared the blessings of her lot with those of others. Little Ruth, too, from her affliction and very delicate health, was often an object of anxiety; but so tenderly was she beloved, that anxiety was scarcely pain in the delight her presence ever caused. Sweet-tempered, loving, and joyous, with a voice of song like a bird's, and a laugh of childlike glee, and yet such strong affections, such deep reverence for all things holy, that who might grieve for her afflictions when she was so happy, so gratified herself? She was the star of that lowly little dwelling, for sorrow, or discord, or care could not come near her.

Joseph, her twin brother, had attracted the notice of a respectable jeweller, who, though he could not take the boy into his house as a regular apprentice till he was thirteen, not only employed him several hours in the day in cleaning jewels, etc., but allowed him small wages—an act of real benevolence, felt by the widow as an especial blessing, rendered perhaps the dearer from the thought, that it was the high character her husband had borne which gave his youngest son so responsible an office, intrusted as it was to none but the strictly honest.

Simeon, now nearly seventeen, was with the same watchmaker who had formerly brought forward his father. It was not a trade he liked; nay, the delicate machinery required was particularly annoying to him, but it was the only opening for him, and he conquered his disinclination. He had long since made a vow to use his every effort to restore his parents to the comfortable estate from which they had unfortunately fallen, and no thought of himself or his own wishes should interfere with its accomplishment. Persevering and resolute, he took a good heart with him to the business; and though his first attempts were awkward, and the laughter of his companions most discouraging, the praise of his master and his own conscience urged him on, and before the two years which we have passed over had elapsed, he had conquered every difficulty, and promised in time to be quite as good a workman as his father.

The extent of suffering which his father's death had been to him no one knew, but he had felt at first as if he could not rouse himself again. It was useless to struggle on; for the beloved parent, for whose sake he had made this solemn vow, was gone for ever. His mother indeed was spared him; but much as he loved and reverenced her, his father had been, if possible, first in his affections. Perhaps it was that his own feelings, his own character, gave him a clue to all that his father had done and endured. He had all his honesty and honour, all his energy, and love for his ancient faith. One difference there was: Perez could bear with, nay, love all mankind—could find excuse for the erring, even for the apostate, much as he abhorred the deed; could believe in the sincerity and piety of others, though their faith differed from his own; but Simeon could not feel this. Often, even in his childhood, his father had to reprove him for prejudice; and as he grew older, his hatred against all those who left the faith, or united themselves in any way with other than Israelites, continued violent. Prejudice is almost the only feeling which reason cannot conquer—religion may, and Simeon was truly and sincerely religious; but he *loved his faith* better than he *loved his God*. He would have started and denied it, had any one told him so, and declared it was impossible—one feeling could not be distinct or divided from the other; yet so it was. An earnest and heartfelt love of God can never permit an emotion so violent as hatred to any of God's creatures. It is no test of our own sincerity to condemn or disbelieve in that of others; and those who do—who are prejudiced and violent against all who differ from them—may be, no doubt are, sincerely religious and well intentioned, but they love their faith better than they love their God.

These peculiar feelings occasioned a degree of coldness in Simeon's sentiments towards his brother Reuben, of whom we have little more to say than we know already.

The death of his father was indeed a fearful shock; yet,

from a few words which fell from him during some of his interviews with Sarah, she fancied that he almost rejoiced that he was bound by no promise to the dying. In the midst of repentant agony that he had arrived too late for his parent's blessing, he would break off with a half shudder, and mutter, "If he had spoken that, he might have spoken more, and I could not have disobeyed him on his death-bed. Whatever he bade me promise I must have promised; and then, then, after a few brief months, been perjured. Oh, my father, my father! why is it my fate to be the wretch I am?"

This grief was violent, but it did not produce the good effect which his parents had so fondly hoped. Even in the days of mourning, it was evident that the peculiar forms which his faith enjoined, as the son of the deceased, chafed and irritated him; and had it not been for the deep, silent suffering of his mother, which he could not bear to increase, he would have neglected them altogether. When he mixed with the world again, he followed his own course and his own will, scarcely ever mixing with those of his own race, but seeking, and at last finding employment with the stranger. He had excellent abilities; and from his having received a better education than most youths of his race, obtained at length a lucrative situation in an establishment which, trading to many different parts of the British Isles, often required an active agent to travel for them. His peculiar creed had been at first against him; but when his abilities were put to the proof, and it was discovered he was in truth only *nominally* a Jew, that he cared not to sacrifice the Sabbath, and that no part of his religion was permitted to interfere with his employments, his services were accepted and well paid.

Had then Reuben Perez, the beloved and cherished son of such good and pious parents, indeed deserted the religion of his forefathers? Not in semblance, for there were times when he still visited the synagogue; and as he did so, he was by many still conceived a good Jew. The flagrant follies of his youth had subsided; he was no longer wild, wavering, and extravagant. Not a word could be spoken against his moral principles; his public, even his domestic conduct was unexceptionable, and therefore he bore a high character in the estimation alike of the Jewish and Christian world. What cause had his mother, then, for the grief and pain which swelled her heart almost to bursting, when she thought upon her first-born? Alas! it was because she felt there was One who saw deeper than the world—One, between whom and himself Reuben had raised up a dark barrier of wrath—One who loved him, erring and sinful as he was, with an immeasurable love, but whose deep love was rejected and abused—even his God, that God who had been the Saviour of his forefathers through so many thousand ages. The mother would have preferred seeing him poor, dependent, obtaining but his daily bread, yet faithful to his faith and to his God, than prosperous, courted, and an alien.

The brothers seldom met, and therefore Simeon was ignorant how powerfully coldness was creeping over his affections for Reuben; how, in violently condemning his indifference and union with the stranger, he was rendering the observance of his promise to his dying father (to bear with and love his brother) a matter of difficulty and pain. Faithful and earnest himself, he could not understand a want of earnestness and fidelity in others. But, however the world might flatter and appear to honour his exemplary moral conduct, one truth it is our duty to record—Reuben was not happy. It was not the mere fancy of his mother and cousin, it was truth; they knew not wherefore—for if he neglected and contemned his religion, he could scarcely feel the want of it —but that he was unhappy, perhaps was the secret cause which held the love of his mother and Sarah so immovably enchained, bidding them hope sometimes in the very midst of gloom.

Of the female members of Perez' family we have little to remark. Leah's good conduct had not only made her the favourite of her mistress, but her liveliness and happy temper had actually triumphed over the sometimes harsh disposition she had had at first to encounter. There was no withstanding her good humour. She had the happy knack of making people good friends with themselves, as well as with each other, and was so happy herself, that, except when she thought of her dear father, and wished that he could but see her and hear her sing over her work, sorrow was unknown. Every Friday evening she went home to remain till the Sunday morning, and that was superlative enjoyment, not only to herself, for her mother looked to the visit of her merry, affectionate daughter as a source of pure feeling, delight, and recreation.

In Sarah there was no change. Still pensive, modest, and industrious, she continued quietly to retain the most devoted affections of her relatives, and the good-will and respect of her employers. Of her own individual feelings we must not now speak, save to say that few, even of her domestic circle, imagined how strong and deep was the under-current of character which her quiet mien concealed.

It was the evening of the Sabbath, and the widow and her daughters were assembled in their pretty little parlour. Simeon and Joseph were not yet returned from synagogue. Reuben, alas! was seldom there on the Sabbath eve. The table was covered with a cloth, which, though not of the finest description, was white as the driven snow; and the Sabbath lamp was lighted, for in their greatest poverty this ceremony had never been omitted. When they had no lamp, and could not have afforded oil, they burnt a wax candle, frequently depriving themselves of some week-day necessary to procure this indulgence. The first earnings of Sarah, Leah, and Simeon had been used to repurchase the ancient Sabbath lamp, the heirloom in their family for many generations. It was silver and very antique, and by a strange chance had escaped the fire, which rendered perhaps the sale of it the more painful to Perez. His gratification on beholding it again had amply repaid his affectionate children. Never being used but on Sabbaths, it seemed to partake of the sanctity of that holy day.

Bread and salt were also upon the table, and the large Bible and its attendant prayer-books there also, open, as if they had just been used. Ruth had plucked some sweet flowers just before Sabbath, and arranged them tastefully in a china cup, and Leah had playfully removed a sprig of rose-buds and wreathed it in the long glossy curls which hung round Ruth's sweet face and over her shoulders. The dresses of all were neat and clean, for they loved to make a distinction between the seventh day and the six days of labour.

"If we were about to pass a day in the presence of an earthly sovereign, my dear children," the widow had often been wont to say, "should we not deserve to be excluded if we appeared rudely and slovenly and dirtily attired? You think we could not possibly do so; it would not only be such marked disrespect, but we should not be admitted. How, then, dare we seek the presence of our heavenly sovereign in such rude and sinful disarray? The seventh day is His day. He calls upon us to throw aside all worldly thoughts and cares, and come to Him, and give our thoughts and hearts to His holy service. If an earthly king so called us, how anxious should we be to accept the invitation—shall we do less for God?"

"But, dear mother," Leah would answer, "will God regard that? Is He not too holy, too far removed from us, too pure too mark such little things?"

"Nothing is too small for Him to remark, if done in love and faith, my child. The heart anxious to mark the Sabbath by increase of cleanliness and neatness in personal attire, as well as household arrangements, must conceive it God's own day, and observing it as such will receive His blessing. It is not the *act* of dressing or the dress He observes. He only marks it as a proof His holy day is welcomed with love and rejoicing, as He commanded; and the smallest offering of OBEDIENCE is acceptable to Him."

"But I have heard you remark with regret, mother, that some of our neighbours are dressed so very smart on Sabbath. If it be to mark the holy difference between that day and the others, why should you regret it?"

"Because, love, there ought to be moderation in all things, and when I see very smart showy dresses, which, if not in material, in appearance are much too fine and smart for our station, I fear it is less a religious than a worldly feeling which dictates them. Have you not noticed that those who dress so gaily generally spend their Sabbath in walking about the streets and exchanging visits, conversing, of course, on the most frivolous topics? I do not think this the proper method of spending our Sabbath day, and therefore I regret to see them devote so much time and thought on mere outward decoration, which is so widely different from obedience to their God."

Leah thought of this little conversation many times. From thoughtlessness and dislike to trouble, she had hitherto been rather negligent than otherwise in her dress; then going to a contrary extreme, felt very much inclined to imitate some young companions in their finery. Her mother's word saved her from the one, and their subsequent misfortunes effectually from the other, as all her earnings were hoarded for one holy purpose, simply to assist her parents; and she would have thought it sacrilege to have spent any portion on herself, except on things which she absolutely needed. But so neat and clean was she invariably in her dress, that her mistress always sent her to receive orders, and, trifling as appearance may seem, it repeatedly gained customers.

"They are coming—I hear their footsteps," said the little Ruth, springing up to open the parlour door. "Oh! I do so love the Sabbath eve, for it brings us all together again so happily."

"Is it only Simeon and Joseph, my child?" inquired the widow, mournfully; for there was one expectation on her heart and that of Sarah, which, alas! was seldom to be fulfilled.

Ruth listened attentively.

"Only they, mother!" she said, checking her voice of glee, and returning to her mother's side, for she knew the cause of that saddened tone, and she laid her little head caressingly on her mother's breast.

Simeon and Joseph at that moment entered, and each advancing, bent lowly before their mother, who, laying her hand upon each dear head, blessed them in a voice faltering from its emotion, and kissed them both. The kiss of love and peace went round, and gaily the brothers and sisters drew round the table, which Sarah's provident love speedily covered with the welcome evening meal. The happy laugh and affectionate interchange of the individual cares and pleasures, vexations and enjoyments of the past week, occupied them delightfully during tea. Sarah had to tell of a new kind of work which had diversified her usual employment, and been most successful; a kind of wadded slipper, which, after many trials, she had completed to her satisfaction, in the intervals of other work; and which not only sold well, but gave her dear aunt an occupation which she could accomplish without pain, in wadding and binding the silk. Leah told of a pretty dress and bonnet which her mistress had presented to her, in token of her approbation of her steadiness in refusing to accompany her companions to some place of amusement, which, from its respectability being doubted, she knew her mother would not approve; and, by staying at home, enabled Mrs. Magnus to finish an expensive order a day sooner than had been expected, and so gained her a new and wealthy customer.

"Dearest mother, you told me how to resist temptation even in trifles," continued the affectionate girl, with tears of feeling in her bright dark eyes. "You taught me from my earliest childhood there was purer and more lasting pleasure in conquering my own wishes than any doubtful recreation could bestow; and that in that inward pleasure our heavenly Father's approval was made manifest. And so, you see, though you were not near me and I could not, as I wished, ask your advice and permission, it was you who enabled me to conquer myself, and resist this temptation. I did want to go, and felt very, very lonely when all went; but when Mrs. Magnus thanked me for enabling her to give so much satisfaction, and said I gained her a new customer, oh, no *circus* or *play* could have given me such happiness as that; and it was all through you, mother, and so I told her."

The happy mother smiled on her animated girl; but her heart did not glorify itself, it thanked God that her early efforts had been so blessed. "And Ruth!" some of our readers may exclaim, "poor blind Ruth, what can she have to say?" And we answer, happy little Ruth had much of industry and enjoyment to dilate on. The straw she had plaited, the hymns she had learnt through Sarah's kindly teaching, the dead leaves she had plucked from the shrubs and flowers, for so delicate had her sense of touch become, she could follow this occupation in perfect security to the plants, distinguishing the dead and dying from the perfect leaves at a touch. Then she told of a poor little orphan beggar girl, whom Sarah had one day brought in cold and crying, because she had been begging all day and had received nothing, and she knew she should be beat when she went home; and how she had said she hated begging, but she could do nothing else; and little Ruth had asked her if she would like to sell flowers; and poor Mary had told her she should like it very very much, but she could not get any. She knew no one who would let her take them from the garden. How she (Ruth) had promised to make her some little nosegays, and Sarah and her mother said they would make her some little nick-nacks, pincushions, and housewives to put with her flowers.

"Ah, we made her so happy!" continued the child, clasping her little hands in delight. "Mother gave her some of my old things, which were quite good to her, and it is quite a pleasure to me to make her nosegays, and feel they give her a few pence better than begging; and Sarah is going to try if I can make her some little fancy things when winter comes. You know I am quite rich to her, for God has given me a home, and such a kind mother, and dear brothers and sisters, and she has neither home nor mother, nor any one to love her. Poor, poor Mary! and then, too, some say the Christians do not like the Jews, and I know she will and does like us, and she may make others of her people like us too."

"Ruth," said her brother Simeon, in a very strange husky voice, "Ruth, darling, come here and kiss me. I wish you would make me as good as you."

"As good!" exclaimed the child, springing on his knee, and throwing her arms round his neck; "dear naughty Simeon, to say such a thing. How much more you can do than I. Do you not work so very much, that dear mother sometimes fears for your health? and it is all for us, to help to support us, mother and me, because we cannot work for ourselves. Ah, I am blind, and can only do little things, and try to make every one happy, that they may love me; but I am only a little girl; I cannot be as good as you."

"Ruth, darling, I could not do as you have done. I cannot love and serve those who hate and persecute us as Israelites."

"They do not persecute us now, brother. Sarah told me sad tales of what we suffered once; but God was angry with us then, and he made the nations punish us. But now, if they still dislike us, we ought not to dislike them, but do all we can to make them love us."

Simeon bent his head upon his sister's; her artless words had rebuked and shamed him. But prejudice might not even then be overcome. He knew she was right and he was wrong, so he would not answer, glad to hear Leah gaily demand a history of his weekly proceedings, as he had not yet spoken. He had little to relate, except that he was now beginning really to understand his business. His master had said that he should soon be obliged to raise his salary; and, what was a real source of happiness, from the care and quickness with which he now accomplished his tasks, he found time for his favourite amusement of modelling, which circumstances had compelled him so long to neglect. Joseph had to tell similar kindness on the part of his master, and industry on his own. He told, too, with great glee, that Mr. Bennet had promised to give him some lessons in the evenings, in the language which of all others he wished most particularly to understand. He knew many were satisfied merely to read their prayers in Hebrew, whether they understood them or not, but he wished to understand it thoroughly; and all the time he was cleaning jewels—for he was now quite expert—he thought over what his master had so kindly taught him; perhaps one day he might be able to know Hebrew thoroughly himself, and oh, what a delight that would be!

By the time Joseph had finished his tale, the table had been cleared; and then the widow opened the large Bible, and after fervently blessing God for His mercy in permitting them all to see the close of another week in health and peace, read aloud a chapter and psalm. Varied as were the characters and wishes of all present, every heart united in reverence and love towards this weekly service—in, if possible, increased devotion towards that beloved parent, who so faithfully endeavoured to support not alone her own duties towards her offspring, but those of their departed father. She had not lost those hours and days, aye, and sometimes long weeks of suffering, with which it had pleased God to afflict her. When confined to her bed, the Bible had been her sole companion, and she so communed with it and her own heart, that many passages, which had before been veiled, were now made clear and light, and her constant prayer for wisdom and religion to lead her offspring in its paths of pleasantness and peace granted to the full. Yet Rachel was no great scholar. Let it not be imagined amongst those who read this little tale, that she was unusually gifted. She was indeed so far gifted that she had a *trusting spirit and a most humble and childlike mind*, and of worldly ways was most entirely ignorant; and it was these feelings which kept her so persevering in the path of duty, and, leading her to the footstool of her God, gave her the strength of wisdom that she needed: and to every mother in Israel these powers are given.

"Well, my dear children, to whom must I look for the text which is to occupy us this evening?" said the widow glancing affectionately round as she ceased to read.

"To me and Ruth, mother; for you know we always think together," answered Joseph, eagerly. "And you don't know how we have both been longing for this evening, for the verse we have chosen has made us think so much, and with all our thinking, we cannot quite satisfy ourselves."

"But what is it, my boy?"

"It is the one our dear father repeated on his death-bed, mother. I have often thought of it since, but feared it would make you sorrowful, if we spoke of it for the first year or two; but as I found Ruth had thought of it and wished it explained also, we said we would ask you to talk about it to-night. You repeat it, Ruth; you pronounce the Hebrew so prettily!"

And timidly, but sweetly, Ruth said, first in Hebrew and

then in English, "'Commit your ways unto the Lord; trust also in him, and he will bring it to pass.' *Ways*," continued the child, "was the word which first puzzled us, but Sarah has explained it to me so plainly, I understand it better now."

"Tell us then, Sarah dear," said her aunt.

"It seems to me," she said, "that the word *ways* has many meanings. In the verse, 'Show me thy ways, O Lord,' I think it means actions. In another verse, 'The Lord made known his *ways* unto Moses, his acts unto the children of Israel,' I think ways mean *thoughts*."

"And there are several in Proverbs," interposed Simeon, "which would make us regard *ways* as the path we are to tread; as for instance, 'Who leaveth the *path* of righteousness, to walk in the *ways* of darkness.'"

"But Ruth and I want to know in which of these ways we are to regard it in our verse," persisted Joseph.

"As meaning both *outward actions and inward thoughts*, my dear children," replied his mother. "I have thought long on this verse, and I am glad you have chosen it for discussion. Perhaps you do not know, my little Joseph, that we *must think to act*; that it is very seldom any good or bad action is performed without previous thought; and, consequently, if we would be pure in act, we must commit our thoughts unto the Lord."

"But how are we to do this, mother?" asked Leah.

"By constant prayer, my love; by endeavouring, wherever we are, or whatever we may be doing, to remember God knows our every thought before it has words, and long before it becomes action. We are apt, perhaps, to indulge in the wildest thoughts, simply because we imagine ourselves secure from all observation. From *human* observation we are secure, but not from our Father who is in heaven; and therefore we should endeavour so to train our thoughts as to banish all which we dare not commit unto our God."

"But are there not some things, dear aunt, too trivial, too much mingled with earthly feelings, to bring before a Being of such ineffable holiness and purity?" inquired Sarah in a voice which, notwithstanding all her efforts, audibly faltered.

"Ah, that is what I want so much to know," added Joseph.

"You must not forget, my dear Sarah," resumed Mrs. Perez, "that our God is a God of love and compassion, as infinite as His holiness; that every throb of pain or joy in the creature His love has formed, is *felt* as well as *ordained* by Him. No nation has a God so near to them as Israel; and we, of all others, ought to derive and realize comfort from the belief that He knows our nature in its strivings after righteousness, as well as in its sin. He knows all our temptations, all our struggles, far better than our dearest earthly friends, and His loving mercy towards us is infinitely stronger. Therefore we can better commit our secret thoughts and feelings unto His keeping, than to that of our nearest friends on earth."

"And may children do this, mother?"

"Yes, dear boy; our Father has children in His tender care and guiding, even as those of more experienced age. Accustom yourselves, while engaged in thought, to ask, 'Can I ask my Father's blessing on these thoughts, and on the actions they lead to?' and rest assured conscience will give you a true answer. If it say, 'No,' dismiss the trifling or sinful meditations on the instant; send up a brief prayer to God for help, and He will hear you. If, on the contrary, conscience approve your thought, encourage it, as leading you nearer, closer, and more lovingly to God."

"But is not this close communion more necessary for women than for men, mother?" inquired Simeon.

"Women may need it more, my dear boy; but believe me it is equally, if not more necessary for man. Think of the many temptations to evil which men have in their intercourse with the world; the daily, almost hourly call for the conquest of inclination and passion, which, without some very strong incentive, can never be subdued. One unguarded moment, and the labour of years after righteousness may be annihilated. Man may not need the *comfort* of this close communion so much as woman, but he yet more requires its *strength*. Nothing is so likely to keep him from sin as committing his thoughts even as his actions unto the Lord."

"Thank you, my dear mother; that first bit is clear," said Joseph. "Now, I want the second: the third is the most puzzling of all, but we shall come to that by and bye."

"You surely know what it means by to 'trust in Him,' Joseph?" said Leah.

"I think I do, sister mine, for it was mother's humble trust in the Lord that supported her in her sorrows; that I saw, I felt, though I was a child; but—" he hesitated.

"Well, my boy?"

"To *trust*, I think, means to have faith. Now, Henry Stevens said the other day, Jews have no faith—and how can we trust then?"

"My dearest Joseph, do not let your companions so mislead you," answered his mother, earnestly. "I know that is a charge often brought against us; but it is always from those who do not know our religion, and who judge us only from those who, by their words and actions, condemn it themselves. The Jew must have faith, not only in the existence of God, but in the sacred history our God inspired, or he is no Jew. He must feel faith—believe God hears and will answer, or his prayers, however fervent, are of no avail. Without faith, his very existence must be an enigma, and his whole life misery. Oh, believe me, my dear children, as no nation has God so near them, so no nation has so much need of faith, and no nation has so experienced the strength, and peace, and fulness which it brings."

"But how does our verse mean that we are to trust in the Lord, mother?" asked Ruth.

"It belongs both to the first and last division of the verse, my love. If we commit our ways unto the Lord, and *trust also in Him* (remember one is of no avail without the other), then He will bring it to pass."

"Ah! that is it. I am so glad we have come to that," eagerly exclaimed Joseph. "Mother, does it mean, *can* it mean that our Father will grant our prayers, will give us what we most wish?"

"If it be for our good, my boy; if our wishes be acceptable in His sight; if they will tend to our eternal as well as our temporal welfare; and we bring them before Him in unfailing confidence, believing firmly that He will answer in His own good time—we may rest assured that He will answer us, that He will grant our prayers."

"But that which is for our good may not be what we most wish for," resumed Joseph, despondingly.

"But, my boy, if what we wish for is *not* for our good, is it not more merciful and kind to deny than to grant it? Remember, God knows us better than we know ourselves; and we may ask what would lead us to evil temporally and eternally. If, for a wise and merciful purpose, even our good desires are not granted, be assured that peace, strength, and healing will be given in their stead."

The little circle looked very thoughtful as the impressive voice of the widow ceased.

Sarah seemed more than usually moved; for, as she bent over her little Bible, which she had opened at the verse, tears one by one fell silently upon the page. Whether Ruth heard them drop, or from her seat close by her cousin, felt that the hand she caressingly held trembled, we know not, but the child rose, and threw her little arms around her neck.

"Do you remember who it was wrote the verse we are considering?" said the widow, after a pause.

"King David," answered Joseph and Simeon together.

"Then you see it was no prosperous monarch, no peaceful lawgiver, but one whose life had passed in trials, compared to which our severest misfortunes must seem trifling. Hunted from place to place, in daily danger of his life, compelled even to feign madness, separated from all whom he loved, from all of happiness or peace, even debarred from the public exercise of his faith, his very prayers at times seemingly unheeded—yet it is this faithful servant of God who exclaims, 'Commit your ways unto the Lord; trust also in him, and he will bring it to pass.' We know not the exact time he wrote these words; but we know he wrote from experience; for did not God indeed bring happiness to pass for him? If we think of the *life* of him who wrote these blessed words, as well as the words themselves, we must derive strength and comfort from the reflection."

"Yes, yes; I see and feel it all now," exclaimed Joseph, eagerly as before. "Oh, mother, I can think about it now without any puzzling at all. I am so glad. Cannot you, Ruth?"

"Hush!" answered the child, as she suddenly started up in an attitude of attentive listening. "Hush! I am sure that is Reuben's step: he is coming, he is coming. Oh, what joy for me!"

"You are wrong, dear; and it only disappoints mother," said Leah, gently.

"No, no! I know I am not. There—listen; do you not hear steps now?"

"Yes: but how can you be sure they are his?" answered Simeon. "It is so very unlikely, I should have thought of everybody else first."

Ruth made no answer; but she bounded from the room, and had opened the street-door, regardless of Leah's entreaties to wait at least till the steps came nearer. A very few minutes more, and all doubts were solved by the entrance of Ruth, not walking, but clinging round her brother Reuben's neck, and almost stifling him with kisses, only interrupting herself to say, "Who was right, Miss Leah and Master Simeon? Ah, you did not have Reuben for long weeks to attend and nurse, as I had, or you would have known his step too."

"You can love me still, then?" murmured her brother, as only to be heard by her; then added aloud, "my mother should have had the first kiss, dearest; let me ask her blessing, Ruth."

She released him, though she still held his hand; and hastening to his mother, he bent his head before her.

"Is it too late to ask my mother's Sabbath blessing?" he said, and his voice was strangely choked. "Bless me, dearest mother, as you used to do."

The widow rose, and, laying her hands upon his head, repeated the customary Hebrew blessing, and then folded him to her heart.

"It is never, never too late for a mother's blessing—a mother's love, my Reuben," she said, her voice quivering with the efforts she made to restrain her emotion. "I could have wished it oftener and earlier asked on the Sabbath eve; but it is yours, my boy, each night and morning, though you hear it not."

"And will it always be? Mother! mother! will you never withdraw it from me? No, no, you will not. You love me only too, too well," and abruptly breaking from her, after kissing her passionately, he turned to greet his brothers and sisters.

All met him cordially and affectionately, except perhaps that there was a stern look of inquiry in Simeon's eyes, which Reuben, from some unexpressed feeling, could not meet; and, looking from him, exclaimed—

"Sarah! where is my kind cousin Sarah? will she not give me welcome?"

"She was here this moment," said Leah; "where can she have vanished?"

"Not very far, dear cousin: I am here. Reuben, can you believe one moment that I do not rejoice to see you once again at home?" said Sarah, advancing from the farther side of the room, and placing her hand frankly in her cousin's, looking up in his face with her clear pensive eyes, but cheeks as pale as marble.

Reuben pressed her hand within his own, tried to meet smilingly her glance, and speak as usual; but both efforts failed, and again he turned away.

"And he has come to stay with us—he will not leave us in a hurry again," said the affectionate little Ruth, keeping her seat on his knee, and nestling her head in his bosom. "I wanted but you to make this evening quite, quite happy."

Reuben kissed her, to conceal a sigh, and controlling himself, he entered cheerfully and caressingly into all Ruth and Joseph had to tell, called for all interesting information from the other members of his family, and imparted many particulars of himself. He was rising high in the world, had been the fortunate means of preventing a great loss to the firm of which he was a servant, and so raised his salary, and himself in the estimation of his employers. Fortune smiled on him, he said, in many ways, and he had had the happiness of securing a trifling fund for his mother, which, though small, was sure, and would provide her yearly with a moderate sum. He had something else to propose, but there would be time enough for that. His mother blessed and thanked him; but her heart was not at rest. Cheerful as the conversation was, happy as the last hour ought to have been, there was a dim foreboding on her spirit which she could not conquer. Something was yet to be told: Reuben was not at peace; and when indeed he did speak that something, it was with a confused more than a joyous tone.

"I do not know why I should delay telling you of my intention, mother," he said at length: "I have had too many proofs of your affection to doubt of your rejoicing in anything that will make my happiness—I am going to be married."

There was a general start and exclamation from all but two in the group—his mother and cousin.

"If it will make your happiness, my son, I do indeed rejoice," the former said very calmly. "Whom do you give me for another daughter?"

"You do not know her yet, mother; but I am sure you will learn to love her dearly: it is Jeanie Wilson, the only child of my fellow-clerk."

"Jeanie Wilson!—a Christian! Reuben, Reuben, how have you fallen!" burst angrily, almost fiercely, from Simeon; "but it is folly to be surprised—I knew it would be so."

"Indeed! wonderfully clear-sighted as you were then, if

you consider such a union humiliation, it would have been more brotherly, perhaps, to have warned me of the precipice on which I stood," answered Reuben, sarcastically.

"Yes! you gave me so fair an opportunity to act a brother's part; never seeking me, or permitting me to seek you, for weeks together; herding with strangers alone—following them alike in the store and in the mart—loving what they love, doing as they do—and, like them, scorning, despising, and persecuting that holy people who once called you son—forgetting your birthright, your sainted heritage—throwing dishonour on the dead as on the living, to link yourself with those who assuredly will, if they do not now, despise you. Shame, foul shame upon you!"

"Have you done?" calmly inquired Reuben, though the red spot was on his cheek. "It is something for the elder to be bearded thus by the younger. Yet be it so. I have done nothing for which to feel shame—nothing to dishonour those with whom I am related. If they feel themselves dishonoured, let them leave me; I can meet the world alone."

"Aye, so far alone, that you will rejoice that others have cast aside the chains of nature, and given you freedom to follow your own apostate path unquestioned and unrebuked."

"Peace, I command you!" exclaimed the widow, with a tone and gesture of authority which awed Simeon into silence, and checked the wrathful reply on Reuben's lips. "My sons, profane not the Sabbath of your God with this wild and wicked contention. Simeon, however you may lament what Reuben has disclosed, it is not your part to forget he is your brother—yes, and an elder brother—still."

"I will own no apostate for my brother!" muttered the still irritated young man. "Others may regard him as they list; if he have given up his faith, I will not call him brother."

"I have neither the will nor occasion to forswear my faith," replied Reuben, calmly. "Mr. Wilson has made no condition in giving me his daughter, except that she may follow her own faith, which I were indeed prejudiced and foolish to deny. He believes as I do; to believe in God is enough—all religions are the same before Him."

"That is to say, he is, like yourself, of no religion at all," rejoined Simeon, bitterly. "Better he had been prejudiced, rigid, even despising us as others do; then this misfortune would not have befallen us."

"Is it a misfortune to you, mother? Leah—Ruth—Joseph, will you all refuse to love my wife? You will not, cannot, when you see and know her."

"As your wife, Reuben, we cannot feel indifference towards her," replied Leah, tears standing in her eyes; "yet if you had brought us one of our own people, oh, how much happier it would have made us!"

"And why should it, my dear sister? Mother, why should it be such a source of grief? *I* do not turn from the faith of my fathers: I may neglect, disregard those forms and ordinances which I do not feel at all incumbent on me to obey, but I must be a Jew—I cannot believe with the Christian, and I cannot feel how my marriage with a gentle, loving, and most amiable girl can make me other than I am. We are in no way commanded to marry only amongst ourselves."

"You are mistaken; we *are* so commanded, my dear son. In very many parts of our Holy Law we are positively forbidden to intermarry with the stranger; and, as a proof that so to wed was considered criminal, one of the first and most important points on which Ezra and Nehemiah insisted, was the putting away of strange wives."

"But they were idolaters, mother. Jeanie and I worship the same God."

"But you do not believe in the same creed, and therefore is the belief in one God more dangerous. We ought to keep ourselves yet more distinct, now that we are mingled up amongst those who know God and serve Him, though not as we do. You do not think thus, my dear son; and therefore all we may do is but to pray that the happiness you expect may be realized."

"And in praying for it, of course you doubt it, though I still cannot imagine why. Sarah, you have not spoken: do you believe me so terrible a reprobate that there is no chance for my happiness, temporally and eternally?"

He spoke bitterly, perhaps harshly, for he had longed for her to speak, and her silence strangely, painfully reproached him. He did not choose to know why, and so he vented in bitter words to her the anger he felt towards himself.

"My opinion can be of little value after my aunt's," she answered, meekly; "but this believe, dear cousin, if you and Jeanie are only as blessed and happy together as I wish you, you will be one of the happiest couples on earth."

"I do believe it!" he said, passionately springing towards

her, and seizing both her hands. "Sarah, dear Sarah, forgive me. I was harsh and bitter to you, who were always my better angel; say *you forgive* me!" He repeated the word, with a strong emphasis upon it.

"I did not know that you had given me anything to forgive, Reuben," she replied, struggling to smile; "but if you think you have, I do forgive you from my very heart."

"Bless you for the word!" he said, still gazing fixedly in her face, which calmly met his look.

"Thank God, one misery is spared me," he muttered to himself; then added, "and you think I may be happy?"

"I trust you will; and if it please God to bless you with prosperity, I think you may."

"How do you mean?"

"That while all things go smoothly, you will not feel the division, the barrier which your opposing creeds must silently erect between you. But if affliction, if death should happen, Reuben, dearest Reuben, may you never repent this engagement then."

The young man actually trembled at the startling earnestness of her words.

"And will you—surely you will not—marry in church, brother?" timidly inquired Joseph.

"He must, he cannot help himself!" hoarsely interposed Simeon, who had remained sitting in moody silence for some time; "and yet he would say he is no apostate, no deserter from our faith."

"You said you had something to ask mother, Reuben," said Ruth, pressing close to his side, for she feared the painful altercation between her brothers might recommence.

"I had," he answered, "but I fear it is useless now. Mother, Jeanie and I hoped to have offered you a home—to have entreated you to live with us, and return to the comforts which were yours; we should seek but to give you joy. But after what has passed this evening, I fear we have hoped in vain."

"I wonder you dared hope it," muttered Simeon. "Would our mother live with any one who lives not as a Jew, whose dearest pride is to seem in all points like the stranger with whom he lives?"

"Thank you for the kind will, my dear son," replied the widow, affectionately, though sorrowfully; "but you are right in thinking it cannot be. I am too old and too ailing to mingle now with strangers. I cannot leave my own lowly dwelling; I cannot give up these forms and ordinances which I have learned to love, and believe obligatory upon me. Bring your wife to me, if indeed she does not scorn your poor Jewish mother; she will meet but love from me and mine.

Reuben flung himself impetuously on her neck, and she felt his whole frame tremble as with choking sobs. His sister, Sarah, and Joseph reiterated their mothers words; Simeon alone was silent. Another half-hour passed—an interval painful to all parties, despite the exertions of Sarah and the widow to make it cheerful, and then Reuben rose to depart. His affectionate embrace, his warm "Good night, God bless you," was welcomed and returned as warmly by all, and then he looked for Simeon. The youth was standing at the farther end of the apartment, in the deepest shadow, his arms folded on his breast, his lip compressed, and eyes fixed sternly on the ground.

"Simeon!" exclaimed Reuben, as he appoached him with frankly extended hand, "Simeon! we are brothers; let us part friends."

"Give up this intended marriage, come back to the faith you have deserted, and we *are* brothers," answered Simeon, sternly. "If not, we are severed, and for ever."

"Be it as you will, then," answered Reuben, controlling anger with a violent effort. "Should you need a brother or a friend, you will find them both in me; the God of our fathers demands not violence like this."

"He does not—He does not. Simeon, I beseech, COMMAND you, do not part thus with your brother; on your love, your duty to me, as your only remaining parent, I command this," his mother said, mildly, but imperatively; but for once she spoke in vain. Leah, Sarah, Joseph, all according to their different characters, sought to soften him; but the dark cloud only thickened on his brow. At that moment a light form pressed through them all, and clasping his knees, looked up in that agitated face, as if those sightless orbs had more than common power—and Ruth it was that spoke.

"Brother," she said, in her clear, sweet voice, "brother, our father bade us love our brother, even if he turned aside from all we hold most sacred and most dear. We stood around his death-bed, and we promised this—to love him to the end. Brother, you will not break this vow? No, no, our father looks upon us, hears us still!"

There was a strong and terrible struggle on the part of Simeon, and a heavy groan of repentant anguish broke from the very heart of Reuben.

"My father, my poor father! did he so love me? And will you still hate me, Simeon?" he gasped forth.

Another moment, and the brothers were clasped in each other's arms.

CHAPTER III.

It had been with the most simple and heartfelt faith, that the widow Perez had sought to instil the beautiful spirit breathing in the verse forming the subject of their Sabbath conversation in the hearts of her children. Yet ere the evening closed, how sadly and painfully had her faith been tried, and how bitterly did she feel that to her prayers there seemed indeed no answer. It was her firstborn whom she had daily, almost hourly "committed to the Lord;" for him she sought with her whole heart, "to trust" that He would, in His deep mercy, awaken her boy to the error of his ways; but did it appear as if indeed the gracious promise would be fulfilled, and the Lord would indeed "bring it to pass?" Alas! farther and farther did it now seem removed from fulfilment. By his marriage with a Gentile what must ensue?—a yet more complete estrangement from his father's faith.

The mother's heart indeed felt breaking; but quiet and ever gentle, who but her loving children might trace this bitter grief? And there were not wanting very many to give the mother all the blame of the son's course of acting. "What else could she expect by her weak indulgence?" was almost universally said. "Why did she not threaten to cast him off, if he persisted in this sinful connection, instead of encouraging such things in her other children, which of course she did, by receiving Reuben as usual? Why had she not commanded him, on peril of a parent's curse, to break off the intended match? Then she would have done her duty; as it was, it would be something very extraordinary if all her other children did not follow their elder brother's example."

The widow might have heard their unkind remarks, but she heeded them little; for she had long learned that the spirit guiding the blessed religion which she and her husband had felt and practised, was too often misunderstood and undervalued by many of her co-religionists; the idea of love bringing back a wanderer was, by the many, thought too perfectly ridiculous ever to be counted upon. But her conscience was at rest. None but her own heart and her God knew how she had striven to bring up her firstborn as he should go, or how agonizing she had ever felt this failure of her struggles and prayers in the conduct of her son, and this last act more agonizing than all. She knew, aye, felt secure, that neither of her other children needed severity towards Reuben to prevent their following his example. In them she saw the fruits of her efforts in their education, and she knew that they felt their brother's wanderings from their beloved faith too sorrowfully ever to walk in his ways. They saw enough of their poor mother's silent, uncomplaining grief, to suppose for a moment that her absence of all harshness towards Reuben proceeded from her *approval* of his marriage; and each and all lifted up the fervent cry for strength always to resist such fearful temptation, and to adhere to the faith of their fathers, even until death.

We are quite aware that, by far the greater number of our readers, widow Perez will be either violently condemned or contemptuously scorned as a weak, mean-spirited, foolish woman. We can only say that if so, we are sorry so few have the power of understanding her, and that the loving piety, the spiritual religion of her character should find so faint an echo in the Jewish heart. The *consequences* of her forbearance will be too clearly traced in our simple tale, to demand any further notice on our own part. We would only ask, with all humility, our readers of every class and grade, to recall any one single instance in which parental violence and severity, even coupled with malediction, have ever succeeded in bringing back a wanderer to his fold; if so, we will grant that our idea of love and forbearance effecting more than hate and violence is both dangerous and false. But to return to our tale:

There was another in that little household bowed like the mother in grief. Sarah had believed that it was her care for Reuben's spiritual welfare which had engrossed her so much —that it was as distinct from him temporally as from herself. A rude shock awakened her from this dream, and oh, so fearfully! The wild tumult of thought pressing on her heart and brain needs no description. From the first year of her residence with her aunt, Reuben had been dear to her; affection so strengthening, increasing with her growth, so mingled with her being, that she was unconscious of its power. And now that consciousness had come—the prayers, the wishes of a lifetime were dashed down unheard and unregarded—could she believe in the soothing comfort of that inspired promise? Had she not committed her ways? had she not trusted? and had it not proved in vain? Sarah was young, had all the inexperience, the elasticity, and consequent impatience of early life; and so it was, that while the mother trusted and believed, despite of all, aye, trusted her boy would yet be saved, to Sarah life was one cheerless blank; her heart so chilled and stagnant, it seemed, as it were, the power of prayer was gone—there could be no darker woes in store. Perhaps her very determination to conceal these feelings from every eye increased the difficulties of self-conquest.

Day after day passed, and her aunt and cousins saw nothing different from her usually quiet, cheerful ways. It might be that they suspected nothing—that even the widow knew not Sarah's trials were yet greater than her own. But at night it was that the effects of the day's control were felt; and weeks passed, and time seemed to bring no respite.

"You can trust, if you cannot pray," the clear, still voice of conscience one night breathed in the ear of the poor sufferer, so strangely distinct, it seemed as if some spiritual voice had spoken. "Come back to the Father, the God, who has love and tenderness for all—who loves, despite of indifference and neglect—who has balm for every wound, even such as thine. Doth He not say, 'Cast your burden on him, and he will sustain you; trust in his word, and sin no more?'" It was strange, almost awful in the dead stillness of night, that low piercing whisper; but it had effect, for the hot tears streamed down like rain upon the deathlike cheek; the words of prayer, faint, broken, yet still trustful, burst from that sorrowing heart, and brought their balm: from that hour the stagnant misery was at an end. Sarah awoke to duty, alike to her God as to herself; and then it was she felt to the full how unutterably precious was the close commune with the Father in heaven, which her aunt's counsels had infused. Where could she have turned for comfort, had she been taught to regard Him as too far removed from earth and earthly things to love and be approached?

Time passed. Reuben's marriage took place at the time

appointed, and still with him all seemed prosperity. It was impossible to see and not to love his gentle wife. Still in seeming a mere child, so delicate in appearance, one could scarcely believe her healthful, as she said she was. It was, however, only with his mother and sisters that Reuben permitted her to associate.

He called himself, at least to his mother, a son of Israel; but all real feeling of nationality was dead within him—yet he was not a Christian, nor was his wife, except in name. They believed there was a God, at least they said they did; but life smiled on them. He was not needed, and so they lived without Him.

Simeon, true to his prejudices, would not meet his brother's wife, nor did his mother demand such from him. It was enough that with Reuben himself, when they chanced to meet, he was on kindly terms. Ruth's appeal had touched his heart, for the remembrance of his father was as omnipotent as his wishes had been during his lifetime. The interests of the brothers, alike temporal as eternal, were, however, too widely severed to permit confidence between them, and so they passed on their separate ways; loving perhaps in their inward hearts, but each year apparently more and more divided.

About six months after Reuben's wedding, Sarah received a letter which caused her great uneasiness. Our readers may remember, at the conclusion of our first chapter, we mentioned Isaac Levison having written to his daughter, stating he was again well to do in the world, and offering her affluence and a cessation from all labour, if she liked to join him. We know also that Sarah refused those offers, feeling that both inclination and duty bade her remain with the benefactors of her youth, when they were in affliction and needed her; and that, irritated at her reply, her father had cast her off, and from that time to the present, nearly three years, she had never heard any thing of him. The letter she now received told her that Levison was in the greatest distress, and seriously ill. His suspiciously-amassed riches had been, like his former, partly squandered away in unnecessary luxuries for house and palate, and partly sunk in large speculations, which had all failed; that he was now too ill to do anything, or even to write to her himself, but that he desired his daughter to come to him at once. She had been ready enough to labour for others, and therefore she could not hesitate for him, who was the only one who had any real claim upon her.

"The only one who can claim my labour," thought the poor girl, as she read the harsh epistle, again and again. "What should I have been without the beloved friends whom he thus commands me to leave? Yet he is my father; he sent for me in prosperity—I could, I did refuse him then, but not now. No, no; I must go to him now, and leave all, all I so dearly love," and letting the paper fall, she covered her face with her hands and wept bitterly.

"Yet perhaps it is better," she thought, after a brief interval of bitter sorrow; "I can never conquer this one consuming grief while I am here, and so constantly liable to see its cause. My heavenly Father may have ordained this in love; and even if it bring new trials I can look up to Him, trust in Him still. I do not leave Him behind me—He will not leave me, nor forsake me, whatever I may be called upon to bear," and inexpressibly strengthened by this thought, she was enabled, without much emotion, to seek her much-loved aunt, to show her letter and its mandate. The widow saw at a glance the duty of her adopted child, and though to part with her was a real source of grief, she loved her too well to increase the difficulty of her trial by endeavouring to dissuade her from it.

"You must go, my beloved girl," she said, folding her to her heart; "but I trust it will be but for a short time. My *home* is yours, remember—always your *home*, wherever else you may be, as only a passing sojourn. Your duty is indeed trying, but fear not, you will be strengthened to perform it."

Yet however determined were the widow and her family to control all weakening sorrow and regret, there was not one who did not feel the unexpected departure of Sarah as an individual misfortune. Each was in some way or other so connected with her, that separation caused a blank in their affections; and what then must have been her own feelings? They parted with but *one* dear friend; she from them all, to go amongst those with whom she had not one thought or feeling in common.

But she who had worked so perseveringly for them, who had felt herself a child in blood as well in heart of the widow's, that she had never thought of making a distinct provision for herself, this unselfish one was not to leave them portionless; and with so much attention to her feelings did her aunt and cousins proffer their gifts, it was impossible, pained as she was, to refuse. They said, it would be long perhaps before she could find employment in her new home, and she might need it; besides, it was not a gift, it was her due; her earnings had all gone for them, and they offered but her rightful share. Reuben and his wife were not at Liverpool when Sarah was compelled to leave it; and she rejoiced that it was so.

We will not linger either on the day of parting or the poor girl's sad and solitary journey. Simeon went with her as far as Birmingham, and when he left her, the scene of loneliness, of foreboding sorrow, pressed so heavily upon her that her tears fell unrestrainedly; but though her heart did feel desolate, she knew she was not forsaken. Her God was with her still, and He would in his own good time bring peace. She was obeying His call, by discharging her duty, and He would lead her through her dreary path.

"Fear not, Abraham, I am thy shield and exceeding great reward," were the words in her little Bible, on which her eyes had that morning glanced, dim with tears—they could see but those; again and yet again she read them, till they seemed to fix themselves upon her heart, as peculiarly and strangely appropriate to herself. Like Abraham, she was leaving home and friends, to dwell in what was to her a strange land, and the same God who had been with him, the God of Abraham and Israel, was her God also. "His arm was not shortened, nor his ear heavy, that he could not save." And oh, what unspeakable comfort came in such thoughts. Century on century had passed; but the descendants of Abraham were still the favoured of the Lord, having, in the simple fact of their existence, evidence of the Bible truth. Sarah had often gloried in being a daughter of Israel, but never felt so truly, so gratefully thankful for that holy privilege as she did when thinking over the history of Abraham, and the promise made to him and his descendants, in her lonely journey, and feeling to the full the comfort of the conviction that Abraham's God was hers.

It was a dull and dreary evening when Sarah entered the great city of London. The stage put her down about half an hour's walk from her destination, and she proceeded on foot, followed by a boy conveying her little luggage. She struggled hard to subdue the despondency again creeping over her, as she traversed the crowded streets, in which there was not one to extend the hand of kindly greeting. She felt almost ashamed, though she could not define why, that the boy should see the low dark alleys which she was obliged to tread before she could discover where her father now lived, and when she did reach it, she stood and hesitated before the door, as if the house she sought could scarcely be there, it was such a wretched-looking place.

Her timid knock was unheard, and the impatient porter volunteered a tap, loud enough to bring many a curious head to the other doors in the alley, and hastily to open the one wanted. A long curious stare greeted Sarah, from an old woman, repulsive in feature and slovenly and dirty in dress, who to Sarah's faltering question if Mr. Levison lived there, somewhat harshly replied—

"Yes, to be sure he does; and who may you be that wants him? He is not at home, whatever your business is."

"Did he not expect me, then? I wrote to say I should be with him to-night," answered Sarah, trying to conquer the painful choking in her throat. "I thought he was too ill to go out."

"Why, sure now, you cannot be his daughter!" was the reply, in a softened tone, and the woman looked at her with something very like pity. "Come in with you, then, if you really are Sarah Levison; send the boy away and come in."

Trembling from a variety of feelings, Sarah mechanically obeyed, giving the boy the customary fee ere she discharged him; a proceeding which caused the woman to look at her with increased astonishment, and to exclaim, when Sarah was fairly in the dirty miserable room called a parlour, "She can do that too, and yet she comes here. Sarah Levison, are you not a great fool?"

The poor girl started, fairly bewildered by the question, and looked at her companion very much as if she thought she had lost her wits. "A fool!" she repeated.

"My good girl, yes. What have you left a comfortable house and kind friends and perhaps a good business for?"

"To obey my father," replied Sarah, simply. "Did he not send to tell me he was ill, and wanted me; that he was no longer the wealthy prosperous man that he was, and I must labour for him now? or have I been deceived, and is it all false," she added, in accents of terror, as she grasped old Esther's arm, "and has some one only decoyed me here?"

"No, child, no; folks about here are bad enough, but not as bad as that. Levison is poor enough, both in health and pocket, and wrote as you say; but for all that, I say you are a fool for coming."

"Was it not my duty?" asked Sarah. "Oh, it was sad enough to leave all I love!"

"I dare say it was, dear, I dare say it was," and the old woman's face actually lost its repulsiveness, in such a strong expression of pity, that the desolate girl drew closer to her, and clasped her hand. "And more's the pity you should have left them at all. Duty—it is a fine sounding word; but I don't know what duty Levison can claim—he has never acted like a father, never done anything for you; how can he expect you should for him?"

"Still he is my father," repeated Sarah. "He sent for me when he was prosperous; and though I did not come, his kind wish was the same, and proved he did not forget me. Besides, even if he had, God's plain command is, to honour our father and mother. We can scarcely imagine any case when this command is not to be obeyed; and surely not when a parent is in distress."

"You have learned fine feelings, my poor child. I hope you will be able to keep them; but I don't know, I tried to do my duty, God knows, when I was young and hearty, but now poverty and old age have come upon me, and I have left off caring for anybody or anything. It is better to take life as we find it, and hard enough it is."

"Not if we believe and feel that God is with us, and will lead us in the end to joy and peace," rejoined Sarah, timidly.

"Why, you cannot be so silly, child, as to believe that God," her voice deepened into awe, "cares for such miserable worms as we are, and would lead us as you say?"

"We are taught so, and I do believe and feel it," replied Sarah, earnestly.

"Taught so; where, child, where?" reiterated old Esther, eagerly.

"In God's own book, the Bible," answered Sarah. The old woman's countenance fell.

"The Bible, child! now that must be your own fancy. I never found it there, and I think I must have read it more than you have."

"Have you looked for it?" inquired Sarah, timidly, for she feared to be thought presumptuous.

"Looked for it—I don't know what you mean. I read it every Saturday, the parts they tell us to read; and I do not find much comfort in them, for they seem to tell me God is too far off to care for such as us."

"Oh, do not, do not say so," replied Sarah, with unaffected earnestness. "Every word of that blessed book brings our God near us as a tender and loving father — tells us we are His children. He loves us, cares for us, bears all our sorrows, feels for us more deeply than any earthly friend. I am not very old, but I have learned this from His holy book; and so, I am sure, will you. Forgive me," she added, meekly, taking the old woman's withered hand, "I am too young perhaps to speak so to one old and experienced as you are."

"Forgive you—you are a sweet angel!" hastily replied Esther, suddenly rising, and pressing Sarah in her arms. "Too good, too good, to come to such a house as this. God forbid you should have such trials as to make you doubt what you now so steadfastly believe; the more you talk, the more I wish you had not come."

"But why do you regret it? What is it I must expect? Pray tell me; be my friend. I have none on earth near me to love me now."

"I wish I could be a friend to you, poor child, but I am of little service now, and you can better tutor me than I can you. It is a hard thing to say to a child of her own father, but you are too good for such as he."

"Oh, no, no; pray do not say so. Tell me, only tell me I may love my father!" entreated Sarah.

"You cannot, child; you have been used to kindness and love, you will find harshness and anger; you have only associated with religion and virtue, you have come to misery and vice. As the niece of the worthy widow Perez, you have been respected, and always found employment; as the daughter of Isaac Levison, you will be shunned, and may be left to starve. It is hard enough to find employment for children of respectable parents amongst us poor Jews; and so how can we expect it for others? Don't cry, dear: it is sad enough, but it is only too true; and so I grieve you have given up even your character to come here."

"But what can I do—what can I do?" repeated Sarah, lifting up her streaming eyes with an expression which almost brought tears to those of Esther. "Could I desert my own father, and I heard he needed me? Is he not in poverty and distress? And is his own child to forsake him because others do?"

"Poor he is, child, and so are most of us. But how can you help him?"

"Can I not work for him as I did for my aunt?"

"Yes; if you can get employment, which will not be very easy. You are known in Liverpool, and you are not in London; and the few trades in which we poor Jews can work are overstocked. Take old Esther's advice—return as you came; your father will never know you have been here, and you may be sure I will not betray you. Go back to your happy home and kind friends: it cannot be your duty to give up happiness for misery; and as he forsook you, your conscience can be quite at rest in your leaving him. Do not hesitate, my good child; go at once: he has no claim upon you."

There are some who doubt the necessity of daily prayer; that we need not pray against temptation, there being so few times in which any great temptation is likely to assail us. Great temptations to sin perhaps we seldom have, but small—oh, of what hour can we be secure? Little did poor Sarah imagine, when she entered that lowly roof, the almost overpowering temptation which was to assail her. The home of peace, cleanliness, and comfort which she had deserted; the beloved friends of her youth; the happy hours that were gone; all rose so vividly before her, conjuring her to return to them, not to devote herself to misery—which, after all, was but a doubtful duty—that her first impulse was indeed to fly from a scene where everything around her confirmed old Esther's ominous words. But Sarah was no weak, wavering child of impulse; her principles were steady, her faith was fixed, and the inward petition arose, with a *fervour* and *faith* which gave it power to penetrate the skies—

"Save me from myself, O God! Do not forsake me now. Teach me my duty, the one straight path, and whatever may befall, let me abide by it."

The brief orison was heard, for the God of Israel has love and mercy for the lowest of his creatures, and strength was given.

"No, Esther, no," she answered mildly, yet firmly; "I will not turn aside, whatever may await me. God sees my heart, knows that I am here to do my duty, even if I be mistaken in the means. He will strengthen me for its performance. Do not try to frighten me away," she added, trying to smile. "I dare say all you tell me may be very true, and it will be difficult to bear; but a good heart and a firm faith may make it lighter, you know. I want a friend sadly, and I feel as if you would be a kind one; your experience may smooth my way."

"Blessings on your sweet face for such words, my darling!" murmured the old woman; "it is long since old Esther has heard anything but abuse and unkindness. I wish I could do for you all my heart tells me; but, deary me, that is a vain wish; for I would take away all sorrow from you, and how can a poor creature like me do that?"

Esther would have run on much more in the same strain, and Sarah felt much too grateful for the kind feeling, however rudely expressed, to check her, had not the old woman suddenly recollected the poor traveller might like some tea, which she hastened to prepare. It was, indeed, a different meal, both in quality and comfort, to that which, even in her uncle's poorest days, she had been accustomed to; but Sarah was too much engrossed in anxiety for her father to heed it, and only made the effort to partake of it, in gratitude to her companion. She had time to conclude her meal, and hear much concerning her father, before he appeared. Esther said he had been ill, but never seriously so; that he could often have procured employment in various humble ways; but for some of them he was too proud, and in others behaved so as to disgust those who would have befriended him, and that he now literally had not a friend in the world, either amongst his superiors or his equals. It was a sad, sad tale; and Sarah's feelings, as she listened, may easily be imagined. But how could he live? Old Esther really did not know. She lodged in the same house with him, but she knew little of his private concerns; she only knew he was a wretched temper, which, of course, daily grew worse and worse. He went to the synagogue regularly; that he did, but it did not seem to benefit him much. How could it, when his actions denied his prayers?

It was late before Levison returned. He was still a good-looking man, but miserably attired, and pale from recent illness. He greeted his daughter with affection; for in the lowest and most debased amongst Israel, that redeeming virtue is seldom found wanting; and Sarah felt, as she looked on him, all the daughter glowing in her heart: that she could love, work for, do anything for him. Little sleep had she that night; not because her bed was hard, its covering coarse and unseemly, but from the many thoughts pressing on her mind. Her path was all dark; nothing but the unexpected warmth of her father's welcome and old Esther's kindness to make it light. She could but trust and pray, not only for strength to meet her trials, but that she might so be blessed as to erase from her heart the pang which lingered in it still.

Weary days passed; often and often did Sarah's spirit so sink within her, that she felt as if it could never rise again. Her father's moroseness returned; affection, in a character like his, could not obtain effective power over the evil habits of long years. Sarah could not realize that he loved her, and had it not been for her firm confidence in the love which was unending, pitying, strengthening, as the gracious Lord from whom it comes, her every energy must have failed. She exerted herself to effect a reformation in their dwelling and in her father's slender wardrobe. To look on him, any one would have believed him a very mendicant; yet there were some few articles of clothing easily to be repaired, and so made decent; and this Sarah did. Struck by her method, her perseverance, and the quiet, easy way in which she did everything, Esther Cardoza, old, and often ailing as she was, did not disdain to profit by her example; she became more tidy, more careful, and was surprised to find that it was just as easy to be clean and neat, however poor her apparel, as the contrary, and for comfort, the one could not be mentioned with the other. One sweet source of pleasure Sarah indeed had. She had excited an ardent desire in the old woman's mind to become thoroughly acquainted with God's holy volume; and many an evening did they sit together, and Esther listened to the sweet pleading voice of her young companion, till she felt with her whole heart that God must be with Sarah; she could not be the good, gentle, yet strong-minded creature she was, without His help; and then came the thought and belief, that if she sought Him, He would be found too of her, unworthy and lowly as she was. Such a rich treasury of promises did Sarah open to her longing heart and eyes, that she often wondered how she could have been blind so long; and she would thank and bless her with such strong feeling, that Sarah would feel with thankfulness, and chastened joy, in the midst of her own sorrows, that she had not left her own dear home in vain.

"I begin to think, dearie," Esther one day said, "that I must have been cross and harsh myself, which made folks abuse me as they did; since you have been here, I feel an altered creature, and now meet with kindness instead of wrong."

"Perhaps you are more inclined to think it kindness," said Sarah, smiling.

"Perhaps so, dear; but that is all your doing. Since you have read to me, and proved to me that God, even Abraham's God, cares for and loves me, I am as happy again, and I think if *He* can love me, why, surely some of my fellow-creatures can too. They cannot be as unjust and harsh as I once thought them. What would have become of me if you had taken my advice, and gone home again?"

"Then you see, Esther, I was not sent here for nothing; humble as I am, I have made one fellow-creature happy."

"You must make every one happy who talks with you, darling; but I want you to be happy yourself, and you have not come here to be that, I'm thinking."

"It is better for me that I should not be happy yet, Esther, or our Father would make me so. You know He could, with a word, and He will in His own good time. I did not think I should find one friend, but His love provided you." Her voice quivered, and she threw her arms round old Esther's neck, to hide and subdue her emotion, which kindness alone had power to excite.

But though for Esther she had been permitted to do so much, her father seemed neither to understand nor appreciate her; and to change the opinions to which he so often gave vent, and which, from their strangeness and laxity, often actually appalled her, seemed to her utterly impossible. The sacred name of God was with him a common interjection, introduced in every phrase; it mattered not whether called for by anger or vexation, or any other feeling. Sarah shuddered with agony as she heard it—that awful name, which she never dared pronounce save with reverence and love, which should be kept far from all moods and tempers of sin—that name, the holiness of which was enjoined as strictly, as solemnly, as "thou shalt not kill," and "thou shalt not steal." She could not conquer the feeling which its constant and sinful use excited, and once so horror-struck was her countenance, that her father marked it and demanded its cause. Tremblingly she told him, and a rude laugh was his reply, coupled with an injunction not to preach to him—words which ever checked her when, in his moments of irritation against the whole world and his own fate, she sought to comfort him by the religion of her own pure mind; she gave up the effort at length, but she did not give up prayer. She would not listen to the agonized supposition that for such as he even the long-suffering of an infinitely compassionate God would be of no avail. She prayed and wept for those who prayed not for themselves, and there was comfort in her prayer.

But to pass her life in idleness was impossible. From the first week of her residence in London, she had sought for employment. Her father would not hear of her living out, and so she endeavoured to find daily occupation, or to work at home. In both of these wishes, as old Esther had foreboded, she failed.

In the low neighbourhood where her father dwelt there was no one to employ her, and she had no friend to speak for her in the higher classes. In vain she had at first urged she must seek for a situation in a private family, as upper housemaid, lady's maid, or nurse. Levison so raged and stormed at the first mention of the plan, that Sarah felt as if she never dared resume it. Yet as weeks passed, and the little fund she had brought from Liverpool would very soon be exhausted, something must be done. Our readers, perhaps, think that her idea of the duty she owed her father went so far as even in this to obey him; they are wrong if they do. Sarah's mind was not of that weak cast which could not discern right from wrong. She knew it was a false and sinful pride which actuated Levison's refusal. "Jews were Jews," he declared, "and one class should not serve the other; his daughter was as good as any in the land, and she should not call any one mistress." Mildly, yet firmly, Sarah resisted his arguments. We have not space to repeat all she said, but her father at length yielded, with an ill grace indeed, and vowing she should go nowhere unless they would let her come to him when he wanted her. But still he yielded, and Sarah thankfully pursued her plan. But, alas! she encountered only disappointment; there were no Jewesses established as milliners, dressmakers, or similar trades in London, and therefore no possibility of her getting occupation with them as she wished. She would not heed old Esther's assurances that no one would take Jewish servants. Unsophisticated and guileless herself, she could not believe that her nation would refuse their aid and patronage to those of their own faith; and she strained every energy, she conquered her own shrinking diffidence, but all without effect. Again and again the fact of her being a Jewess completed the conference at once. One said, Jewish servants were more plague than enough, they should never enter her house. Another, that their pride and ignorance were beyond all bounds, and as for a proper deference towards their superiors, a willingness to be taught or guided, it was not in their nature. Another, that a Jewish cook might be all very well, but for anything else it was quite out of the question; they knew the low habits, the laziness and insolence that characterized such kind of people, and they certainly would not expose themselves to it with their eyes open. In vain Sarah pleaded for a trial—that she was willing, most willing to be taught her duty; that she was not wholly ignorant, and humbly yet earnestly trusted she was not proud. Her duty to her God had, she hoped, taught her proper deference towards her superiors on earth. Some there were who, only her superiors in point of fortune, stared at her with stupid surprise, and utterly unable to understand such pure and truthful feelings, sharply terminated their conference at once. Others would not even hear her. Some there were really superior in something more than fortune, and anxiouly desirous to alleviate distress and aid their poorer brethren, but they shrank from being the *first* to engage a Jewess as lady's maid or nurse. Some, touched by her respectful and gentle manner, would have waived this, but when the question who was her father, was asked and answered, the most kindly intentioned shrank back—it could not be. In vain she told them she had never been under his care, and offered references to many respectable families in Liverpool. A daughter of Levison was no fit servant for any respectable family; they were sorry, but they could do nothing for her.

Day after day, week after week thus passed, till even months had elapsed, and, despite her unwavering faith, Sarah's weary spirit flagged.

"But why should it be?" she asked one day, as she sat by the rude bed to which poor old Esther was confined, and in answer to her observation, it was only what she had feared; "But why should it be?" there must be some reason for our being so shunned. Those of the stranger faith, of course, could not employ us; but our own?—how much better and happier we might be if they would take us into their families, and unite us by kindness on the one hand, and obedience and faithfulness on the other."

"It certainly would make us happier, but we must be better fitted for it, Sarah, dear, before it can be accomplished," replied the old woman. "You don't know anything of the majority of us here; how many of us hate the very idea of going into service. What a dreadful deal of pride is amongst us, and such false pride; we very often throw away those that would be our friends, and repay sometimes with abuse any kindness. Then, again, we want to be taught our proper duties. It is not enough to read our Bibles and prayer-books, because a great many are blinded to what they tell us. We want some one to explain them, and tell us plainly what we ought to do, and may do, without breaking our religion. Because you see, dear, when we were in Jerusalem, some things must have been different to what they can be now; and, as servants, we might be called upon to do some things which we think we ought not. Then, it is all very true about being lazy and sometimes insolent. We must set about doing all we can to be *kinder to ourselves*, before we can expect anybody to be kinder to us. I see that now quite clearly, though I did not once; but for you, darling, you are good enough for anybody to find a treasure in you. I wish I could help you; there is one good, kind, charitable lady that I would send you to, but a sister of mine behaved so ungratefully to her, that I do not like intruding on her again. She nearly clothed my sister's little girl, and, would you believe it, Becky went to her house and abused her. What right, forsooth, had she to know that her child wanted clothes."

Sarah uttered an exclamation of surprise.

"Indeed, and yes, dear; and so you see, though I had nothing to do with it, I don't much like to go to Miss Leon again; but you might, though. I am sure she would do what she could for you."

Sarah eagerly inquired who this Miss Leon was.

"None of your very rich carriage people, dear; indeed I don't know how she contrives to do all the good she does, for she is not half as rich as many who think themselves poor. She finds out those who want help; she employs all she possibly can; she gets us work from others; makes our interests hers; teaches our girls all sorts of useful knowledge; gives many a very poor family the meal on which they break their fast, and all such good acts; comes amongst us, and, somehow or other, always does us good. I don't know how many people she cured of rheumatism last winter, by supplying them with some doctor's stuff and warm clothing. Then, as for the girls' schools, I don't know what would become of them without her; she gets them work, cuts out all they want, and teaches them often herself. She is a good creature, God bless her! I lost a kind friend by Becky's behaving as she did, for I never had the face to go to her again, and I would not have her come to this low place; but that she would not mind, as she does not care for the world in doing good."

Sarah listened eagerly; had she indeed found a friend? yet she checked her rising hopes. Miss Leon might do her service, but might not have the power. Before she could make up her mind to seek her, she received, as was her custom, every month at least, a long letter from the dear home she had left; she had stated her many disappointments to her aunt, and that beloved relative entreated her to return.

"Tell your father," she wrote, "two-thirds you earn shall be honestly sent to him; and you can better, much better, support him here than in London. Entreat him to let you return to us—all our happiness is damped when we think of your heavy trials. Come to us, my love; it can scarcely be your duty to remain any longer where you are."

Sarah read this letter to her father, hoping more than she dared acknowledge to herself, that he would see how much better it would be for her to return. But for this he was far too selfish. Sarah had so riveted all the affection which he was capable of feeling, that he would not let her leave him. He was jealous and angry that she should so love her absent friends, and swore that they should not take any more of her heart from him; he would rather remain as he was, than she should work for him at Liverpool; he did not want her labour, he wanted her love, and that she would not give him. Sarah submitted with a strange feeling of consolation amidst her sorrow —did he indeed want her love? Oh, if she could but believe it, she might have some influence over him yet.

Not long after this, as she was sitting reading one morning to poor old Esther that holy book, which was now as great a comfort to Esther as to herself, a lady unexpectedly entered, and before even she heard her name, Sarah guessed who she was. There was the decided manner and kind speech of which Esther had spoken; the plain attire with which, to avert notice, she ever went her rounds of charity; and even had there been none of these peculiarities, the very fact of her coming to that poor place at all proclaimed Miss Leon. She gently upbraided the poor old woman for not letting her know she was ill and needed kindness; would not accept her plea that after her sister's ungrateful conduct she could have no right to appeal to her, and by a very few judicious words set Esther's heart to rest. She inquired what her ailing was, seemed to understand it at once, and promised soon to get her about again.

"God bless you, lady dear!" exclaimed the grateful creature, fervently; "only the other day was I talking about you and all you did; not that I wanted you—for you see my threescore and ten years are almost run out, and it signifies little now if I suffer more or less—but for this poor girl, bless you, lady, you could do so much for her. I ought not to call her poor though, for in one sense God has made her rich enough, and she has been a good angel to me."

With a vivid blush of true modest feeling, that attracted Miss Leon's penetrative eye at once, Sarah tried to check the old woman's garrulity, but in vain. She would pour out all that Sarah had done for her, and wanted and suffered for herself, and who she was, and how brought up, and where she came from. Miss Leon meanwhile had quietly taken a seat, and, without the smallest symptom of impatience or failing interest, listened to the tale. When it was concluded, she put some questions to Sarah, the answers to which appeared much to please and satisfy her. She promised to do what she could, making, however, no professions that could excite delusive hopes, yet somehow, leaving such comfort behind her, that on her departure Sarah sought her own room to pour forth her swelling thanksgiving to God.

Miss Leon never made professions, but she always acted. When it was known amongst her friends where she had been, and whose daughter she intended, if possible, to befriend, a complete storm of advice and warning and censure had to be encountered, but Adelaide Leon was not to be daunted; for advice she was grateful, but timidity and selfish consideration never entered her code of charity. She felt no fear of consequences whatever; even had she to come in contact with Levison himself, she saw nothing very dreadful in it, and as for the censure, she smiled very quietly at the idea; but when her conscience told her she was right, it mattered little what other people said. In a word, she did as most strong-minded, right people do—finally carried her point. She went to see Esther three times that week, and before a month had passed the old woman was able to sit up, doing a little knitting, which Miss Leon herself had taught her; and Sarah went sometimes four days in the week to work at the Square.

A very brief period of intercourse convinced Miss Leon that Sarah certainly was a superior person, and her benevolent intentions did not terminate in merely getting her daily work. She had not enough in her own family to occupy her sufficiently, and many in her circle were too prejudiced to follow her good example.

Now it so happened Miss Leon had a widowed sister, a Mrs. Corea, who had four little girls, and was in want of a young woman to attend on and work for them, and take care of them when they were not with her or their governess. Genteel and modest in her manners, without a portion of pride or insolence, truly and unostentatiously pious, and withal better informed on many subjects than very many who profess a great deal, Sarah was just the very person whom Miss Leon could desire to be with her nieces; but the difficulties she had to contend with, before she accomplished the end, we have no space to dilate on. Mrs. Corea was about as weak-minded, prejudiced, and foolish as Miss Leon was the contrary. First, she had a horror of all low-born people, however they might be brought up; and no one could say but that, if Sarah was Levison's child, she was the very lowest of the low. Secondly, she could not have a Jewess; she would give the children all sorts of superstitious, ignorant ideas, and was as helpless and exacting as any fine lady. And thirdly, and most convincing of all, in her own ideas, she did not like the plan, and would not have her; what would people say too—doing what nobody else did?

Fortunately for our poor Sarah, Miss Leon never desponded when determined to do good; the more difficulties she had to contend with, the more determined was she to carry her point, and, to the surprise of everybody, even in this she succeeded. Mrs. Corea yielded to perseverance. It was too much trouble to say "no" any longer. She had seen no one that would do, and Adelaide had promised she would take all the blame, and answer everybody who meddled and found fault; and if Sarah did not suit, why Adelaide would take the blame for that too, and never torment her to take a Jewess again.

Sarah did not know all that Miss Leon had encountered in her cause, but she knew it was to her she owed the comfortable situation in which she was at length installed; and the grateful girl not only prayed God to bless her benefactress, but to bless her own efforts, that she might do her duty to her young charge, and, in serving them, prove her gratitude to their aunt.

With her father she had had at first a difficult part to play. He, of course, could not be allowed to come to the house to see her, and he had sworn she should go nowhere, where he might not be admitted. A voiceless prayer that his heart might be changed rose from Sarah's heart, as she attempted to tell him of her plans; and the prayer was heard, for, to her own astonishment, her gentle arguments and meek persuasions were successful. His anger subsided at first into sullenness, then he seemed endeavouring to conceal some strong emotion, and at last, as she drew closer to him, trembling and fearful, conjuring his reply, he caught her in his arms, kissed her again and again, bade God bless her and spare her till he was a better man, when she would love him more. He knew she could not as he was; but for her sake there was nothing she could not persuade him to do; she did not know how much he loved her, and, as Sarah sobbed from many varied feelings on his bosom, she thanked God that He had called her to her father, and permitted her even in the midst of sorrow and sin to cling to him still.

CHAPTER IV.

OUR readers must imagine a period of eighteen months since we bade them farewell. But few changes had taken place. Leah, Simeon, and Joseph continued in their respective situations, every year increasing their wages, and riveting the esteem and good-will of their employers.

The widow might have had another home in a gayer part of the town, but she refused to leave the lowly dwelling she had so dearly loved, until Leah or one of her sons had a home, to keep which she was needed. One change in the widow's household had indeed taken place, for Ruth was in London. Sarah's excellent conduct had interested Miss Leon not only in herself, but in her family. As they were all comfortably providing for themselves, Miss Leon could find no object for her active benevolence but the little Ruth. The poor child had not indeed so many resources as many similarly afflicted, for though all were desirous, none knew how to teach her. It so happened Miss Leon was peculiarly interested in Ruth, because she had once had a sister who was blind; one whom she had so dearly loved, that she had learned the whole method of tuition for the blind simply for that sister's sake. She died just when she was of an age to know all that affection had done for her; and Miss Leon now offered to impart all she knew to Ruth, to give her board and lodging at her house till she was enabled to earn something for herself, when she would herself send her to her mother.

It was a hard struggle before the widow could consent to part with her darling; but the representations of Leah and Simeon, and Ruth's own yearnings to be able to do something for herself, overcame all selfish considerations. She could not feel Miss Leon a stranger, for her kindness to Sarah had made her name never spoken without a blessing, and Sarah would always be near Ruth to watch over and write of her; and so with tears of thankfulness the widow consented. Leah was often permitted to take her work to the widow's cottage and pursue it there; and the little Christian girl, to whom Ruth and Sarah had been so kind, was delighted to come and do any cleaning or scouring in the house, or sit with the widow and work and read for her, to prove how grateful she was.

And where was Reuben Perez all this while? Were his mother's prayers for him still unanswered? Alas! farther and farther did they seem from fulfilment. He had left Liverpool to accept, in conjunction with his father-in-law, the management of a bank, in one of the smaller towns of Yorkshire, and, of course, even his casual visits were discontinued. Not that they were of much avail, going as he did; but still his mother had hoped against her better reason, that while near her he would never entirely take himself away. Now that hope was at an end. He was thrown entirely amongst Gentiles, and Sabbaths and holidays seemed wholly given up. He did not often write home, but when he did, always affectionately; and his mother's allowance was regularly paid. She yearned to see and bless him once again, but months, above a year passed, and his foot had never passed her threshold.

With regard to Sarah, a very few months' association with her, though only in the relative position of mistress and servant, had completely conquered Mrs. Corea's prejudices; and the very indolence and foolishness, which had originally been so difficult to overcome, were now as likely to ruin as they formerly had been to oppose. But fortunately Sarah was not one for indulgence and confidence to spoil; indeed she often regretted her mistress's indolence, from the responsibility it devolved on her. Mrs. Corea had repeatedly allowed herself to be cheated and deceived, because it was too much trouble to find fault. She often permitted the most serious annoyances in her establishment—keys and even money repeatedly lying about, her children neglected, their clothes often thrown aside long before they were worn out. In a very few months Sarah's ready mind discovered this state of things. One only she had the power of herself to remedy—the neglect of her charge; and so admirably did she do her duty by them, that Miss Leon felt herself amply rewarded. Finding it was of no use to entreat Mrs. Corea to have more regard to her own interest, and not allow herself so repeatedly to be deceived, Sarah in distress appealed to Miss Leon, who quietly smiled, and assured her she would soon settle matters entirely to Mrs. Corea's satisfaction. She did so, by giving to Sarah's care almost the entire charge of the housekeeping, with strict injunctions to take care of her mistress's keys and purse, whenever she saw them lying about. Sarah at first painfully shrunk from the responsibility, knowing well it would expose her yet more to the dislike of her fellow-servants, who, as a Jewess, already regarded her with prejudice. Mrs. Corea was charmed that such a vast amount of trouble was spared her; telling everybody Sarah was a treasure, and she only wondered there were not more Jewish servants.

But our readers must not imagine that Sarah's situation was all delightful. She had many painful prejudices to bear with, many slights and unkindness in her fellow-servants to forgive and forget, many jests at her peculiar religion, and ridicule at its forms—much that, to a character less gently firm and forbearing, would have led to such domestic bickering and misery, that she would have been compelled to leave her place, or perhaps have been induced weakly to hide, if it did not shake her reverence for, the observance of her ancient faith. But Sarah had not read her Bible in vain. She had not now to learn that such prejudice and scorn were of God, not of man. That He permitted these things, in His wisdom, to teach His people, though they were still His own, still His beloved, their sins had demanded chastisement, and thus received it. That the very prejudice in which by the ignorant they were held, was proof of the Bible's truth—proof that they were His chosen and His firstborn; and more consolatory still, that as the *threatenings* were thus fulfilled, so, in His own good time, would be His *promises*. Sarah never wavered in the line of duty which she had marked out for herself—to make manifest that her faith was of God by *actions*, not by *words;* and she so far succeeded, that after a while peace was established between her and her fellow-servants. They began to think, even if she were a heathen, she was a very harmless and often a very kind one, and there was not so much difference between them as at first they had fancied.

These are but trifling things to mention; but we most particularly wish our readers to understand that though good conduct will inevitably find reward even on earth, it is not to be expected that it will have no trials. Virtue and religion will *not* exempt us from suffering, but they teach us so to bear them, that we can derive consolation and unfailing hope even in the darkest hours; and, instead of raising a barrier between us and our God, they draw us nearer and nearer to Him, till we can realize His immeasurable love towards us; and, tracing every suffering from His hand sent for our good, to love Him more and more, and in that very love find comfort. Do not then let us practise religion and virtue because we think they have power to shield us from all trial and sorrow, but simply for the love of Him who bids us practise them, and who has promised, if we seek Him, He will heal our sorrows and heighten our joys.

One unspeakable source of comfort Sarah had: it was that her influence with her father rather increased than lessened with him. Once every month she spent the Sabbath evening with him, and she felt that indeed he loved her. Old Esther told her, even that when she was absent he was an altered man. He sought employment, and after some difficulty found it, though it was of a kind so humble, that before Sarah came to town he would have spurned it as so derogatory to his pride, he would rather starve than have it; but now it was welcome, because he would not be a burden on his Sarah. His Sarah! —every dormant virtue seemed to spring into life with those dear precious words. The very interjections of that sacred name of God, which had been once ever on his lips, were now constantly checked. "She does not like it, my angel Sarah, and I *will* not say it," Esther heard him mutter when the accustomed phrase broke from him; and many other evil habits, that thought—" my angel Sarah "—had equal power to remove. The bad man seemed fast breaking from his sins, and it was from the influence of his gentle pious child. The father was at work within him, and God blessed him through that feeling, and through his daughter's unceasing prayers. Every time Sarah visited him she saw more to hope, more for which with grateful tears to bless her God; and each time to love him more, and feel she was yet more beloved.

On Sarah's returning home one afternoon, after a brief visit to old Esther, who was not quite well, she was informed a young man had called to see her, and stayed some time; but as she did not come as soon as they expected, he had gone away, promising to return in the course of the evening. He had not left his name, they added; but he seemed a gentleman, quite a gentleman, though one of her own nation, and was in the deepest mourning. Sarah was not one given to speculation or curiosity, though she did wonder who this gentleman could be, but quietly continued her usual employments. She had just finished dressing her young ladies to go with their mother to the theatre, and ran down to see them safely in the carriage, when the footman called out—

" Sarah, the gentleman has come again, he is waiting for you in the housekeeper's room."

She went accordingly; but her self-possession almost deserted her when, on looking up in the face of the stranger as she entered, she recognised at once her cousin Reuben—pale, thin, and worn indeed, but still himself, and it required a powerful effort, even in that strong and simple mind, to evince no feeling but surprise and welcome.

Few words, however, at the first moment passed between them. Reuben sprang forward as she entered, and clasped both her hands in his, which were cold and trembling; and she saw his lips quiver painfully, and, to her grief and almost terror, as she spoke to him he gradually let go her hands, and, sinking on the nearest chair, covered his face with his handkerchief, and wept like a child.

" I terrify you, dear cousin, do forgive me," he said at length, as he heard the gentle voice which sought to soothe him falter in spite of herself. " Sarah, dear Sarah, I do not know why your kind voice should affect me thus. I cannot tell you why I have come to grieve you with my grief, except that when I least desired it, you were always kind and good and feeling, and gave me comfort when I could not console myself; and my heart has so yearned to you now—now, when your own word has come to pass, to tell you you were right. In prosperity I might be happy, though God knows it was but a strange unnatural happiness; but in affliction—Sarah, do you remember your own words?"

She did remember them; but she had no voice to repeat them then, and her quivering lip alone gave answer. Her cousin continued, almost choked with many emotions—

"'If affliction, if death—may you never repent your engagement then.' These were the words you said; and oh, how often, the last few months, have they returned to me. Affliction has come, my own cousin; affliction, oh, such affliction that God alone could send—death, even death!" The word was almost inaudible.

"Death!" repeated Sarah, startled at once into perfect consciousness. She looked at his dress—the deepest mourning—and the words more fell from her than were spoken. "Not Jeanie, your own Jeanie—tell me, it is not she?" Then, as she read his answer in the tighter pressure of his hand, the convulsive movement of his lips, she threw her arms round him, and faintly exclaiming, "Reuben, my poor Reuben, may God grant you His comfort!" burst into tears.

Nothing is so true a balm to the afflicted as unaffected sympathy; and Reuben roused himself from his own sorrow, to bless his cousin for her tears, yet bid her not weep for him.

"It is better thus, my gentle cousin. The God of my parents has revealed Himself to their sinful offspring, even in His chastening. I cannot tell you all now, dear Sarah; how, even when life seemed all prosperous around me, there was still a void within—I was not happy. I had returned to virtue, turned aside from all irregular and sinful pursuits, kept steady to business, and in doing kind acts towards men; and more still, I had a gentle being who so loved me, that she forced me into loving her more than when I first sought her; for then, then—Sarah, do not hate me—I did but seek her, because I thought a union with a Christian would put a final barrier between me and the race I had taught myself to hate—would mark me no more a Jew; and so for this, this dreadful sin, I banished feelings which had once been mine.

Sarah, do not ask me what they were. Yet still, still, even when I did love my fair and gentle wife, when she lavished on me such affection it ought to have brought but joy, I was not happy. I was away from all who knew my birth and race; the once hated name, a Jew, no longer hurt my ears; courted, flattered, admired, Sarah, Sarah, was it not strange there was still that gnawing void?"

She looked up with streaming eyes. "It was a void no man could fill, dear cousin. You thought its cause was of earth, and sought with earth to fill it; but now, oh, let us thank God, His image fills it now."

"You have guessed aright, my Sarah, as you always do; but, oh, you know not all I endured before it was so filled. I tried to believe with my Jeanie and her father, but I could not. I attended their church at times, I listened to their doctrines, I read their books; but no, no, God's finger was upon me. I could not believe in any Saviour, any Redeemer, but Himself; and then that holy name, that sacred subject, which should be the dearest link between those that love, never found voice. We dared not read each other's thoughts. When we married, you know Jeanie thought little of those things; but she became acquainted with a good and holy man, a pious minister of her own faith, and he made her think more seriously: and what followed? She loved me more and more, but she knew I did not believe in that Saviour whose recognition she deemed necessary for my salvation, and so she drooped and drooped at the very time when nature demanded greater sustenance and support. In a few months I was a father. O God, the agony of that hour which should have been all bliss! Then I felt in all its fulness there was a God, and I had neglected Him. My innocent babe might be snatched from me, as David's was, for its father's sin; and how was I to avert this misery—how devote it to its God, as its mother believed? I shuddered. From that hour my Jeanie sunk, even though they said she had recovered all effects of her confinement. Month after month I watched over her. I heard her clinging to a faith, a Saviour, which to me was mockery. I heard her call aloud for help and mercy from Jesus, not from God. Sarah, it is vain, I cannot tell you what those hours were. You can tell their anguish, for you warned me such might be." He paused, every limb trembling with his emotion; and Sarah, almost as much affected, entreated him not to harrow his feelings by such recollections any more.

"Bear with me, dear cousin; I shall be better, happier when all is told. I saw her look on our infant (thank God, it was a girl!) with the big tear stealing down her pale face, and I knew of what she thought; yet I could not, I dared not give her the only promise that might be her comfort, and her love for me was so strong, so intense, she had no voice to ask it. At length, one evening, after Mr. Vaughan, the clergyman, had been urging on her the necessity of her child receiving baptism, she called me to her, and, laying her head on my bosom, conjured me to grant her last request, the only one, she said, she had ever feared to ask me. Her voice was faint from weakness, yet it thrilled so on my heart, that it was a struggle to reply, and conjure her not to say more. I knew what she would ask, but she interrupted me by sinking on her knees before me, and wildly reiterating her prayer, 'My child, my child! let her be made pure—let me feel I shall look upon her again. Reuben, my husband, have mercy on us all!' Sarah, had that moment been all my punishment, it would have been enough. Why could I not feel then, as I had so often declared before, that all faiths were the same in the sight of God? Why could I not make this promise to the dying and beloved? I know not, I know not now, save that I felt myself a father, and the immortal spirit of my child was of more value than my own had ever been. I raised her: I solemnly vowed that I would study both faiths—I would read with and listen to Mr. Vaughan, and *if I could believe*, my child should be reared a Christian, and be baptized with myself. She raised her sweet face to mine with such a smile. 'Bless you, bless you, my own husband! we shall all meet again, then. Oh, you have made me so happy! Jesus will save—will bring us all to——' Her sweet voice sunk, and her head drooped down on my bosom; and thinking she was exhausted, I clasped her closer to me, and kissed her again and again. Nearly half an hour passed, and I felt no movement, heard no breath. It was quite dark, and with sudden terror I called aloud for lights. They were brought: I lifted the bright curls from her dear face, and raised her head. It was vain, vain."

He ceased abruptly, and there was silence, for Sarah could not speak. Reuben hastily paced the room; then, reseating himself by his cousin, continued more calmly; but, limited as we are for space, we are forbidden to continue the conversation, though it deepened in interest, even as it subsided in emotion. Reuben told how he had faithfully kept his promise—how, for two months, he had remained with his father-in-law, studying the word of God, and listening to all the instructions of Mr. Vaughan, whose very kindness and true piety in spirit made his arguments more difficult to resist, than had they been harshly and determinately enforced. A year was the period Reuben had promised to devote to the fulfilment of his vow; and if, at the end of that time, he could believe in Jesus, he and his child would, of course, be made Christians; but if his studies had a contrary effect, no more, either by Mr. Wilson or the clergyman, would be said to him on the subject.

"Sarah, my dear cousin, do not fear for me. My God did not forsake me, even when I forsook Him. He will not then forsake me now that I seek Him, and night and day implore Him to reveal that path, that faith, which is most acceptable to Him. I have already read and felt enough to glory in the faith I once despised—to feel it is a privilege, aye, and a proud one, to be a Jew: for the rest, let us trust in Him."

"And your child, dear Reuben—where is she?"

"With Mrs. Vaughan, at present. At the conclusion of the year, God willing, and my mother is spared, she shall be cared for by the same tender love which her erring father only now knows how to value and return."

"And does my aunt know this?"

"No, Sarah, no. I cannot tell her. I feel as if I had no right to go to her again, until I have indeed returned with heart and soul to the faith in which all her gentle counsels had not power to retain me. No, no, no; I cannot, cannot claim the solace of her love till I am worthy to be called her son in faith as well as love."

The cousins were long together, and much, much was spoken between them, which we would fain repeat, as likely to be useful to our readers, but we are warned to desist: enough to know that Sarah prevailed on Reuben to write to his mother and tell her all, even if the story of his inward life were otherwise kept secret.

Reuben said he had given up his place in the bank, and intended, for the remainder of the year, to endeavour to obtain a situation in some Jewish counting-house as clerk, for some hours in the day; and thus allow him evenings, Sabbaths, and holidays for his sacred purpose. It was with this intention he had come up to London, as though he might have procured employment in Liverpool or Manchester, he shrunk from all remark, even kindness, from his own nation, until he had in truth returned to them. He had brought with him letters of high recommendation, which had obtained a capital situation in a thriving house of his own nation; a branch of which resided in Birmingham, to which place it was likely he should go.

"It is not that I fear the temptations of this large city, dearest Sarah, that I would rather live elsewhere. No, I shrink from all scenes of pleasure now with sensation of loathing; but I feel as if it would be better for me to be alone, even away from those I most love, till this one year is passed. Sarah, will you think of me, pray for me?" he took both her hands, and looked pleadingly in her face. "It would be a comfort, such a comfort to come to you for sympathy, for counsel; for you it was, when we watched together by my sick mother's bed, who first made me feel that were all like you, the name 'a Jew' would cease to be reproached; but no, no, it is better for me—perhaps, too, for your character, dear girl—that we should not meet yet awhile. I threw away happiness once when it might perchance have been mine; and now—but it is better thus."

He had spoken incoherently, and he broke off abruptly. Sarah only answered by the simple assurance that she never ceased to pray for his happiness, nor would she now; and soon after they separated affectionately, confidingly, as in long past years, perchance yet more so; for then a barrier was between them, now there was none; their rock of refuge, the shield of their salvation, was the same.

To define Sarah's feelings, as she prostrated herself before her God in prayer that night, is indeed impossible; nor is there need—surely the coldest, the most callous, can imagine them, and give her sympathy. Not indeed that hope was dawning for her long-tried, long-hidden affection; for Reuben never dreamed he was so loved. It was simply thanksgiving, the purest, most heartfelt, that her prayers were heard—the beloved one of her heart brought back to his God.

Yet many were the secret tears she shed, as she pictured her cousin's anguish. She gave not one single thought to those words, which a less guileless heart might have believed related to herself. She never thought of the consequences which Reuben's return to his faith might bring to her individually. It was enough of happiness to feel he had sought her in his sorrow, had felt her as his friend.

But sorrow was at hand, as unexpected as terrible. About four or five months after her interview with Reuben, old Esther came to her one day in such extremity of grief and horror, that even her little share of discretion vanished before it, ard she imparted her tidings to Sarah so suddenly, that the poor girl stood stunned and paralysed, preserved only by a strong though almost unconscious effort from fainting. Levison had been taken up and carried to Newgate as an accomplice in act of burglary and robbery, which, attended by circumstances of unusual notoriety, had been lately committed in the neighbourhood of Epping. Levison had loudly and fiercely asserted his innocence; but of course his asseverations had been disregarded.

"But he has said it—he has said it! He has declared he is innocent, and he is—he is!" reiterated poor Sarah, with a violent burst of tears, which restored sense and energy. Esther, however, seemed to derive no comfort from the assertion.

"Yes, dear, yes; I do believe he is not guilty—bad as some of us are, we do not do such things. Who ever heard of a Jew being a housebreaker or a thief? But who will believe him? Who will take his word, his oath? Oh, what will become of us?" and the old woman rocked herself to and fro, in the misery of the thought. Sarah was in no state to offer the usual comfort; but stunned, bewildered as she was, her thought formed itself into unconscious prayer for help and strength. Her plan of action was decided on the instant; she would, she must go to him. In vain Esther bade her think of the consequences; what would her mistress say, if she knew that Sarah was any way related to Levison, the reputed housebreaker, much less that she was his daughter?

"Would you then advise me, if this misery come to her knowledge, deny my father, now that he may need me more than ever? Oh, Esther, I cannot do this," replied Sarah mournfully, though firmly. "My mistress need not know my errand now perhaps, and this terrible trial may be permitted to pass away before it comes to the worst. But should it indeed reach her ears, I cannot deny him; he has only me, and if it cause me the loss of my situation, of my character in the opinion of my fellow-creatures, my God will love me, care for me still. I cannot desert my father."

And while she seeks him, we must inform our readers, briefly as may be, how the matter really stood. Levison had been seen and recognised talking to a party of men the evening previous to the night's robbery. No one could swear to his person as accessory to the act by having seen him in the house, but in such earnest conversation with those who were taken in the fact, that he was, in consequence, committed as one of the gang, for the apprehension of whom a large reward had been offered. It was true, none of the stolen property had been found on his person, or in his dwelling; but these facts were little heeded in his favour.

He was a Jew—a man who had been noted for his dishonest practices in business, and consequently there was no one to come forward with such report of his former character as could be taken in his favour.

He persisted that he was innocent; that though he had been talking to the men as was alleged, he knew nothing of their real character or intentions; that he had been acquainted with them formerly, but only in the way of business; that they knew he had separated from them, at seven o'clock that evening, to proceed several miles in a contrary direction, to the burial-ground of his people, where he had been engaged to watch beside the grave of one that day interred; the person who had been engaged to do so having been suddenly taken ill, and asked him, Levison, to watch in his stead. How could he prove this? he was asked.

The unhappy man groaned aloud for answer—he had no proof. Some one, a gentleman, had indeed visited the grave at break of day, had demanded who he was, and why he was there instead of the person engaged; and he answered, giving his full name. The gentleman had thrown him money, and hastily departed; but who or what he was, except a Jew, as himself, Levison did not know.

Of course, such a tale, and from such a person, was not to be believed, and he was committed to Newgate, with his supposed accomplices, to take his trial.

It was with great difficulty Sarah gained admittance to his cell; but it was not till in his presence, till the door was closed upon her for a specified time, that the energy which supported her throughout gave way.

She could but throw herself on her knees before him, but fling her arms round him, and sob forth, "Father!" the convulsions of agony and fear which shook her every limb depriving her at once of power and of voice.

The effect of her presence on Levison was terrible. He

gave vent to a wild, shrill cry, then catching her to his bosom, gasped forth, " My daughter! oh, my daughter! the God of wrath and justice will withdraw his hand, if you are near," and then sunk back in a strong convulsive fit. Perhaps it was as well that the poor girl was thus compelled to exertion. Terrified as she was, she knew to call for help was useless, for who could hear her? But by unloosening his collar, and the application of cold water, which happened to be in the room, after a few minutes of intense terror, she saw the convulsive struggles gradually give way, and he lay sensible, but exhausted. It was then she saw the ravages either illness or imprisonment had made; it seemed as if even death itself was upon him. He had never quite recovered the illness which had originally called her to London, and the last few days seemed to have brought it back with increase of suffering and complete prostration of physical power. His black hair had whitened, and his form was bent, as if a burden of many years had descended upon him; his features were contracted, and wan as death.

" Sarah, Sarah, I thought God had forsaken me; but I see you, and I know he has not. Miserable and guilty as I am—guilty of many sins, as I know, I feel now—but not of this: no, no, no; my child, my child, I am innocent of this. I turned away from vice and sin for your sake. I made a vow to try and become worthy of such an angel child; and see, see what has come upon me! I have been deceiving and dishonest in former days, but even then I never, never turned aside to steal—to join a gang of thieves. Sarah, Sarah, I thought to make you happy at last; and I shall be but your curse, your misery. Perhaps you too will not believe me, but I am innocent of this crime; my child, my child, I am indeed!"

It was long ere Sarah's gentle soothings and earnest assurances of her firm belief in his perfect innocence could calm the fearful agitation of her unhappy father. Still her presence, the pressure of her hand was such comfort, that a light appeared to have gleamed on the darkness of his despair, and he poured forth his agonizing thoughts, his terrors, alike of life and death and eternity, as if his child were indeed the ministering angel of hope and faith and comfort which his deep love believed her.

" Had I not you, my daughter, oh, there would be no hope, no mercy for one like me. I have disobeyed and profaned my God, and taken His holy name in vain, and called down on me His wrath, His vengeance; and how can I, how dare I hope for mercy? I cannot repent—I cannot seek righteousness now; it is too late, too late! Yet God has given me you; and is He then all wrath, all punishment? Tell me, tell me, there is mercy for the sinner, even now."

"Father, dear father, there is! Has He not said it? Yes, and reiterated it in His holy book, till the most doubting of us must believe. 'He hath no pleasure in the death of the wicked, but rather that he should turn from his wickedness and live;' bidding us repent and believe, and that in the day we did so our guilt should not be remembered—should not appear against us; telling us but to confess our sin, to throw ourselves on His mercy, that mercy all perfect to purify, redeem, and save—that He is merciful and gracious, long-suffering, abundant in mercy and love—showing mercy unto thousands! My father, oh, my father, there is no sin so infinite as His mercy—no sin for which repentance and love and faith in Him will not in His sight atone."

"But I can make no atonement, my child. I can do nothing to prove repentance—that I would serve and love Him now—nothing to make reparation for past sin: too late, too late!" and he groaned aloud.

"He does not ask works, my father, when He knows they cannot be performed. Have you not sought Him this last year, in penitence and prayer, and amendment of your ways? and does He not record this, though man may not? and now, oh, do but believe in Him, in His will and power to forgive and save—do but call upon Him with the faith and repentance of a sorrowing child. Oh, my father, God asks no more than we can do. His sacrifices are a broken heart and a contrite spirit, which we all have power to bestow. He has told us this blessed truth, through the lips of one who had the power to do and give much more in atonement for his sin, that we, who can do nothing but believe and repent, may be comforted. Father, my own dear father, if indeed you repent and love, and believe, oh, God is near you, will save you still!"

Much, much more did Sarah say, as she sat on the straw pallet where her unhappy father half reclined, her dark, truthful eyes, often swelling in large tears, fixed on his face as she spoke. It was impossible for one whom her influence the last twelvemonth had already, through God's mercy, changed in heart, to listen to her healing words, and look on her sweet pleading face, and yet retain the doubts and terrors of despair. It seemed to Levison that if such a being could love and pity him, and cling to him thus even in a prison cell, he could not be cut off from all of heavenly hope—the all-pitying love and consoling promises of God appeared to him through her as if by a voice from heaven. They could not deceive, and even in the depth of repentant agony—for it was true repentance—there was comfort. Sarah was summoned away only too soon, but she promised to visit him often again. The piece of gold which she had slid into the turnkey's hand, she knew, would be her passport; but to do this unknown to her mistress was an act of injustice towards her, which her pure mind rejected.

Yet how to tell her? The determination was made, but on the manner of fulfilling it poor Sarah thought some time. Perhaps it was fortunate she was roused to exertion. On entering the kitchen for something she wanted, she saw her fellow-servants congregated in a knot together, the footman reading aloud the account of the robbery, and the committal of the gang, from the newspapers. He stopped as she entered, and every eye turned on her. Her cheek grew white as ashes, and her lip quivered, so as to be remarked by all. The footman seemed about to speak, but the housemaid laid her hand on his arm, with an imploring look to forbear. It was enough. Sarah felt she could better leave her mistress than encounter the questions or suspicions of her fellow-servants, and that instant she sought the parlour. Miss Leon was with her sister. The ghastly paleness and agonized expression of the poor girl's face struck her at once, and with accents of earnest kindness she inquired what was the matter. Bursting into tears, Sarah almost inarticulately related the heavy trial which had befallen her, and her intention to give up her situation. Confidential, happy as it was to devote herself to her unfortunate father, feeling that the child of one suspected as he was could bring but disreputableness to a respectable family, Sarah felt her story was incoherent; but that it was understood was visible in its effects. Mrs. Corea, selfish and weak as her wont, thought only of the trouble and annoyance Sarah's resignation of her situation would bring her; and overwhelmed her with reproaches, as ungrateful and capricious. Miss Leon spoke calmly and reasonably. There was no need for any decisive parting. Sarah might leave them for a time, if she were desirous of doing so, though she did not think it wise; that if Mrs. Corea valued her so much, she could have no objection to her returning. "What! the daughter of a pickpocket, a housebreaker! No, no, if Sarah were fool enough to say she was the daughter of such a person, she would have nothing more to do with her; but there was no need for her to do so. What was to prevent her disclaiming all relationship; and what good could she do to him or herself by going to him? It was all folly. There were plenty of Levisons in the world. Nobody need know this Levison was Sarah's father, if the girl herself were not such a fool as to betray it."

"And can you advise this, Miss Leon?" implored Sarah, turning towards her. "Oh, do not, do not say so. I would not displease one so kind and good as you are. I would do anything, everything to show you I am grateful; but I cannot, oh, I cannot deny my father! I should never know a happy day again."

Miss Leon was not at all a person to evince useless emotion, but there was certainly something rising in her throat, which made her voice husky ere she replied. Reasonable and feeling, however, as her arguments were, that, without actually denying or deserting her father, she need not ruin her own reputation for ever, by proclaiming it was to visit him in prison, she left her place. Sarah could at that moment only *feel;* her future was bound up in her father's.

We have not, however, space to dilate on all Miss Leon urged or Sarah felt. Suffice it, that the next morning Sarah turned away from the house which for nearly two years had been a happy home. She knew not if she should ever be welcome there again. Miss Leon was indeed still her friend; but how could even she aid her now? She returned to that dilapidated dwelling where old Esther still lived, feeling that heavy as she had thought her trial when she had first entered those doors, it was light, it was joy to that which was hers now.

Day after day, in the brief period intervening before Levison's final trial, did his devoted daughter visit his cell, and not in vain. The terror, the anguish which had possessed him were passing from his soul. He did believe in the saving power of his God. He did approach His throne with a broken and contrite heart; and it was the prayers, the faith, the forbearing devotion of his child, which brought him there.

Sarah had told all his story to Miss Leon, who had listened attentively, though she herself feared that to remedy this and prove him innocent was, even to her energetic benevolence, impossible.

The morning of the trial came, the court was crowded; for the extensive robberies traced home to this gang occasioned unusual excitement. The trembling heart of the daughter felt that to wait to hear of its termination, and her father's sentence, was impossible, the very effort would drive her mad. In vain old Esther remonstrated; offered, infirm as she was, to go herself, if Sarah would but remain quietly at home. Sarah insisted on accompanying her, muffled up so as not to be recognised. They mingled with the thronging crowds, jostled, pushed, and otherwise annoyed, yet Sarah knew it not—seemed conscious of nothing till her eyes rested on her misguided father. What was it she hoped? She knew not, except a strange undefined belief that even now, in the eleventh hour, his innocence would be made evident. Alas, poor girl! the summary proceedings of a court of justice on a gang of noted criminals allowed no saving clause. He was sworn to as having been seen with them, and that was sufficient. All he said was unheeded, perhaps unheard; and sentence of transportation for life was pronounced on every man by name, Isaac Levison included.

Sarah did not scream; she thought she did not faint, for the words rung in her ears as repeated by a hundred echoes, each one louder than the other; but except this power of hearing, every other sense seemed suddenly stilled. She did not know whose arm led her from that terrible scene—who was conducting her hastily yet tenderly towards home. She walked on quick, quicker still, as if the rapidity of movement should hush that mocking sound. It would not, it could not; and when she was at home, she sunk down powerless, conscious only of misery that even faith might not remove.

"Sarah, my own Sarah! look up, speak to me, this silence is terrible!" exclaimed a voice which roused her as with an electric shock. Reuben Perez was beside her, his arm around her; the ice of misery, the restraint of long-hidden feelings, were broken by the power of that voice, and laying her head on his shoulder, she sobbed in uncontrollable agony. He told her how he had seen the name of Levison in the papers, and his defence, and how he had trembled lest it should be her father; how anxiously he had wished to come up at once to

London, but was unavoidably prevented leaving Birmingham till the previous night. How he had proceeded to the court; at once recognised Levison, and at the same moment, guided by some strange instinct, looked for and found Sarah, muffled as she was.

He had gradually and with difficulty made his way through the crowd towards her, and reached her just as the sentence was pronounced. Old Esther had begged him to take care of Sarah home, as she could follow more slowly. He tried to speak comfort respecting her father; but in this he failed. Shudderingly, she reiterated the sentence. "Transportation, and for life—to be sent away to work, to die, untended, unloved," and then, as with sudden thought, she started up—

"No, no, no!" she exclaimed, a hectic glow tinging her pallid cheek. "Why cannot I go too? not with him, they will not let me do that; but there are ships enough taking out emigrants, and I can meet him there—be with him again. They shall not separate the father from his child; and he is innocent! My father, my poor father, your Sarah will not forsake you even now!" and she wept again, but less painfully than before. Startled as he was, Reuben could yet feel this was scarcely a resolution to be kept, and with argument and persuasion sought to turn her from her purpose. Her father could not need such sacrifice; how could she aid him in his far distant dwelling?

"He has but me—he has but me!" she reiterated; "who is there that has claim enough to keep me from him? I have thought a former trial heavy to be borne; but had it not been for that, my poor father might have died in sin, for perhaps I could not have come to him as I did when free. No, no, I was destined to be the instrument, in the hands of mercy, in bringing him back to the God he had offended, and I may do so still. Reuben, Reuben, who is there has such claim upon me, as my poor, poor father? Others love me, and oh, God only knows how I love them! but they are happy and prosperous, they do not need me."

"Sarah," answered Reuben, his voice choked with emotion, "Sarah, you spoke of a former heavy trial, one hard to bear. Oh, answer me, speak to me! Was not I its cause? I deceived myself when I thought I had not injured your peace when I wrecked my own."

"It matters little now," replied Sarah, turning from his look, while her cheek again blanched to marble; "my path is marked out for me. I may not leave it, even to think of what has been or might be; it cannot, must not matter now."

"It must—it shall!" exclaimed Reuben, with more than wonted impetuosity. "Sarah, Sarah, you ask me who needs you as your father does—to whom you can be as you are to him? I answer, there is one, one to whom, as to your father, you have been a guardian angel, winning him back even by your memory, when far separated, to the God he had forsaken. I trampled on the love I bore you—my own feelings as well as yours—to unite myself with a stranger race, to bid all who knew me cease to regard me as a Jew. I sought to believe I had nothing to reproach myself with, as I had not caused you grief, and yet—conscience, conscience! Oh, Sarah, my poor Jeanie's very love was constant agony, for I could not return it. I never loved her as I loved you, even though she wound herself about my very heart, and her death seemed misery. I looked to the end of this twelvemonth to feel myself worthy to tell you all my sin, my misery, and, if you could forgive me, to conjure you to become mine. Oh, do not sentence me to increase of trial! I looked to you to train up my motherless Jeanie, as indeed a child of God, according to your own pure belief; and to bind me to Him by links I could never, even in the strongest temptation, turn aside. And now, now, when my heart tells me I was deceived and I had injured you—for you did love me, you do love me—oh, will you leave me—for a doubtful duty, part from me for ever? I care not how long I serve to win you. Sarah, Sarah, only tell me you can still love me, you will be mine."

"Too late, too late, oh, it is all too late!" replied Sarah, firmly, though her voice was choked with tears.

"Reuben, dear Reuben, why have you spoken thus, and at this moment? It was a weak and idle folly to deny that to be your wife would be the dearest happiness which could be mine; that I have loved you, long before I knew what love could mean; and prayed for you, wept for you—but I must not think of these things now. Months ago, such words from you would have been all joy; but now—do not speak them, dearest Reuben—they increase my trial, but cannot change my purpose. My poor father is innocent, condemned unjustly. Were he guilty, I might decide otherwise; for perhaps it were then less a positive duty to tend him to the last."

And in vain did Reuben combat this determination. In vain, rendered more eloquent from his conviction that he was beloved, did he speak and urge, and speak again. He desisted at length; not from lack of argument, but because he saw it only increased the anguish of her feelings.

"If it must be so, dearest—yet indeed, indeed, it is a mistaken duty; do not look on me so beseechingly, I will urge no more. For myself I know I did not merit the joy I had dared to picture; yet still, still to resign it thus, to know you love me spite of all—Sarah, how may I struggle on, with every hope and promise blighted?"

"Do not say so, Reuben. Our Father will not leave you lonely. Seek Him, love Him, and He will fill up all the void which my absence may create; and do not think we part for ever. Oh, Reuben the love borne in my heart so long can know no cloud or change, and though years may pass on—my first duty be accomplished—yet when it is, and my poor father's weary course is ended, if you be still free, may I not return to you, all, all your own?"

She lifted up her pale face to his with such a look of confidence and love, that Reuben's only answer was to fold her to his heart and bid God bless her for such words.

Days passed on, and though all who heard her resolution were against it, though she had to encounter even Miss Leon's arguments and entreaties that she would forego a purpose as uncalled for as misguided, Sarah never for one moment wavered. Vainly Miss Leon sketched the miseries that would await her in a savage land; the little chance there was of her even being permitted to be near her father; the little she could do for him, even if they were together. She reasoned well and strongly and even feelingly, but there are times and duties when the heart hears only its own impulses, its own feelings, and must follow them. Had she wavered before she again met her father after his condemnation, which, however, she did not, her first interview would have strengthened her yet more. There was a wild and haggard look about him, a hollow tone and wandering words, that made her at the first moment tremble for his reason.

"Sarah, my daughter! they have banished me from my God! they have sentenced me to return to sin. Better, better had they said I was to die, for then I should have gone direct from you to judgment, and your prayers, your angel words, had turned me from my sin: but they will send me from you, and I shall sin again. I shall fall away from all the good you taught me. With you, with you only I am safe —my daughter, oh, my daughter !"

"And I will not leave you, father—I go with you, not in the same ship, but I will meet you in a strange land. We shall be together there as here. I will not leave you while you need me. Do not look so, father, I have sworn it to my God."

She threw herself upon his neck, and the sinful but repentant man wept as an infant on her shoulder; and from that hour her dread that his reason was departing never tormented her again.

The evening before Levison's removal with his fellow-convicts to Portsmouth—the ship awaiting them there—the influence of a larger bribe than usual from Reuben to the turnkey had secured to Sarah a few uninterrupted hours with her father in a separate cell. There was something strange in Levison's countenance which rather alarmed him when he joined them; it was flushed and excited, and as he walked across the cell his limbs seemed to totter beneath him.

They had not much longer to be together, when an unusual number of footsteps crowded along the passage; and, soon after, the turnkey, a sheriff, and a gentleman whom neither Sarah nor Reuben knew, though he was evidently of their own nation, entered the cell. There was still quite daylight sufficient to distinguish persons and features, and the very instant Levison's eye caught the stranger, he started with a shrill cry to his feet, endeavoured to spring forward, but failed, and would have fallen had not Reuben caught him in his arms, where he remained in a fit of trembling, which almost seemed convulsion. "Now, be quiet, my good fellow, you will do well enough," whispered the turnkey, as he stepped forward to assist in supporting Levison upon his feet. "Here is this here gemman come to swear to your person, as having seen you in the burial-ground, just as how you said, that there night; proving an alibi d'ye see. They'll let you go even now—who'd ha' thought it?"

"You said, sir, that you saw and spoke to a man named Isaac Levison, of the Jewish nation, in the burial-ground of your people, on the morning of Wednesday, the 14th of May, exactly as the clock of Mile End Church chimed three," deliberately began the pompous sheriff, on whose blunted sensibilities the various attitudes of agonized suspense, hope, and terror delineated in the group before him excited no emotion whatever. "I have troubled you to come here to see this man, who calls himself by that name, and tells the same tale, seeing, that if you can swear to his person, he must be detained from accompanying the rest of the gang, and undergo a second trial, that your assertion in the court may publicly prove it."

"I do not see much use in that," interrupted the gentleman, who, no lawyer, did not quite comprehend technicalities; "I should think my oath as to his person quite enough to free him. I did not appear on his trial, simply because I was abroad, and only heard of it through a friend sending me a newspaper and the particulars of the case—a friend of his wishing the man's innocence to be proved. He wrote to me, knowing that either I or some one belonging to me had employed a watcher that night, and vague as the tale was, I might help to clear it; this, however, is nothing to the purpose. If the robbery you speak of was committed at Epping on the 14th of May, just about three o'clock in the morning, that man, Isaac Levison, is as innocent as I am; for I can take my oath as to seeing and speaking with him that very morning, at that very hour, in the burial-ground of our people at Mile End. I particularly remarked him, as he was not the person I had engaged. There is no justice in England if you do not let him go—he is innocent."

"Innocent—innocent—innocent! My child, you are right; there is a God, and a God of love! Blessed—blessed—forgiven!" He bounded from the detaining arms of Reuben and the turnkey, clasped Sarah to his heart with strange unnatural strength, and fell back a corpse!

CHAPTER V.

A small but most comfortably-furnished parlour of a new, respectable-looking dwelling, in one of the best streets of Liverpool, is the scene to which we must conduct our readers about two years after the conclusion of our last chapter. The furniture all looked new, except a kind of antique silver lamp, which stood on an oaken bracket opposite the window. It was a room thrown out from the usual back of the house, opening by a large French window, and one or two steps into a small but beautifully laid-out flower garden, divided by a passage and another parlour from the handsome shop which opened on the street. It was a silversmith and watchmaker's, with the words "Perez Brothers," in large but not showy characters, over the door. The shop seemed much frequented, there was a constant ingress and egress of respectable people; but there was no bustle, nothing going wrong, all seemed quietness and regularity; orders received and questions answered, and often articles of particularly skilful workmanship displayed with that gentle courtesy and good feeling which can spring but from the heart.

But we are forgetting—it is the parlour and not the shop with which we have to do. The room and its furniture may be strangers to us—perhaps one of its inmates—but not the other. The still infirm and aged, but the thrice-blessed, thrice-happy mother was still spared to bless God for the prosperity, the well-doing, and the unchanging faith and piety of her beloved children. Simeon's wish was fulfilled—his mother was restored to her former station, nay, raised higher in the scale of society than she had ever been; but meek in prosperity as faithful in adversity, there was no change in that widowed heart, save, if possible, yet deeper love and gratitude to God. And a beautiful picture might that gentle face have made, bending down with such a smile of caressing love on the lovely infant of nearly three years, who had clambered on her knee, and was folding its little round arms about her neck. It was a touching contrast of age and infancy, for Rachel looked much older than she really was, but there was nothing sad in it. The unusual loveliness of the child cannot be passed unnoticed; the snowy skin, the rich golden curls, just touched with that chestnut which takes away all insipidity from fairness, might have proclaimed her not a child of Israel; but then there was the large, lustrous, black eye and its long fringe, the subdued, soul-speaking beauty of the other features—that was Israel's, and Israel's alone! Full of life and joyousness, her infant prattle amused her grandmother, till at the closing, about six in the evening, her son Simeon joined her. We should perhaps have said that an elderly Jewess, remarkably clean and tidy in her person, had very often entered the parlour to see, she said, if the dear widow were comfortable or wanted anything, or little Jeanie were troublesome, etc. It was old Esther, who fulfilling all sorts of offices in the family, acting companion and nurse to the widow and Jeanie, cleaning silver—in which she was very expert—seeing to the cooking of the dinner, and taking care of the lads' clothes, delighted herself, and more than satisfied those with whom she lived.

To satisfy our readers' curiosity as to how this great change in the widow's condition had been brought about, we will briefly narrate its origin. When Reuben's year of probation was over, and he felt he was a Jew in heart and soul and reason, as well as name, he returned to Liverpool, to delight his mother with the change. He was met with love and with rejoicing, no reference was made to the past, and between himself and Simeon not a shadow of estrangement remained. The latter had at first hung back, feeling self-reproached that he had wronged his brother; but Reuben's truly noble nature conquered these feelings, and soon after bound him to him with the ties of gratitude as well as love. Simeon's talent for modelling in silver was now as marked as his dislike to that trade, which, despite of disinclination, he had perseveringly followed. Reuben, on the contrary, retained all his father's instructions in watch-making, and had determined, when he returned to Liverpool, to set up that business, which, from the excellent capital he had amassed and laid by, was not difficult to accomplish. He had determined on this plan, feeling as if he thus tacitly acknowledged and followed his lamented father's wishes, and atoned to him, even in death, for former disregard. He, of course, wished to associate Simeon in the business; but as the young man's desires and talents seemed pointed otherwise, he placed him for a year with a first-rate silversmith in London. Morris, Simeon's late master, had given up business, and this in itself was a capital opening for Reuben. He made use of it, and flourished. In less than eighteen months after his return to Liverpool, "Perez Brothers" opened their new shop as silversmiths and watchmakers, and from the careful, economical, and strictly honourable way in which the business was carried on —the name, too, with its associations of the honest hard-working man of whom these were the sons, adding golden weight—a very few months' trial proved that industry, economy, and honesty must carry their own reward.

But why was the widow alone? Was not Reuben married, and should not Sarah have been with her? Gentle reader, Reuben is not yet married; he has now gone to fetch his Sarah, for the term of probation for both is over. The morrow is the thirteenth birthday of the twins; and the widow is expecting the return of Reuben and Sarah and Ruth, as she sits with her darling Jeanie in her little parlour, the evening we meet her again.

Levison's innocence and his sudden death had, of course, been made public, not only in an official way, but through the eagerness of Reuben that not a shadow of shame should ever approach his Sarah. When the first month of mourning had expired, Sarah returned to her situation; her mistress quite forgetting former anger, and ready to declare Sarah had only done just as she ought towards her poor innocent father; that she was a pattern of Jewish daughters, and poured forth a volume of praises, all in the joy of getting her back.

Reuben had been anxious for their marriage as soon as he had completed two years from poor Jeanie Wilson's early death. Sarah fully sympathised in his feelings towards Jeanie, and they would often talk of her as a being dear to and cherished by them both. When the two years were completed, the marriage was still delayed, Mrs. Corea entreating Sarah to remain with her till she went on the Continent with her daughters, which she intended to do in about six or eight months. She had been too indulgent a mistress, and Miss Leon too sincere a friend, for Sarah to hesitate a moment in postponing her own happiness. Besides, the delay, though Reuben did not like it, might be beneficial to him, in allowing him time to get settled in his business. Before the period elapsed, Sarah and Reuben too were rejoiced that she was still in London, for Ruth needed her; the wherefore we shall find presently.

"Are they not late, mother?" inquired Simeon, as he joined his mother in her own parlour. "Troublesome loiterers! I wish they would arrive—I want my tea."

"And is that all you want, Simeon?" said the widow, smiling; "because that may easily be satisfied."

"No, no; not quite so voracious as that comes to. I want the loiterers themselves, though I have seen them later than you have, you know. You won't find Sarah a whit altered; she is just the gentle yet energetic creature she always was, only more animated, more happy, I think. Then Ruth, darling Ruth—oh, how much I owe to her! I never shall forget her reminding me of my promise to my poor father—her compelling me, as it were, to love my brother; and now, what is not that brother to me? Mother, is it not strange how completely prejudice has gone?"

"No, my dear son; your heart was too truly and faithfully pious, too desirous really to love its God, for prejudice long to obtain the ascendant. It comes sometimes in very early youth, when we are apt to think we alone are quite right, but, unless encouraged, cannot long stand the light of strengthening reason and real spiritual love."

"But does it not seem strange, mother, that I alone of my family should have been the one selected to receive such extreme kindness from a Christian—one of those whom, in former days, I was more prejudiced against than I dared acknowledge? I was very ill on my way home from London, and, as you know, Mr. Morton had me conveyed to his house, instead of leaving me to the care of heartless strangers at the public inn—had a physician to attend me, nursed me as his own son—would read and talk to me, even after he knew I was a Jew, on the *spirit* of religion, which we both felt. Never shall I forget the impressive tone and manner with which he said, when parting with me, 'Young man, never forget this important truth—*that heart alone in sincerity loves God, who can see, in every pious man, a brother, despite of difference of creed. That difference lies between man and his God: to do good and love one another is man's duty unto man*, and can, under no circumstances and in no places, be evaded. Learn this lesson, and all the kindness I have shown you is amply rewarded.' Is it not strange this should have occurred to me?"

"I do not think it strange, my dear son," replied Mrs. Perez, affectionately, though seriously. "I believe so firmly that God's eye is ever on us, that He so loves us, that He guides every event of our lives as will be most for our eternal good. He saw you sought to love and serve Him—that the very prejudice borne towards others had its origin in the ardent love you bore your faith, and His infinite mercy permitted you to receive kindness from a Gentile and a stranger, that this one dark cloud should be removed, and your love for Him be increased in the love you bear your fellow-creatures."

"May I believe this, mother? It would be such a comfort, such a redoubled excitement to love and worship," answered Simeon, fixing his large dark eyes beseechingly on his mother's face. "But can I do so without profaneness, without robbing our gracious God of the sanctity which is so imperatively His due?"

"Surely you may, my dear boy. We have the whole word of God to prove and tell us that we are each individually and peculiarly His care—that He demands the *heart;* for dearer even than a mother's love for her infant child is His love towards us. How may we give Him our heart, if we never think of Him but as a Being too inexpressibly awful to approach? How feel the thanksgiving and gratitude He loves to receive, if we do not perceive His guiding hand, even in the simplest events of our individual lives? How seek Him in sorrow, if we do not think He has power and will to hear and to relieve?—in daily prayer, if we were not each of us especially His own? My boy, if the hairs of our head are numbered, can we doubt the events of our life are guided as will be but for our eternal good, and draw us closer to our God? Think but of one dear to us both; did it not seem, to our imperfect wisdom, that Reuben's marriage must for ever have divided him from his nation? Yet that very circumstance brought him back. Our Father in mercy permitted him to follow his own will, to be prosperous, to lose even the hated badge of Israel, that his own heart might be his judge. Affliction also, sent from that same gracious hand, deepened the peculiar feelings which becoming a parent had already excited. Then the year of research put the final seal on his return to us. His mind could never have believed without calm, unimpassioned, steady examination. He has examined not alone his own faith. Mr. Vaughan, from being the explainer, was forced to become the defender of his own creed. He drew back, avowing, with a candour and charity which proved how truly of God was the *spirit* of religion within him, spite of the mistaken faith, that Reuben never could become a convert. And we know what true friends they are, notwithstanding Mr. Vaughan's disappointment. They have strengthened themselves in their own peculiar doctrines, without in the least shaking each other's."

"Yes, yes; you are quite right, mother dear, as you always are," replied Simeon, putting his arm round her, and affectionately kissing her. "What a blessing it has been for me to have such a mother. Why, how now, master Joseph, what has happened? have you lost your wits?"

"If I have, it is for very joy!" exclaimed the boy, springing into the parlour, flinging his cap up to the ceiling, and so stifling his mother with kisses, as obliged her to call for mercy. "Mother, mother, how can I tell you the good news? I must scamper about before I can give them vent."

"Not another jump, not another step, till you have told

us," exclaimed Simeon, laughing heartily at the boy's grotesque movements, and catching him midway in a jump that would not have disgraced a harlequin. "Now, what is it, you overgrown baby? Are you not ashamed not to meet joy like a man?"

"No baby ever felt such joy, Simeon; and though I am a man to-morrow, I am not ashamed to act the madcap to-night. Mother, have I not told you the notice Mr. Morales has always taken of me, and the books he has lent me? Well, my master must have said such kind things of me; for what, what do you think he has offered?—that is, if you will consent; and I know, oh, I know you love me too well to refuse. He will call on you himself to-morrow about it."

"About what?" reiterated Simeon. "My good fellow, it is of no use his calling. You are gone distracted, mad, fit for nothing!"

"What does he offer, my love?" anxiously rejoined the widow.

"To take me home with him, as companion and friend to his own son, a boy just about my age—and such a fellow! He has often come to talk with me about the books we have both read. And Mr. Morales said I shall learn all that Conrad does. That I shall go abroad with them, and receive such an education, that years to come, if I still wish it, I may be fitted to be, what of all others I long to be, the *Hazan* of our people. Hebrew, the Bible and the Talmud, and Latin, and Greek, and every thing that can help me for such an office; besides the lighter literature and studies, which will make me an enlightened friend for his son. Oh, mother! Simeon! is it not enough to make me lose my wits? But I must not though, for I shall want them more than ever. You do not speak, my own dear mother; but you will not, oh, I know you will not refuse."

"Refuse!" repeated the grateful widow, whose voice returned. "No, no! I would deserve to lose all the friends and blessings my God has given me, could I be so selfish to refuse, because for a few years, my beloved child, I must part with you. I do not fear for you; you will never forget to love your mother, or to remember and obey her precepts!"

"Give you joy, brother mine! though, by my honour, I had better not wish you any more joy, for this has well-nigh done for you," laughingly rejoined Simeon; for he saw that both Joseph and his mother's eyes were wet with grateful tears, and he did not wish emotion to become pain.

"Yes, one more joy, but one: it is almost sinful to wish more, when so much has been granted me," replied Joseph, almost sorrowfully. "Would that Ruth, my own Ruth, could but *look on* me once more; could but have sight restored, that I might think of her as happy, independent, not needing me to supply her sight. Oh, I should not have one wish remaining; but sometimes I think, afflicted as she is, and bound so closely as we are, I ought not to leave her."

"Then don't think any more silliness, my boy. Reuben and your humble servant are much obliged to you for imagining, because we do not happen to be her twin brothers, we cannot be to her what you are—out on your conceit! Make haste, and be a *Hazan*, and give her a home, and then you shall have her all to yourself; till then we will take care of her!"

Joseph's laughing reply was checked by the entrance of Leah, attended by a young man of very prepossessing appearance. It was Maurice Carvalho, the son and heir of a thriving bookseller and fancy stationer, of Liverpool, noted for a very devoted attendance on the pretty young milliner.

"Not arrived yet! why, I feared they would have been here before me, and thought me so unkind," said Leah, after affectionately greeting her mother. "Are we not late?"

"Dreadfully!" replied Simeon, mischievously. "Mrs. Valentine said you were at liberty after five; what have you been doing with yourselves?"

"Taking a walk, and went further than we thought," said

widow's betrayed at once that the bachelor was quite at liberty to talk and amuse himself at their expense; their love was acknowledged to each other, and hallowed by a parent's blessing and consent.

Joseph had scarcely had time to tell his joyful tale to his sister, before a loud shout from Simeon, who had gone to the front to watch, proclaimed the anxiously-desired arrival. Joseph and Maurice darted out, and in less than a minute Reuben and Sarah entered the parlour.

"Mother, dearest mother, she is here—never, never, with God's blessing, to leave us again!" exclaimed Reuben, as Sarah threw herself alternately in the arms of the widow and Leah, and then again sought the embrace of the former, to hide the gushing tears of joy and feeling on her bosom, without the power of uttering a single word.

"My child, my own darling child! oh, what a blessing it is to look on your dear face again! Still my own Sarah, spite of all the cares and trials you have borne since we parted!" exclaimed the widow, fondly putting back the braids of beautiful hair, to look intently on that sweet gentle face.

"And your blessing, mother, dearest mother; oh, say as you have so often told me, you could wish and ask no dearer, better wife for your Reuben; and such blessing may give my Sarah voice!" He threw his arm round her as he spoke, and both bent reverently before the widow, whose voice trembled audibly as she gave the desired blessing, and told how she had prayed and yearned that this might be, and Sarah's voice returned, with a tone so glad, so bird-like in its joy, it needed but few words.

"My Ruth, where is my Ruth? and where are Joseph and Simeon gone?" asked the widow, when one joy was sufficiently relieved to permit her thinking of another.

"She will be here almost directly, mother. She was rather tired with the journey, and so I persuaded her to rest quiet at the inn close by, till I sent Simeon and Joseph with a coach for her and our luggage; they will not be long before they return. But tell me, where is my Jeanie? not in bed I hope, though we are late?"

"No; Esther took her away about half an hour ago, to amuse and keep her awake—not very difficult to do, as she is as lively as ever." Reuben was off in a moment.

"And Esther, dear Reuben, bid her come and see me," rejoined Sarah; and then clasping her aunt's hand, "oh, my dear aunt, what have I not felt, since we last met, that I owe you! I thought I was grateful, felt it to the full before; but not till I was tried, not till I learned the value of strong principles, steady conduct, and firm control, did I know all you had done for me. My God, indeed, was with me throughout; but this would not have been, had not your care and your affection taught me how to seek and love Him. Oh, will a life of devotion to our Reuben, and to you, and to his offspring, in part repay your kindness, dearest aunt?"

The widow's answer we leave our readers to imagine, fearing they should accuse us of again becoming sentimental. Old Esther speedily made her appearance, and her greeting was second only in affection to the widow's own.

"Father, dear father, come home, come home!" was the next sweet lisping voice that met the delighted ears of Sarah, and in another moment Reuben appeared with the child in his arms, her little rosy fingers twisted in his hair, and her round soft cheek resting against his.

"This is my poor motherless babe, for whom I have bespoken your love, your protection, your guiding hand, my Sarah," he whispered, in a low, earnest voice. "Will you love her for my sake?"

"And for her own and for her mother's; do not doubt me, Reuben. If she is yours, is she not, then, mine?" she answered, in the same voice. The child looked at her as if half inclined to spring into the caressing, extended arms, but then, with sudden shyness, hid her face on her father's shoulder.

"Jeanie, darling, what was the word I taught you to say? Look at her and say it, and kiss her as you do me."

The child still hesitated; but then, as if emboldened by Sarah's sweet voice calling her name, she looked full in her face and lisped out, "Mother," held up her little face to kiss her, and was quite contented to be transferred from Reuben's arms to those of Sarah.

"Ruth, Ruth—I think I hear her coming!" joyfully exclaimed Leah, a few minutes afterwards.

"Go to her then, dear—detain her one minute," hastily whispered Reuben, in a tone and manner that made his sister start. "Do not ask me why now—you will know the moment you see her—only go. I must prepare my mother. I did not think she would have been here so soon."

Leah obeyed him, her heart beating, she did not know why, and Reuben turned to his mother. Sarah had given little Jeanie to Esther's care, and was kneeling by her as if to intercept her starting up.

"What is it—what is it? Why do you keep my child from me? why send her brothers and sisters to her, instead of letting her come to me? Reuben, Sarah! what new affliction has befallen my angel child?"

"Affliction? None, none!" repeated Sarah and Reuben together. "It is joy, dearest aunt, all joy. Oh, bear but joy as you have borne sorrow, and all will be well."

"Joy!" she repeated, almost wildly; "what greater joy can there be than to have my children all once again around me? I have heard my Ruth has been ill, but that she was quite well, quite strong again, and have blessed God for that great mercy."

"But there may be more, my mother, yet more for which to bless Him. Oh, are not all things possible with Him? He who in His wisdom once deprived of sight, can He not restore it?"

"Reuben, Sarah! what can you mean? My child, my Ruth!" but voice and almost power failed, for such a trembling seized her limbs that Reuben was compelled to support her as she sat. It was but for a moment, for the next a light figure had bounded into the room, followed by Simeon and Joseph, Maurice and Leah.

"Mother! mother! mother! They need not tell me where you are. You need not come to your poor blind Ruth. I can SEE your dear face—see it once again.

The widow had sprung up from her chair; but ere she had made one step forward her child was in her arms—was fixing those long-closed eyes upon her face as if they would take in every feature with one delighted gaze. One look was sufficient. A deadly faintness, from over-excited feelings, passed over the widow's heart; but as she felt Ruth's passionate kisses on her lips and cheeks, life returned in a wild burst of thanksgiving, and the widow folded her child closer and yet closer to her heart, and, overpowered by joy as she had never been by sorrow, "she lifted up her voice and wept."

Reader, our task is done—for need we say it was the benevolent exertion of Miss Leon, under a merciful Providence, which procured the last most unlooked-for blessing to the widow and her family? She had remarked there was a slight change in the appearance of the child's eyes, had taken her without delay to the most eminent oculist of the day, and received his opinion that sight might be restored. The rest, to a character such as hers, was easy; and thus twice was she the means of materially brightening the happiness of the Perez family; for, though we had not space in our last chapter to dilate on it, it had been actually through her means the innocence of Levison had been discovered, though she herself was at the time scarcely conscious how. She had mentioned it to everybody she thought likely to be useful in discovering it, had been laughed at for her folly in believing such a tale, warned against taking up the guilt or innocence of such a person's character; and, in short, almost every one dissuaded her from mentioning the subject; it really would do her harm. But she had persevered against even her own hope of effecting good, and was, as we have seen, successful.

Before we quite say farewell, we would ask our readers if we have indeed been happy enough in this simple narration to make one solemn and most important truth clear as our own heart would wish—that, however dark may be our horizon, however our prayers and trust may for a while seem unheeded, our eager wishes denied us, our dearest feelings the mere means of woe, yet there is an answering and pitying God above us still, who, when He bids us "commit our ways unto Him, and trust also in Him," has not alone the power, but the will, the loving-kindness, the infinite mercy, to "bring it to pass." My friends, that God is still our God; and though the events of our simple tale may have no origin in real life, is there one amongst us who can look back upon his life, and prayers, and thoughts, and yet say that overruling Providence is but fiction, for we feel it, know it not? Oh, if so, it is his own heart, not the love and word of his God, at fault. All may not be blessed so visibly as the widow and her family, but all who wait on and trust in the Lord will have their reward, if not on earth, yet dearer, more gloriously in heaven.

The Stone-Cutter's Boy of Possagno.

A SKETCH FROM HIS LIFE.

It was evening in Venice. The queen of the Adriatic, her marble palaces and princely halls, her stately bridges and her dreary prisons, lay sleeping in gorgeous beauty, flushed by the glowing splendour of the setting sun, lingering as loath to fade away and be lost in the more sombre hues of twilight, which, rising from the east, was softly and balmily stealing over the expanse of heaven, bearing silence, and repose, and quiet loveliness on her meekly pensive brow. It was an hour of deep calm—the pause of life and nature, when the business of the day was done, the gay festivities of night not yet begun. Now and then the sound of a guitar, or the thrill of melody from music-gushing voices, echoed from the water; or whispered accents, in the passioned tones of Italy, betraying some tale of happy love; and then, again, might be traced a muffled figure, with shadowed brow and stern-closed lip, holding himself aloof, as if his world were contained in the mighty passions, the deep secrets of his own heart; and thus, from hate, or guile, or scorn, contemning all his fellows. And then would come by, with measured oar and evening hymn, the fisher's humble skiff; and then, in strange contrast, the decorated bark of patrician pride, with noble freight and liveried attendants. Presently, light after light gleamed up from palace, and hall, and bridge, rivalling the stars of heaven, spangling earth and water. Sunset faded into twilight; and twilight, resting a brief interval on the bosom of night, gave up to her the care of earth, and disappeared. But not with the marble palaces and their princely honours—not with the midnight intrigue, the lovers' meeting—not with the pirate of the seas, the brigand of the land; all of which seem springing up, more vivid than memory, more tangible than fancy, in that one magic word, Venice—not with these have we to treat.

In a small, rudely furnished apartment, scattered round with implements of sculpture, half-finished models in clay and stone, sketches, both in chalk and colouring, and some few volumes of miscellaneous lore, sat one, a boy in years, but bearing on his brow and in his eye somewhat far—oh! far beyond his age. Clothed as he was in the simplest, most homely attire, his peculiarly graceful and well-proportioned figure marked him noble; his intelligent, nay more, his soul-breathing features, the light of MIND illumining his full dark eye, and resting on the broad, high forehead, even the beautiful hair of glossy black, curling so carelessly round the peculiarly well-shaped head:—could these characteristics belong to the stone-cutter's boy of Possagno, whose first twelve years had been passed in the mud-walled cabin of his poor and hard-working grandfather? It was even so; but the lowliness of birth was, even at this early period of his life, lost in the nobility of Genius. Her voice had breathed its thrilling whisper within him; and he heard, but as yet understood it not—was unconscious of the deep meanings, the glorious prophecy, the mighty shadows of an unborn future, of which those thrilling whispers spoke. He only knew there was a spirit within him, urging, impelling, he scarce knew what: a longing for the Infinite which pressed so heavily upon him, that he felt, to use his own impressive words, "He could have started on foot with a velocity to outstrip the wind, but without knowing whither to direct his steps; and when activity could no longer be supported, he would have desired to lie down and die." He would hurry to the haunts of Nature—the wildest, most boundless scenes, gazing on the distant mountain, the rushing torrent, the dark, mysterious forest; and then up to the gorgeous masses of cloud, sailing over the transparent heaven of his own bright land, watch intently each light, each shade, each fleeting change, longing to soar to them, to penetrate the mysteries of Nature. And at such moments he was happy; for the sense of Infinity seemed taken from his own overcharged heart to be impressed on Nature, to linger around, below, above him, to breathe its tale aloud, from the voice of the torrent to the glistening star reflected in its depths—from the radiant star to the lowly flower, trembling beneath its burning gaze; and the voice was less painfully oppressive then than when it came, in the still, the lonely hour, to the deep recesses of his own young heart. And from these scenes he would turn again to the work of his own hand; and despondency and darkness, at times, clouded up his spirit, for they gave not back the impress of the beauty, the infinity, with which his soul was filled. He knew not the wherefore of this deep-seated joy and woe; and had there been one to whisper it did but prophesy immortal fame, the boy would have smiled in disbelief.

But on this fair eve neither the hurrying impulse nor desponding sadness was upon him. The boy sat beside the open casement, looking forth on the gradual approach of night and her starry train, on the still waters slumbering beneath, or flashing in passing light from illuminated skiffs; but his thoughts were not on these. An open volume lay upon his knee, which had so absorbed alike heart, mind, and fancy, that darkness had stolen around him unconsciously; and when compelled to cease reading, there was a charm in the thoughts created, too entrancing, too irresistible, to permit their interruption, even by a movement.

"Why, Antonio, lad, what holds thee so tranced, even thine own Guiseppe stands beside thee, rudely and inhospitably unnoticed? Shame on thee! The Falieri had not welcomed Tonin thus."

With a start of joyful surprise, the boy turned to grasp the extended hands of his noble friend, to welcome him again and again, and then to ask and answer so many questions interesting to none but themselves, that some time passed ere Guiseppe Falieri found leisure to ask what had so engrossed his friend when he entered.

"Up in the skies again, Tonin, lad—riding on a star, or reposing on a cloud—yonder one, perchance, so exquisitely silvered by the moon?"

"No, Guiseppe mio, I was more on earth than in heaven that moment."

"Thou on earth! and with such a sky, such a moon, above us! Marvellous! Ah, a book!" And, attracted by Antonio's smile to the volume, he took it up, and read by the clear moonlight, "'Life of Dante.' Only his life! Nay, had it been his Divina Commedia, his soul-thrilling poesy, I could better have forgiven thy neglect."

"Yet, perchance, had his life no Beatrice, Guiseppe, Italy had had no poet."

"It was Beatrice, then, that so enchanted thee! Come, that's some comfort for my pride. I give thee permission to neglect me for her. Yet," he added, after a brief pause, "how know we it was not all illusion—a vision of the poet—a fancy—a beautiful creation? I have often thought it too shadowy, too much of the ideal, for dull, dark reality."

"Illusion or reality, oh! it was blessed for Italy, thrice blessed for the poet!" answered Antonio, with such unaffected fervour, that it extended to his companion. "Without Beatrice, what had Dante been? A poet, perchance, but wanting the glow, the life, the thrilling beauty, now gushing so eloquently from every line. Beauty, and such as hers, ethereal from first to last, till nought but his own heart and heaven retained her. Oh, Guiseppe, the glance of her eye, the touch of her hand, was all sufficient to ignite the electric lamp of genius, which, without such influence, perchance, had been buried in its own smouldering gloom, and never flung its rays upon a world."

"Thinkest thou, then, Tonin, that the influence of beauty could, indeed, be so experienced by one who, though so mighty in intellect, was still only a boy in years?"

"Do I think so, Guiseppe?—yes, oh, yes! It filled up all the yearning void so dark before; it threw a sunshine and a glory over all of life and earth; it gave a semblance and a shape to all the glowing images of mind; and as the countless rays down-gushing from one sun, it poured into the poet's breast infinity from one!"

Guiseppe Falieri looked on the enthusiast, feeling far more than Antonio himself the glorious gifts that boyish heart enshrined; and loved, aye, reverenced him—him, the peasant boy, though he himself was noble, the younger son of an illustrious Venetian house. But what, he felt, was rank of birth compared to rank of intellect? and with that peasant boy the youthful noble remained for hours, only leaving that lowly room to wander forth with him, as their souls had freer, more delicious communion, under the blue vault of heaven than in confining walls. To enjoy the society of his humble friend in their brief visits to Venice, Guiseppe Falieri ever relinquished the more exciting pleasures of the boon companions of his rank and station; and ere the mantle of age descended upon him, how did he glory in the penetration of his boyhood!

II.

It was morn in Venice: her seventy islets were lighted up with a flood of sunshine of transparent brilliance, known only to fair Italy, but falling with soft and mellowed rays within the gallery of the proud Farsetti Palace. Thrown open to the youth of both sexes studying the fine arts, private munificence had gathered together the most perfect specimens of ancient and modern art—all that could forward the eager student in his darling pursuit, ensuring priceless advantages even to the poorest and the humblest, fostering in every individual breast the gift peculiarly his own. Oh, truly is that country where such things are, the nurse of Genius! Truly may her children decorate her with the fruits of those resplendent gifts with which Heaven has endowed them! Truly may her poets breathe forth lays to mark her as themselves—immortal! Italy, beautiful Italy, how doth the heart burn, the spirit love, when we write of thee!

To this gallery the young Antonio was a constant visitor, and he was so persevering in his studies as to attract the attention and rivet the friendship of its noble owner, at whose order he executed the first specimen of that sculpture which was to enroll his lowly name amid the mighty spirits of his native land, and bear to distant shores the echoes of his fame. Morning after morning found him in the Farsetti gallery, engaged either in drawing, modelling, or painting from antique casts, or from those modern ones to which the possessors of the establishment directed his notice. No difficulty could deter, no more tempting model could allure. Severely, faithfully true to the path marked out, every other student shrunk from competition with him, as pigmies from a giant.

Wrapt as Antonio ever was in his task, however severe or little interesting, generally so absorbed as to be unconscious of all outward things, it was strange that a voice had power to rouse him from such preoccupation, and bid him, half-unconsciously yet inquiringly, look round. Soft, low, silvery, it thrilled to the boy's soul, as a voice that had haunted his dreams, and was yet to reality unknown. And the being from whom it came? Had he ever seen one like to her, or was it the mere embodying of all those visions of beauty, which, sleeping or waking, haunted his soul? He knew not. He only knew he sat entranced, breathless, awestruck, as though some angelic being had stood before him, demanding adoration. Young, very young, she seemed yet older than himself; and pale, but oh! so exquisitely lovely—with all of heaven, nought of earth! E'en the deep feeling resting on that full bright lip; the dark, lustrous, deep-souled eye; the rich, the glorious intellect sitting throned upon that beauteous brow; the smile flitting round that chiselled mouth, as an emanation from the soul; nay, every movement of the sylph-like form, too light, too spirit-like, for coarser earth—all whispered to the boy's full heart with power, eloquence, unfelt though often dreamed before. And matter of astonishment it was to him, that the other students so calmly continued their labors, content with one glance of admiration on the stranger.

Leaning on the arm of a friend or attendant, she advanced up the gallery, and took her seat as one of the students. The model was selected, her drawing materials arranged, and silently she pursued her task.

Little more did Antonio do that day; for the strange, tumultuous emotions of his bosom seemed from that time to paralyse his hand. He worked on, indeed, mechanically till the hour of closing, and then, oh! how grateful was the fresh breeze of heaven, the free, active movement of a rapid walk. Yet even then—strange incongruity of feeling—he yearned for the morrow to find himself anew by her side; and then a trembling was upon him, that it was all illusion, all a sweet, bright vision, which would fade as it had come.

But such it was not. The hours of study came and passed, and each morning found that frail, ethereal being in the Farsetti gallery, attended on her entrance and departure, but left to pursue her studies, as was the custom, alone; and, irresistibly, the young sculptor chose those casts which drew him closer to her side, that even as he worked he might glance on that surpassing beauty, might watch each graceful movement; and this was happiness, inexpressible happiness, although he knew not wherefore. He could not speak it, even to his dearest friend. He felt it all too sacred, too deeply shrined for voice, as if the first breath that gave it utterance would bid it fly for ever. He shrunk deeper and deeper within himself; not moodily, not sadly, but only sensible that "with such a being he should be for ever happy;" for even her silent presence shed a glow around him, fading not even when she was no longer near. He was feeling what his own lips had so vividly described as Beauty's influence on Dante; but the guileless, unsophisticated boy knew not that such it was.

Silently he felt, and silently he worked; for those new, strange, yet delicious feelings weakened not his mighty powers; nay, new light suffused them, even to his own impartial, often desponding eye. Once she stood by his side, leaning on the arm of her attendant. He felt the glance of those lovely eyes was fixed admiringly on the work of *his* hand; and that hand trembled for the first time. Her voice reached his ear in its sweet music, and though it simply praised his work as "*assai bello*," it lingered on his heart as a never-forgotten melody, thrilling through the deeper, louder, mightier voice of Fame, of monarchs' praise, of world's applause, as an angel's whisper midst the crashing storm. He only bowed his head in low acknowledgment, in voiceless answer. He could not summon strength to breathe one word, or meet that gentle glance; but, oh! the deep, full, gushing joy which was upon him from that hour, inspiring more air of beauty in his labours, for her eye might rest on them again.

Days, weeks, thus passed, and still, as by magnetic influence, those youthful students were ever side by side; but ere the second moon had wholly waned, Antonio sat alone; that lovely one had vanished from her usual haunt, and mournfully, darkly, the hours, once so joyous, passed—for the sunlight had departed from them.

Day after day, hope returned to the boy's heart, but not its beauteous object to his eye, and heavily this silent adoration lay upon his soul. Another and another day, and still she came not; a week, another, and how might he inquire her fate, when, even could he speak that yearning sorrow, he had no trace—no clue to her identity? She had come with nought but her own loveliness to steal upon his heart, and he could not violate the sanctuary her image filled by one word of question. He shrunk from every eye, as if he feared his treasure were discovered, and the notice of his fellows would sully its ethereal purity by mingling it with earth.

Still he laboured indefatigably as before; for her voice was sounding in the still depths of his own soul, and perhaps it might sound again—her praise might hallow the work, even of his impotent hand, and mark it blessed!

A ray of sunshine had fallen upon the work of the young sculptor, giving it that peculiar light and shadow which it had worn that never-to-be-forgotten day, when his eye first marked the loveliness his soul had visioned. Such as the ray had reached him from its fount, flashed back every feeling, every pulsation of that hour, till, in its magic, the very form of the beloved, the worshipped one, stood, or seemed to stand, before him, tangible, palpable as life, save that the smile, the shadowy form, were as if all of earth had gone. Breathless, pale, motionless, Antonio's trembling hand refused to guide the pencil—his fixed and starting eye to move, lest all should fade away, and leave him desolate. A noise among the students aroused him, and with a sudden start and heavy sigh he awoke to consciousness. It was but vacancy on which he gazed, or his spirit held commune with beings not seen of earth.

Another week, and Antonio looked on the faithful attendant of his spirit's idol; but she was alone, and pale and sad, and robed in all the sable draperies of woe. His heart throbbed, his voice failed, a sickness as of death crept over him; yet, as she passed to seek and remove the portfolio of the missing one, he struggled to subdue that inward trembling, and speak, but only a few brief, faltering accents came.

"The Signora—her friend—was she well?—had she quitted Venice?"

A burst of agonizing tears answered him, and then the mournful confirmation: "The Signora Julia had gone to that heaven whose child she was; earth would see her sweet face, list her glad laugh, feel her light step, no more." And the mourner passed on: and Antonio leaned his head upon his hands, as if some invisible stroke had crushed him. Gone! and for ever! Oh! the unutterable agony to the young, the loving, contained in those brief words!

And never more did the young sculptor hear that name. Never did he know the birth, the rank, the story of her who so like a spirit had crossed his path! Men knew not, dreamed not, the tide of feeling on that young boy's soul. Now in him were working the silent influences of beauty, of hopeless love. They saw him engaged each day, studying his art, laboriously working under his master, Ferrari, on some still, cold, soulless statues, still to be seen in the villa of Trepoli; and how could they imagine the glowing visions of beauty, of poetry, at work within? No! It was in after years, when such forms of unrivalled loveliness, of immortal beauty, sprung in almost breathing life beneath the magic chisel of ANTONIO CANOVA, that the vision of early boyhood might be traced; and even now, in the perfection to which his art attained, man may behold the realization of those vague yet impelling yearnings after Beauty, Infinity, all that Genius craves, which had started into life and being from the lovely vision of his first and only love.

Amète and Yafèh.*

AN ALLEGORY.

Far in the illimitable space, seeming to earth as one of those bright yet tiny stars, which even the most powerful telescope will not increase in size, so immeasurable is the distance between them and us, two Spirits sat enthroned, each intrusted with an attribute of the Creator, with which to renew His image in man and vivify the earth. Their work was one, each so aiding each that, though in outward form distinct, their inward being was the same. The one, known in the language of heaven as Amête—and who, were there measurement of Time in the children of Eternity, might seem the elder—was in aspect grave, almost stern, but those who could steadily gaze upon him, and receive his image within their hearts (and man did so a thousand and a thousand times, though the Spirit's visible form was unrevealed), loved him, with such deep, earnest love, as to forget the seeming sternness in the deep calm and still security his recognition ever brought. A coronet of light circled his brow, his wings were of living sapphire, and in his hand he held a transparent spear. Wherever he moved, darkness and mist fled from before him; and error sunk annihilated, before one touch of that crystal lance. Change and mutability touched him not; coeval with Creation, he endured to Everlasting—ever presenting the same exquisite aspect, producing on earth the same effect, and through every age aiding to mould man for Immortality. Distinct from his companion, yet the same; reflecting his every changeful hue of loveliness, yet retaining undisturbed his own.

Not such was the outward appearance of Yafèh. Less majestic, less grave, Earth and Heaven ever hailed him with rejoicing. The latter, indeed, knew him not apart from Amête; and the former, in her darkness, sometimes greeted

* Two Hebrew words, whose translations will be found in the concluding paragraph.

his semblance, not himself. Robed in light, drawn not from the ethereal fount which circled Amête, but from those dazzling iris-coloured rays, the reflection of which we sometimes catch when the sun shines upon a prism, the various changes of his exquisite loveliness were impossible to be defined. But it was only when in close unity with Amête he was seen to full perfection, and his glittering garb endowed with vitality and glory; apart those iris rays shone forth resplendent and most dazzling, but without the light glistening on the brow of his companion were too soon merged in gloom.

But this Yafèh himself knew not, and in his young ambition besought permission to work alone. His revealed form was more visible on earth than that of Amête. As he looked down, and around, and above him, the attribute of which he was the guardian seemed so powerfully and palpably impressed, that he could not trace the invisible workings of his companion, and in his presumption he deemed it all his own, and chafed and spurned the bond which, since their creation, had entwined and marked them one. Mournfully and earnestly Amête conjured him to check the impious prayer; that which the All-Wise had assigned them was surely best and safest. But Yafèh would not heed, and ceased not his murmuring supplication till it was granted. With the work already done, the work of Creation, he might not interfere; but the archangelic minister bade him "Go down to earth, and in the workshop of man, be his creation of hand or brain, display thy power; thou art free to work alone," and with a glad burst of triumphant song, and the brilliant velocity of a falling star, the Spirit darted down to earth.

"Follow him not!" commanded the archangel, answering Amête's imploring gaze; "once convinced of his nothingness alone, he will never leave thee more. That lesson learned, thou mayest rejoin him; meanwhile, look down upon his course," and sorrowingly Amête obeyed.

He beheld him, arrayed in even more than his wonted loveliness, enter the several habitations of man; his invisible but felt presence greeted with wild joy, and his inspirings followed in the new creative genius of all whom he touched. In the lowly homes of the mechanic and the artisan he lingered, and their work grew beneath their hand; and at first it seemed most lovely, but still something was wanting, and they toiled and toiled to find it, but in vain; and despair and ruin usurped the place of glad rejoicing.

"They are of too low a grade, too dull a mind," murmured the Spirit, and he flew to the easel of the painter, the workshop of the sculptor; and new conceptions of loveliness floated so vividly in their minds, that day and night unceasingly they toiled to give them embodied form, and sweet dreams of fame mingled with their creation, till life itself seemed brighter than before. And Yafèh rejoiced, for surely now he was triumphant; here at least perfection would vitalize his presence, and prove how little needed he Amête. He mingled invisibly with the judges of the works, and he beheld them scorned—contemned as dreams of madmen; and the artists fled, disgraced and miserable, to their homes, with difficulty restrained from shivering their work to atoms.

Terrified, yet still not humbled, Yafèh winged his flight to the studio of the musician, and harmonies of heaven floated in his ear, entrancing him with their exquisite perfection, and hour after hour he laboured to bring them from their impalpable essence to the bondage of note and phrase, but in vain—in vain! The sounds he did produce were wild, discordant, unconnected, and in passionate agony he refused to listen more.

The poet, the philosopher, the historian—wherever genius lay—Yafèh touched with his quivering breath, and to all came the same dream of marvellous loveliness—the same ideal perfection. On all burst the torrent of inspiration, compelling toil and work, to give words to the pressing thought, and all for awhile believed it perfect; and their burning souls throbbed high in the fond hope that each glorious lay, each novel discovery, each startling hypothesis—clothed in such glowing imagery and thrilling words—must last for ever. And Yafèh triumphed, for surely here he was secure, and in these prove that he could work alone, and needed the aid of none.

A brief, brief while, and the burning lays of the poet were forgotten and unread. The theory of the philosopher, lovely as it had seemed, quivered into darkness before the test of usefulness and reason. The new discoveries, new thoughts of the historian met with scorn and laughter in the vain search for their foundation. And, in their deep despair, Yafèh heard the names by which he was known to earth accursed and scorned; his presence banished; his inspirations rudely checked, as bringing not loveliness and joy, but misery and ruin; and the Spirit fled, in his wild agony, far, far from the homes of earth and the hearts of men; and, shrinking from his starry home and light-clad brother, sought to pierce through and through the vast realms of unfathomable space, and lose himself in darkness. His iris rays seemed fading from his lovely form, lost in denser and denser gloom. Above, below, and around him thunder rolled, and the glittering Hosts of Heaven trembled, lest his proud wish were to be chastised still further. But soon the majestic form of the Spirit Amête stood beside his brother, and before the touch of his glittering spear, Error and Despair, about to claim Yafèh, fled howling.

"Yafèh, beloved! we will descend together," he said, in tones clear, distinct, and liquid, impossible to be withstood. "Thy work shall yet live, and be immortal."

"Nay, 'twill be thine," murmured the repentant Spirit, his darkened loveliness resuming light and glory, from the effulgent brow so pityingly bent down on his. "What need hast thou for me? Go forth and work alone; I have no part on earth."

"Thou hast; for without thee I have no power. Man trembles at my form, when, at the Eternal's mandate, I must go forth alone; but with thee, perchance because my sterner self is hidden, he loves and hails me, and permits my work ascendency. Without thee, I could but bind to earth; with thee, I lead to heaven. Brother, we are ONE, though earth may deem us twain. We cannot work for Immortality apart."

Side by side, so closely twined that even their brother spirits could with difficulty distinguish their individuality, Amête and Yafèh stood within the dwellings of man. The mechanic and the artizan started from their desponding trance; the neglected work was resumed. The form, the inspiration was the same; but as if a flash of light had touched it, it gave back that perfect image of the mind for which before they had so toiled, and toiled in vain. On to the artist, the sculptor, the musician, and one touch from that crystal spear, and the misty cloud dispersed, and the senseless canvas gave back the perfected thought; the cold marble sprung into the warmth of actual being; the impalpable but exquisite harmonies, the ethereal essence of sound, at the word of Amête, resolved itself into the necessary bondage of note and form, and breathed forth to admiring thousands the music lent to one. Hovering over the poet, again the thrilling words burst forth, and fraught with such mighty meanings every heart responded, as to the voice of the Immortal; folding his azure pinion round the panting soul of the philosopher, the shrouding cloud dispersed, and science, deep, stern, lasting, took the place of the mere lovely dream; and on the page of the historian, light from the brow of Amête so flashed, as to mark him gifted reader of the Future, by the wondrous record his spirit-thought unfolded of the Past. Wherever the Spirits lingered, man worked for Immortality; it mattered not under what guise, or in what rank. From the highest to the lowest, each creative impulse, fashioned by Yafèh, received perfection from Amête. The former, indeed, alone was *visible*, but never more he sought to work alone. Within his outward work was the vital essence breathed by Amête, without which the most exquisite form was incomplete—the most lovely thought imperfect—the fairest theory a dream.

And so it is even now. Up, up in yon distant star, gleaming so brightly through the immeasurable space, as may be their throne, still does their glorious and united Presence walk the earth. Their semblance may be found apart, but not themselves. Twain as they are in name and aspect, in essence they are ONE. TRUTH is the vital breath of BEAUTY; BEAUTY the outward form of TRUTH; the REAL the sole foundation of the IDEAL; the IDEAL but the spiritualized essence of the REAL.

The Fugitive.

A TRUE TALE.

JUDAH AZAVEDO was the only son of a rich Jewish merchant, settled in London. His grandfather, a native and resident of Portugal, having witnessed the fearful proceedings of the Inquisition on some of his relations and friends, secretly followers of Israel, as himself, fled to Holland, bearing with him no inconsiderable property. This, through successful commerce, swelled into wealth; and when, on his death, his son, with his wife and child, removed to England, and settled in the metropolis, they were considered, alike in birth, education and riches, one of the very highest families of the proud and aristocratic Portuguese.

But the situation of the Jews in England, some eighty or ninety years ago, was very different to their situation now. Riches, nay, even moral and mental dignity, were not then the passport to society and friendliness. Lingering prejudice, still predominant in the hearts of the English, and pride and nationality equally strong in the Hebrew, kept both parties aloof, so that no advance could be made on either side, and each remained profoundly ignorant of the other, not alone on the subject of opposing creeds, but of actual character.

This though certainly a social evil, was, in some respects, as concerned the Israelites, a national good. It drew them more closely, more kindly together; aliens and strangers to the children of other lands, the true followers of their persecuted creed were as brothers. Rich or poor, it mattered not. Hebrews and Portuguese were the ties in common, and the joy or grief of one family was the joy or grief of all. Fashion was little thought of. Heartlessness, and that false pride which forswears relation to or connection with poverty, were unknown. Faults, no doubt they had; but a more kindly, noble-hearted set of men, in their own sphere, than the Spanish and Portuguese Jews, nearly a hundred years ago, never had existence.

The restless and over-sensitiveness of Judah Azavédo was

a subject of as much surprise to his nation as of regret to his father. Sole heir to immense wealth—unencumbered with business—nothing to occupy him but his own pleasure—gifted with uncommon mental powers—dignified in figure—a kindly and most winning manner, when he chose to exert it; yet was his whole life embittered by the morbid sensitiveness with which he regarded his most unfortunate lack of all attraction in face and feature. He was absolutely and disagreeably plain; we would say ugly, did we not so exceedingly dislike the word. Yet there were times when the glow of mind, or still more warmly of heart, would throw such a soft and gentle expression over the almost deformed features, that their natural disfigurement ceased to be remembered. Those who knew him never felt any difference between him and his fellow-men, save in his superior heart and mind; but Azavédo himself always imagined that, wherever he went, he must be an object of derision or dislike. He shrunk from all society, particularly from that of females, who, he was convinced, would be terrified even to look at him. Entreaties, commands, and remonstrances were vain. Could he have known more, mingled more with the world at large, these morbid feelings would, in time, have been rubbed off; but in his very limited circle of familiar friends this was impossible, and the evil, in consequence, each year increased.

To the Israelites of ninety years ago, the idea of travelling for pleasure was incomprehensible; they were too happy, too grateful to the land which gave them rest and peace, to think of quitting it for any other. That Judah Azavédo should restlessly desire to leave England, and seek excitement in foreign lands, was in accordance with all his other extraordinary feelings; but that his father, the wise, sedate, contented old man, whose every hope and affection were centred in this son, should give his consent, was more extraordinary still; and many, in kindness, sought to dissuade him from it. But Azavédo loved his son too well to permit old habits and prejudices to interfere with the only indulgence Judah had ever asked; he gave him his blessing and *carte blanche* with regard to gold, and the young man forthwith departed.

He was absent three years, having travelled as far as the East, and visited every scene endeared to him as one of that favoured race for whom the sea itself had been divided. He had looked on misery, in so many varied forms, as the portion of his nation, that he felt reproached and ashamed at his own repinings. He learnt that only crime and sin could authorize the misery he had endured; that he was an immortal being, and one whose earthly lot was blessed so much above thousands of his brethren, that he only marvelled his sin of discontent had not called down on him the wrath of God. His soul seemed suddenly free from fetters, and he moved among his fellow-men fearless and unabashed.

Notwithstanding the danger of such a route—for, if known, or even suspected as a Hebrew, he would inevitably have perished—Judah chose to return home through Spain and Portugal, making himself known to some friends of his family still dwelling in the latter kingdom. With them he remained some few months, and then it was that a new emotion awoke within him, chaining him effectually, ere aware of its existence. From his earliest youth Judah had dreaded, and so forsworn love, feeling it next to impossible for him ever to be loved in return; but Love laughs at such forswearers. Before he could analyse why that bitterness against his unhappy ugliness should return, when he had thought it so successfully conquered, he loved with the full passionate fervour of his race and his own peculiar disposition, and loved one of whom he could learn nothing, trace nothing, know nothing, save that she was so surpassingly lovely, that though he had seen her but three times, never near, and only once without her veil, her beauty both of face and form lingered on his memory as indelibly engraved as if it had lain there for years, and then had been called into existence by some strangely awakening flash. She was as unknown to his friends as to himself; only at the Opera had she been visible; no inquiry, no search could elicit information. Once only he had heard the sound of her voice, and it breathed music as thrilling and transporting as the beauty of her face. Yet was she neither saintlike nor angelic; it was an arch witchery, a shadowless glee, infused with the nameless, descriptionless, but convincing charm of mind.

Judah Azavédo returned home an altered man, yet still no one could understand him. He no longer morbidly shunned society, nor even cared to eschew the company of females, seeming as wholly careless and insensible to the effects of his presence as he had before thought too much about it. Some said he was scornfully proud; others that it was impenetrable reserve; all agreed that he was changed, but only his most intimate friends could perceive that he was unhappy, and from some deep-seated sorrow essentially distinct from the feelings engrossing him when he left England, and that this one feeling it was which rendered him so totally indifferent to everything else.

Three, nearly four years elapsed, and Azavédo, in character and habits, remained the same. His father was dead, leaving him immense wealth, which he used nobly and generously, winning "golden opinions" from every class and condition of men, who, at the same time, wished that they could quite understand him; and so we must leave him to waft our readers over the salt seas, and introduce them to a more southern land and a very different person.

In a luxuriously furnished apartment of a beautiful little villa, a few miles from Lisbon, was seated a lady of that extraordinary beauty which ever fastens on the memory as by some strange spell. Not more than three or four and twenty, all the freshness of girlhood was so united to the more mature graces of woman, that it was often difficult to say to which of these two periods of life she belonged. Her large, lustrous, jet-black eye, and the small pouting mouth, alike expressed at will either the mischievous glee of a mirth-loving girl, or the high-souled intellectuality of maturer woman. Hair of that deep dark brown, only to be distinguished from black when the sunshine falls upon it, lay in rich masses and braids around the beautifully shaped head, and giving, from the contrast, yet more dazzling fairness to the pure complexion of face and throat which it shaded; the brow, so "thought-thronged" when at rest, yet lit up, when eye and mouth so willed, with such arch, laughter-loving glee; but we must pause, for the pen can never do beauty justice, and even if it did, would be accused of exaggeration, although there yet remain those who, from personal acquaintance, can still bear witness to its truth.

A gentleman was standing near her as she sat on her sofa, in the busy idleness of embroidery; and as part of their conversation may elucidate our tale, we will record it briefly as may be.

"Then you refused him?"

"Can you ask?" and the lightning flash of the lady's dark eye betrayed unwonted indignation. "He who would have so tempted a helpless girl of seventeen—I was then no more, though I had been married nearly a year—under such spacious reasoning, that I dreamed not his drift till the words of actual insult came; sought to sow suspicion and distrust in my heart against my husband, his own brother, to serve his vile purposes; and you ask me if I refused him, when, being once more free to wed, he dared pollute me with his abhorred addresses! Julian, my fair cousin, have you so forgotten Inez?"

"If I had, that indignant burst would have recalled her; but of insult, remember, I knew nothing. You were married when so young, to a man so much older than yourself, that when I heard of his death, three years ago, I fancied, as you know is often the case with us, you would have married his younger brother, so much more suitable in point of qualities and years."

"More suitable! Wrong again, cousin mine. If I did not love my husband, I respected, honoured him—yes, loved him too as a father; but as for Don Pedro, as men call him, Julian, I would rather have trusted the tender mercies of the Inquisition than I would him, and so I told him."

"You could not have been so mad!"

"In sober truth, I was feeling too thoroughly indignant to weigh my words. It matters not, he dare not work me harm, for the secret on which alone he can, involves his safety as well as mine."

"I wish I could think so; there are many to say that he is in truth what he appears to be, and therefore one most dangerous to offend."

"I fear him as little as I scorn him much. I have heard this report before, but heed it not at all. Our holy cause loses little in the apostasy of sush a member."

"It may be so, Inez; but he holds the lives of others in his keeping, and therefore revenge is easily obtained."

"You will not frighten me, Julian, try as you may. They say Pedro Benito is ill, almost to death—I am sorry for him, for I know no one more unfit to die; but I have far too much pride to fear him, believe me. Better he should injure me, than I my own soul in uniting it with his. See," she continued, laughing, as she pointed to the portly figure of a Dominican priest pushing his mule up the steep ascent leading to the villa, in such evident haste and trepidation as to occasion some amusement to his beholders; "there is more fear there than I shall ever feel. What can the poor priest need? Do you know him, Julian? comes he to you or me?"

"I trust to neither, Inez, for such hot haste bodes little good."

"Why, now, what a craven you have grown! I will disown you for my cousin if you pluck not up more spirit, man!"

Julian Alvarez tried to give as jesting a reply, but succeeded badly, his spirits feeling strangely anxious and oppressed. He was spared further rallying on the part of Inez, by the sudden reappearance of the priest (whom they had lost sight of by a curve in the ascent), without his mule, at the private entrance of Inez's own garden, and without ceremony or question neared the window. Inez addressed him courteously, though with evident surprise; the priest seemed not to heed her words, but, laying his hand on her arm, said, in a deep, low tone—

"Donna Inez, this is no time for courtesy or form. Daughter, fly! even now the bloodhounds are on the track. The scent has been given; a dying man proclaimed you Jewess in hearing of others besides his confessor, else had you been still safe and free. Ere two hours, nay, in less time, they will be here. Away! pause not for thought; seek to save nothing but life, too precious for such sacrifice. A vessel lies moored below, which a brisk hour's walk will reach. She sails for England the moment the wind shifts; secure a passage in her, and trust in the God of Israel for the rest."

"And who are you who thus can care for me, knowing that which I am?" answered the lady, in accents low as the supposed priest's, but far less faltering, and only evincing the shock she had sustained by the sudden whiteness of cheek and lip.

"Men call me—think me, Padre José, my child; but were I such you had not seen me here. *That which you are am I*, and because I thought Pedro Benito the same, I stood beside his death-bed. Vengeance and apostasy went hand in hand. Ask no more, but hence at once; how may those fragile limbs bear the rack—the flames? Senor Alvarez, shake off this stupor, or it will be too late!"

Julian did indeed stand as paralysed, so suddenly and fearfully were his worst fears confirmed. Fly! and from all, home, friends, luxury, to be poor and dependent in a strange land? It was even so; the voice of vengeance had betrayed the fatal secret of race and faith, the very first whisper of which consigned to the Inquisition—but another word for torture and death. In two short hours, part of which had already gone, Inez had to find the vessel, be received on board, and leave no trace whatever of her way. Her very domestics must suspect nothing, or discovery would inevitably ensue. And yet, in the midst of all this sudden accumulation of misfortune, Inez but once betrayed emotion.

"Julian, Julian, my boy!" she exclaimed, her sole answer to the reiterated entreaties of her companions for her to depart at once; "what will they not do to him?"

"Nothing, lady; he shall be with me till he can rejoin you. Who will suspect Padre José of harbouring an Israelite save to convert him to the Holy Faith?"

Inez caught the old man's hand, her lip and eyelids quivering convulsively; but even the passion of choking tears was conquered by the power of mind. In less than half an hour she was walking, at a brisk pace, through the shrubberies, in direction of the river, enveloped in mantilla and veil, and Julian Alvarez carrying a small parcel, containing the few jewels which she could collect, and one or two articles of clothing, the all that the mistress of thousands could save from the rapacious hands which, under the garb of religion, were ever stretched out to confiscate and to destroy.

Scarcely had they quitted the shrubberies, after nearly an hour's brisk walking, and entered the high road, their only path, when about a dozen men, in the full livery of the Holy Office, were clearly discernible, on a slight rising not half a mile beyond them, pushing their horses so as directly to face them, and advancing at full speed. To turn back, was to excite suspicion; to meet them, tempt discovery. Fortunately a small inclosure of tall larches and thick firs lay forward, a little to the left, and there Inez impelled her bewildered companion, walking as carelessly, to all appearance, as taking a saunter for amusement. They saw the troop rapidly advance, pause exactly in front of their hiding-place, look round inquiringly; one or two spurred forward, as to beat the bushes; a man's step at the same time sounded in their rear—his dress fanned them as he passed: it was one of Donna Inez's own labourers. They heard him hailed as he appeared, and questions asked, of which they heard nothing, but that wordless sound of voices so torturing to those who deem that life or death are hanging on the words. A few minutes—feeling hours—the conference lasted; some direction, loudly repeated along the file, betrayed that their questions only related to their further route to the Villa Benito, and the horses galloped on.

Without exchanging a syllable, Inez and her companion hurried forward. It was still full half-an-hour's walk to the river; the sun was declining, and the wind had risen fresh and balmy; but while Julian rejoiced in its reviving power, he trembled lest it should be bearing his cousin's only chance of safety farther from them. Their pace was brisk as could be, yet every step seemed clogged with lead, and weary felt the way, till the river's brink was gained. Bathed in the lingering glow of a magnificent sunset, the bright waters lay before them, and every sail spread, gliding softly yet swiftly on her course, they beheld the longed-for vessel receding from their sight.

For one minute they stood, gazing on the departing ship, as mute, as feelingless as stone, save to the horrible consciousness that flight was over, all hope of escape must be vain. But great emergencies prevent the continuance of despair. Ere Julian had recovered the stupor of alike disappointment and dread, Inez had hailed a boatman, and drawing a diamond ring of immense value from her hand, bade him place her in safety on board the English vessel, and it should be his. The man hesitated, then swore it was worth the trial, and very speedily a boat was ready, manned by four stout rowers impatient as herself.

"And now farewell, dear Julian!" she said, calmly, taking the parcel from his hand, and looking in his astonished face with her own sweet smile. "You go no farther; I will not risk your life, so precious to your wife and children, because I weakly fear to meet my destiny alone. Do not attempt to argue with me; it will be useless, as you ought to know. Look to my poor boy; he needs you more than I do." Her voice sunk to a thrilling whisper: "The God we *both* serve bless you, and keep you from a similar fate."

She wrung his hand, and lightly springing into the boat, it was pushed off, and rapidly cutting the yielding waters, ere Julian Alvarez recovered sufficiently from his emotion to speak even a farewell word. And now, with feelings wrought almost to agony, he watched a chase seemingly so utterly vain. For some time the vessel still kept ahead, but the efforts of the rowers in no degree relaxed. He heard their stentorian hail repeated by the innumerable echoes on the shore, but still there seemed no answer. Again, and yet again! It is fancy.

No, the sails are lowered, the vessel's speed is diminished, till the boat appears almost alongside. Julian strained his gaze, while his very heart felt to have ceased beating, in the sickening fear that even now her flight might be prevented by a refusal to receive her. He could discern no more, for twilight had gathered round him, and interminable seemed the interval till the boat returned with the blessed assurance that the Senora was safe on board.

Night fell; the lovely southern night, with its silvery moonshine on the gleaming waters, its glistening stars, appearing suspended in the upper air as globes of liquid light, with its fresh, soft breezes, bearing such sweet scents from the odoriferous shores, that a poet might have fancied angelic spirits were abroad, making the atmosphere luminous with their pure presence, and every breeze fragrant with their luscious breath.

Inez sat upon the deck, a fugitive, and alone. She who, only the evening previous, had been the centre of a brilliant group, whose halls had sounded with the voice of revelry, the blithesome dance, whence aught of sorrow seemed so far away as to be but a name, not a reality. To us, looking back on the extraordinary fact of the most Catholic kingdoms being literally peopled with secret Jews, whose property and life might be sacrificed from one hour to another, it appears incomprehensible that security or happiness could ever have existed, and still more difficult to understand what secret feeling it was which thus bound them to a country where, acknowledged or discovered, Judaism was death, when there were other parts of the globe where they could be protected and received. Yet so it was; and there are still families in England to trace their descent from those who, like the Senora Benito, were compelled to fly at an hour's warning, saving little else than life.

Some spirits would have sunk under a misfortune so sudden, so overwhelming in its details; but Inez rose above it. She had nothing to look to but her own resources; the few valuables she had secreted would, she knew, soon be exhausted, did she depend on them alone. She was going to a land where she knew not one, her only credentials being a letter hurriedly written by her cousin to one of his friends in London. Loneliness, privation, care, and even manual toil, all awaited her, child as she had been of luxury and wealth, lavish as it was believed exhaustless; yet, as she looked forth on the glorious night, with her starlit dome, as she inhaled the sweet breath of a thousand flowers floating on the breeze, she knew she was not forsaken. He who cared for all nature, would still more care for her, and, when the spirit is at peace, how lightly is all of sorrow borne.

The unusual stir in the harbour, which they reached about midnight, attracted the attention not only of Inez, but of the captain and crew. On stopping at the quay for passengers and freight, he was told that the vessel must remain at anchor, no English ship being allowed to leave the harbour until it had received a visit from the officers of the Inquisition, in search of a female fugitive suspected of Judaism, who, having effectually disappeared from her home, was supposed to have taken refuge in some English vessel, the general receivers of heretics and unbelievers.

"I halt not at any man's beck or bidding!" was the proud reply. "England owns no Inquisitional supremacy. Had any such fugitive taken refuge in my ship, no power of the Inquisition, backed by the whole kingdom, should force me to give her up."

Time for reply or seizure there was none. Every sail spread at the word of command, and almost bending beneath her weight of canvas, the gallant ship, with her right English-hearted crew, sped on to sea.

Inez had seen all, felt all; but though her heart beat quicker, no word or sign betrayed it. She saw the captain look hastily on her, and for a terrible moment she knew not whether the glance of discovery—for such it was—would be followed by her surrender or her safety. His words speedily reassured her, and sent her to the berth provided for her comfort, with more care than for any other passenger, with the grateful feeling that all of danger was indeed at end. She was in England's keeping, and no Inquisition could work her harm.

Nor was it the mere excitement of misfortune which so endowed her with courage to endure. She retained not only firmness but liveliness during the voyage, and when received in England with the most hospitable kindness by Julian's friends, gaily consulted them on the best means of subsistence—whether to take in plain work or enter upon the business of fancy confectionary, for both of which her convent education had well fitted her. And what with her brilliant beauty, her sparkling wit, and readiness of repartee, ere two days had passed she had completely fascinated old and young.

The evening of the third day Mr. Nunez's family had been engaged to spend with a friend living a few miles from London. On sending to state that a Portuguese lady staying with them would prevent their going, an entreaty was instantly forwarded that she would accompany them.

"What, go! and my whole wardrobe consists of this one dress?" was her laughing reply. "I shall bring shame on your fashionable reputation, my kind friends."

They assured her that dress was of little consequence, and, even if it were, she need not be alarmed, being more likely to bring them fame by the fashion of her face than shame by the plainness of her robe; which, by the way, a rich black velvet, set off the dazzling clearness of her complexion more becomingly than the most carefully assorted garb.

To the house of their friend, in consequence, they went; and the beautiful stranger, with her broken English, sweetly spoken Portuguese, and most romantic story, soon commanded universal attention.

Towards the middle of the evening a rapidly approaching carriage, followed by a thundering rap, announced the arrival of some new guest.

"That is Azavédo," observed one, "I know him by the sound of his four horses. A strange fancy that, always sporting a carriage and four, when in everything else he has no pretension whatever. Did you expect him, Cordoza?" he asked of his host.

"He said he might look in on his way to Epping," was the reply.

"What a changed man he is," said another; "I remember when he literally loathed society, and shrunk from beauty, male or female, as if it stung him by the contrast with himself."

"I have never heard him admire a woman yet though," rejoined the first speaker. "I wonder if he will notice the beauty of to-night?"

Azavédo entered as he spoke, and after addressing his host and hostess, began an earnest conversation with a friend near them.

A low musical laugh from the centre of a merry group at the opposite end of the large drawing-room caused Azavédo suddenly so to start, with such an indescribable change of countenance, as to impel the anxious query whether he were ill. He answered hurriedly in the negative, but his friend perceiving his eye fixed on the group, eagerly entered on the story of the stranger, from whom the laugh had come, inviting him to join the circle round her. Somewhat hesitatingly he did so. Inez, in compliance with the customs of her own country, still wore her veil, which, in answer to the inquiry of some one near her as to the different fashions of wearing it in Portugal, she had drawn so closely round her as to hide every feature.

"Tell her that it is not the custom of English ladies to wear veils," whispered Azavédo to his hostess, in tones of such strong and most unusual excitement, that she looked at him as if in doubt of his identity. His hint was acted upon, however, and Inez, with winning courtesy, soon after laid aside her veil.

Azavédo had become in some degree a man of the world; and it was well he was, or he might have found it difficult so to suppress inward emotion as to conceal it from those around him. He looked once more on the being who for four long years had in secret so occupied his heart, as never to permit the entrance of another image, or the faintest thought of another love. She was there, not only yet more radiant in finished lovliness than when he had first beheld her, but free, and of his own race and creed. And so exquisite were the feelings of the moment, that he feared to be introduced, lest her first glance upon his face, if it revealed the horror that he believed it would, should sentence him to misery.

That he had trembled needlessly was proved by his never leaving her side that evening. The lively spirits of the young stranger appeared, by some extraordinary species of mesmerism, to call forth the same from him; and he conversed more brilliantly, more unreservedly, than he had ever before been known to do.

Judah Azavédo pursued his journey to his country-house, and Inez quietly fixed her residence with a Jewish family in London, and pursued her intention of taking in plain work; giving no more thought of her former affluence, save to wish that part had been spared for her boy, who, through the efforts of Padre José and Julian Alvarez, joined her about three weeks after her flight, bringing the information that every article belonging to her had been seized and confiscated.

Twice a week, then three times, and at length every day,

did Azavédo, on some pretence or other, visit the fair fugigive. Folks talked and wondered, but for once he heeded neither. But why prolong our tale, claimed as it is by truth, however it may read like fiction? Not six weeks after Inez left Portugal, a fugitive for her very life, she became the wife of Judah Azavédo, the richest Hebrew in London, and the possessor of a love as warm and unwavering as was ever felt by man. But did she—could she—return it? Reader, we will not blazon the simplicity of truth with the false colouring of romance. *She did not* love him, in the general acceptation of the term, and she told him so, beseeching him to withdraw his offer, if his heart could not rest satisfied with the respect and gratitude which alone she felt. He thanked her for her candour, but the hand was not withdrawn, and they were married. Some biographers stop here, bidding the curious reader probe not too deeply into the history of wedded life. As regards our heroine, however, we shrink not from the probe. The *romance* of love *before* marriage she might not have known, but its *reality afterwards* she made so manifest, even when disease, joined to other infirmities, so tried her husband as to render him fretful and irritable, that there are still living some to assert that never was wife more tenderly affectionate, more devotedly faithful than was Inez Azavédo. Her extraordinary beauty seemed invulnerable to age, for I have heard it said that even in her coffin, and she lived to the full age of mortality, she retained it still.

The Edict.

A TALE OF 1492.

"The love that bids the patriot rise to guard his country's rest,
With deeper mightier fulness thrills in woman's gentle breast."—MS.

"And we must wander witheringly,
In other lands to die;
And where our father's ashes be,
Our own may never lie."—BYRON.

"THEN thou wouldst not leave this beautiful valley even with me, Josephine?"

"Nay, thou knowest thou dost but jest, Imri; thou wouldst not give me such a painful alternative?"

"How knowest thou that, love?" Perchance I may grow jealous even of thy country, an it hold so dear a place in thy gentle breast, and seek a home elsewhere—to prove if thy love of Imri be dearer than thy love of land."

"I know thou wouldst do no such thing, my Imri; so play the threatening tyrant as thou mayest, I'll not believe thee, or lessen by one throb the love of my land, which shares my heart with thee. I know too well, thy heart beats true as mine; thou wouldst not take me hence."

"Never, my best beloved. Our children shall rove where we have roved, and learn their father's faith uninjured by closer commune with its foes. Here, where the exiles of Israel for centuries have found a peaceful home, will we rest, my Josephine, filling the little hearts of our children with thanksgiving that there is one spot of earth where the wandering and the persecuted may repose in peace."

"And surely it is for this cause the love we bear our country is so strong, so deep, that the thought of death is less bitter than the dream of other homes. We stand alone in our peculiar and most sainted creed, alone in our law, alone in our lives on earth, in our hopes for heaven. Our doom is to wander accursed and houseless over the broad earth, exposed to all the misery which man may inflict, without the power to retaliate or shun. Surely, oh, surely then, the home that is granted must be doubly dear—so sheltered from outward ill, so blessed with inward peace, that it might seem we alone were the inhabitants of Spain. Oh! it is not only memory that hallows every shrub and stream and tree—it is the consciousness of safety, of peace, of joy, which this vale enshrines, while all around us seemeth strife and gloom. Dearest Imri, is it marvel that I love it thus?"

The speaker was a beautiful woman of some two or three and twenty summers. There was a lovely finished roundness of form, a deep steady lustre in her large black eye, a full ripe red on her beautiful lip, a rose soft yet glowing as the last tinge of sunset beaming, in the energy of her words, upon a cheek usually more pale—all bespeaking a stage of life somewhat past that generally denominated girlhood, but only pressing the threshold of the era which follows. Life was still bright and fresh, and buoyant as youth would paint it; but in the heart there were depths and feelings revealed that were never known to girlhood. Her companion, some three or four years her senior, presented a manly form, and features more striking from their frankness and animation than any regular beauty. But there was one other individual, seated at some little distance from the lovers (for such they were), whose peculiar and affecting beauty would rivet the attention to the exclusion of all else. He was a slight boy, who had evidently not seen more than ten years, though the light in the dark blue eye, so deep, so concentrated in its expression, that it seemed to breathe forth the soul; the expression ever lingering round his small delicately pencilled mouth appeared to denote a strength and formation of character beyond his years. His rich chestnut hair, long and gracefully curling, fell over his light blue vest nearly to his waist, and, parted in the centre, exposed a brow of such transparent fairness, so arched and high, that it scarce appeared natural to his Eastern origin and Spanish birth. Long lashes, much darker than his hair, almost concealed the colour of the eye, save when it was fixed full on those who spoke to him, and shaded softly, yet with a mournful expression, the pale and delicate cheek, to which exertion or emotion alone had power to bring the frail and fleeting rose. An indescribable plaintiveness pervaded the countenance; none could define wherefore, or why his very smile would gush on the heart like tears. He was seated on the green sward, weaving some beautiful flowers into a garland or wreath, in perfect silence, although he was not so far removed from his companions as to be excluded from their conversation, could he have joined in it. Alas! those lips had never framed a word; no sound had ever reached his ear.

An animated response from Imri followed his Josephine's last eager words; and the boy, as if desirous of partaking their emotion whatever it might be, bounded towards them, placing his glowing wreath on the brow of Josephine with a fond admiring glance, calling on Imri by a sign to admire it with him; then nestling closer to her bosom, inquired in the same manner the subject of their conversation; and when told, there was no need of language to speak the boy's reply. He glanced eagerly, almost passionately, around him; he stretched forth his arms, as if embracing every long-loved object, and then he laid his hand on his heart, as if the image of each were reflected there, and stretched himself on the mossy earth, as if there should be his last long sleep. He pointed to distant mountains, made a movement with his hands, to denote the world beyond them, then turned shudderingly away, and laid his head on the bosom of his nearest and dearest relative on earth.

The situation of the valley of Eshcol was in truth such as to inspire enthusiasm in colder hearts than Josephine's. Formed by one of the many breaks in the Sierra Morena, and sharing abundantly the rich vegetation which crowns this ridge of mountains nine months in the year, it appeared set apart by Nature as a guarded and blessed haven of peace for the weary wanderers of Israel; who, when the Roman spoiler desolated their holy land, tradition said there found a resting-place. Lofty rocks and mountains hemmed it round, throwing as it were a natural barrier between the valley and the world beyond. The heath, the rosemary, the myrtle, and the cistus grew in rich profusion amidst the cliffs; while below, the palm, the olive, the lemon, orange and almond, interspersed with flowering shrubs of every variety, marked the site of the hamlet, and might mournfully remind the poor fugitives of the yet richer and holier land their fathers' sins had forfeited. To the east, a thick grove of palm, cedar, and olive surrounded the lowly temple, where for ages the simple villagers worshipped the God of Israel as their fathers did. Its plain and solid architecture resisted alike the power of storm and time; and it was the pride of every generation to preserve it in the primitive simplicity of the past. Innumerable streams, issuing from the mountains, watered the vale: some flowing with a silvery murmur and sparkling light, others rushing and leaping over crags, their prominences hid in the snowy foam, creating alike variety and fertility. The brilliant scarlet flower of the fig-marigold mingled with the snowy blossoms of the myrtle, peeping forth from its dark glossy leaves, formed a rich garland around the trunks of many a stalwart tree; and often at the sunset hour the perfume of the orange and almond, the balsamic fragrance of the cistus, mingling with, yet apart from the others, would float by on the balmy pinions of the summer breeze, adding indescribably to the soothing repose and natural magic of the scene.

But it was not the mere beauty of nature which sunk so deeply on the hearts of the Eshcolites, as to create that species of *amor patriæ*, of which Josephine's ardent words were but a faint reflection; it was the fact that it was, had been, and they fondly hoped ever would be, to them a second Judea. Its very name had been bestowed by the unhappy fugitives from the destruction of Jerusalem, who hailed its natural loveliness as their ancestors did the first-fruits of the land of promise. Throughout the whole of Spain, indeed, the sons of Israel were scattered, far more numerously and prosperously than in any other country. Despite her repeated revolutions, her internal wars, her constant change of masters, the Hebrews so continued to flourish that the whole commerce of the kingdom became engrossed by them; and occupying stations of eminence and trust—the heads of all seminaries of physic and literature—they commanded veneration even from the enemies and persecutors of their creed.

With the nation at large, however, our simple narrative does not pretend to treat. Century after century found the little colony of Eshcol flourishing and happy; acknowledging no law but that of Moses, no God but Him that law revealed. It mattered not to them whether Mahommedan or Nazarene claimed supremacy in Spain. Schism and division were unknown amongst them; the same temple received their simple worship from age to age; for if it chanced that the more eager, the more ambitious spirits sought more stirring scenes, they returned to the simplicity of their fathers, conscious they had no power to alter, and satisfied that they could not improve.

Varying in population from three to five hundred families, actuated by the same interests, grief and joy became as it were the common property of all—the one inexpressibly soothed, the other heightened by sympathy—the vale of Eshcol seemed marked out as the haven of peace. The poet, the minstrel, the architect, the agriculturist, even the sculptor, were often found amongst its inmates, flourishing, and venerated as men more peculiarly distinguished by their merciful Creator than their fellows. The sins that convulse kingdoms and agitate a multitude to them were unknown; for the seditious, the restless, the ambitious sought a wider field, bidding an eternal farewell to the vale, whose peaceful insipidity they spurned. Crimes were punished by banishment, perpetual or for a specified time, according to the guilt; liable indeed to death, if the criminal returned, but of this the records of Eshcol present no example.

Situated in the southern ridge of the Sierra Morena, on the eastern extremity of Andalusia, and consequently at the very entrance of the Moorish dominions, yet Nature's care had so fortified the vale, that it had remained both uninjured and undiscovered by the immense armies of Ferdinand and Isabella, who for ten years had overrun the beautiful province of Grenada, and now, at the commencement of our narrative, had completed its reduction, and compelled the last of the Caliphs to acknowledge their supremacy in Spain. Misery and death were busy within ten miles of the Hebrew colony, but there they entered not. Some aspiring youths had in truth departed to join the contending hosts; but by far the greater number, more indifferent to the fate of war, cared not on which side the banner of victory might wave—their affections centred so strongly on the spot of earth at once their birthplace and their tomb, that to depart from it seemed the very bitterness of death.

Tedious as this digression may seem, it is necessary for the clear comprehension of our narrative; for the appreciation of that feeling of *amor patriæ* which is its basis; an emotion experienced in various degrees by every nation, but by the Jew in Spain with a strength and intensity equalled by none and understood but by a Jew.

Josephine Castello, in whom this feeling was resting yet more powerfully than in her compeers, was regarded as an orphan, and as such peculiarly beloved; yet an orphan she was not. The youth of her father, Simeon Castello, had been marked by such ungovernable passions, as to render him an object of doubt and dread to all; with the sole exception of one—the meekest, gentlest, most timid girl of Eschol. Perhaps it was the contrast with herself—the generous temper, the frank and winning smile, the bold character of his striking beauty, or the voiceless magic which we may spend whole lives in endeavouring to define, and which only laughs at our wisdom—but Rachel Asher loved him, so faithfully, so unchangeably, that it stood the test of many months, nay years, of wandering on the part of Simeon, who on each return to the vale appeared more restless, more wayward than before.

Men said he was incapable of loving, and augured sorrow and neglect for the gentle Rachel, even when, seemingly touched by her meek and timid loveliness, he bent his proud spirit to woo her love, and was accepted. They were married; and some few years of quiet felicity appeared to belie the prognostics of the crowd. But soon after the birth of a daughter, the wandering propensities of her father again obtained ascendency; and for months, and then years, he would be absent from his home.

Uncomplainingly Rachel bore this desertion, for he was ever fond when he returned; and even when she once ventured to entreat permission to accompany him, it was with soothing affection, not harsh repulse, he refused, assuring her, though honoured and trusted by the Nazarene, he was seldom more than a month at one place; and he could not offer delicate females the quiet settled home they needed. Rachel could have told him that privation and hardship with him would be hailed as blessings, but she knew her husband's temper, and acquiescing, sought comfort in the increasing intelligence and beauty of her child.

Ten years thus passed, and then Simeon, as if involuntarily yielding to the love of his wife and child, declared his intention of never again seeking the Nazarene world, and for two years he adhered to his resolution; at the end of that time hailing with pleasure the promise of another little one, to share with Josephine the affection he lavished upon her. This sudden change of character could not pass unnoticed by his fellows; and no man being more tenacious of his honour than Simeon Castello, it was of course exposed to many aspersions, which his passionate temper could not brook.

It happened in a jovial meeting of youngsters when somewhat heated by excitement and wine, that the character and actions of Castello were canvassed somewhat more freely than sobriety would have ventured. One of them at length remarked, that in all probability he was glad to avail himself of the retreat of Eshcol, to eschew the hundred eyes of justice or revenge.

"Then die in thy falsehood, liar!" were the words that, uttered in thunder, startled the assembly. "The man lives not who dares impugn the honour of Castello!" and the hapless youth sunk to the earth before them, stricken unto death. The speechless horror of all around might easily have permitted flight, but Castello scorned it. He knew his doom, and met it in stern unflinching silence;—to wander forth alone, with the thoughts of blood clinging to his conscience, till the mandate of his God summoned him to answer for his crime; —death, if he ever ventured to insult the sacred precincts of his native vale by seeking to return.

The voice of his father faltered not, as from his seat of judgment, amid the elders of his people, he pronounced this sentence. His cheek blanched not as the wife and child of the murderer flung themselves at his feet, beseeching permission to accompany the exile. It could not be. Nay more, did he return, the law was such, that his own wife or child must deliver him up to justice, or share the penalty of his crime. Hour by hour beheld the wretched suppliants pleading for mercy, but in vain.

Nor did this more than Roman firmness (for it was based on love not stoicism) desert him when, in agonized remorse, his son besought his forgiveness and his blessing. He confessed his sin, for he felt it such. No provocation could call for blood. And headstrong and violent as were the passions of Simeon Castello, his father believed in his remorse, his penitence; for he knew deeds of blood were foreign to his nature. He raised his clasped hands to heaven, he prayed that the penitence of the sinner might be accepted, he spoke his forgiveness and his blessing, and then flinging his arms around his son, his head sunk upon his shoulder. Minutes passed and there was no sound—the Hebrew father had done his duty: but his heart had broken—he was dead!

From the moment she was released from the parting embrace of her doubly-wretched husband, and her strained eyes might no longer distinguish his retreating figure, no word escaped the lips of Rachel. For the first time, she looked on the sorrow of her poor child, without any attempt to soothe or console. She resumed her usual duties, but it was as if a statue had been endowed with movement. Nor could the entreaties of her aged grandfather, her sole remaining relative, nor the caresses of Josephine, wring even one word of suffering from her lips.

A week passed, and Josephine held a little brother in her arms; the looks of her mother appeared imploring her to cherish and protect him, and kneeling, she solemnly swore to make him the first object of her life;—belief beamed in the eyes of the dying—her look seemed beseeching the blessing of heaven on them both; but Josephine yearned in vain for the sweet accents of her voice—she never spoke again.

From that hour, the gay and sprightly child seemed changed into premature and sorrowing womanhood. She stood alone of her race. Alone, with the sole exception of that aged relative, who had seen his children and children's children fall around him, and her infant brother. She shrunk in her sensitiveness, from the young companions who would have soothed her grief. She did not fear that the crime of her father would be visited upon her innocent head, for such feelings were unknown to the simple government of Eshcol; but her loneliness, the shock which had crushed every hope and joy of youth, caused her to cling closer to her aged relative, and direct every energy to the welfare of her young and—as, alas! she too soon discovered—afflicted brother. She watched his increase in strength, intelligence, and loveliness, and pictured in vivid colouring the delight which would attend his instruction; she longed intensely for the moment when her ear should be blessed by the sweet accents of his voice. That moment came not! the affliction of her mother had descended to the child she bore, and Josephine, in irrepressible anguish, became conscious that not only was his voice withheld from her, but hers might never reach his ear.

Her deep affection for him, however, roused her from this mournful conviction; and energetically she sought to render his affliction less painful than it had appeared, and she succeeded. She led him into the fields of nature—every spot became to the child a fruitful source of intelligence and love, providing him with language, even in inanimate objects; by his mother's grave she instilled the thoughts of God and heaven, of their peculiar race and history; of the God of Israel's deep love and long-suffering; and she was understood—though to what extent she knew not, imagined not, till the hour of trial came. That she was inexpressibly assisted by the child's rapid conception of the good and evil, of the sublime and beautiful—by his extraordinary intellect and truly poet's soul, is true, but the lowly spirit of Josephine felt as if a special blessing had attended her task, and urged yet further efforts for his improvement.

By means of waxen tablets, formed by the hand of Imri Benalmar, she taught him to read and write. Leading his attention to familiar objects, she would write down their appropriate names, and familiarising his eye to the writing, he gradually associated the written word with the visible object. The rest was easy to a mind like his. The flushed cheek and sparkling eye denoted the intense delight with which he perused the manuscripts collected, and often adapted for his use by Imri, and poesy became his passion; breathing in the simplest words, on his waxen tablets, the love he bore his devoted sister, and the pure, beautiful sentiments which filled his soul.

The kindness of Imri to her Aréli, passed not unfelt by the heart of Josephine. Tremblingly she became conscious that an emotion towards him was obtaining ascendency, which she deemed it her duty to conquer, or at least profoundly to hide. She could not forget the stigma on her name, and believed none could seek her love. The daughter of a murderer (for though the crime was involuntary, such he was) was lonely upon earth. Dignified and reserved, they would have thought her proud, had not her constant kindness, her total forgetfulness of self, in continually serving others, belied the thought; but this they did think (and Imri Benalmar himself, so well did she hide her heart), that her affections were centred in her aged relative and her young brother.

But when the magic words were spoken, when Imri Benalmar, whose unwavering piety and steady virtue had caused him to stand highest and dearest in the estimation of his fellows, young and old, conjured her with a respectful deference, which vainly sought to calm the passionate affection of his soul, to bless him with her love, her trust—the long hidden feelings of Josephine were betrayed, their inmost depths revealed. Blessed, indeed, was that moment to them both. Fondly did Imri combat her arguments, that she had no right to burden him with the aged Asher and her helpless Aréli, yet from them she could never consent to part.

"Had not Aréli ever been dear to him as a brother—had he not always intended to prove himself such?" he asked, with many other arguments of love; and how might Josephine reply, save with tears of strong emotion to consent to become his bride?

Josef Asher heard of their engagement with delight; but he would not consent to burden them with his continued company. True, he was old, but neither infirm nor ailing. He would retain possession of his own dwelling, which had descended to him from many generations; but the nearer his children resided, the greater happiness for him.

Imri understood the hint, and, as if by magic, a picturesque little cottage, not two hundred yards from her native home, rose before the wondering eyes of Josephine; and Aréli, as he watched its progress, clapped his hands in childish joy, and sought to aid the workmen in their tasks. Presents from all, as is the custom of the Hebrew nation, were showered on the youthful couple, to enable them to commence housekeeping with comfort, or add some little ornament or useful article of furniture to the house or its adjoining lands. The more the *fiancées* were beloved, the greater source of public joy was a wedding in Eshcol.

The conversation which the commencement of our tale in part records took place a few evenings previous to the day fixed for the nuptials.

On leaving his sister and her betrothed, Aréli betook himself, as was his custom, ere he joined the evening meal, to his mother's grave, to water the flowers around it, and peruse, in his simple and innocent devotion, the little Bible which Josephine and Imri's love had rendered into the simplest Spanish, from the Hebrew Scriptures of their race. The shades of evening had already fallen around the leafy shadowed place of tombs, but there was sufficient light remaining for the boy to discern a cloaked and muffled figure prostrate before his mother's grave, the head resting in a posture of inexpressible anguish on the cold marble of the tomb. The stranger's form moved convulsively, and though Aréli could distinguish no sound, he knew that it was grief on which he gazed. Softly he approached, and laid his little hand on that of the stranger, who started in evident alarm, looking upon that angelic face with a strange mixture of bewilderment and love. He spoke, but Aréli shook his head mournfully, putting his arm around his neck caressingly, as if beseeching him to take comfort; then, as if failing in his desired object, he hastily drew his tablets from his vest, and wrote rapidly—

"Poor Aréli cannot speak nor hear, but he can feel; do not weep, it is so sad to see tears in eyes like thine!"

"And why is it sad, sweet boy?" the stranger wrote in answer, straining him as he did so involuntarily closer to his bosom.

"Oh, man should not weep, and man like thee, who can list the sweet voice of nature, and the tones of all he loves; who can breathe forth all he thinks, and feels, and likes. Tears are for poor Aréli, and yet they do not come now as they did once; for I have a father who loves, and who can hear me too, though none else can."

"A father?" wrote the stranger. "Who is thy father, gentle boy? Thou bearest a name I know not. Tell me who thou art."

"Oh, I have no father that I may see and hear—none, that is, on earth; but I love Him, for He smiles on me through the sweet flowers, and sparkling brooks, and beautiful trees; and I know he loves me and cares for me, deaf and dumb and afflicted as I am, and He hears me when I ask Him to bless me and my sweet sister, and reward her for all she does for me. He is up—up there, and all around." He stretched out his arms, pointing to the star-lit heavens and beautiful earth. "My Father's house is everywhere; and when my body lies here, as my mother's does, my breath will go up to Him, and Aréli will be so happy—so happy!"

"Thy mother!" burst from the stranger's lips, as though the child could hear him; and his hand so trembled that he could hardly guide the steel pencil which traced the wax. "Who is thy mother—where does she lie?"

Aréli laid his hand on the tomb, pointing to the name of Rachel Castello, there simply engraved. The effect almost terrified him. The stranger caught him in his arms—he pressed repeated kisses on his cheek, his brow, his lips—clasping him, as if to release him were death. The child returned his caresses without either impatience or dissatisfaction. After a while the stranger again wrote—

"Thy sister, sweet boy—is it she who hath taught thee these things—doth she live—is she happy?"

"Oh, so happy! and Imri, kind Imri, will make her happier still. Aréli loves him next to Josephine, and grandfather and I am to live with them, and we are all happy. Oh, how I love Josephine! I should have been so sad—so sad, had she not loved me, taught me all; but come to her—she will make thee happy too, and thou wilt weep no more. The coming meal waits for us both—wilt thou not come? Josephine will love thee, for thou lovest Aréli."

A deep agonized groan escaped from the stranger, vibrating through his whole frame. Several minutes passed ere he could make reply, and then he merely wrote, in almost illegible characters—

"I am not good enough to go with you, my child. Pray for me—love me: I shall remember thee."

And then again he folded him in his arms, kissed him passionately, and disappeared in the gloom, ere Aréli could detain him or perceive his path, though he sprang forward to do so.

The child watered his flowers more hastily than usual, evidently preoccupied by some new train of thought, which was shown by a rapid return to his grandfather's cottage, and an animated recital, through signs and his tablets, of all that had occurred, adding an earnest entreaty to Imri to seek and find him.

Josephine started from the table—the rich glow of her cheek faded into a death-like paleness, and, without uttering a syllable, she threw her mantle around her and hastily advanced to the door. Imri and even the aged Josef threw themselves before her.

"Whither wouldst thou go, Josephine, dearest Josephine? this is not well—whom wouldst thou seek?"

"My *father*," she replied, in a voice whose low deep tone betrayed her emotion. "Shall he be lingering near, unheeded, uncared for by his child? Imri, stay me not; I *must* see him once again."

"Thou must not, thou shalt not!" was Imri's agonized reply, clasping her in his arms to prevent her progress. "Josephine, thy life is no longer thine own, to fling from thee thus as a worthless thing; it is mine—mine by thine own free gift; thou shalt not wrest it from me thus."

"My child, seek not this stranger; draw not the veil aside which he has wisely flung around him. The penalty to both may not be waived—thou mayst not see *him*, save to proclaim—or die. My child, my child, leave me not in my old age alone"

The mournful accents of the aged man completed what the passionate appeal had begun. Josephine sunk on a seat near him, and burst into an agony of tears. Aréli clung round

6*

her, terrified at the effect of his simple tale; and for him she roused herself, warning him to repeat the tale to none, but indeed to grant the stranger's boon, and remember him in his lowly prayers. Fearfully both Imri and Asher waited the morning, dreading lest its light should betray the stranger; and thankfully did they welcome the close of that day and the next without his reappearance. A very different feeling actuated the afflicted Aréli; he sought him with the longing wish to look on his face again, for it haunted his fancy, lingered on his love—and a yet more hallowed spot became his mother's tomb.

The intervening days had passed, the affection of Imri bearing from the heart of Josephine its last lingering sadness, and enabling her to feel the anguish her impetuosity might have brought not only on her father and herself, but on all whom she loved. The first of May, her bridal morn, found her composed and smiling like herself. She had placed her future fate, without one doubt or fear, in the keeping of Imri Benalmar, for the tremors and emotions of modern brides were unknown to the maidens of Eshcol; once only her calmness had been disturbed, when her young brother had approached her, and clasped his arms about her neck, and with glistening eyes had written his boyish love.

"Look at the sun, sweet sister; how brightly and beautifully he shines, how soft and blue the sky, and the sweet flowers, and the little birds! Oh, they all love thee, and can smile and sing their joy! and gentle friends throng round thee, and speak loving words. Oh, why is poor Aréli alone silent, when his heart is so full? But he can pray, sweet sister; pray as thou hast taught him; and he will pray his Father to give back to thee all which thou hast done for him."

Was it marvel that Josephine's tears should fall over those fond words? But the boy's caresses turned that dewy joy to softer smiles, as surrounded by her youthful companions she waited the entrance of her aged relative to conduct her to the temple.

Three hours after noon the nuptial party there assembled, marriages among the Hebrews seldom being performed at an earlier hour. Twenty young girls dressed alike, and half that number of matrons, attended the bride; and proudly did old Josef gaze upon her, as she leaned on his arm in all the grace and loveliness of beautiful womanhood, unconscious how well it contrasted with his sinewy and athletic form ; his silvery beard and hair alone betraying his four-score and fourteen years. There was no shadow of age upon his features, beaming as they were, in his quick sympathy, with all around him. The path was strewed with the fairest flowers, and the freshest moss, of varied hues, while rich garlands, interwoven with the blushing fruits, festooned the trees. The whole village wore the aspect of rejoicing, and every shade passed from the brow of the young Aréli ; the flush deepened on his fair cheek, the intense blue of his beautiful eye so sparkled in light, that the eyes of all were upon him, till they glistened in strange tears.

The bridegroom awaited the bride and her companions in the temple, attended by an equal number. The little edifice was filled, for marriages in Eshcol were ever solemnized in public ; the number that attended evincing the feelings with which the betrothed were regarded. The ceremony commenced, and, save the voice of the officiating priest. there was silence so profound, that the faintest sound could have been distinguished.

As Josephine flung back her veil, at once to taste the sacred wine, and prove to Imri that no Leah had been substituted for his Rachel, a distant trampling fell clearly on the still air. The service continued, but many looked up to the high casements as if in wonder. The sun still poured down his golden flood of light ; no passing cloud announced an approaching storm, so to explain the unwonted sounds as distant thunder. They came nearer and nearer still ; the trampling of many feet seemed echoing from the mountain ground ; and at the moment Imri flung down the crystal goblet on the marble at his feet, as the conclusion of the solemn rites, the shrill blast of many trumpets and the long roll of the pealing drum were borne on the wings of a hundred echoes, far and near. Wild birds, whose rest had never before been so disturbed, rose screaming from their haunts, darkening the air with their flapping wings. Again and again, at irregular intervals, this unusual music was repeated ; but though alarm blanched many a maiden's cheek, and the brows of the sterner sex became knit with indefinable emotion, the afternoon service, which ever follows the Jewish nuptials, continued undisturbed.

The eyes of Josephine were fixed on Imri more in wonder than alarm, and Benalmar had folded his arm round her and whispered, "Mine, mine in woe or in weal; mine thou art, and wilt be, love! whatever ill these martial sounds forebode."

A smile so bright, so confiding, was the answer, that even had he not felt her cling closer to his heart, Imri would have been satisfied. A sudden paleness banished the rich flush from the cheek of the deaf and dumb; he relinquished his station under the canopy which had been held over the bride and bridegroom during the ceremony, and drew closer to them. He had *heard* indeed no sound; but so keen are the other senses of the deaf and dumb, that many have been known *to feel* what they cannot hear. Aréli could read, in a moment's glance, the countenances of those around him, and at the same instant he became conscious of a thrilling sensation creeping through his every vein. He took the hand of Imri and looked up inquiringly in his face. The answer was given, and the child resumed the posture of devotion, which his strange feelings had disturbed.

The last words of the presiding priest were spoken, and there was silence; even the sounds without were hushed, and a voiceless dread appeared to withhold those within from seeking the cause. There was evidently a struggle ere the usual congratulations could be offered to the young couple; and so preoccupied was the attention of all, that the absence of Aréli was unnoticed, till, as trumpet and drum again pierced the thin air, he darted back, and with hasty and agitated signs related what he had beheld.

"Soldiers, many soldiers? It may be so; yet wherefore this alarm, my children?" exclaimed the aged Asher, stepping firmly forward, and speaking in an accent of mild reproof. "What can ye fear? Nazarene and Mahommedan have ofttimes found a shelter in this peaceful valley; fearlessly they came, uninjured they departed. Wrong we have never done to man; peace and goodwill have been our watchword; wherefore, then, should we tremble to meet these strangers? My children, the God of Israel is with us still."

The cloud passed from the brows of his hearers. The young maidens emulated the calm firmness of the bride, and gathering round her, followed their male companions from the temple. The spot on which the sacred edifice stood commanded a view of the village market-place, which, from its occupying the only level ground half a mile square, was surrounded by all the low dwellings of the artizans, and was often the place of public meeting, when any point was discussed requiring the suffrages of all the male population. This space was now filled with Spanish soldiers, some on horseback, others on foot; while far behind, scattered in groups amongst the rocks, many a steel morion flung back the sun's glistening rays. The villagers startled and amazed, had assembled on all sides, and even Josef Asher for a moment paused, astonished.

"Let us on, my children," he said, "and learn the meaning of this unusual muster. Yet stay," he added, as several young men hastened forward to obey him: "they are about to speak; we will hear first what they proclaim."

Another flourish of drums and trumpets sounded as he spoke, and then one of the foremost cavaliers, attired as a herald, drew from his bosom a parchment roll. The officers around doffed their helmets, and he read words to the following import:—

"From the most high and mighty sovereigns, Ferdinand and Isabella, joint-sovereigns of Arragon and Castile, to whose puissant arms the grace of God hath given dominion over all heretics and unbelievers, before whose banner of the Holy Cross the Moorish abominations have crumbled into dust—to our loyal subjects of every principality and province, of every rank, and stage, and calling, of every grade and every state, these—to which we charge you all in charity give good heed.

"Whereas we have heard and seen that the Jews of our state induce many Christians to embrace Judaism. particularly the nobles of Andalusia; for THIS they are BANISHED from our domains. Four months from this day, we grant them to forswear their abominations and embrace Christianity, or to depart; pronouncing DEATH on every Jew found in our kingdom after that allotted time.

"(*Signed*) FERDINAND AND ISABELLA.

"*Given at our palace of Segovia this thirtieth day of March, of the year of grace one thousand four hundred and ninety-two.*"

As a thunderbolt falling from the blue and cloudless sky—as the green and fertile earth yawning in fathomless chasms beneath their feet. so, but more terribly, more vividly still, did this edict fall on the faithful hearts who heard. A sudden pause, and then a cry, an agonized cry of horror and despair, burst simultaneously from young and old, woman and child; and then, as awakened from that stupor of woe, wilder shouts arose, and the fiery youth of Eshcol gathered tumultuously together, and shrill cries of "Vengeance, vengeance! cut them down—rend the lying parchment into shreds, and scatter it to the four winds of heaven—thus will we defend our rights!" found voice, amid groans and hisses of execration and assault. A volley of stones fell among the Spaniards, who, standing firmly to their arms, appeared in the act of charging, when both parties were arrested by the aged patriarch of Eshcol rushing in their very centre, heeding not, nay, unconscious of personal danger, calling on them to forbear.

"Are ye all mad?" he cried. "Would ye draw down further ruin on your devoted heads? Think ye to cope with those armed by a sovereign mandate, backed by a mighty kingdom? Oh, for the love of your wives, your children, your aged, helpless parents, keep the peace, and let your elders speak!"

Even at that moment their natural veneration for old age had influence. Reproved and sorrowful, they shrunk back—the angry gesture calmed, the muttered execration silenced. Surrounded by his brother elders, Asher drew near the Spaniards, who, struck by his venerable age and commanding manner, consented to accompany him to the council-room near at hand, desiring their men on the severest penalties to create no disturbance. The edict was laid before them, its purport explained, enforced emphatically, yet kindly; for the Spaniards felt awed, in spite of themselves. But vainly the old men urged that the given cause of their banishment could not extend to them. They had had no dealing with the Nazarene; they lived to themselves alone; they interfered not with the civil or religious government of the country, which had sheltered them from age to age; they warred with none, offended none; their very existence was often unsuspected; they asked but liberty to live on as they had lived; and would the sovereigns of Spain deny them this? It could not be. The Spaniards listened mildly; but the edict had gone forth, they said, unto all and every class of Jews within the kingdom, and not one individual was exempt from its sentence, save on the one condition—their embracing Christianity. It was true that many of their nation might be faithful subjects; but even did their banishment involve loss to Spain, her sovereigns, impressed with religious zeal, welcomed the temporal loss as spiritual gain. If, indeed, they could not comply with the very simple condition, they urged the old men instantly to depart, for one month out of the four had already elapsed, the edict bearing date the last day but one of the month of March. They added, the secluded situation of the valley had caused the delay, and might have delayed its proclamation yet longer, had not chance led them to these mountains in search of an officer of rank, who had wandered from them, and they feared had perished in the hollows.

Even at that moment a chilling dread shot through the heart of the aged Asher. Could that officer be he whom Aréli had seen but seven days previous? He dared not listen to his heart's reply, and gave his whole attention to that which followed. A second edict, the Spaniards continued to state, had been issued, prohibiting all Christians to supply the fugitives with bread or wine, water or meat, after the month of April.

The old men heard; there was little to answer, though much to feel; and the sorrowing council occupied some time after the officers had retired. They wished to learn the condition of their wretched countrymen, and the real effects of this most cruel edict. The blow had descended so unexpectedly, it seemed as if they could not, unless from the lips of an eyewitness, believe it true, and they decided on sending twenty of their young men to learn tidings, under the control of one, calm, firm, and dispassionate enough to restrain those acts of violence to which they had already shown such inclination. But who was this one? How might they ask *him?*

The old men together sought the various groups, and expressing their wishes, all were eager to obey. Josef Asher alone approached his children, who sat apart from their companions. He related all that had passed between them and the Spaniards, and then awhile he paused.

"Imri," he said at length, "my son, thou hast seen the misguided passion of our youth; they must not go forth on this mission of unimpassioned observation alone. Our elders, the wise and moderate, must husband their little strength for their weary pilgrimage. Thou, my son, hast their wisdom, with all the activity and energy of youth. We would that thou shouldst head this band; but a very brief absence is needed. Canst thou consent?"

A low cry of suffering broke from the pale lips of Josephine, and she threw her arms round Imri, as thus to chain him to her side. "In such an hour wilt thou leave me, Imri?" His lip quivered, his cheek paled, and the few words he uttered were heard by her alone. "Yes, yes, thou shalt go, my beloved; heed not my woman's weakness. Thou wilt return; and then—then we will *depart* together." Oh, what a world of agony did that one word speak.

The instant departure of the younger villagers occasioned some surprise, but without further interference. The Spaniards began to pitch their tents amongst the rocky eminences, as preparing for some months' emcampment. Had not the inhabitants of Eshcol felt that their cup of bitterness was already full to the brim, the appearance of an armed force in the very centre of their peaceful dwellings would have added gall; but every thought, feeling, and energy were merged in one engrossing subject of anguish. Some there were who rejected all belief in the edict's truth. They could not be banished from the scenes in which they and their fathers had dwelt, from age to age, in peace and bliss. Others felt their minds a void; they asked no question of their elders, spoke not to each other, but in strange and moody silence awaited the return of Imri and his companions. Nor could the obnoxious sight of a huge wooden crucifix, which the next morning greeted the eyes of every villager, rouse them effectually from the lethargy of despair.

And Josephine, did she weep and moan, now that the fate she so instinctively dreaded had fallen? Her tears were on her heart, lying there like lead, slowly yet surely undermining strength, and poisoning the gushing spring of life. In sobs and tears her young companions gathered round her, and she spoke of comfort and resignation, her gentle kindness soothing many, and rousing them to hope, on the return of the young men, things might not be found so despairing as they now seemed. But when twilight had descended and all was hushed, Josephine led her young brother to her mother's grave. She looked on his sweet face, paled with sympathetic sorrow, though as yet he knew not why he wept; and she sought to speak and tell him all, but the thought that his young joys, yet more than her own, were blighted—that, weakly and afflicted as he was, he too must be torn from familiar scenes and objects which formed his innocent pleasures, and encounter hardships and privations that stood in dread perspective before her—oh, was it strange that that noble spirit lost its firmness for the moment, and that sinking on the green sward, she buried her face in her hands, and sobbed in an intensity of suffering which found not its equal even midst the deep woe around her? Aréli knelt beside her; he clasped her cold hands within his own; he hid his head in her lap—seeking by all these mute caresses, which had never before appealed in vain, to restore her to composure. For his sake she roused herself; she raised her tearful eyes to the star-lit heavens in silent prayer, and drawing him closer to her, commenced her painful task. Too well his ready mind conceived her meaning. His beautiful lip grew white and quivering—the dew of suffering stood upon his brow; but he shed no tear—nay, he sought to smile, as thus to lessen his sister's care. But when she told him the condition which was granted, and bade him choose between the land of his love or the faith of his fathers—a change came over his features; he started from her side, the red flush rushing to his cheek; he drew his little Bible from his bosom, pressed it fervently to his lips and heart, shook his clenched fist in direction of the Spanish encampment, and then laid down beside the grave. "My boy, my boy, there spoke the blessed spirit of our race!" and tears of inexpressible emotion coursed down the cheek of Josephine, as she clasped him convulsively to her aching heart. "Death and exile, aye, torture, thou wilt brave rather than desert thy faith. My God, my God, thou wilt be with us still!"

It was not till the ninth day from their departure that Imri Benalmar and his companions returned. One glance sufficed to read their mournful tale. On all sides, they said, they had beheld but cruelty and ruin, perjury or despair. From every town, from every province, their wretched brethren were flocking to the sea-coast—their homes, their lands left to the ruthless spoiler, or sold for one-tenth of their value. They told of a vineyard exchanged for a suit of clothes—a house, with all its valuables, for a mule. Their gold, silver, and jewels, prohibited either to be exchanged or carried away with them, became the prey of their cruel persecutors. Famine and horror on every side assailed them; many they had seen famishing on the roads, for none dared give them a bit of bread or a draught of water; and even mothers were known to slay their own children, husbands their wives, to escape the agony of watching their lingering deaths. Their illustrious countryman, Isaac Abarbanel, Imri said, had offered an immense sum to refill the coffers of Spain, emptied as they were by the Moorish war, would his sovereigns recall the fatal edict. They had appeared to hesitate, when Thomas de Torquemada, advancing boldly into the royal presence, raised high before them a crucifix, and bade them beware how they sold for a higher price Him whom Judas betrayed for thirty pieces of silver—to think how they would render an account of their bargain before God. He had prevailed, and the edict continued in full force.

On a towering rock, in the centre of the mourning populace, the aged Asher stood. He stretched forth his hands in an attitude of supplication, and tears and groans were hushed to a voiceless pause. There was a deep-red spot on the old man's either cheek, but his voice was still firm, his attitude commanding.

"My children," he said, "we have heard our doom, and even as our brethren we must go forth. Let us not in our misery blaspheme the God who so long hath blessed us with prosperity and peace, and pour down idle curses on our foes. My children, cruel as they seem, they are but His tools; and therefore, as to His decree, let us bow without a murmur. Have we forgotten that on earth the exiles of Jerusalem have no resting—that for the sins of our fathers the God of Justice is not yet appeased? Oh, if we have, this fearful sentence may be promulgated to recall us to Himself, ere prosperity be to us, as to our misguided ancestors, the curse, hurling us into eternal misery. We bow not to man; it is the God of Israel we obey! We must hence; for who amongst us will deny Him? Tarry not, then, my children; we are but few days' journey from the sea, and in this are blest above our fellows. Waste not, then, the precious time allowed us in fruitless sorrow. There are some among ye who speak of weakness and timidity, in thus yielding to our foes without one blow in defence of our rights. Rights! unhappy men, ye have no rights! Sons of Judah, have ye yet to learn we are wanderers on the face of the earth, without a country, a king, a judge in Israel? My children, we have but one treasure, which, if called upon, we can DIE to defend—the glorious faith our God himself hath given. To Him, then, let us unite in solemn prayer, beseeching His guidance in our weary pilgrimage—His forgiveness on our cruel foes; and fearless and faithful we will go forth where His will may lead."

The old man knelt, and all followed his example; and silence, deep as if that wild scene were desolate, succeeded those emphatic words. A fervent blessing was then pronounced by the patriarch, and all departed to their homes.

And now day after day beheld the departure of one or two families from the village. We may dwell no longer on their feelings, nor on those of their brethren in other parts of Spain. We envy not those who feel no sympathy in that devotedness to a persecuted faith which could bid men go forth from their homes, their temples, the graves of their fathers, the schools where for centuries they had presided, honored even by their foes, and welcome exile, privation, misery of every kind, woes far worse than death, rather than depart from it. If they think we have exaggerated, let the skeptic look to the histories of every nation in the middle ages, and they will acknowledge this simple narrative is but a faint outline of the sufferings endured by the persecuted Hebrews, and inflicted by those who boast their religion to be peace on earth and good-will to all men.

Reduced from affluence to poverty, from every comfort, to the dim vista of every privation, without the faintest consciousness where to seek a home, or how to cross the ocean, did Imri Benalmar regret that he had now a wife and a young, helpless boy for whom to provide? Nay; that Josephine was his, ere this dread edict was proclaimed, was even at this moment a source of unalloyed rejoicing. He knew her noble spirit, and that, had not the solemn service been actually performed, she would have refused his protection, his love, and, rather than burden him with such increase of care, have lingered in that vale to die. That she was inviolably his own, endowed him, however, with an energy to bear, which, had he been alone, would have failed him. He thought but of her sufferings; for, though from her lips they had never found a voice, he knew what she endured. He told her there were some of their unhappy countrymen, who, rather than lose the honourable situations they enjoyed, the riches they possessed, had made a public profession of Christianity, and received baptism at the very moment they made a solemn vow, in secret, to act up to the tenets of their fathers' faith.

"Alas! are there indeed such amongst us, thus doubly perjured?" was the sole observation of Josephine, looking up sorrowfully in his face.

"They do not think it perjury, my beloved: they say the God of Israel will pardon the public falsehood, in consideration of their secret allegiance to Himself."

"But thou, Imri, canst thou approve this course of acting? Couldst thou rest in such fatal security?"

"Were I alone, my Josephine, with none to love or care for, death itself were preferable; but oh, when I look on thee, and remember thy deep love for this fair soil—when I think on Aréli, on all that he must suffer—the misery we must all endure—I could wish my mind would reconcile itself to act as others do; that to serve my God in secret, and those of wood and stone in public, were no perjury."

"Oh, do not say so, Imri; think not of me, my beloved: I love not my home better than my God; I would not accept peace and prosperity at such a price! Had I been alone, death, even by the sword of slaughter, would have been welcome, would have found me here, for I could not have gone forth. But now I am thine, Imri, thine; and whither thou goest I will go; and thou shalt make me another home than this, my husband, where we may worship our God in peace and joy, and there shall be blessing for us yet."

She had spoken with a smile so inexpressibly affecting in its plaintive sweetness, that her husband could only press her to his heart in silence, and inwardly pray it might be as she said. Of Aréli she had not spoken, and he guessed too truly wherefore. From the hour of their banishment, a change had come over the spirit of the boy; his smiles still greeted those he loved, but he was longer away than was his wont, and Imri, following him at a distance, could see him ever lingering amid his favourite haunts; and when far removed, as he believed, from the sight of man, he would fling himself on the grass, and weep, till sometimes, from very exhaustion, sleep would steal over him, and then, starting up, he would make hasty sketches of some much-loved scenes, to prove to his sister how well he had been employed.

These painful proofs of the poor boy's sorrow Imri could conceal, but not the decay of bodily strength; or deny, when Josephine appealed to him, that his frame became yet more shadowy in its beautiful proportions,—that the rose which had spread itself on either cheek, the unwonted lustre of the eye, the increased transparency of his complexion, told of the loveliness of another world: yet for him how might they grieve?

It happened that one of the Spanish soldiers, a father himself, and less violently prejudiced than his fellows, had taken a fancy to the beautiful and afflicted boy always wandering about alone; and he thought it would be doing a kind action to prevent his accompanying the fugitives, by adopting him as his own; believing it would be easy to rear him to the Catholic church, as one so young, and, moreover, deaf and dumb, could have imbibed little of the Jewish misbelief. Kindly and tenderly he sought and won the child's affection, and found means to converse with him intelligibly.

Incapable of thinking evil, Aréli doubted not his companion's kindness, and though aware he was a Spaniard and a Catholic, artlessly betrayed the deep suffering his banishment engendered. Fadrique worked on this; he told him he should not leave them, that he would bring his family and live there, and Aréli should be loved by all. He worked on the boy's fancy till he felt he had gained his point, then erecting a small crucifix, bade him kneel and worship.

The film passed from the eyes of the child, indignation flashed from every feature, and springing up, he tore the cross to the earth, and trampled it into the dust. Ten or twelve soldiers, who had been carelessly watching Fadrique's proceedings from a distance, enraged beyond measure at this insult from a puny boy, darted towards him, flung him violently to the earth, and pointed their weapons at his throat. At that instant Josephine stood before them; for she too had watched, with the anxious eye of affection, the designs of Fadrique.

"Are ye men!" she exclaimed, and the rude soldiers shrunk abashed from her glance, "that thus ye would take the blood of an innocent, helpless child—one whose very affliction should appeal to mercy, denied as it may be to others? On yourselves ye called this insult to your faith. How else could he tell ye he refused your offers? You bade him acknowledge that which his soul abhors; and was it strange his hand should prove that which he hath no voice to speak? And for this would ye take his life? Oh, shame, shame on your coward hearts!"

Sullenly the men withdrew, at once awed by her mien, and remembering that in assaulting any Hebrew before the time specified in the edict was over, they were liable to military severity. Fadrique lingered.

"This was not my seeking," he said respectfully; "I

sought but the happiness of that poor child: I would save him from the doom of suffering chosen by the elders of his race. Leave him with me, and I pledge my sacred word his life shall be a happy one."

"I thank thee for thine offer, soldier," replied Josephine, mildly, "but my brother has chosen his own fate; I have used neither entreaties nor commands."

The boy, who had betrayed no fear even when the deadly weapons were at his throat, now took the hand of Fadrique, and by a few expressive signs craved pardon for the insult he had been led to commit, and firmly and expressively refused his every offer.

"Thou hast yet to learn the deep love borne to our faith by her persecuted children, my good friend," said Josephine, perceiving the man's surprise was mingled with some softer feeling; "that even the youngest Jewish child will prefer slavery, exile, or death, to forswearing his father's God. May the God of Israel bless thee for the kindness thou hast shown this poor afflicted boy, but seek him not again."

She drew him closer to her, and they disappeared together. A tear rose to the Spaniard's eye, but he hastily brushed it away, and then telling his rosary, as if it were sin thus to care for an unbeliever, rejoined his comrades.

The family of Imri Benalmar was the last to quit the vale. Each was mounted on a mule, and there were two led or sumpter mules, on which was strapped as much clothing as they could conveniently stow away, and provisions which they hoped would last them till they reached the vessel, knowing well they could procure no more. Some few valuables Imri contrived to secrete, but his fortune, principally consisting in land and its produce, was of necessity irretrievably ruined.

Josef Asher accompanied them; he had been active in consoling, encouraging, and assisting his weaker brethren. Not a family departed without receiving some token of his sympathy and love; and young and old crowded round him, ere they went, imploring his blessing and his prayers.

It was, however, observed that of his own departure, his own plans, Asher never spoke. That he would accompany his children all believed, and so did Josephine herself; but all were mistaken.

On the evening of their first day's journey, as they halted for rest and refreshment, some unusual emotion was observable in the mien and features of the old man. He asked them to join him in prayer, and as he concluded, he spread his hands upon their heads, and blessed each by name emphatically, unfalteringly, as in his days of youth.

"And now," he said, as they arose, "farewell, my beloved children. The God of Israel go with ye, and lead ye, even as our ancestors of old, with the daily cloud and nightly pillar. I go no further with ye."

"No further! what means our father?" exclaimed Imri and Josephine together.

"That I am too old to go forth to another land, my children. The God of Judah demands not this from his old and weary servant. Fourscore and fifteen years I have served Him in the dwelling-place of mine own people, and there shall His Angel find me. My sand is well-nigh run out, my strength must fail ere I reach the shore. Wherefore, then, should I go forth, and by my infirmities bring down danger and suffering on my children? Oppose me not, beloved ones; refuse not your aged father the blessing of dying beside his own hearth."

"Alone, untended, and perchance by the sword of slaughter? Oh, my father, ask us not this!" exclaimed Josephine, with passionate agony throwing herself at his feet, and clinging to his knees.

"My child, the Spirit of my God will tend me: I shall not be alone, for His ministering angels will hover round me ere He takes me to Himself; and if it be by the sword of slaughter, 'twill be perchance an easier passage for this sorrowing soul than the lingering death of age."

"Then let me return and die with thee!"

"Not so, my child! thy life has barely passed its spring; 'twould be sin thus to sport with death. The God who calls me to death, bids thee go forth to serve Him—to proclaim His great name in other lands. Thy husband, thy poor Aréli, both call on thee to live for them; thou wouldst not turn from the path of duty, my beloved child, dark and dreary as it may seem. See, thine Imri weeps; and thou, who shouldst cheer, hast caused these unmanly tears."

She turned towards her husband, and with a painful sob, sunk into his extended arms. Asher gave one long lingering look of love, folded the weeping Aréli to his bosom, and ere Imri could sufficiently recover his emotion to speak, the old man was gone.

The death he sought was speedily obtained. The Spanish officers and several of the men had quitted Eshcol, leaving only the lowest rank of soldiery to keep watch lest any of the fugitives should return, and, taking advantage of the secluded situation of the vale, set the edict at defiance. Effectually to prevent this, the men were commanded to turn the little temple to a place of worship for true believers. Workmen, with images, shrines, and pictures, were sent to assist them. and a pension promised to every Catholic family who would reside there, thus to exterminate utterly all trace of heresy and its abominations.

The men thus employed, ignorant and bigoted, exulted in the task assigned them, and only lamented that no human blood had been shed to render their holocausts to their patron saints more efficacious still. The return of Asher excited some surprise, but believing he would depart ere the allotted period had expired, they took little heed of his movements. The work continued, crosses were affixed to every side, images decked the interior, and all promised fair completion, when one night a wild cry of fire resounded, and hurrying to the spot, they beheld their work in flames. It was an awful picture. The night was pitchy dark, but far and near the thick woods and blackened heavens suddenly blazed up with lurid hue. There were dusky forms hurrying to and fro; oaths and execrations mingled with the stormy gusts which fanned the flames into greater fury, and, amidst them all, calmly looking on the work his hand had wrought, there stood an aged man, whose figure, in that glow of light, appeared gigantically proportioned, his silvery hair streamed back from his broad unwrinkled brow, and stern, unalterable resolution was impressed upon his features. He was seen, recognised, and with a yelling shout the murderers darted on their prey.

"Come on!" he cried, waving his arms triumphantly above his head. "Come on, and wreak your vengeance on these aged limbs; 'tis I have done this. Better flames should hurl it to the dust, than the temple of God be profaned by the abominations He abhors. Come on, I glory in the deed!"

He spoke, and fell pierced with a hundred wounds. A smile of peculiar beauty lighted up his features. "Blessed be the God of Israel, the sole One, the Holy One!" he cried, and his spirit fled, rejoicing, to the God he served.

Slowly and painfully did Imri's little family pursue their way. They chose the most secluded paths, but even there traces of misery and death awaited them, and they shrank from suffering they could not alleviate. There might be seen a group dragging along their failing limbs, their provisions exhausted, and the pangs of hunger swallowing up all other thoughts. There lay the blackening bodies of those who had sunk and died, scarcely missed, and often envied by the survivors. Often did the sound of their footsteps scare away large flocks of carrion birds, who, screaming and flapping their heavy wings, left to the travellers the loathsome sight of their half-devoured prey. And they saw, too, the fearful fascinated gaze of those in whom life was not utterly extinct, as they watched the progress of these horrible birds, dreading lest they should dart upon them ere death had rendered them insensible. Josephine looked on these things, and then on her young brother, whose strength each day too evidently declined.

Aréli's too sensitive spirit shrank in shuddering anguish from every fresh scene of human suffering. He, whose young life had been so full of peace and bliss, knowing but love and good-will passing from man to man, how might he sustain the change? He had no voice to speak those feelings, no time to give them vent in the sweet language of poesie, which, in happier hours, had been the tablet of his soul. As the invisible worm at the root of a blooming flower, secretly destroying its sap, its nourishment, and the flower falls ere one of its leaves hath lost its beauty, so it was with the orphan boy. Each day was Imri compelled to shorten more and more their journey, for often would Aréli drop fainting from his mule, though the cheek retained its exquisite bloom, his eye its lustre. Imri became fearfully anxious; from the comparative vicinity of the sea-shore, he had believed their provisions would be more than sufficient to last them on their way, but from these unlooked-for delays, the horrors of famine, thirst, that most horrible death, stood darkly before him. Josephine, his own, his loved, would she encounter horrors such as they had witnessed? Imri shuddered.

One evening, Aréli lay calmly on the soft bed of moss and heath his sister's love had framed; his hand clasped hers; his eyes seemed to speak the unutterable love and gratitude he felt. They were in the wildest part of a thick forest in the Sierra Nevada; and Imri, unable to look on the sufferings of his beloved ones, had wandered forth alone. Distant sounds of the chase fell at intervals on the ears of Josephine; but they were far away, and her soul was too enwrapt to heed them. Suddenly, however, her attention was effectually roused by the loud crashing of the bushes near them, accompanied by low yet angry growls. Aréli marked the sudden change in her features, his eye too had caught an object by her still unseen. He sprang up with that strength which energy of feeling so often gives when bodily force has gone, and grasped tightly the hunting spear he held; scarcely had he done so, when a huge boar sprung through the thicket, his flanks streaming with blood, his tusks upraised, his mouth gaping, covered with foam, and uttering growls, denoting pain and fury yet more clearly than his appearance. He stood for a second motionless, then, as if startled by the agonized scream of terror bursting from Josephine, he sprung upon the daring boy. Undauntedly Areli met his approach. His spear, aimed by an eye that never failed, pierced him for a second to the earth, but, alas! the strength of the boy was not equal to his skill. The boar, yet more enraged, tore the weapon from the ground which it had not pierced above an inch. Once more he fell, struck down by a huge stick, which Areli, with the speed of lightning, had snatched up. Again he rose, and fastened on the child. A blow from behind forced him to relax his stifling hold; furious, he turned on the slight girl who had dared attack him, and Josephine herself would have shared her brother's fate, when the spear of Imri whizzed through the air, true to its mark, and the huge animal, with a cry of pain and fury, rolled lifeless on the ground.

The voice of his beloved had startled Imri from his mournful trance; the roar which followed explained its source, and winged by terror, he arrived in time. Josephine was saved indeed, but no word of thankfulness broke from that heart, which, in grateful devotion, had never been dumb before. She knelt beside the seemingly lifeless body of her Aréli, scarcely conscious of the presence of her husband; his hands, his neck, his brow, were deluged in blood; she bathed him plentifully with cold water. Could she remember at such a moment that no springs were near, and that, if overwhelmed with thirst, the pure element would be denied them? Oh, no, no; she saw only the helpless sufferer, to whom her spirit clung with a love that, in their affliction, had with each hour grown stronger.

But death was still a brief while deferred, though so fearfully had Aréli been injured, they could not move him thence.

His wounds were numerous and painful, and strength to support himself even in a sitting position, never again returned. Yet never was that sweet face sad; his smiles, his signs were ever to implore his sister not to weep for him—to take comfort and be happy in another land; that the blissfulness of heaven was already on his soul—that if it might be, he would pray for her before his God, and hover like a guardian spirit over her weary wanderings, till he led her to a joyous home. For him, indeed, Josephine might not grieve, but for Imri she felt the deepest anxiety. The horrors to which this unlooked-for delay exposed him had startled her into consciousness, and on her knees she besought him to seek his own safety; she would not weakly shrink, but when all was over she would follow him, and, in all probability, they would meet again in another land; not to risk his precious life and strength by lingering with her beside the dying boy. She pleaded with all a woman's unselfish love, but, need we say, in vain?—that Imri's sole answer was to lift his right hand to heaven and swear, by all they both held most sacred, NEVER to leave her—they would meet their fate together? Days passed; their small portion of food and water, economised as it was, dwindled more and more away, and so did the strength of Aréli. It was a night of unclouded beauty; millions and millions of stars spangled the deep blue heavens; the moon in her full glory walked forth to silver many a dark tree, and dart her most refulgent rays on that little group of human suffering. Yet all was not suffering; the purest happiness beamed on the features of the dying, and an unconscious calm pervaded the weary spirit of these lonely watchers. Nature was so still, they spoke almost in whispers, as fearing to disturb her.

A sudden change spread on the features of the dying boy. Imri started; "Josephine, the chains are rent—he HEARS us!" he cried; and Josephine, raising him in her arms, almost involuntarily spoke in uttered words, "Aréli, my own, my beautiful!"

He HEARD; the film was removed one brief moment from his ear; her voice, sweet as thrilling music, fell upon his soul; his lips moved, and one articulate word then came, unearthly in its sweetness, "JOSEPHINE!" He raised his clasped hands to heaven, and sunk back upon her bosom; his soul had hovered on the earth one moment FREE, then fled for ever.

Imri and Josephine joined in prayer beside the loved. They neither mourned nor wept, and calmly Josephine wrapped the fadeless flower in the last garments of mortality, while Imri formed his resting-place. They laid him in that humble grave, strewed flowers and moss upon it, prayed that their God would in mercy guard his body from the ravening beasts, then turned from that hallowed spot, and silently pursued their journey.

It wanted but two days to the completion of the allotted period, when, faint, weak, and well-nigh exhausted, Imri and his Josephine stood on the sea-shore, and there horrible indeed was the sight that presented itself. Hundreds of the wretched fugitives lay famishing on the scorching sands. Many who had dragged on their failing limbs through all the horrors of famine, of thirst, of miseries in a thousand shapes, which the very pen shrinks from delineating, arrived there but to die; for there were but few vessels to bear them to other lands, and these often sailed with half their number, either because the bribes they demanded were refused (for the wretched victims had nought to give), or that their captains swore so many heretics would sink their ships, and they would take no more. Then it was that, with a crucifix in one hand, and bread and wine in the other, the Catholic priests advanced to the half-senseless sufferers, and offered the one, if they acknowledged the other. Was it marvel that at such a moment there were some who yielded? Oh, there is a glory and a triumph in the martyr's death! Men look with admiring awe on those who smile when at the stake; but the faith that inspired courage and firmness and constancy 'mid suffering which we have but faintly outlined—'mid lingering torments 'neath which the *heart*, yet more than the frame, was crushed—that FAITH is regarded with scorn as a blinded, wilful misbelief. Could man endow his own spirit with this devotedness? Pride might lead him to the stake, but not to bear what Israel had borne, aye, and will bear till the wrath of his God is turned aside. No; the same God who strengthened Abraham to offer up his son, enables His wretched people to give up all for Him. Would He do this, had they denied and mocked Him?

Imri saw the cold shuddering creeping over the blighted form of his beloved, and he led her to the sheltering rock, whose projecting cliffs partly concealed the wretched objects on the beach. There was one vessel on the broad ocean, and in her he determined at once to secure a passage, if to do so cost the forfeit of the few valuables he had been enabled to secrete. He lingered awhile by the side of his Josephine, for he saw, with anguish, the noble spirit, which had so long sustained and consoled her, now for the first time appear to droop. The sudden appearance of a Spanish officer, and his apparent advance towards them, arrested him as he was about to depart. He was attired richly, his whole bearing seeming to denote a person of some rank and consequence. Josephine's gaze became almost unconsciously riveted upon him. He came nearer, nearer still; they could trace his features, on which sorrow or care had fixed its stamp. A moment he removed the plumed cap from his head, and passed his hand across his brow. An exclamation of recognition escaped the lips of Imri, and in another moment Josephine had bounded forward and was kneeling at his feet. "My father! my father!" she sobbed forth. "O God, I thank Thee for this unlooked-for mercy. I have seen him once again."

"Thou—art thou my child, my Josephine, whom I left in such bright, blooming beauty—whom I have sought in such trembling anguish from the moment I might reach these shores? Child of my Rachel, art thou, canst thou be? Oh, yes, yes, yes! 'Twas thus she looked when I departed. Could I hope to see thee as I left thee, when blight and misery fell upon thy native vale, as on all the dwellings of thy wretched race? And I—O God!—my child, my child, curse me, hate me—I hurled down destruction on thy house."

But even as he spoke in those wild accents of ungovernable passion, but too familiar to the ears that heard, he had raised and strained her convulsively to his breast, covering her cheek and lips with kisses, till his burning tears of agonized remorse mingled with those of softer feelings on the cheeks of Josephine. But not long might she indulge in the blessed luxury of tears; shuddering, she repeated his last words, gazing up in his face with eyes of horrified inquiry.

"Yes, I, even I, my child. I was not sufficiently wretched—the bitter cup of remorse was not yet full. The edict was proclaimed. On all sides there was but wretchedness and unutterable misery, beyond all this woe-built world hath known. Then came a wild yearning to look again upon my native vale—to know if in truth its concealed and sheltered caves had escaped uninjured by the wide-spreading, devastating scourge that edict brought—to look on thee, my child, if I might without endangering that precious life—to know the fate of my unborn babe. I dared not dream my wife yet lived. Josephine, I looked upon her tomb, and by its side beheld my own, my beautiful, my unknown boy. O God! O God! my crime was visited upon his innocent head; and where—oh, where is he? Why may I not look upon his sweet face again?"

He ceased, choked by overwhelming emotion, and some minutes passed ere either of his agitated listeners could summon sufficient composure to reply. But the anguish of Castello seemed incapable of increase. For several minutes, indeed, he was silent; the convulsive workings of his features denoting how deeply that simple narrative had sunk. When he spoke, it was briefly and hurriedly to relate how he had lingered in the vicinity of Eshcol, till at length discovered by a party of Spaniards sent to seek him, with a message from the sovereigns. His wanderings had been tracked, and that which he had most desired to avert he had been the means of accomplishing—the discovery of the vale. And then convulsively clasping the hands of Josephine and Imri in his own, he besought them to remove in part the load of misery from his heart—to say they would not leave him more.

"Goest thou then forth, my father? Hast thou indeed tarried for us, that we may seek a home together?" The father's eyes shrunk beneath those mild inquiring eyes.

"My child, I go not forth," he said at length, and his voice trembled. Josephine gently withdrew herself from his arms, and laid her hand on her husband's.

"My child! my noble child," he said, in smothered accents, "I am not perjured. I am still a son of Israel, though to the world a Catholic. Oh, do not turn from me. Come with me to my home, and thou shalt see how the exiled and the persecuted can defy the power of their destroyers. Life, with every luxury, shall be thy portion; thine Imri shall have every dream of ambition and joy fulfilled. The children of Sigismund Castello will be courted, cherished, and loved. 'Tis but to kneel in public before the cross of the Nazarene—in private, we are sons of Israel still."

"Father, urge me not; it cannot be," was her calm and firm reply.

"Hast thought on all that must befall thee in other, perchance equally hostile, lands? My child, thou knowest not all thou mayest have to endure."

"It is welcome," she answered; "the more rugged the path to heaven, the more blessed will seem my final rest."

"And thou wilt leave me to all the agonies of remorse; to struggle on with the blackening thought, that not only have I murdered those I love best on earth—my wife, my boy—but sent ye forth to poverty, privation and misery. Josephine, Josephine, have mercy!" and the father threw himself before his child, grovelling in the sand, and clasping his hands in the wild energy of supplication.

"Father, father, drive me not mad! I cannot, cannot bear this. Imri, my husband, if thou wouldst save my heart from treachery, raise him—in mercy raise him. I cannot answer with him there! God, God of Israel! leave me not now. My brain is reeling—save me from myself."

She staggered back, and terrified at those accents of almost madness, her father sprang from the ground, he caught her again in his arms, while Imri, kneeling beside her, chafed her cold hands in his, imploring her to speak, to look on him again.

"My child, my child, wake, wake! I will not grieve thee thus again. But oh, thy husband's look would pray thee not to go forth! The God of love, of pity, demands not this self-sacrifice. Imri, one word from thee would be sufficient. Look on her. Think to what thou bearest her, when peace, comfort, and luxuries await ye, with but one word. Speak, speak! Thou canst not, wilt not take her hence."

Though well-nigh senseless, well-nigh so exhausted alike in body and mind that further exertion seemed impossible, Josephine roused herself from that trance of faintness to gaze wildly and fearfully on the face of her husband. It was terribly agitated. She threw herself on his neck, and gasped forth, "Canst thou bid me do this thing, my husband?" He struggled to answer, but there came no word. Strength, the mighty strength of virtue, returned to that sinking frame. She stood erect, and spoke without one quivering accent or one failing word.

"Imri, my husband! by the love thou bearest me, by all we both hold sacred, by that great and ineffable name we are forbidden to pronounce, I charge thee answer me truly. Didst thou stand alone—were Josephine no more—how wouldst thou decide? The eye of God is upon thee—deceive me not!"

He turned from that searching glance, his strong frame shook with emotion; his voice was scarcely audible, yet these words came—

"I NEVER could deny my God! Exile and death were welcome—but for thee!"

"Enough, my husband!" she exclaimed, and throwing her arms around him, she turned again to her father, a glow of holy triumph tinging her pallid cheek. "And wouldst tempt him to perjury for my sake? Oh, no, no! father, beloved, revered, from the first hour I could lisp thy name, oh, pardon me this first disobedience to thy will! Did I linger, how might I save thee from remorse; when each day, each hour, thou wouldst see me fade beneath the whelming weight of perjury and falsity? No, no! Bless me, oh bless me, ere I go, and the prayers of thy child shall rise each hour for thee!"

Again she knelt before him, and Castello, inexpressibly affected, felt he dared urge no more. How might he agonize that heart; when in neither word, nor hint, nor sign did she utter reproach on him? Again and again he reiterated blessings on her sainted head; and when he could release her from his embrace, it was to secure their speedy passage in the vessel, which his command had detained in her moorings; though the hope that he should once more look upon his child had well-nigh faded ere she came.

The exiles stood upon the deck. A hundred other of the miserable fugitives had found a refuge in this same vessel, whose captain, somewhat more humane than many of his fellows, and richly bribed by Castello, set food before the famishing wanderers directly they had weighed anchor. But even the cravings of nature were lost in the one feeling, that they gazed for the last time on the land they loved. There were dark thunder-clouds sweeping over the sky, mingled with others of brilliant colouring, that proclaimed the hour of sunset. The ocean-horizon seemed buried in murky gloom; but the shores of Spain stood forth bathed in a glow of warm red light, as if to bid the unhappy wanderers farewell in unrivalled brilliance. For awhile there was silence on the vessel, so deep, so unbroken, that the flapping of the sails against the masts was alone distinguishable. It was then a wild and wailing strain burst simultaneously from the fugitives; the young and the old, the strong man and exhausted female, joined almost unconsciously. In the language of Jerusalem they chanted forth their wild farewell, which may thus be rendered into English verse.

Farewell! farewell! we wander forth,
Doom'd by th' Eternal's awful wrath;
With nought to bless our lonely path,
  Across the stormy wave.
Cast forth as wanderers on the earth;
Torn from the land that hailed our birth,
From childhood's cot, from manhood's hearth,
  From temple and from grave.

Farewell! farewell! thou beauteous sod,
Which Israel has for ages trod;
We leave thee to th' oppressors' rod,
  Weeping the exiles' doom.
We go! no more thy turf we press;
No more thy fruits and vineyards bless;
No land to love—no home possess,
  Save earth's cold breast—the tomb.

Where we have roamed the strangers roam;
The stranger claims each cherished home;
And we must ride on ocean's foam,
  Accursed and alone.
False gods pollute our holy fane;
False hearts its sacred precincts stain;
False tongues our fathers' God profane;
  But WE are still HIS OWN.

Farewell! farewell! o'er land and sea,
Where'er we roam, our soul shall be,
Land we have loved so long, with thee,
  Though sad and lone we dwell.
Thou land, where happy childhood played;
Where youth in love's sweet fancies strayed;
Where long our fathers' bones have laid;
  Our own bright land—farewell!

Wilder and louder thrilled the strain until the last verse, when mournfully the voices for a few seconds swelled, and then gradually died away to silence, broken only by sobs and tears. Imri and Josephine alone sat apart; they had not joined the melody, but their souls in silence echoed back its mournful wailing. Josephine half sat, half reclined on a pile of cushions, where she might command the last view of Spain. Imri leaned against a mast, close beside her; but few words passed between them, for each felt the effort to speak was made only for the other, and they ceased to war thus with nature.

A sudden gloom darkened the heavens. The glow passed from the beautiful shores. A heavy fall of dense clouds hung over them, and concealed them from the eyes which in that direction lingered still. The last gleam of light disclosed to Imri his Josephine in the attitude of calm and happy slumber. Her head reclined upon her arm, and the long dark curls had fallen over her face and neck. He rejoiced; for he thought nature had at length found the repose she so much needed. His own eyelids felt heavy, and his limbs much exhausted; but he remained watching, untired, the sleep of his beloved. Heavy gusts now at intervals swept along the ocean. The blackened waves rolled higher and higher at the call, now crested by the snowy foam. The vessel rocked and heaved, and speedily driven from her course, mocked every effort to guide her southward, one moment riding proudly on the topmost wave, the next sinking in a deep valley, as about to be whelmed by huge mountains of roaring water. Distant thunder, mingled with the moaning gusts, coming nearer and nearer, till it burst above their heads, louder and longer than the discharge of a hundred cannons. The forked lightning streamed through the ebon sky, illumining all around for above a minute by that blue and vivid glare, and then vanishing in darkness yet more terrible.

The elements were at war around them, cries of human terror joined with the roar of the ocean, the rolling thunder, the groaning blasts; but there was no movement in the form of Josephine. Could she still sleep? Could exhaustion render her insensible to sounds like these? Imri knelt beside her and called her by name:—"Josephine, my beloved! Oh, waken!"

There was no answer. At that moment a bright flash darted through the gloom, and sea and sky appeared on fire. A strange and crashing sound succeeded, followed by a cry of agony, which, bursting from a hundred throats, echoed far and near, drowning even the noise of the raging storm, for it was the deep tone of human terror and despair. The topmast fell, shivered by the lightning, in the very centre of the deck; flames burst forth where it fell, and on went the devoted vessel a blazing pile on the booming waters.

Imri Benalmar moved not from his knee—he heard not the cries of suffering echoing round—he knew not the cause of that livid glare, which had so suddenly illumined every object —he knew nothing, felt nothing, save that he gazed on the face of the DEAD.

* * * * *

* * * * *

A fearful sound, seeming distinct from the warring elements, called forth many of the hardy inhabitants of Malaga from their homes. They hurried to the beach, and appalled and startled, beheld one part of the horizon completely bathed in living fire; sea and sky united by a sheet of flame. Presently it appeared to divide, and borne onwards by the winds and waves, a ball of fire floated on the water. It came nearer—and horror and sympathy usurped the place of superstition, as a burning vessel rose and fell with every heaving wave. The storm was abated though the sea yet raged, and many a hardy fisherman pushed out his boat in the pious hope of saving some of the unfortunate crew. Their efforts were in vain; ere half the distance was accomplished, there came a hissing sound; the flames for one brief moment blazed with appalling brilliance—then sunk, and there was a void on the wide waste of waters.

The Escape.

A TALE OF 1755.

> "Dark lowers our fate,
> And terrible the storm that gathers o'er us;
> But nothing, till that latest agony
> Which severs thee from nature, shall unloose
> This fixed and sacred hold. In thy dark prison-house;
> In the terrific face of armed law;
> Yea! on the scaffold, if it needs must be,
> I never will forsake thee."—JOANNA BAILLIE.

ABOUT the middle of the eighteenth century, the little town of Montes, situated some forty or fifty miles from Lisbon, was thrown into most unusual excitement by the magnificence attending the nuptials of Alvar Rodriguez and Almah Diaz: an excitement which the extraordinary beauty of the bride, who, though the betrothed of Alvar from her childhood, had never been seen in Montes before, of course not a little increased. The little church of Montes looked gay and glittering, for the large sums lavished by Alvar on the officiating priests, and in presents to their patron saints, had occasioned every picture, shrine, and image to blaze in uncovered gold and jewels, and the altar to be fed with the richest incense, and lighted with tapers of the finest wax, to do him honour.

The church was full; for, although the bridal party did not exceed twenty, the village appeared to have emptied itself there; Alvar's munificence to all classes, on all occasions, having rendered him the universal idol, and caused the fame of that day's rejoicing to extend many miles around.

There was nothing remarkable in the behaviour of either bride or bridegroom, except that both were decidedly more calm than such occasions usually warrant. Nay, in the fine, manly countenance of Alvar ever and anon an expression seemed to flit, that in any but so true a son of the church would have been accounted scorn. In such a one, of course, it was neither seen nor regarded, except by his bride; for at such times her eyes met his with an earnest and entreating glance, that the peculiar look was changed into a quiet, tender seriousness, which reassured her.

From the church they adjourned to the lordly mansion of Rodriguez, which, in the midst of its flowering orange and citron trees, stood about two miles from the town.

The remainder of the day passed in festivity. The banquet, and dance, and song, both within and around the house, diversified the scene and increased hilarity in all. By sunset, all but the immediate friends and relatives of the newly wedded had departed. Some splendid and novel fireworks from the heights having attracted universal attention, Alvar, with his usual indulgence, gave his servants and retainers permission to join the festive crowds; liberty, to all who wished it, was given for the next two hours.

In a very brief interval the house was cleared, with the exception of a young Moor, the secretary or book-keeper of Alvar, and four or five middle-aged domestics of both sexes.

Gradually, and it appeared undesignedly, the bride and her female companions were left alone, and for the first time the beautiful face of Almah was shadowed by emotion.

"Shall I, oh, shall I indeed be his?" she said, half aloud. "There are moments when our dread secret is so terrible; it seems to forebode discovery at the very moment it would be most agonizing to bear."

"Hush, silly one!" was the reply of an older friend; "discovery is not so easily or readily accomplished. The persecuted and the nameless have purchased wisdom and caution at the price of blood—learned to deceive, that they may triumph—to conceal, that they may flourish still. Almah, we are NOT to fall!"

"I know it, Inez. A superhuman agency upholds us; we had been cast off, rooted out, plucked from the very face of the earth long since else. But there are times when human nature will shrink and tremble—when the path of deception and concealment allotted for us to tread seems fraught with danger at every turn. I know it is all folly, yet there is a dim foreboding, shadowing our fair horizon of joy as a hovering thunder-cloud. There has been suspicion, torture, death. Oh, if my Alvar—"

"Nay, Almah; this is childish. It is only because you are too happy, and happiness in its extent is ever pain. In good time comes your venerable guardian, to chide and silence all such foolish fancies. How many weddings have there been, and will there still be, like this? Come, smile, love, while I rearrange your veil."

Almah obeyed, though the smile was faint, as if the soul yet trembled in its joy. On the entrance of Gonzalos, her guardian (she was an orphan and an heiress), her veil was thrown around her, so as completely to envelope face and form. Taking his arm, and followed by all her female companions, she was hastily and silently led to a sort of ante-room or cabinet, opening, by a massive door concealed with tapestry, from the suite of rooms appropriated to the private use of the merchant and his family. There Alvar and his friends awaited her. A canopy, supported by four of the youngest males present, was held over the bride and bridegroom as they stood facing the east. A silver salver lay at their feet, and opposite stood an aged man, with a small, richly-bound volume in his hand. It was open, and displayed letters and words of unusual form and sound. Another of Alvar's friends stood near, holding a goblet of sacred wine; and to a third was given a slight and thin Venetian glass. After a brief and solemn pause, the old man read or rather chanted from the book he held, joined in parts by those around; and then he tasted the sacred wine, and passed it to the bride and bridegroom. Almah's veil was upraised, for her to touch the goblet with her lips, now quivering with emotion, and not permitted to fall again. And Alvar, where now was the expression of scorn and contempt that had been stamped on his bold brow and curling lip before? Gone—lost before the powerful emotion which scarcely permitted his lifting the goblet a second time to his lips. Then, taking the Venetian glass, he broke it on the salver at his feet, and the strange rites were concluded.

Yet no words of congratulation came. Drawn together in a closer knot, while Alvar folded the now almost fainting Almah to his bosom, and said, in the deep, low tones of intense feeling, "Mine, mine for ever now—mine in the sight of our God, the God of the exile and the faithful; our fate, whatever it be, henceforth is one;" the old man lifted up his clasped hands, and prayed.

"God of the nameless and homeless," he said, and it was in the same strange yet solemn-sounding language as before, "have mercy on these Thy servants, joined together in Thy Holy name, to share the lot on earth Thy will assigns them, with one heart and mind. Strengthen Thou them to keep the secret of their faith and race—to teach it to their offspring as they received it from their fathers. Pardon Thou them and us the deceit we do to keep holy Thy law and Thine inheritance. In the land of the persecutor, the exterminator, be Thou their shield, and save them for Thy Holy name. But if discovery and its horrible consequences—imprisonment, torture, death—await them, strengthen Thou them for their endurance—to die as they would live for Thee. Father, hear us! homeless and nameless upon earth, we are Thine own!"

"Aye, strengthen me for him, my husband; turn my woman weakness into Thy strength for him, Almighty Father," was the voiceless prayer with which Almah lifted up her pale face from her husband's bosom, where it had rested during the whole of that strange and terrible prayer; and in the calmness stealing on her throbbing heart, she read her answer.

It was some few minutes ere the excited spirits of the devoted few then present, male or female, master or servant, could subside into their wonted control. But such scenes, such feelings were not of rare occurrence; and ere the domestics of Rodriguez returned, there was nothing either in the mansion or its inmates to denote that anything uncommon had taken place during their absence.

The Portuguese are not fond of society at any time, so that Alvar and his young bride should after one week of festivity, live in comparative retirement, elicited no surprise. The former attended his house of business at Montes as usual; and whoever chanced to visit him at his beautiful estate, returned delighted with his entertainment and his hosts; so that, far and near, the merchant Alvar became noted alike for his munificence and the strict orthodox Catholicism in which he conducted his establishment.

And was Alvar Rodriguez indeed what he seemed? If so, what were those strange mysterious rites with which in secret he celebrated his marriage? For what were those many contrivances in his mansion, secret receptacles even from his own sitting-rooms, into which all kinds of forbidden food were conveyed from his very table, that his soul might not be polluted by disobedience? How did it so happen that one day in every year Alvar gave a general holiday—leave of absence for four and twenty hours, under some well-arranged pretence, to all save those who entreated permission to remain with him? And that on that day, Alvar, his wife, his Moorish secretary, and all those domestics who had witnessed his marriage, spent in holy fast and prayer—permitting no particle of food or drink to pass their lips from eve unto eve; or if, by any chance, the holiday could not be given, their several meals to be laid and served, yet so contriving that, while the food looked as if it had been partaken of, not a portion had they touched? That the Saturday should be passed in seeming preparation for the Sunday, in cessation from work of any kind, and in frequent prayer, was perhaps of trivial importance; but for the previous mysteries—mysteries known to Alvar, his wife, and five or six of his establishment, yet never by word or sign betrayed; how may we account for them? There may be some to whom the memory of such things, as common to their ancestors, may be yet familiar; but to by far the greater number of English readers, they are, in all probability, as incomprehensible as uncommon.

Alvar Rodriguez was a Jew. One of the many who, in Portugal and Spain, fulfilled the awful prophecy of their great lawgiver Moses, and bowed before the imaged saints and martyrs of the Catholic, to shrine the religion of their fathers yet closer in their hearts and homes. From father to son the secret of their faith and race descended, so early and mysteriously taught, that little children imbibed it—not alone the faith, but so effectually to conceal it, as to avert and mystify all inquisitorial questioning, long before they knew the meaning or necessity of what they learned.

How this was accomplished, how the religion of God was thus preserved in the very midst of persecution and intolerance, must ever remain a mystery, as, happily for Israel, such fearful training is no longer needed. But that it did exist, that Jewish children, in the very midst of monastic and convent tuition, yet adhered to the religion of their fathers, never by word or sign betrayed the secret with which they were intrusted; and, in their turn, became husbands and fathers, conveying their solemn and dangerous inheritance to their posterity—that such things were, there are those still amongst the Hebrews of England to affirm and recall, claiming among their own ancestry, but one generation removed, those who have thus concealed and thus adhered. It was the power of God, not the power of man. Human strength had been utterly inefficient. Torture and death would long before have annihilated every remnant of Israel's devoted race. But it might not be; for God had spoken. And, as a living miracle, a lasting record of His truth, His justice, aye, and mercy, Israel was preserved in the midst of danger, in the very face of death, and will be preserved for ever.

It was no mere rejoicing ceremony, that of marriage, amongst the disguised and hidden Israelites of Portugal and Spain. They were binding themselves to preserve and propagate a persecuted faith. They were no longer its sole repositors. Did the strength of one waver all was at an end. They were united in the sweet links of love—framing for themselves new ties, new hopes, new blessings in a rising family—all of which, at one blow, might be destroyed. They existed in an atmosphere of death, yet they lived and flourished. But so situated, it was not strange that human emotion, both in Alvar and his bride, should on their wedding-day, have gained ascendency; and the solemn hour which made them one in the sight of the God they worshipped, should have been fraught with a terror and a shuddering, of which Jewish lovers in free and happy England can have no knowledge.

Alvar Rodriguez was one of those high and noble spirits, on whom the chain of deceit and concealment weighed heavily; and there were times when it had been difficult to suppress and conceal his scorn of those outward observances which his apparent Catholicism compelled. When united to Almah, however, he had a stronger incentive than his own safety: and as time passed on, and he became a father, caution and circumspection, if possible, increased with the deep passionate feelings of tenderness towards the mother and child. As the boy grew and flourished, the first feelings of dread, which the very love he excited called forth at his birth, subsided into a kind of tranquil calm, which even Almah's foreboding spirit trusted would last, as the happiness of others of her race.

Though Alvar's business was carried on both at Montes and at Lisbon, the bulk of both his own and his wife's property was, by a strange chance, invested at Badajoz, a frontier town of Spain, and whence he had often intended to remove it, but had always been prevented. It happened that early in the month of June, some affairs calling him to Lisbon, he resolved to delay removing it no longer, smiling at his young wife's half solicitation to let it remain where it was, and playfully accusing her of superstition, a charge she cared not to deny. The night before his intended departure his young Moorish secretary, in other words, an Israelite of Barbary extraction, entered his private closet, with a countenance of entreaty and alarm, earnestly conjuring his master to give up his Lisbon expedition, and retire with his wife and son to Badajoz or Oporto, or some distant city, at least for a while. Anxiously Rodriguez inquired wherefore.

"You remember the Senor Leyva, your worship's guest a week or two ago?"

"Perfectly. What of him?"

"Master, I like him not. If danger befall us it will come through him. I watched him closely, and every hour of his stay shrunk from him the more. He was a stranger?"

"Yes; benighted, and had lost his way. It was impossible to refuse him hospitality. That he stayed longer than he had need, I grant; but there is no cause of alarm in that—he liked his quarters."

"Master," replied the Moor, earnestly, "I do not believe his tale. He was no casual traveller. I cannot trust him."

"You are not called upon to do so, man," said Alvar, laughing. "What do you believe him to be, that you would inoculate me with your own baseless alarm?"

Hassan Ben Ahmed's answer, whatever it might be, for it was whispered fearfully in his master's ear, had the effect of sending every drop of blood from Alvar's face to his very heart. But he shook off the stagnating dread. He combated the prejudices of his follower as unreasonable and unfounded. Hassan's alarm, however, could only be soothed by the fact, that so suddenly to change his plans would but excite suspicion. If Levya were what he feared, his visit must already have been followed by the usual terrific effects.

Alvar promised, however, to settle his affairs at Lisbon as speedily as he could, and return for Almah and his son, and convey them to some place of greater security until the imagined danger was passed.

In spite of his assumed indifference, however, Rodriguez could not bid his wife and child farewell without a pang of dread, which it was difficult to conceal. The step between life and death—security and destruction—was so small, it might be passed unconsciously, and then the strongest nerve might shudder at the dark abyss before him. Again and again he turned to go, and yet again returned; and it was with a feeling literally of desperation he at length tore himself away.

A fearful trembling was on Almah's heart as she gazed after him, but she would not listen to its voice.

"It is folly," she said, self-upbraidingly. "My Alvar is ever chiding this too doubting heart. I will not disobey him, by fear and foreboding in his absence. The God of the nameless is with him and me," and she raised her eyes to the blue arch above her, with an expression that needed not voice to mark it prayer.

About a week after Alvar's departure, Almah was sitting by the cradle of her boy, watching his soft and rosy slumbers, with a calm sweet thankfulness that such a treasure was her own. The season had been unusually hot and dry, but the apartment in which the young mother sat opened on a pleasant spot, thickly shaded with orange, lemon, and almond trees, and decked with a hundred other richly-hued and richly-scented plants; in the centre of which a fountain sent up its heavy showers, which fell back on the marble bed, with a splash and coolness peculiarly refreshing, and sparkled in the sun as glittering gems.

A fleet yet heavy step resounded from the garden, which seemed suddenly and forcibly restrained into a less agitated movement. A shadow fell between her and the sunshine, and, starting, Almah looked hastily up. Hassan Ben Ahmed stood before her, a paleness on his swarthy cheek, and a compression on his nether lip, betraying strong emotion painfully restrained.

"My husband! Hassan. What news bring you of him? Why are you alone?"

He laid his hand on her arm, and answered in a voice which so quivered that only ears eager as her own could have distinguished his meaning.

"Lady, dear, dear lady, you have a firm and faithful heart. Oh! for the love of Him who calls on you to suffer, awake its strength and firmness. My dear, my honoured lady, sink not, fail not! O God of mercy, support her now!" he added, flinging himself on his knees before her, as Almah one moment sprang up with a smothered shriek, and the next sank back on her seat rigid as marble.

Not another word she needed. Hassan thought to have prepared, gradually to have told, his dread intelligence; but he had said enough. Called upon to suffer, and for Him her God—her doom was revealed in those brief words. One minute of such agonized struggle, that her soul and body seemed about to part beneath it; and the wife and mother roused herself to do. Lip, cheek, and brow vied in their ashen whiteness with her robe; the blue veins rose distended as cords; and the voice—had not Hassan gazed upon her, he had not known it as her own.

She commanded him to tell her briefly all, and even while he spoke, seemed revolving in her own mind the decision which not four and twenty hours after Hassan's intelligence she put into execution.

It was as Ben Ahmed had feared. The known popularity and rumoured riches of Alvar Rodriguez had excited the jealousy of that secret and awful tribunal, the Inquisition, one of whose innumerable spies, under the feigned name of Leyva, had obtained entrance within Alvar's hospitable walls. One unguarded word or movement, the faintest semblance of secrecy or caution, were all sufficient; nay, without these, more than a common share of wealth or felicity was enough for the unconscious victims to be marked, tracked and seized, without preparation or suspicion of their fate. Alvar had chanced to mention his intended visit to Lisbon; and the better to conceal the agent of his arrest, as also to make it more secure, they waited till his arrival there, watched their opportunity, and seized and conveyed him to those cells whence few returned in life, propagating the charge of relapsed Judaism as the cause of his arrest. It was a charge too common for remark, and the power which interfered too mighty for resistance. The confusion of the arrest soon subsided; but it lasted long enough for the faithful Hassan to escape, and, by dint of very rapid travelling, reached Montes not four hours after his master's seizure. The day was in consequence before them, and he ceased not to conjure his lady to fly at once; the officers of the Inquisition could scarcely be there before nightfall.

"You must take advantage of it, Hassan, and all of you who love me. For my child, my boy," she had clasped him to her bosom, and a convulsion contracted her beautiful features as she spoke, "you must take care of him; convey him to Holland or England. Take jewels and gold sufficient; and—and make him love his parents—he may never see either of them more. Hassan, Hassan, swear to protect my child!" she added, with a burst of such sudden and passionate agony, it seemed as if life or reason must bend beneath it. Bewildered by her words, as terrified by her emotion, Ben Ahmed gently removed the trembling child from the fond arms that for the first time failed to support him, gave him hastily to the care of his nurse, who was also a Jewess, said a few words in Hebrew, detailing what had passed, beseeching her to prepare for flight, and then returned to his mistress. The effects of that prostrating agony remained, but she had so far conquered, as to seem outwardly calm; and in answer to his respectful and anxious looks, besought him not to fear for her, nor to dissuade her from her purpose, but to aid her in its accomplishment. She summoned her household around her, detailed what had befallen, and bade them seek their own safety in flight; and when in tears and grief they left her, and but those of her own faith remained, she solemnly committed her child to their care, and informed them of her own determination to proceed directly to Lisbon. In vain Hassan Ben Ahmed conjured her to give up the idea; it was little short of madness. How could she aid his master? why not secure her own safety, that if indeed he should escape, the blessing of her love would be yet preserved him?

"Do not fear for your master, Hassan," was the calm reply; "ask not of my plans, for at this moment they seem but chaos, but of this be assured, we shall live or die together."

More she revealed not; but when the officers of the Inquisition arrived, near nightfall, they found nothing but deserted walls. The magnificent furniture and splendid paintings which alone remained, of course were seized by the Holy Office, by whom Alvar's property was also confiscated. Had his arrest been deferred three months longer, all would have gone—swept off by the same rapacious power, to whom great wealth was ever proof of great guilt—but as it was, the greater part, secured in Spain, remained untouched; a circumstance peculiarly fortunate, as Almah's plans needed the aid of gold.

We have no space to linger on the mother's feelings, as she parted from her boy; gazing on him, perhaps, for the last time. Yet she neither wept nor sighed. There was but one other feeling stronger in that gentle bosom—a wife's devotion—and to that alone she might listen now.

Great was old Gonzalos' terror and astonishment when Almah, attended only by Hassan Ben Ahmed, and both attired in the Moorish costume, entered his dwelling and implored his concealment and aid. The arrest of Alvar Rodriguez had, of course, thrown every secret Hebrew into the greatest alarm, though none dared be evinced. Gonzalos' only hope and consolation was that Almah and her child had escaped; and to see her in the very centre of danger, even to listen to her calmly proposed plans, seemed so like madness, that he used every effort to alarm her into their relinquishment. But this could not be; and with the darkest forebodings, the old man at length yielded to the stronger, more devoted spirit with whom he had to deal.

His mistress once safely under Gonzalos' roof, Ben Ahmed departed, under cover of night, in compliance with her earnest entreaties, to rejoin her child, and to convey him and his nurse to England, that blessed land, where the veil of secrecy could be removed.

About a week after the incarceration of Alvar, a young Moor sought and obtained admission to the presence of Juan Pacheco, the secretary of the Inquisition, as informer against Alvar Rodriguez. He stated that he had taken service with him as clerk or secretary, on condition that he would give him baptism and instruction in the holy Catholic faith; that Alvar had not yet done so; that many things in his establishment proclaimed a looseness of orthodox principles, which the Holy Office would do well to notice. Meanwhile he humbly offered a purse containing seventy pieces of gold, to obtain masses for his salvation.

This last argument carried more weight than all the rest. The young Moor, who boldly gave his name as Hassan Ben Ahmed (which was confirmation strong of his previous statement, as in Leyva's information of Alvar and his household the Moorish secretary was particularly specified), was listened to with attention, and finally received in Pacheco's own household, as junior clerk and servant to the Holy Office.

Despite his extreme youthfulness and delicacy of figure, face, and voice, Hassan's activity and zeal to oblige every member of the Holy Office, superiors and inferiors, gradually gained him the favour and goodwill of all. There was no end to his resources for serving others; and thus he had more opportunities of seeing the prisoners in a few weeks, than others of the same rank as himself had had in years. But the prisoner he most longed to see was still unfound, and it was not till summoned before his judges, in the grand hall of inquisition and of torture, Hassan Ben Ahmed gazed once more upon his former master. He had attended Pacheco in his situation of junior clerk, but had seated himself so deeply in the shade that, though every movement in both the face and form of Alvar was distinguishable to him, Hassan himself was invisible.

The trial, if trial such iniquitous proceedings may be called, proceeded; but in nought did Alvar Rodriguez fail in his bearing or defence. Marvellous and superhuman must that power have been which, in such a scene and hour, prevented all betrayal of the true faith the victims bore. Once Judaism confessed, the doom was death; and again and again have the sons of Israel remained in the terrible dungeons of the Inquisition—endured every species of torture during a space of seven, ten, or twelve years, and then been released, because no proof could be brought of their being indeed that accursed thing—a Jew. And then it was that they fled from scenes of such fearful trial to lands of toleration and freedom, and there embraced openly and rejoicingly that blessed faith, for which in secret they had borne so much.

Alvar Rodriguez was one of these—prepared to suffer, but not reveal. They applied the torture, but neither word nor groan was extracted from him. Engrossed with the prisoner, for it was his task to write down whatever disjointed words might escape his lips, Pacheco neither noticed nor even remembered the presence of the young Moor. No unusual paleness could be visible on his embrowned cheek, but his whole frame felt to himself to have become rigid as stone; a deadly sickness had crept over him, and the terrible conviction of all which rested with him to do alone prevented his sinking senseless on the earth.

The terrible struggle was at length at an end. Alvar was released for the time being, and remanded to his dungeon. Availing himself of the liberty he enjoyed in the little notice now taken of his movements, Hassan reached the prison before either Alvar or his guards. A rapid glance told him its situation, overlooking a retired part of the court, cultivated as a garden. The height of the wall seemed about forty feet, and there were no windows of observation on either side. This was fortunate, the more so as Hassan had before made friends with the old gardener, and pretending excessive love of gardening, had worked just under the window, little dreaming its vicinity to him he sought.

A well-known Hebrew air, with its plaintive Hebrew words, sung tremblingly and softly under his window, first roused Alvar to the sense that a friend was near. He started, almost in superstitious terror, for the voice seemed an echo to that which was ever sounding in his heart. That loved one it could not be, nay, he dared not even wish it; but still the words were Hebrew, and, for the first time, memory flashed back a figure in Moorish garb who had flitted by him on his return to his prison, after his examination.

Hassan, the faithful Hassan! Alvar felt certain it could be none but he; though, in the moment of sudden excitement, the voice had seemed another's. He looked from the window; the Moor was bending over the flowers, but Alvar felt confirmed in his suspicions, and his heart throbbed with the sudden hope of liberty. He whistled, and a movement in the figure below convinced him he was heard.

One point was gained; the next was more fraught with danger, yet it was accomplished. In a bunch of flowers, drawn up by a thin string which Alvar chanced to possess, Ben Ahmed had concealed a file; and as he watched it ascend, and beheld the flowers scattered to the winds, in token that they had done their work, for Alvar dared not retain them in his prison, Hassan felt again the prostration of bodily power which had before assailed him for such a different cause, and it was an almost convulsive effort to retain his faculties; but a merciful Providence watched over him and Alvar, making the feeblest and the weakest, instruments of his all-sustaining love.

We are not permitted space to linger on the various ingenious methods adopted by Hassan Ben Ahmed to forward and mature his plans. Suffice it that all seemed to smile upon him. The termination of the garden wall led, by a concealed door, to a subterranean passage running to the banks of the Tagus. This fact, as also the secret spring of the trap, the old gardener in a moment of unwise conviviality imparted to Ben Ahmed, little imagining the special blessing which such unexpected information secured.

An alcayde and about twenty guards did sometimes patrol the garden within sight of Alvar's window; but this did not occur often, such caution seeming unnecessary.

It had been an evening of unwonted festivity among the soldiers and servants of the Holy Office, which had at length subsided into the heavy slumbers of general intoxication. Hassan had supped with the gardener, and plying him well with wine, soon produced the desired effect. Four months had the Moor spent within the dreaded walls, and the moment had now come when delay need be no more. At midnight all was hushed into profound silence, not a leaf stirred, and the night was so unusually still that the faintest sound would have been distinguished. Hassan stealthily crept round the outposts. Many of the guards were slumbering in various attitudes upon their posts, and others, dependent on his promised watchfulness, were literally deserted. He stood beneath the window. One moment he clasped his hands and bowed his head in one mighty, piercing, though silent prayer, and then dug hastily in the flower-bed at his feet, removing from thence a ladder of ropes, which had lain there some days concealed, and flung a pebble with correct aim against the bars of Alvar's window. The sound, though scarcely loud enough to disturb a bird, reverberated on the trembling heart which heard, as if a thousand cannons had been discharged.

A moment of agonized suspense, and Alvar Rodriguez stood at the window, the bar he had removed, in his hand. He let down the string, to which Hassan's now trembling hands secured the ladder and drew it to the wall. His descent could not have occupied two minutes, at the extent; but to that solitary watcher what eternity of suffering did they seem! Alvar was at his side, had clasped his hands, had called him "Hassan! brother!" in tones of intense feeling, but no word replied. He sought to fly, to point to the desired haven, but his feet seemed suddenly rooted to the earth. Alvar threw his arm around him, and drew him forwards. A sudden and unnatural strength returned. Noiselessly and fleetly as their feet could go, they sped beneath the shadow of the wall. A hundred yards alone divided them from the secret door. A sudden sound broke the oppressive stillness. It was the tramp of heavy feet and the clash of arms; the light of many torches flashed upon the darkness. They darted forward in the fearful excitement of despair; but the effort was void and vain. A wild shout of challenge—of alarm—and they were surrounded, captured, so suddenly, so rapidly, Alvar's very senses seemed to reel; but frightfully they were recalled. A shriek, so piercing, it seemed to rend the very heavens, burst through the still air. The figure of the Moor rushed from the detaining grasp of the soldiery, regardless of bared steel and pointed guns, and flung himself at the feet of Alvar.

"O God, my husband—I have murdered him!" were the strange appalling words which burst upon his ear, and the lights flashing upon his face, as he sank prostrate and lifeless on the earth, revealed to Alvar's tortured senses the features of his WIFE.

How long that dead faint continued Almah knew not, but when sense returned she found herself in a dark and dismal cell, her upper garment and turban removed, while the plentiful supply of water, which had partially restored life, had removed in a great degree the dye which had given her countenance its Moorish hue. Had she wished to continue concealment, one glance around her would have proved the effort vain. Her sex was already known, and the stern dark countenances near her breathed but ruthlessness and rage. Some brief questions were asked relative to her name, intent, and faith, which she answered calmly.

"In revealing my name," she said, "my intention must also be disclosed. The wife of Alvar Rodriguez had not sought these realms of torture and death, had not undergone all the miseries of disguise and servitude, but for one hope, one intent—the liberty of her husband."

"Thus proving his guilt," was the rejoinder. "Had you known him innocent, you would have waited the justice of the Holy Office to give him freedom."

"Justice!" she repeated, bitterly. "Had the innocent never suffered, I might have trusted. But I knew accusation was synonymous with death, and therefore came I here. For my faith, mine is my husband's."

"And know you the doom of all who attempt or abet escape? Death—death by burning! and this you have hurled upon him and yourself. It is not the Holy Office, but his wife who has condemned him;" and with gibing laugh they left her, securing with heavy bolt and bar the iron door. She darted forwards, beseeching them, as they hoped for mercy, to take her to her husband, to confine them underground a thousand fathoms deep, so that they might but be together; but only the hollow echo of her own voice replied, and the wretched girl sunk back upon the ground, relieved from present suffering by long hours of utter insensibility.

It was not till brought from their respective prisons to hear pronounced on them the sentence of death, that Alvar Rodriguez and his heroic wife once more gazed upon each other.

They had provided Almah, at her own entreaty, with female habiliments; for, in the bewildering agony of her spirit, she attributed the failure of her scheme for the rescue of her husband to her having disobeyed the positive command of God, and adopted a male disguise, which in His eyes was abomination, but which in her wild desire to save Alvar she had completely overlooked, and she now in consequence shrunk from the fatal garb with agony and loathing. Yet despite the haggard look of intense mental and bodily suffering, the loss of her lovely hair, which she had cut close to her head, lest by the merest chance its length and luxuriance should discover her, so exquisite, so touching, was her delicate loveliness, that her very judges, stern, unbending as was their nature, looked on her with an admiration almost softening them to mercy.

And now, for the first time, Alvar's manly composure seemed about to desert him. He, too, had suffered almost as herself, save that her devotedness, her love, appeared to give him strength, to endow him with courage, even to look upon her fate, blended as it now was with his own, with calm trust in that merciful God who called him thus early to Himself. Almah could not realise such thoughts. But one image was ever present, seeming to mock her very misery to madness. Her effort had failed; had she not so wildly sought her husband's escape—had she but waited—they might have released him; and now, what was she but his murderess?

Little passed between the prisoners and their judges. Their guilt was all-sufficiently proved by their endeavours to escape, which in itself was a crime always visited by death; and for these manifold sins and misdemeanours they were sentenced to be burnt alive, on All Saints' day, in the grand square of the Inquisition, at nine o'clock in the morning, and proclamation commanded to be made throughout Lisbon, that all who sought to witness and assist at the ceremony should receive remission of sins, and be accounted worthy servants of Jesus Christ. The lesser severity of strangling the victims before burning was denied them, as they neither repented nor had trusted to the justice and clemency of the Holy Office, but had attempted to avert a deserved fate by flight.

Not a muscle of Alvar's fine countenance moved during this awful sentence. He stood proudly and loftily erect, regarding those that spake with an eye, bright, stern, unflinching as their own; but a change passed over it as, breaking from the guard around, Almah flung herself on her knees at his feet.

"Alvar! Alvar! I have murdered—my husband, oh, my husband, say you forgive—forgive—"

"Hush, hush, beloved! mine own heroic Almah, fail not now!" he answered, with a calm and tender seriousness, which seeming to still that crushing agony, strengthened her to bear; and raising her, he pressed her to his breast.

"We have but to die as we have lived, my own! true to that God whose chosen and whose first-born we are, have been, and shall be unto death, aye, and *beyond* it. He will protect our poor orphan, for He has promised the fatherless shall be His care. Look up, my beloved, and say you can face death with Alvar, calmly, faithfully, as you sought to live for him. God has chosen for us a better heritage than one of earth."

She raised her head from his bosom; the terror and the agony had passed from that sweet face—it was tranquil as his own.

"It was not my own death I feared," she said, unfalteringly, "it was but the weakness of human love; but it is over now. Love is mightier than death; there is only love in heaven."

"Aye!" answered Alvar, and proudly and sternly he waved back the soldiers who had hurried forward to divide them. "Men of a mistaken and bloody creed, behold how the scorned and persecuted Israelites can love and die. While there was a hope that we could serve our God, the Holy and the only One, better in life than in death, it was our duty to preserve that life, and endure torture for His sake, rather than reveal the precious secret of our sainted faith and heavenly heritage. But now that hope is at an end, now that no human means can save us from the doom pronounced, know ye have judged rightly of our creed. We ARE those chosen children of God, by you deemed blasphemous and heretic. Do what you will, men of blood and guile, ye cannot rob us of our faith."

The impassioned tones of natural eloquence awed even the rude crowd around; but more was not permitted. Rudely severed, and committed to their own guards, the prisoners were borne to their respective dungeons. To Almah those earnest words had been as the voice of an angel, hushing every former pang to rest; and in the solitude and darkness of the intervening hours, even the thought of her child could not rob her soul of its calm or prayer of its strength.

The 1st of November, 1755, dawned cloudless and lovely, as it had been the last forty days. Never had there been a season more gorgeous in its sunny splendour, more brilliant in the intense azure of its arching heaven than the present. Scarcely any rain had fallen for many months, and the heat had at first been intolerable, but within the last six weeks a freshness and coolness had infused the atmosphere and revived the earth.

As it was not a regular *auto da fé* (Alvar and his wife being the only victims), the awful ceremony of burning was to take place in the square, of which the buildings of the Inquisition formed one side. Mass had been performed before daybreak, in the chapel of the Inquisition, at which the victims were compelled to be present, and about half-past seven the dread procession left the Inquisition gates. The soldiers and minor servitors marched first, forming a hollow square, in the centre of which were the stakes and huge faggots piled around. Then came the sacred cross, covered with a black veil, and its body-guard of priests. The victims, each surrounded by monks, appeared next, closely followed by the higher officers and inquisitors, and a band of fifty men, in rich dresses of black satin and silver, closed the procession.

We have no space to linger on the ceremonies always attendant on the burning of Inquisitorial prisoners. Although, from the more private nature of the rites, these ceremonies were greatly curtailed, it was rather more than half an hour after nine when the victims were bound to their respective stakes, and the executioners approached with their blazing brands.

There was no change in the countenance of either prisoner. Pale they were, yet calm and firm; all of human feeling had been merged in the martyr's courage and the martyr's faith.

One look had been exchanged between them—of love spiritualized to look beyond the grave—of encouragement to endure for their God, even to the end. The sky was still cloudless, the sun still looked down on that scene of horror; and then was a hush—a pause—for so it felt in nature, that stilled the very breathing of those around.

"Hear, O Israel, the Lord our God, the Lord is ONE—the Sole and Holy One; there is no unity like His unity!" were the words which broke that awful pause, in a voice distinct, unfaltering, and musical as its wont; and it was echoed by the sweet tones from woman's lips, so thrilling in their melody, the rudest nature started. It was the signal of their fate. The executioners hastened forward, the brands were applied to the turf of the piles, the flames blazed up beneath their hand—when at that moment there came a shock as if the very earth were cloven asunder, the heavens rent in twain. A crash so loud, so fearful, so appalling, as if the whole of Lisbon had been shivered to its foundations, and a shriek, or rather thousands and thousands of human voices, blended in one wild piercing cry of agony and terror, seeming to burst from every quarter at the self-same instant, and fraught with universal woe. The buildings around shook, as impelled by a mighty whirlwind, though no sound of such was heard. The earth heaved, yawned, closed, and rocked again, as the billows of the ocean were lashed to fury. It was a moment of untold horror. The crowd assembled to witness the martyrs' death fled, wildly shrieking, on every side. Scattered to the heaving ground, the blazing piles lay powerless to injure; their bonds were shivered, their guards were fled. One bound brought Alvar to his wife, and he clasped her in his arms. "God, God of mercy, save us yet again! Be with us to the end!" he exclaimed, and faith winged the prayer. On, on he sped; up, up, in direction of the heights, where he knew comparative safety lay; but ere he reached them, the innumerable sights and sounds of horror that yawned upon his way! Every street, and square, and avenue was choked with shattered ruins, rent from top to bottom; houses, convents, and churches presented the most fearful aspect of ruin; while every second minute a new impetus seemed to be given to the convulsed earth, causing those that remained still perfect to rock and rend. Huge stones, falling from every crack, were crushing the miserable fugitives as they rushed on, seeking safety they knew not where. The rafters of every roof, wrenched from their fastenings, stood upright a brief while, and then fell in hundreds together, with a crash perfectly appalling. The very ties of nature were severed in the wild search for safety. Individual life alone appeared worth preserving. None dared seek the fate of friends—none dared ask, "Who lives?" in that one scene of universal death.

On, on sped Alvar and his precious burden, on, over the piles of ruins; on, unhurt amidst the showers of stones, which, hurled in the air as easily as a ball cast from an infant's hand, fell back again laden with a hundred deaths; on, amid the rocking and yawning earth, beholding thousands swallowed up, crushed and maimed, worse than death itself, for they were left to a lingering torture—to die a thousand deaths in anticipating one; on over the disfigured heaps of dead, and the unrecognised masses of what had once been magnificent and gorgeous buildings. His eye was well-nigh blinded with the shaking and tottering movement of all things animate and inanimate before him; and his path obscured by the sudden and awful darkness, which had changed that bright glowing hue of the sunny sky into a pall of dense and terrible blackness, becoming thicker and denser with every succeeding minute, till a darkness which might be felt, enveloped that devoted city as with the grim shadow of death. His ear was deafened by the appalling sounds of human agony and Nature's wrath; for now, sounds as of a hundred waterspouts, the dull continued roar of subterranean thunder, becoming at times loud as the discharge of a thousand cannons; at others, resembling the sharp grating sound of hundreds and hundreds of chariots driven full speed over the stones; and this, mingled with the piercing shrieks of women, the hoarser cries and shouts of men, the deep terrible groans of mental agony, and the shriller screams of instantaneous death, had usurped the place of the previous awful stillness, till every sense of those who yet survived seemed distorted and maddened. And Nature herself, convulsed and freed from restraining bonds, appeared about to return to that chaos whence she had leaped at the word of God.

Still, still Alvar rushed forwards, preserved amidst it all, as if the arm of a merciful Providence was indeed around him and his Almah, marking them for life in the very midst of death. Making his rapid way across the ruins of St. Paul's, which magnificent church had fallen in the first shock, crushing the vast congregation assembled within its walls, Alvar paused one moment, undecided whether to seek the banks of the river or still to make for the western heights. There was a moment's hush and pause in the convulsion of nature, but Alvar dared not hope for its continuance. Ever and anon the earth still heaved, and houses opened from base to roof and closed without further damage. With a brief fervid cry for continued guidance and protection, scarcely conscious which way in reality he took, and still folding Almah to his bosom—so supernaturally strengthened that the weakness of humanity seemed far from him—Rodriguez hurried on, taking the most open path to the Estrella Hill. An open space was gained, half-way to the summit, commanding a view of the banks of the river and the ruins around. Panting, almost breathless, yet still struggling with his own exhaustion to encourage Almah, Alvar an instant rested, ere he plunged anew into the narrower streets. A shock, violent, destructive, convulsive as the first, flung them prostrate; while the renewed and increased sounds of wailing, the tremendous and repeated crashes on every side, the disappearance of the towers, steeples, and turrets which yet remained, revealed the further destructiveness which had befallen. A new and terrible cry added to the universal horror.

"The sea! the sea!" Alvar sprung to his feet and, clasped in each other's arms, he and Almah gazed beneath. Not a breath of wind stirred, yet the river (which being at that point four miles wide appeared like the element they had termed it) tossed and heaved as impelled by a mighty storm—and on it came, roaring, foaming, tumbling, as every bound were loosed; on, over the land to the very heart of the devoted city, sweeping off hundreds in its course, and retiring with such velocity, and so far beyond its natural banks, that vessels were left dry which had five minutes before ridden in water seven fathoms deep. Again and again this phenomenon took place; the vessels in the river, at the same instant, whirled round and round with frightful rapidity, and smaller boats dashed upwards, falling back to disappear beneath the booming waters. As if chained to the spot where they stood, fascinated by this very horror, Alvar and his wife yet gazed; their glance fixed on the new marble quay, where thousands and thousands of the fugitives had congregated, fixed, as if unconsciously foreboding what was to befall. Again the tide rushed in—on, on, over the massive ruins, heaving, raging, swelling, as a living thing; and at the same instant the quay and its vast burthen of humanity sunk within an abyss of boiling waters, into which the innumerable boats around were alike impelled, leaving not a trace, even when the angry waters returned to their channel, suddenly as they had left it, to mark what had been.

"'Twas the voice of God impelled me hither, rather than pausing beside those fated banks. Almah, my best beloved, bear up yet a brief while more—He will spare and save us as he hath done now. Merciful Providence! Behold another wrathful element threatens to swallow up all of life and property which yet remains. Great God, this is terrible!"

And terrible it was: from three several parts of the ruined city huge fires suddenly blazed up, hissing, crackling, ascending as clear columns of liquid flame; up against the pitchy darkness, infusing it with tenfold horror—spreading on every side—consuming all of wood and wall which the earth and water had left unscathed; wreathing its serpent-like folds in and out the ruins, forming strange and terribly beautiful shapes of glowing colouring; fascinating the eye with admiration, yet bidding the blood chill and the flesh creep. Fresh cries and shouts had marked its rise and progress; but, aghast and stupified, those who yet survived made no effort to check its way, and on every side it spread, forming lanes and squares of glowing red, flinging its lurid glare so vividly around, that even those on the distant heights could see to read by it; and fearful was the scene that awful light revealed. Now, for the first time could Alvar trace the full extent of destruction which had befallen. That glorious city, which a few brief hours previous lay reposing in its gorgeous sunlight—mighty in its palaces and towers—in its churches, convents, theatres, magazines, and dwellings—rich in its numberless artizans and stores—lay perished and prostrate as the grim spectre of long ages past, save that the fearful groups yet passing to and fro, or huddled in kneeling and standing masses, some bathed in the red glare of the increasing fires, others black and shapeless—save when a sudden flame flashed on them, disclosing what they were—revealed a strange and horrible PRESENT, yet lingering amid what seemed the shadows of a fearful PAST. Nor was the convulsion of nature yet at an end;—the earth still rocked and heaved at intervals, often impelling the hissing flames more strongly and devouringly forward, and by tossing the masses of burning ruin to and fro, gave them the semblance of a sea of flame. The ocean itself, too, yet rose and sunk, and rose again; vessels were torn from their cables, anchors wrenched from their soundings and hurled in the air—while the warring waters, the muttering thunders, the crackling flames, formed a combination of sounds which, even without their dread adjuncts of human agony and terror, were all-sufficient to freeze the very life-blood, and banish every sense and feeling, save that of stupifying dread.

But human love, and superhuman faith, saved from the stagnating horror. The conviction that the God of his fathers was present with him, and would save him and Almah to the end, never left him for an instant, but urged him to exertions which, had he not had this all-supporting faith, he would himself have deemed impossible. And his faith spake truth. The God of infinite mercy, who had stretched out His own right hand to save, and marked the impotence of the wrath and cruelty of man, was with him still, and, despite of the horrors yet lingering round them, despite of the varied trials, fatigues, and privations attendant on their rapid flight, led them to life and joy, and bade them stand forth the witnesses and proclaimers of His unfailing love, His everlasting providence!

With the great earthquake of Lisbon, the commencement

of which our preceding pages have faintly endeavoured to portray, and its terrible effects on four millions of square miles, our tale has no further connection. The third day brought our poor fugitives to Badajoz, where Alvar's property had been secured. They tarried there only long enough to learn the blessed tidings of Hassan Ben Ahmed's safe arrival in England with their child; that his faithfulness, in conjunction with that of their agent in Spain, had already safely transmitted the bulk of their property to the English funds; and to obtain Ben Ahmed's address, forward tidings of their providential escape to him, and proceed on their journey.

An anxious but not a prolonged interval enabled them to accomplish it safely, and once more did the doubly-rescued press their precious boy to their yearning hearts, and feel that conjugal and parental love burned, if it could be, the dearer, brighter, more unspeakably precious, from the dangers they had passed; and not human love alone. The veil of secrecy was removed, they were in a land whose merciful and liberal government granted to the exile and the wanderer a home of peace and rest, where they might worship the God of Israel according to the law he gave; and in hearts like those of Alvar and his Almah, prosperity could have no power to extinguish or deaden the religion of love and faith which adversity had engendered.

The appearance of old Gonzalos and his family in England, a short time after Alvah's arrival there, removed their last remaining anxiety, and gave them increased cause for thankfulness. Not a member of the merchant's family, and more wonderful still, not a portion of his property, had been lost amid the universal ruin; and to this very day, his descendants recall his providential preservation by giving, on every returning anniversary of that awful day, certain articles of clothing to a limited number of male and female poor.*

* A fact.

Red Rose Villa, and its Inhabitants.

A SKETCH.

On the outskirts of a certain country town, which for euphony we will call Briarstone, from its being situated in one of the most picturesque but least known parts of old England, and almost imbedded in hills and lanes, where the wood or briar-rose grew redundantly, was a certain castellated-looking mansion, glowing with red bricks and bright blue slates, storied with large-paned windows, framed with such fresh green, that it would seem as if the painter's brush could never have been absent above a month together. The entrance-door, of most aristocratic dimensions, was of bright glazed yellow, never sullied by dust or dimness. Below the portentous-looking circular knocker (Briarstone was yet in happy ignorance of the *un*-aristocracy of knockers) was a large brass plate, glittering in the sunshine like burning gold, and bearing thereon, in large and dignified letters, as if the name was of such importance in itself that it required no engraver's ornament, the monosyllables—portentous in their very brevity—Miss Brown. The gravel walk which led up to the imposing flight of steps (white as the most scrupulous care could make them) that the yellow door surmounted, was kept so particularly neat, that the very birds feared to alight upon it, lest they should be swept off for some intrusive leaf or twig, quicker even than their voluntary flight. It was impossible to look upon the exterior of the mansion without being impressed with a grand idea of its as yet invisible interior.

Standing, as Red Rose Villa did, in a spacious garden, full ten minutes' walk out of the town, it was marvellous how the daily events of this said town became known within its walls, as if a train had been laid—a sort of electrical conductor—to the interior of every dwelling, which conveyed back to its starting-place all the information required. However invisible the *means* of communication, the *effects* were certain; for Miss Brown knew everything, even before the persons affected knew it themselves.

Now, Miss Brown, though her dignified name appeared on the brass plate solus, was not the sole inmate of this stately mansion by any means. She was, in fact, one of a multitude; for there were times when the capacious walls of Red Rose Villa enshrined no fewer than fifty living souls. The truth must out on our paper, though Miss Brown would have been shocked almost to annihilation had any one suggested the propriety of permitting it to speak on her cherished brass plate —Miss Brown kept a first-rate finishing academy for young ladies of the first families, and a boarding-house for all who needed kind friends, cheerful lodgings, and comfortable board. Then she had an English, and a French, and an Italian, and of course a German teacher—all exemplary young women. Masters were rarely admitted, it being a gross impropriety in Miss Brown's educational code to accustom young ladies to male tuition.

One indeed there was, a Mr. Gilbert Givevoice; but then Miss Brown and his lamented mother had been such friends, that at one time they had thought of becoming another Miss Ponsonby and Lady Eleanor Butler, and causing a sensation by retiring to live on friendship; but, unfortunately, before this could be carried into effect, a Mr. Givevoice appeared, and Miss Brown was left to mourn the inconsistency of those professions which had declared friendship all-sufficient for life. The offence was not forgiven for many years; but when Mrs. Givevoice was left a widow, Miss Brown generously relented, and Gilbert showing some musical talent (magnified by the Briarstonians into marvellous genius), he was gradually installed as music-master general, and aid extraordinary in all the concerns of Red Rose Villa.

Besides five-and-twenty pupils, a dozen boarders, four teachers, and half-a-dozen servants, Miss Brown was blessed with two brothers and two sisters, to all of whom she had performed most inimitably a mother's part. Many marvelled that such grown men as Mr. Gustavus and Mr. Adolphus Brown should so contentedly succumb to female domination, and not seek homes for themselves; but petticoat government was so supreme in Red Rose Villa, that even the hint of such a thing would have been far too great a stretch of masculine audacity; and, in fact, they were very well contented where they were. Mr. Adolphus was a banker's clerk, and was only known at home as going to sleep upon the sofa. Mr. Gustavus had been (according to his own account), at one time a land-surveyor, at another, an architect, and then an engraver; but he was, he declared, one of the unlucky ones, and so quietly sunk down in his sister's establishment, as merely a domestic man, who could set his hand to anything. He taught writing and arithmetic, and oriental tinting, and a variety of finishing accomplishments; and copied music, and invented patterns for all the young lady-boarders who were worth something more than smiles. Mr. Adolphus was always asleep. Mr. Gustavus never seemed to sleep at all; thin as a lath, he was here, there, and everywhere, busying himself in everybody's concerns, but never succeeding in forwarding his own.

Miss Brown, portly and majestic in carriage as of imperturbable gravity in look, possessed a fund of high-sounding, choice-worded, conversational powers—that is to say, her speech, once entered upon, flowed on in such a continuous gently-murmuring stream, that to break or interrupt it by a rejoinder was utterly impossible. The voice was as imperturbable and unvarying as the face. She was wondrously learned; schooled in the lore of the ancient, and wise in the ways of the modern world. No scheme could be set afloat at Briarstone unless Miss Brown had been consulted; no shop was the fashion unless Miss Brown had patronised; no case of distress worth relieving, unless forwarded by Miss Brown; and, in sober truth, Miss Brown was benevolent—was generous—did the kindest deeds imaginable; but as she never left her pinnacle of ice to look into human hearts, lest their warmth should thaw hers, she received neither the regard nor esteem which her sterling qualities in reality merited. Miss Wilhelmina Brown was her antipodes—all sweetness—all graciousness—all fascination! Miss Brown was learned, and not accomplished; Miss Wilhelmina accomplished and not learned. Miss Brown was all sobriety, Miss Wilhelmina all smiles. At thirty, she learnt the harp; at five-and-thirty the guitar; at forty, she discovered she had a voice, and could sing inimitably—all the Briarstone *soirées* said so, and of course it must be true. Whole scenes from the French tragedians—stanzas from Dante—long lines from Schiller—Miss Wilhelmina would recite with such pathos, such expression, there was no occasion to understand the languages to enter into such charming recitations. English poetry was not ventured upon; Byron and Moore *were* charming, certainly; but then her sister's responsible position—she dared not admit them upon the drawing-room tables of Red Rose Villa—she could only indulge herself strictly in private.

Miss Angelica, the youngest of the family by some years, was different to either sister. Nature had not been very bountiful in the powers of the brain, but, in their stead, had endowed her with powers of housewifery in no common degree. She managed all the domestic concerns of this human Noah's ark as no one else could. From morning till night she was moving; so overlooking every department, that at the farthest sound of her footsteps (none of the lightest, for Miss Angelica was as short and stout as Miss Wilhelmina was tall and languidly slim) every brush and broom seemed endowed with double velocity. Jingle, jingle, went a huge bunch of keys—pat, pat, her substantial feet, from kitchen to attic—scullery to roof. Even if she sat down, her fingers continued the same perpetual motion, in the creation of sundry caps, bonnets, head-dresses—all the paraphernalia of female elegancies. No one dressed so becomingly as the Misses Brown; and Miss Angelica was considered the originator and inventor of fashions which all Briarstone followed.

The pupils were like most misses in their teens. Originality of character always succumbed to system in Red Rose Villa. Miss Brown's was a finishing academy for manners as well as morals; and so in the weekly *soirées* of her mansion, the young ladies, by alternate eights, appeared in the drawing-room, dressed very becomingly, to sit down and smile, and answer in monosyllables; to play their last specimen of Herz or Thalberg, or sing their last bravura, or make one in a quadrille; but in all they did to bear witness to the admirable code of tuition and government carried out in Red Rose Villa.

The boarders presented a variety of characters; but as our sketch only extends over one evening, we can merely mention them generally. Officers' widows, on half-pay, who, by a residence in Miss Brown's establishment, combined first-rate education for their daughters, and society for themselves; ancient spinsters, who had not given up the idea of becoming middle-aged matrons, well knowing that Miss Brown's philanthropic disposition gave them opportunities for the cultivation of the tender passion, when any one else would have imagined the time for such juvenilities was over. In the fortnightly *soirées*, one, two, or three pairs of lovers were always found among Miss Brown's guests—unfortunates, whose interminable engagements, from pecuniary difficulties, or the stern dissent of cruel guardians, would have seemed hopeless to all but for the energetic encouragement of the benevolent Miss Brown, who always acted on the idea

"Passion, I see, is catching."

And, still more urgent reason, never did a wedding-party issue from the well-glazed portals of Red Rose Villa (and such events did really occur) but an accession of pupils and boarders immediately followed.

Amongst the boarders were two young ladies, sisters' children, and both orphans, but the similitude went no further. Isabel Morland, the eldest by two years, was a sparkling brunette—satirical—clever ; eccentric in habits, uneven in temper, and capricious as the wind. But what did all this signify? She was an heiress ; and, reckoning according to the estimation of Briarstone, a rich one. She had been a pupil, and her love of display, a coquetry, and determination to get a husband, had occasioned her resolve to remain with a family whom in heart she detested, rather than reside with the only relations she possessed, old respectable folks in the country. She had sense enough to know that her fortune, inexhaustible as it seemed in Briarstone, would not endow her with the smallest consequence elsewhere. And though so highly gifted by nature as, had she selected the society of superior minds, to have become both estimable and happy ; yet her love of power—of feeling herself superior to any one with whom she associated—made her voluntarily become a member of a family whom she lost no opportunity of turning into objects of satire and abuse ; receiving the marked attentions of Mr. Gustavus Brown so graciously, when no better offered, as to give him every hope of ultimate success ; but cold, distant, and disdainful, at the remotest chance of achieving a more desirable conquest.

Very different was Laura Gascoigne. Unusually retiring in manner, the peculiar charm hovering around her could better be felt than described. Possessing neither the wit nor the cleverness, or, as Coleridge so happily expresses it, "the brain in the hand," which characterised her cousin, she had judgment, feeling, thought—the rare power of *concentration*, which enabled her to succeed in all she attempted—the quiet, persevering energy which leads to completion, even in the simplest trifles, and prevents all mere superficial acquirement. Perhaps early sorrow had deepened natural characteristics. From the time her mother became widowed, no pen can describe the devotedness which was the tie between them. The failing health of Mrs. Gascoigne had, during the last year of her life, compelled a residence in the south of England; and, when in the neighbourhood of Briarstone, the real kindness to the mother and daughter received from the Misses Brown induced Laura, after Mrs. Gascoigne's death, to make their house her home, till she could decide on her future plans. She was indeed lonely upon earth; and the straitened means which had urged her to teach many hours in the day, to supply her mother with luxuries and comforts, by stamping them as poor, prevented her being known in those circles where her gentle virtues would have gained her real appreciating friends.

All that she had sacrificed in her filial devotion even her mother never knew, though that mighty sacrifice had been made full two years before her death. An invalid, whose life might pass from night till morning with none on earth to love and tend her but her child, Laura could not leave her. And when she had said this, her lover, in all the jealous irritation of an angry, passionate nature, reproached her that she did not, could not love him, else every other consideration would be waived—that the reports of her affections having been transferred to another were true, and therefore it was better they should part. She had meekly left him to resume her sad duties by her mother's side, and they had never met again. She knew he had been on the eve of leaving England for an honourable appointment in the West Indies, to which he had been nominated. But the wish would rise that he would write; he could not continue in anger towards her; time must show the purity, the justice, of her motive in her refusal, at such a moment, to leave England. And gladly would she have remained in one spot, hoping, believing on; but her mother needed constant change, and they had gone from place to place, that perhaps, even if he had written, no letter could have reached her. Three years had passed; and if the *hope* to prove her truth still lingered, the *expectation* had indeed long gone. And so Laura's early youth had passed, with not one flower cast upon it save those her own sweet disposition gave. Miss Brown's establishment was not, indeed, a congenial home; but she had her own room, her own pursuits; and though often yearning—how intensely!—for sympathy and intellectual companionship, could be thankful and contented. She could not love the Miss Browns, but she respected their sterling qualities, and regretted their eccentricities; and so found some good point to dilate on when others quizzed and laughed at them, that her presence always checked ill-nature.

"What is the cause of all this unusual confusion and excitement, Isabel?" inquired Laura one morning, entering her cousin's apartment: "do enlighten me. You always know everything as thoroughly as Miss Brown herself."

"And you always know nothing, my most rustic cousin. Fortunate for you, you have so superior a person as myself to come to. There is to be a grand assembly in the lower regions to-night, and so of course sweet Wilhelmina is practising and tuning enough to terrify away all harmony, and Angelica is buried in all the mysteries of supper craft. Don't look unbelieving, it is true."

"And it is Wednesday, not Saturday, Isabel."

"Granted, Laura; but such a grand event as receiving a baronet and his sister demands everything uncommon, even to a change of night. It would be doing him no honour to receive him on a usual *soirée* night. Learned Lucretia is deep in the last novel and this month's most fashionable magazine. Folks report that Sir Sydney Harcourt likes literary conversation. I mean to try if Isabel Morland will not have more effect in captivating than the three graces, Lucretia, Wilhelmina, and Angelica altogether, backed by their whole corps of spinsters and schoolgirls. What has seized you, Laura, that you do not scold me, as usual, for my self-conceit? Do you begin to feel it is breath wasted? My dear, you shall see me in perfection to-night. Sir Sydney shall not depart heart-whole from Briarstone, though he does look as if nobody within it could be worth speaking to."

Isabel was standing before a large mirror, much too engrossed in admiring her own face and studying various attitudes, and the best mode of arranging her glossy black hair, to notice how strangely and fitfully Laura's colour varied, and the voice in which she said, "Sir Sydney Harcourt, is he a new resident at Briarstone?" was not sufficiently agitated to cause remark, save to a much quicker perception than Isabel's.

"Yes, within the last few days; such a sensation has his arrival made, you must have heard of it even in your sanctum."

"My dear Isabel, have I not been staying out the last fortnight, and only returned last night?"

"Oh, by-the bye, so you have."

"How much you must have missed me!"

"I did the first few days; but, my good child, how could I think of anything but the new lion, splendid as he is, too? He is only here for a month. Will you dare me to the field, Laura, to make that month two, or six, or something more into the bargain?"

"No, Isabel, you need no daring. Only remember your own peace may be endangered too."

"My peace! my dear foolish child. I shall see Sir Sydney at my feet long before any such catastrophe. Lady Harcourt! how well it sounds!"

"And Mr. Brown, Isabel?"

"The wretch! we have quarrelled irretrievably."

"And when I left you were giving him every encouragement you could."

"Nonsense, Laura! You are always preaching of my giving encouragement. The poor wretch would die in despair if I did not relent sometimes."

"Better, as I have always told you, put an end to his attentions at once. I am certain he would cease to persecute, if you did not encourage him, as you know you do."

"I know I do. Poor dear Gussy—he is very well, when I can get no one else."

"But indeed, Isabel, you are very wrong; your manner to him is the talk of every one."

"I do not care for what every one thinks, as I have told you hundreds of times. I will just pursue my own inclination, whether the world approve of it or not. What is the world to me? You cannot possibly imagine I mean ever to become Mrs. Brown. Why, the very name is enough to make me drown myself first. No, I am free to receive all Sir Sydney's attentions, which I fully mean to win. You know I have some power, Laura."

"To attract, but not to keep, Isabel."

"Laura, if you were not a thorough simpleton, I should say you had designs on Sir Sydney yourself. Come, will you run a tilt with me for him? I will be generous, and keep back some of my fascinations, that we may try as equals, if you will."

"Thank you for the proposal, but it would hardly be fair. You will burst upon Sir Sydney in the freshness and brilliancy of novelty, in addition to all your other attractions. I have not even novelty to befriend me, for I rather think I have met him before."

"Sir Sydney Harcourt! How sly of you not to tell me all this time. When?—how?—where?"

"How could I tell you, before, Isabel, when you have scarcely given me breathing space?"

"But do you know anything of his former life? Report says he was jilted by a poor insignificant girl, and has been a professed woman-hater ever since. I do believe there he is in his curricle. What a splendid set-out!—do look, Laura. Stay—I shall see him better in the next room."

And to the next room she flew, so engrossed with Sir Sydney's splendid driving, that she did not perceive that Laura had not accepted the invitation, but had quietly retired to her own room.

"Miss Gascoigne, I trust you will join us to-night. I expect the honour of Sir Sydney Harcourt's and his accomplished sister's company. Your manners and appearance are so completely *comme il faut* that they will, no doubt, be glad to meet you. I do not approve of young ladies hunting after gaiety and dissipation; but it is a great advantage to mix in such society as I can offer you to-night. I shall expect to see you, of course," and without waiting for a reply—for such a thing as dissent to Miss Brown's commands was not to be thought of—Miss Brown, or learned Lucretia, in Isabel Morland's phraseology, majestically floated onwards.

"Laura, my sweet Laura, play over the accompaniment to this luscious 'Ah te o cara.' Mr. Givevoice will be here to-night, so I shall not want you; but now, if you will assist me, you will do me such a favour. The music is so mellifluous, it will quite repay you for the trouble." And Laura complied, regretting most sincerely that a person possessing such real sense and goodness as Miss Wilhelmina should so expose herself to ridicule, but feeling that, young as she was, it was more her duty to bear with folly than reprove it.

"Laura, dear, put the finishing bows to Lucretia's cap for me, there's a love. I have such innumerable things to see after and get done before seven o'clock to-night, that I have no time to breathe."

"You are always busy, my dear Miss Angelica. I wish you would make me of use. I shall finish this in ten minutes; so you had better give me something else to do."

"You are the best girl in the world, Laura, my dear; but you can't assist me in household concerns. No one can; they worry me to death—but I don't grow thin upon them, that's one comfort. Come, I am glad you are smiling, Laura, my dear. What a pity you are not more merry. By-the-bye, you may help me very much—I shall never get through the tea-making all by myself."

"Let me take it off your hands entirely. I will with pleasure."

"Thank you—thank you, my dear; but nothing would go right if I were not there too, depend upon it. If there is not Molly only going now to dust the rooms—the lazy huzzy!" and off trotted Miss Angelica, to scold and dust by turns.

The evening at length arrived. Confusion and noise, and sundry domestic jars, had subsided into silence and solemnity actually portentous. The pupils, with the exception of six most highly favoured, had been dismissed to their dormitories, and the school-room fitted up for the supper, which, under Miss Angelica's auspices in the culinary department, Miss Wilhelmina's in the elegant arrangement of fruit and flowers, and Miss Lucretia's in the selection of sweets and solids least hurtful to the gastronomic and digestive powers, was to be unequalled.

In the front drawing-room the Misses and Messrs. Brown and their train of boarders sat in imposing state. The covers had all been removed from the couches, *chairs-longues*, ottomans, etc., displaying a variety of embroidery by the fair fingers of Miss Wilhelmina, and the splendid designs of Mr. Gustavus. The harp was uncovered; the guitar, with its broad blue ribbon, laid carelessly on the grand piano-forte, which was open; and at his post on the music-stool sat Mr. Gilbert Givevoice, fair and famous, smiling very sweetly on his tall pupil, Miss Wilhelmina, who was in earnest conversation by his side. Miss Brown was on the sofa, looking wiser and grander than ever. A vacant place was left beside her, which no one thought of taking, for that it was designed for Miss Harcourt, being as well known as if the name had been chalked up on the wall behind. Presently all the presentable inhabitants of Briarstone flocked in, attired in their very best, and satisfying Miss Brown as to the imposing appearance of her saloon. The back drawing-room, somewhat less brilliantly lighted, was occupied, as usual, by three or four sets of lovers. The blue room opened from it, and Laura was there ensconced as Miss Angelica's aid extraordinary. The door being thrown open permitted a full view of the two drawing-rooms and all their proceedings, though from the blue room occupying a sort of angular corner, its inmates could not even be observed. Isabel Morland, looking actually dazzling from her becoming dress and indescribable *tournure*, had chosen to settle down into a regular flirtation with a Mr. Manby, a young man she sometimes deigned to notice, at others deemed too little even to be visible. Mr. Gustavus looked black as a thunder-cloud; his thin form moving in and out the circle, but always hovering nearest Isabel, who took no more notice of him than of his vacant chair.

At length the magic words, "Sir Sydney and Miss Harcourt," were pronounced, and the door flung back as if its very hinges should suffer martyrdom to do them honour; and the whole roomful rose, as by one movement, except Isabel, who carelessly remained seated. Then came sundry flourishes and introductions, and mutual bows and curtseys, till Miss Harcourt fairly sank down on her seat of honour, casting a rueful glance at her brother, who returned it with one so irresistibly comic, that Isabel, to whom alone the look was visible, was compelled to smile too. Sir Sydney, whose eye was wandering round the room, caught the look, eagerly bowed recognition, and in another minute was at her side, leaving Mr. Gustavus with half his tale untold.

That Sir Sydney was handsome, and had all the ease and elegance of a polished gentleman, there could not be two opinions about; but there was something more about him, no one could exactly define what. He was too well bred to be haughty or repulsive when he had quite willingly accepted Miss Brown's invitation; yet he certainly did not seem in his element. He did smile and talk well; but Miss Wilhelmina whispered to an intimate friend to observe how very melancholy his countenance was when at rest; she was certain he was not a happy man, and what could be the reason? Miss Harcourt was pronounced, after a trial of ten minutes, a most charming, accomplished, elegant girl; she was in reality merely an unaffected, genteel, quiet, little personage, without any pretension whatever, and somewhat past what she deemed girlhood.

The evening proceeded most harmoniously. Tea was accomplished elegantly, under Miss Angelica's active surveillance. She was in the blue room, back and front drawing-rooms, so quickly, one after the other, that she seemed gifted with ubiquity for the evening. Then Miss Brown proposed music and dancing; she thought they were such delectable adjuncts to young people's amusement—such social pleasures, etc.; to all of which Miss Harcourt gracefully assented. She would be happy to perform her part; her brother seldom danced. A general lamentation followed. What a loss to the dancers: perhaps he would prefer music; they could offer him some very passable; and a concert commenced, in appearance very naturally given, but in reality performed in exact accordance with well-cogitated arrangements beforehand.

Whether Sir Sydney benefited by the succession of "sweet sounds," or not, remained a problem; as Isabel, to Miss Brown and Mr. Gustavus's excessive annoyance, kept him so exclusively her attendant, that it required all his acquaintance with worldly tact to save him from rudeness to his hostesses, at the same time that he fully encouraged his companion. The only thought Isabel could spare from Sir Sydney was for Laura to witness her triumph; but Laura was nowhere to be seen. If Isabel could have known that her cousin saw her and Sir Sydney too, and the sickness of heart that vision gave, she might have triumphed more.

Dancing was at length accomplished, and Sir Sydney actually joined in it, dancing two quadrilles successively with Isabel, and then remaining standing with her, leaning against the piano, in such apparent earnest conversation as allowed attention to nothing else. Mr. Manby and several other beaux of Briarstone, whom Isabel never disdained at the public balls, when none superior were to be had, came in humble adoration entreating the honour of her hand. The toss of the head and curl of the lip with which they were refused elicited an expression in Sir Sydney's eye and very handsome mouth which must have startled Isabel, had she not been too engrossed with her own apparent conquest to perceive it.

"Sydney, you are wrong," whispered Miss Harcourt, as Isabel, for an instant, disappeared to find a musical album on which she much prided herself.

"Mary, I am right," was the reply. "If young ladies choose to play the coquette, it is but fair in us to pay them back in their own coin. How ungracious I should be to let all these graceful arts be wasted."

Miss Harcourt still looked disapproval, but further rejoinder was impossible; for Isabel, flushed with conquest, had returned, more animated and engrossing than before.

"Of course you sing, Miss Morland?"

"No, Sir Sydney; I abhor all pretension; and as I knew I could never sing like a professor, I never attempted it."

"Pardon me, but I think you are wrong. There can be no necessity for private performers to equal professors; indeed, I would banish all Italian bravuras from private rooms."

"You will think my brother a sad Goth, Miss Morland; but he prefers a simple English ballad to anything else."

"I admire his taste; but you surely do not think ballad-singing an easily-accomplished matter?"

"Easy enough for any one with natural feeling," replied Sir Sydney, somewhat hastily, "and with boldness sufficient to express it. I would rather hear 'Go, forget me,' as I have heard it, than the finest Italian scena by a prima donna."

"I am delighted, Sir Sydney, that we have it in our power to afford you that gratification," energetically interposed Miss Wilhelmina. The baronet made her a graceful bow, looking at his sister, however, with eyes that plainly said, "Save me from this."

"Laura!" (Sir Sydney actually started, but recovered himself so rapidly that the sudden flushing of his brow was unremarked even by Isabel.) "Dear me, where can the dear girl have hid herself? I assure you, Sir Sydney, though she sings very seldom, she is considered first-rate in English ballads," and away gracefully glided Miss Wilhelmina in search of her.

"Who is this 'dear girl,' Miss Morland? Can she really sing that song? I would rather she chose any other," said Sir Sydney, in a tone almost of irritation.

Isabel looked up with one of her most mischievous smiles, which recalled him instantly to his artificial self; but before he could rally sufficiently to speak again, Miss Wilhelmina's voice, in its most dulcet tones of encouragement, was close beside him.

"Come, Laura, my dear; we are all friends, you know—no one to be afraid of. Sir Sydney is so particularly partial to 'Go, forget me:' I am sure you will favour him."

"Or any other song the young lady likes. I would not be so arbitrary as to select for her," he exclaimed, springing up, with gentlemanly politeness, to relieve Miss Wilhelmina of the music-book she carried, and, as he took it from her, coming in close contact with the fair girl behind her, whom her flowing drapery had till then completely concealed.

"Laura! Miss Gascoigne! Is it possible?" he articulated, in a tone which, though suppressed, must, to any perception less obtuse than the Misses Brown's have betrayed intense emotion; but Miss Wilhelmina only read casual acquaintanceship, and supposed an introduction had taken place in the early part of the evening. Laura bowed, Sir Sydney thought, coldly, and quietly passed on to the piano. The song was selected and sung. She had often been heard before, but her voice had never seemed the same as at that moment. It might have been that what a baronet and his sister listened to with such interest, that the former had moved himself some distance from Miss Morland's fascinations to look at and listen to the singer unobserved, must be of greater value than it had ever before been supposed, or that there really was some spell in the song which Laura had never been heard to sing before (Miss Wilhelmina seeing it amongst her music, had spoken on supposition merely); but it fell upon the most thoughtless, the most obtuse, with such unaccountable power, that even when the strain ceased the sudden and unusual hush continued, until rudely broken by Mr. Gustavus Brown and Mr. Gilbert Givevoice clapping their hands most vehemently, exciting an uproar of applause, under which Laura tried to make her escape; but she was prevented by the friendly advance of Miss Harcourt, who, with both hands extended, exclaimed, so as to be heard by all, "Miss Gascoigne, will you permit me to thank you for your beautiful song and claim your acquaintance in the same breath? We have, in truth, never met before; but if you knew me as well as I know you from report, we should be friends—nay, more, allies—already. You need not look so very terrified," she added, with laughing earnestness; "I am not a very formidable person, though my want of ceremony may really be rather startling; but I am so glad to have found you, that I must entreat Miss Brown's kind permission to excuse me, if I do forget everybody but you for a little while."

Her ready tact met with the rejoinder she desired: she was entreated by all the sisters to make herself quite at home; they were delighted she should know their dear Laura. The blue room was quite deserted, and they could chat there quite comfortably; and to the blue room Miss Harcourt eagerly led her companion, who so trembled that she feared for the continuance of her composure. The door was not closed; to do so would have occasioned remark; but, as we said before, the room was so situated for its inmates to be completely retired from all observation.

Isabel Morland was furious. She had seen Sir Sydney's suppressed emotion, and, with the quickness of thought, connected that and Miss Harcourt's eager address with the floating rumours of Sir Sydney's early life; but that her insignificant, unfashionable cousin could be the heroine of the tale, and retain such hold of his recollection as to drive all her present fascinations from his mind, was a degradation not to be passively endured; in fact, it was impossible—she would not think about it—Sir Sydney should be caught yet; but at present there certainly was little hope of it. He had deserted her, and was in earnest, if not agitated, conversation with Miss Lucretia and Miss Wilhelmina Brown, who were listening and answering, and then gradually entering into detail, with so much interest, that all superficial folly gave way, for the time, before the real goodness of heart which they in general so strenuously contrived to conceal.

"Disagreeable, designing old women!" Isabel thought, "what can he see in them to hold his attention so chained? He shall not listen any longer," and she glided close to the sofa where the two were seated. Sir Sydney rose, and offered her his seat. No; she would rather stand. Sir Sydney bowed, and quietly sat down again. Something seemed the matter with Isabel's bracelet; she clasped and unclasped it vehemently, but the movement did not disturb the earnest conversation which Sir Sydney, in a low voice, still continued. The trinket broke, and fell at his feet. He gracefully raised and presented it, regretting the accident, and turned again to the Misses Brown. An exclamation of "What could have become of her beautiful bouquet?" was the young lady's next effort to recall the deserter to his allegiance; but Sir Sydney did not even seem to hear it, or, if he did, before he could make a move to seek it, it was presented to her by the officious Gussy, with a most malicious bow. Isabel did not quite throw it at his head, as inclination prompted, but in a very few seconds every flower lay in fragments at her feet; one beautiful exotic fell, uninjured, so close to Miss Wilhelmina, that she raised it with an expression of lamentation; but Isabel snatched it from her, and hastily stamped her pretty little foot upon it, with such a very unequivocal expression of temper, that Sir Sydney almost unconsciously fixed an astonished gaze upon her. It was too much to be borne quietly; she turned angrily away, sauntering through the rooms, deigning to hold converse with none, and would have so far sacrificed all propriety, as to enter the blue room to solve the mystery at once, had not Laura and Miss Harcourt at that instant reappeared. The countenance of the latter bore such evident traces of emotion, spite of the strong control she was practising, that Isabel was on the point of making some bitterly satirical remark, but those dark reproving eyes were again upon her, and Sir Sydney spoke before she did; but it was to Laura, not to her.

"Has my sister pleaded in vain, or may I indeed claim an old friend—and forgiveness?" he added, speaking the last word in so low a tone as only to be heard by his sister, Laura and Isabel. Laura's lip so quivered, that no word would come; but her hand was unhesitatingly placed in that which Sir Sydney so eagerly extended, and her eyes met his. He drew her arm in his, and led her, to all appearance, so easily and naturally to a quadrille that was forming, that few suspected more than that they had been old friends; and how strange it was they should meet there and then; and, if he should talk to her, and make her sing twice again, during the short remainder of the evening, it was nothing remarkable!

Isabel had thrown herself moodily on one of the sofas in the blue room, half concealed by the curtains of the window, trying, in vain, to connect Sir Sydney's conduct and the report of his former life. It seemed clear enough, but she would not believe it. There was nothing in his manner but old acquaintanceship: she would conquer him yet. How could Laura vie with her? Alas, for the delusion! Miss Harcourt's shawl, by the provident care of Miss Angelica, had been brought to the blue room, and there, with Laura, she repaired; the Misses Brown, in trio, assembled to do them great honour; and Isabel remained wholly unperceived. After being well shawled, Miss Harcourt disappeared with her body-guard of Browns. Sir Sydney, who had come ostensibly to hurry her, lingered—

"Laura! my own beloved! forgiven—loved through all! How could I doubt—how could I make myself and you so miserable? Can I ever repay you, even by a long life of love? If you but knew the remorse, the wretchedness I have endured, you would forgive still more," were the somewhat incoherent sentences that fell distinctly on Isabel's ear; and, though there was no answer, no words, she could see Sir Sydney's arm thrown round her cousin, and that she shrunk not from his parting kiss. Another moment, and both had disappeared; Sir Sydney to take such farewell of the really worthy women who had befriended his Laura, that he left them in perfect raptures; and Laura to fly to the security of her own room, where, burying her face in her hands, the tears burst forth like a torrent, giving relief, vent, calm to a heart which, though so sustained in grief, had been so unused to joy, that its presence had well-nigh prevented its realization.

Our readers must imagine all the various crosses and vexatious *contretemps* which had prevented Sir Sydney Harcourt from discovering Laura, as he had so ardently desired to do; for ours is a mere sketch, not a tale. They must recollect he had, only the last six months, returned from the West Indies, a residence in which had entirely frustrated his wishes for a reconciliation, even by letter; for, as we have said before, Mrs. Gascoigne's constant removals had prevented the possibility of any letter from such a distance finding them. When he had first loved her he was dependent on a coarse-minded, worldly relation, to whom an affection for a poor girl dared not be breathed. He had sought an appointment abroad, to escape a matrimonial connection which was being forced upon him, and he had wished Laura to consent to a private marriage, and accompany him abroad as the companion of his sister, who preferred daring the miseries of the West Indies with her brother, to remaining in England without him. Sir Sydney (then plain Sydney Harcourt, with little hope of the baronetcy and independence for many years), naturally of a fiery and somewhat jealous temper, materially increased from the privations and checks he was constantly enduring, chose to believe Laura's calm, reasoning indifference, and her refusal to leave her ailing mother, only a cover to reject his affection for that of some richer love. Time, his sister's representations, and the bitter pain of separation cooled these unjust suspicions, and he only recollected Laura's look of suffering and tone of suppressed agony, with which she had bade him farewell.

The unexpected demise of his relation, the baronetcy, and a moderate independency recalling him to England much sooner than he had dreamed of, every effort was put in force to find Laura, but in vain, till chance led him to Briarstone, and some magnetic instinct urged him to accept an invitation which it was more in his nature to have travelled some miles to avoid. He always declared his belief in mesmeric influences henceforward.

Isabel's schemes to prevent the course of true love from running smooth were fruitless. The old adage had already had its more than quantum of fulfilment, and Laura Gascoigne became Lady Harcourt before she was two months older. The delight and self-complacency of the Misses Brown were beyond description; Miss Lucretia looked grander, Miss Wilhelmina more gracious, and Miss Angelica more bustling than ever. An accession of pupils and boarders was almost the immediate consequence of Laura's marriage, and the fair fame of Red Rose Villa was so well established, as fortunately to receive no diminution from an affair which so scandalized Miss Brown, that she herself could not rally from it for months. After alternately encouraging Mr. Gustavus Brown and Mr. Gilbert Givevoice, till each gentleman so believed himself the favoured individual as to be ready to call his rival out, if he dared to deny it, Isabel Morland, one fine summer morning, eloped with an Italian emigrant count, who, much against Miss Brown's ideas of propriety, she would have to teach her Italian, leaving both lovers in the somewhat disagreeable predicament of having been most egregiously deceived and laughed at, at the very moment they were anticipating the *gold*, far more than the hand, of an heiress; and as such was the origin of their dreams and the source of their disappointment, we can better forgive Isabel's conduct to them, than we can her conduct to herself. Alas, indeed, for those whom Nature has so gifted, and over whom principle has no sway!

Gonzalvo's Daughter.

I.

"Constance, my child! take comfort; all is not lost to thee, though I must leave thee sooner than I expected," were the almost inarticulate words of a dying warrior, as, supported in the arms of an attendant, he bent over a beautiful girl who had flung herself on her knees beside his rude pallet, burying her face in his hand in all the abandonment of grief. It was a low-roofed, rudely-furnished chamber in the olden castle of Ruvo, supporting on its panelled walls and divisions of the ceiling many specimens of the warlike implements of the time. Shields of massive workmanship, with the overhanging helmet, the long sword, and *misericorde* or dagger, interspersed with spears and iron caps, were suspended on all sides; while jars and flasks, a bugle horn, an unsheathed sword and belt, and such like gear, were scattered on the floor. The dying man was stretched on the only couch the room afforded; a wooden pallet serving alike for bed and chair, one part of which was occupied by two of the warrior's men-at-arms, their eyes fixed alternately on their beloved commander and the fair being on whom his last thoughts seemed centred. On their left stood two venerable monks; the one holding aloft the cross, the other bearing on a silver salver the consecrated bread and wine, which the warrior had received in lowly faith, convinced his last moment was at hand. Two other armed figures, sturdy cavaliers, finished the group. Individual sorrow was deepened by the thought, that with Duke Manfred died the last lingering hopes of Naples. He had refused to follow his brother, the voluntarily-exiled monarch Frederic, to the court of France, hoping still to preserve his ill-fated country from being trampled on, even if its liberty were gone; struggling against Spain, and her great captain, simply because he thought France less likely to look on Naples as a slave, though for him individually life had lost all joy—for he felt his country would never again rise, beautiful and free, as she had been. Mortally wounded in an unexpected skirmish with the Spaniards, Manfred would yet have met death calmly, if not willingly, had not the deep grief of the fair girl, who had clung to him as to a second father—preferring to linger by his side in the roughest part of Naples, to accompanying her own royal parent to the luxurious court of Louis—distracted him to the forgetfulness of all, save how to comfort her. He knew it was no small loss she mourned;—the young, impoverished, yet noble Luigi Vincenzio, to whom the first freshness of her young affections had been given, with all the fervid warmth of an Italian heart, was dear to Manfred as his own son, and he had promised to plead for Vincenzio with her father, in lieu of the gay Duke de Nemours, whom Frederic favoured, but whom Constance instinctively abhorred. No marvel the words of the dying man fell vainly and discordantly upon her ear,—that she clung to him as if that wild embrace should fetter life within;—he should not, must not leave her! Fainter and fainter became the voice of Manfred, —and then all was silent, save the convulsive sobs of the kneeling girl, whose tears had so bedewed the rough hand she clasped that she knew not how cold it grew, and the deep yet suppressed breathings of those around. A quick step made its way through the groups of mourning Neapolitans, who thronged the chamber, and a tall manly form stood reverentially and mournfully beside the pallet.

"Alas! alas! too late,—he has gone! his look, his voice of kindly blessing—all denied me! Constance! my beloved!"

The voice aroused her; she started to her feet, looked shudderingly on the face of the dead, and then sinking in the arms of Vincenzio, wept less painfully upon his bosom. But, brief as was that upward glance, it displayed a face so youthful, and of such touching loveliness, that tears should have been strangers there; childlike as it was, yet there was something in its sweet expression which told the threshold of life was past; she had looked beyond, and tasted the magic draught whose first drop transforms the being, and influences the whole of after life. Her rich golden hair hung loose and dishevelled over her pale cheek, and her deep blue beautifully-formed eye was swollen with weeping, yet she was lovely despite of all.

But short communion was allowed the youthful pair, for the last wish of the dying warrior had been that his niece should seek the convent of St. Alice, twenty miles distant, there to remain till happier hours dawned for Naples, or she could more securely rejoin her father.

"Yes, better there than lingering here, where Nemours may deem himself privileged to seek thee when he lists," resumed the young Neapolitan, when his words of gentle soothing had had effect, and Constance was comforted. "Sweetest! it shall be but a very brief farewell; the thought that thou art in safety shall soothe the hours of absence, and thou wilt promise to think of me—my own!"

"Think of thee!" she repeated, and a smile lit up that sweet face, till to say in which it looked more lovely, smiles or tears, would have been difficult. "There is no need to make me promise that, my Luigi; I could not, if I would, think of aught other, save" (her voice faltered) "of the kind heart gone!" She paused a moment, then added, sorrowfully, "My father, my poor father! I should wish to join him—yet I cannot. Luigi, dearest Luigi, 'tis my turn to chide now, if thou lookest doubtingly and sad; our best friend has gone! Oh, we cannot weep too long for him! yet, canst thou think if Frederic knew whom his Constance loved he would still deny her? No! no! smile on me, love, and trust me, Constance of Naples will have none other lord but thee."

He did trust her; and the brief period left them passed in such sweet and hopeful converse, that sorrow itself was soothed, and both were strengthened for the parting hour.

Luigi himself headed the gallant little troop of native warriors, collected to convey her with all honour to the convent. He dreaded that Nemours, obtaining notice of the intended movement, would attempt the capture of the princess by force, and otherwise annoy them; but to his surprise not a trace of the French army awaited them.

Quartered as they were almost all over Calabria, generally presenting their steel fronts as strong lines of defence for the towns and castles round, this desertion appeared extraordinary; particularly as their aim had been to incapacitate the Spaniards from leaving their entrenchments within the fortified city of Barletta, twelve miles to the south of Ruvo, where they were at present quartered.

Night was falling when Vincenzio returned to Ruvo; but there was still light enough for him to distinguish more than usual military bustle within the walls; soldiers were hurrying to and fro; arms were burnishing; lances and swords sharpening; large fires blazing up; bands of armed men assembling; the heavy harness and unsheathed weapons forming in heaps and lines to be donned and grasped at a moment's warning. Anxious and curious, Vincenzio hastened to the quarters of the Sire de La Palice, governor of the town, and found him, though joyous and laughter-loving as was his wont, alternately giving orders to several officers, who seemed to appear and disappear with a glance, and muttering oaths and execrations on some extraordinary act of folly, the nature of which, or by whom committed, Luigi found some difficulty in comprehending.

Our limits will not permit our becoming personally acquainted with La Palice, which a conversation might accomplish. We must confine ourselves to a brief relation of historical facts. It appeared that the inhabitants of Castellanata, enraged beyond all measure at the licentious and insulting conduct of the French troops quartered in their vicinity, had risen in sudden revolt, and finally betrayed the town into the hands of the Spaniards. Nemours, thinking more of his own dignity, which he imagined had been outraged in this revolt, than of the real interests of his sovereign, swore the most signal vengeance, and marched his whole force northward, disregarding the representations of more experienced officers, that it would be the height of folly to leave all Calabria unguarded, for the reduction of one paltry town. The character of Gonzalvo was too well known to admit a thought of his neglecting this opportunity of attack; and La Palice therefore, on his part, determined to be on the alert, though he guessed not how soon or whence the attack would come.

There were many sad thoughts on the young Neapolitan's heart, as he returned to his own chamber. Alas! it little signified to Naples who were her masters, French or Spaniards; but he recalled that period of his country's brief prosperity, when the celebrated Captain Gonzalvo had been his monarch's guest and honoured friend, and grieved that Frederic had chosen France, instead of Spain, for refuge; perhaps his instinctive hatred to Nemours, as the encouraged aspirant to the hand of his Constance, increased these regrets; but still to La Palice he was bound by all the chivalric ties of military companionship, and he determined, if danger threatened, to forget his nationality awhile, and fight in his friend's defence.

The night was peculiarly mild and lovely; and the soft

silvery halo flung down from the full moon on the clustering olives and vineyards, stretching beneath the young Italian's window, over some miles of fertile country, seemed to whisper tranquillity and peace, that war had not yet disturbed; and Luigi looked forth lingeringly till the calm sank into his own soul, and Constance alone stood forth amid those troubled visions like a star gleaming through clouds on the trembling waves.

It was near daybreak ere he sought his couch and slept; but not for long. One pale streak of dawn alone was visible; but there were sounds on the still air little in accordance with the lingering night. A dull, heavy, monotonous roar, as of a continued cannonade close at hand, was accompanied by sharp, vivid flashes of light playing athwart the casement; then followed the roll of many drums,—the shout "to arms,"—"the foe! the foe!"—the clash of the alarum bell—the heavy trampling of a hundred feet—the shrill shrieks of woman's terror, and other sounds of tumult and war. Vincenzio listened a moment as one still dreaming; but then La Palice's warning flashing on his mind, he sprang to his feet and glanced beneath him. Far, far as his eye could reach, trampling down that fair scene of fertility and peace, there came band after band of armed men, rolling onward in such dense masses, that he felt at a glance resistance was in vain. Marvellous as it seemed, Gonzalvo de Cordova himself was upon them; and that name in its mighty eloquence was paralysing terror! A very brief interval sufficed to banish every thought from Luigi's mind but fears for La Palice, by whose side he speedily was. The noise waxed louder, closer, but there was no trace of disturbance, or even anxiety, on the governor's open brow, as he gaily marshalled his little band of three hundred lances, to throw themselves into the first breach which Gonzalvo's unceasing cannonade was rapidly making in the walls.

"Ha! welcome, comrade mine!" he cried, grasping Vincenzio's hand. "Mark La Palice as a true prophet, and Nemours the most egregious blockhead that ever wrote himself a man. Ha! all compact there; ready! that's well—to the right, forward!" and on they rushed through the town. Already every wall was manned, and showers of arrows and stones galled the Spaniards at every turn, but had no power on the immense mass at work against the ramparts. Already the walls were tottering, falling, borne down by the heavy cannonade. On the opposite side the walls had been scaled, and Spanish and

French fought hand to hand on the summit. A yell of triumph soon after proclaimed the formation of an immense breach, into which Gonzalvo himself and his choicest troops poured like a mountain torrent, increasing, swelling, as it came, as if utterly to overwhelm the compact little phalanx which La Palice threw forward to oppose him. A very brief struggle sufficed to show how fruitless was every effort of the French; the immense odds speedily forced the breach; but still, hemmed in on all sides so closely that their swords had scarcely room for full play, there was no word of surrender or defeat; struggling only to preserve their honour in their death, man after man fell, without yielding an inch, around his leader. Presently wilder and more deafening sounds arose; mingling indiscriminately the roar of artillery, the clang of steel, the rush of a hundred chargers, the shrill shrieks of women, so that not one could be distinguished from another. The town was forced, and every street, for a brief interval, became the scene of combat. Another hour, and the strife was at an end. La Palice, who had striven as if his individual efforts could avert defeat, had been overwhelmed with numbers, and brought to the ground with the crushing blow of a battle-axe; yet even then, with his own gay laugh, he flung his sword over the heads of his captors, that none should claim him as an individual prize. Vincenzio shared his fate, the capture of his friend removing from him all inclination to prolong the fruitless combat, and yet more exasperate the Spaniards against his ill-fated countrymen.

The close of that day beheld Ruvo deserted; the heavy banner of Spain waving above the ruined ramparts alone marked what had been; for the riches of Ruvo,—gold, treasure, horses and arms, the French prisoners, almost all of whom were badly wounded, and the principal Neapolitan citizens, were conveyed under strong detachments to Barletta, the head-quarters of the great captain and his troops.

II.

Twenty-four hours after his daring reduction of Ruvo, Gonzalvo de Cordova was seated in one of the best furnished apartments of Barletta, bearing little traces either of the eager warrior or sagacious general; all other emotions merged in that one which, even in his glorious campaigns, reigned uppermost—love for the lovely, the transcendent being, who, in woman's freshest, most beautiful prime, was seated at his feet, her arm reclining caressingly on his knee, and her dark, splendid orbs, all their flashing passion stilled in filial love, fixed on his face as he narrated his last triumph. It was his daughter Elvira, for whom so deep was the hero's love, that even in his foreign wars she was never known to be parted from his side.

"Trust me, they shall be seen to, my father," she said, in answer to his entreaty that her woman's tenderness and care would look to the comfort of his wounded prisoners, whom he had already luxuriously installed, with his own surgeon to attend them. "La Palice is in truth a champion to gain guerdon of woman's care."

"But not of woman's heart, my gentle one; thine must not pass to the wardance of our foes."

"Nor shall it, father; it is thine, all thine!" and the rich burning flush resting on her cheek as she spoke, was deemed by her father but the glow of sunset which played around her. He kissed her fondly, vowing he would accept such devotedness only till another and a dearer sought it. "Find but one deserving of thy love, my child, and no selfish pangs shall bid me keep thee by my side; yet, methinks, thou as myself art difficult to please; the noblest and the best have bowed to thee in vain,—thy heart was ice to all, and selfish as I am, I have rejoiced it was so."

Her face was buried in his hand, and he saw not how painfully its colour varied. He did not feel the full quick throb of that maiden heart: if her fond father penetrated not its secret, how may we?

In obedience to Gonzalvo's command (in those days no strange one), Elvira, attended by her women, herself visited the apartments of the wounded prisoners, administered to their wants, superintended the healing of their wounds, speaking words of comfort and of hope, till—veiled as she was, her rank, even her name often unknown—the sound of her voice, the touch of her gentle hand, were hailed by each sufferer with such feelings of devotion and gratitude, as might have marked her indeed the angel visitant their fevered fancies deemed her.

"And I have seen all?—thou art sure none other needs my tending?" she asked of an attendant. "Methinks those rooms we have not visited."

"There are no prisoners of moment there, lady; but one

room tenanted;—a poor Italian—Neapolitan, I should say—who, as he may bring little honour and less ransom to our leader's coffers, scarce needs your gracious care; he will do well enough."

"Peace, slave! it is well Gonzalvo hears you not;" he crouched beneath her flashing scorn. "Poor—friendless; the more he needs his captor's care: lead on!"

She was obeyed, and the apartment gained. A young man was reclining on a rude couch—his limbs stretched out, his head bent forward, resting on his arm in all the abandonment of complete repose; his long jetty hair had fallen as partly to shade his face, but there was just enough visible of his cheek and brow to startle by their ghastly whiteness, gleaming out in fearful contrast with the crimson cloak he had drawn around him. The opening of the door had not aroused him, and a moment the intruders paused; there was a start, a quick and choking breath, as if respiration had been suddenly impeded; and the Lady Elvira stood beside the slumberer, and lifted the damp curls from his brow. Why did she so pause, so stand, pale, rigid, breathless?—feared she to break those peaceful slumbers?—if so, her caution was in vain: the young man started, looked wildly round, then heavily and painfully arose, as if conscious he was in the presence of rank and beauty, and struggled to give them homage.

"Nay, fair sir, we come to thee as leech, not queen, and must refuse all homage but obedience," the lady said, calmly. "We must condemn thee to thy couch, not to thy knee."

"Who is it that speaks? Lady, that voice comes to my ear laden with happy memories, bringing a vision of one whose faintest smile was chivalry's best fame—aye, e'en to Naple's sons."

"And is it marvel, Signor Vincenzio, the daughter of Gonzalvo should be with her father still, though Naples no longer calls him friend? Nay, we have refused thine homage, as little suited to thy weakness, gentle sir. Resign thee for a brief while to the leech's art, and take comfort; Gonzalvo wars with France, not Naples. We will visit thee again."

Luigi Vincenzio rose from his knee, where he had sunk simply in greeting to one whose resplendent gifts in happier days had excited his young imagination in no ordinary degree; and the calm unimpassioned posture in which he stood till she departed, betrayed no warmer feelings than reverence and admiration. Days passed, merging into weeks; but long before that period, Luigi Vincenzio was not only convalescent, but permitted and enabled to roam at large about Barletta and its environs; unguarded, even by his parole. Whence came this extraordinary indulgence none knew; but all supposed, that as the great captain had repeatedly declared he warred not with the Neapolitans—not at least with those who chose to accept his friendship, and own the supremacy of his sovereigns, Ferdinand and Isabella—the young nobleman had accepted these conditions, and had been thus received into favour. Again, as had been the case before the capture of Ruvo, chivalric games agreeably diversified the dull routine of military duty. Nemours, overcome with shame, at the consequences of his own folly, had retired to Canosa; and as Gonzalvo had not received the expected reinforcements, enabling him to change his mode of attack to the offensive, his officers, and many of the Neapolitans friendly to his interests, entered with spirit into all their general's plans for military recreation, while the Lady Elvira resumed her station, as queen of the revels, crowning the victor with her own fair hands. Her influence had led Vincenzio there; she rallied him on his deep gloom, playfully demanding why he alone should scorn the prize she gave; he had professed such deep gratitude for the tender care she had so silently lavished on his sufferings, soothing him by the charm of her voice to health, more powerfully than the leech's art, and yet he refused such trifling boon. And he obeyed; he joined the combatants, received bright wreaths of glory from her hand, and lingered by her side, but the smile she sought was not upon his lips; her step, her voice, however unexpected, had no power to flush his cheek, or light his eye with joy; but his to her!—the *echo* of *his* footstep, the faintest whisper of *his* voice, as the smouldering fire in the bosom of the volcano, seeming so still, so silent, till, roused to whelming might, they lay upon her heart.

Fiercely and terribly the thunder-cloud of wrath had gathered on the brow of Gonzalvo de Cordova, as with heavy strides he paced his private cabinet about a month after Ruvo's capture. He chafed not at fair and open fight, nay, gloried in the heat, the toil, the press of war; but conspiracy, treachery, or that which in the present excited state of his mind he deemed as such, he could not brook. A plot had been discovered—ill formed, ill digested. but if correct in its details, in the names of its principals, involving many of those whom Gonzalvo had treated and trusted as friends—amid the Neapolitans to throw off the yoke of the Spaniards, to be free, and preserve their liberty at the sword's point, till seconded by other cities, and encouraged by Nemours' inactivity, Frederic himself might be recalled; this seemed their object, pledged to by the most solemn oaths. Gonzalvo's name was found upon their lists of victims, but all was dark and little tangible. Still warrants had been issued; those supposed the principal conspirators arrested and secured; and the great captain now chafed and fumed, unwilling to believe the whole tale true, from the heavy judgment it demanded, yet feeling to the full the tremendous responsibility devolved upon himself.

"My father! God in heaven! the tale is not false, then—yet—yet, they have dared to connect the innocent! Luigi—Vincenzio—he is not, he cannot be, of these! speak—speak, in mercy!" and the proud, the majestic daughter of Spain, whom it had seemed no human power, no human emotion could bow, sunk in powerless agony on the earth, grasping the robe of her father, and gazing on his face, as if her life depended on his answer. Startled, amazed, Gonzalvo, who had been unconscious that for several minutes she had been in his presence reading his brow, ere she found words, vainly sought to raise and soothe her; she reiterated but those words, her tone becoming wilder and shriller in its agony, as the reply was evidently evaded.

"Aye, even he!" at length it came, and Gonzalvo sternly pointed to the young nobleman's name upon the list. "Elvira, Gonzalvo's daughter! away with this engrossing weakness; well it is for thee, none but thy father marks it. I have heard, and in return for that kind confidence would, had the fates decreed, have sought, fixed, gloried in thy happiness, though the choice had been other than mine own; but now—with this damning proof. My child! my child! away with the unworthy weakness; it shall not so debase thee!"

"Weak! debased! who dares to say these words to me—to me? Am I not still Elvira? she sprang to her feet, standing erect in all her majesty, but with cheeks of marble whiteness, gleaming out from that night-black hair, as if their rich current had rushed back to her heart. "What is it they said—that he was guilty?—false! 'tis false! yet if 'tis not—misled—misguided—father, is there no pardon?—there must—there SHALL be. What is his doom? speak! there is no weakness now!"

"Death. or the galleys!—what else befits the ingrate

traitors?" in a deep concentrated voice the answer came. "Ha! Holy Virgin! my child! my child!" She had tottered —fallen—and lay without voice or motion at his feet.

III.

Luigi Vincenzio denied none of the charges brought against him, save that of the intended murder of the principal Spaniards in Italy. Such baseness he strenuously denied; they had decoyed him into the conspiracy, working on all his peculiar feelings of love of land and of his exiled king; who was not alone regally but personally dear to him. The conspiracy appeared to him but a noble effort of some few bold hearts to throw off the hated yoke of the foreigner; and therefore he had joined it, and even now, in danger of death, of worse than death—the galleys, he persisted in the glory, the virtue of his cause. It was rumoured that Gonzalvo, in his still continued desire to conciliate the Neapolitan nobles had offered to Vincenzio, not alone pardon but riches, and connection by marriage with one of the most powerful and noble families of Castile, though its name never transpired, if he would take a solemn oath to be true to the interests of Ferdinand of Arragon, and never seek Naples again, save in pursuance of that monarch's interests; and these offers, more than usually magnanimous even for Gonzalvo, were, to the utter bewilderment of all, refused.

Scarcely a week after Vincenzio's arrest, the unusually strict retirement of the Lady Elvira was disturbed by an earnest petition for a private interview, on the part of a Neapolitan boy, who, the attendant said, had been so urgent, and appeared so exhausted, that he could not refuse him entrance. He would not tell his business to any save the Lady Elvira. Permission was given, and he was conducted to her presence, clothed in a coarse folding cloak of Neapolitan cloth, with the red picturesque cap of the country slouched upon his brow. He stood at the threshold of the apartment, his arms folded in his mantle, his hand bent on his breast, as if either physical or mental strength had for the moment utterly failed him. "Retire," was the first word that met his ear; and he perceived that Lady Elvira addressed her attendants, who still lingered. "Retire, all of you. The boy asked a private audience, and I have promised it. Treachery! danger!—I fear them not !—begone !" and they obeyed. One searching glance the boy cast around, and ere the lady could address him, he had darted across the room, and flung himself at her feet, clasping her knees with the convulsive grasp of agony, struggling for words, but so ineffectually that nought but quivering anguish convulsed those parched lips, nought but agonized sobs found vent. Mantle and cap had both fallen in the quickness of the movement, and though the inner dress was still the boy's, that exquisite face, that swelling bosom told a different tale.

" Ha ! who art thou ? What wouldst thou ?—speak, silly trembler," and even at the moment that an indescribable thrill passed through the heart of Gonzalvo's daughter, she struggled to speak playfully. " In sooth, thou art too lovely to wander forth alone, save in this strange guise ; speak—what is thy boon ?

" A life ! a life they say is forfeited ! Lady, kind, generous lady, oh, have mercy ! I thought I had words to plead his cause, to beseech, implore, adjure thee, but I have none—none !—Mercy, oh, have mercy !"

" Mercy ! I am no sovereign to give life or death, poor child ! How may I serve thee, and whom is it thou wouldst save ?"

" Art thou not Elvira ?—art thou not Gonzalvo's daughter ?—and will he not pardon at thy word ? Oh, seek him ! Tell him Constance, princess of Naples, is in his power ! yields herself his prisoner, to be dealt with as he lists, let him but spare Luigi—Luigi, my own noble love ! Give him but pardon, life, liberty ! Lady, lady ! plead for him ! let them hold me prisoner in his stead. Wherefore lookest thou thus ? Mercy, oh, have mercy—save him !"

" WHOM saidst thou, girl ? WHOM wouldst thou save ?—speak, I command thee !" exclaimed Elvira, in a voice so changed, so unnatural, that Constance shuddered, vainly endeavouring to shrink from the heavy hand that grasped her shoulders, the eyes that flashed upon her, as if fire had dwelt within their depths. " As thou hopest for mercy, speak !"

" Save ! whom but my own, my plighted lord ! Is there one in the wide world to love me now as Luigi—Luigi Vincenzio, he who hath honoured Constance with his troth ? Oh, save—"

" Love ! thou DAREST not tell me that he loves thee !—false—false—he does *not* love thee !" She sprang up, cheek, lip, brow, flushing for a single instant crimson, then fading into a white so ghastly, it seemed as if life itself must have passed, save for the mighty passion which held it chained.

"Thee! one like thee, poor foolish child! art thou one to bid Luigi Vincenzio love, to hold his heart enchained? Yet thou art lovely, good God of Heaven, how exquisitely lovely! Poor child, poor child, I have appalled thee!—does he so love thee?" She had sunk back on the cushion, her hands convulsively pressed together, as to conceal their trembling, but the wild light of those eyes, now still movelessly fixed on Constance, who had risen from that posture of entreaty, as if the deep emotion of another had stilled her into composure.

"Love me! yes, as none but Luigi can love; daughter of a ruined, a persecuted house, with little to make me worthy of such love, yet doth he love me, as I in truth were all in all to him, as he is all to me—love me! Oh! did they bid me die, or wander forth an exile, an outcast, like all of my race, yet queens might envy Constance for Luigi Vincenzio's love!"

"And thou wouldst save him?"

"Aye, with my life—with all that they may deem precious. Constance of Naples is no common prize; 'tis said, Ferdinand would give a jewel from his coronet for all of Frederic's unhappy offspring placed within his power; I am here; bid Gonzalvo send me a state prisoner, as he so nobly did my brother. Ha! lady, noble lady, forgive the word; 'tis not for the captive, the suppliant, to arraign the captor and the judge. Grief makes the speech unwary—heed it not, heed it not; take my life, my liberty for his!"

"Constance of Naples, thou mayst save both! Gonzalvo wars not with women!" The princess threw herself at her feet, with a wild cry of gratitude: the strangeness of that voice, the rigid expression of that face, she heeded not, knew not, she only dreamed of hope.

"Aye, but I have not said *how*, girl; pardon, life, liberty, all have been offered to him for whom thou pleadest, on the sole condition of swearing allegiance to Ferdinand, fealty to Spain."

"And he hath refused," she interrupted; "oh! give me entrance to him—I will plead, kneel, move not from his feet till he hath done this; he will submit for me, he will hear me, live for Constance—let me but plead."

"Peace! there is more; he must be naturalized in Spain, WED one of her noblest daughters, aye, one that LOVES him; let him do this, and he shall have life, riches, honour, all that can make life glad. Ha! dost thou fail? bid him do this, and he shall live."

"Yes, even this!" was the reply, after one single moment's pause; and the quivering lip, the ashy cheek, the trembling frame, alone betrayed that young heart's agony. "Let Luigi Vincenzio be free, be happy—for if she whom he must wed in truth thus love him, the dream of his youth will fade beneath the glory of his manhood, and he shall, he must be blessed—if such things be, what recks it that Constance droops alone? I shall have saved him, have given him back to life, to his fellows, to honour, to glory, and my death will be happy, oh! so happy! Lady, I will do this."

"Death! who spoke of death for thee? bid Luigi thus accept his life, and thine is secured, is free."

"Free! speakest thou of love, yet dreamest thou life could exist apart from him—peace, peace—let me but save him, let him but live, give me but admission to his presence, let me but speak with him. Lady, lady, wherefore tarry? I will do this, take me but to him."

"Thou wilt SWEAR?" That low terrible whisper was a more fearful index of passionate agony in the speaker than even that which crushed her who stood in such meek, mournful, yet heroic suffering before her: one only feeling prompted Constance, but in Elvira it was the fierce contest of the evil and the good; one whelming passion struggling for dominion over all that had been so fair, so bright, so beautiful before.

"Swear to sacrifice my all of selfish bliss for him? aye, without one moment's pause! Oh! lady, thou knowest not love, if thou deemest it needs oath to hallow that which I have said. If thou doubtest me, bid one thou mayst trust, be witness of my truth; but oh! keep me no longer from him; let me save his life!"

Without a word or notice in reply, the Lady Elvira sat a moment in deep thought, then rose, and signed to the princess to follow her.

IV.

The prison of Luigi Vincenzio had been changed from the dark loathsome dungeon, in which he had first been cast, to a low-roofed, rambling apartment, in that wing of the citadel of Barletta which generally served as a barrack for infantry.

An iron grating, however, running in the centre from roof to floor, cut the chamber in two, one portion generally serving as a guardroom, when any important prisoner demanded unusual care. This annoyance had been spared Vincenzio; although the evening following the interview above described about ten soldiers were then assembled, occupying the farthest corner of the chamber, grouped in a circle enjoying their pipes and cups, seasoned by many a jest, which effectually turned their attention alike from their own officer and their prisoner. The former, closely muffled in a military cloak, and cap, with a heavy plume of black feathers, stood leaning against the stone pillar to which the grating was affixed by thick iron rings, parted only by that open railing from the prisoner, and consequently enabled not alone to hear all that passed between him and the lovely being whom he was holding convulsively to his breast, but to mark every change in the countenance of each.

What had already passed between those loving ones it is needless to record; nor the deep suffocating emotion which had for several minutes utterly deprived Vincenzio of voice, when his Constance so strangely, so unexpectedly sprang into his arms. What cared he now that his guards were present; that she was not permitted to see him alone, save to smile at Gonzalvo's idle fear that she could bring him means to escape? He felt nothing but her presence, drinking in for the first few moments the sweet faint accents of her beloved voice, as if nothing of ill or misery could touch him more. But soon, oh! how much too soon, the sweet dream fled, and but one truth remained—that he was doomed to death, to close his eyes on that beloved one, and for ever! A shudder had convulsed his frame, a deep groan had been wrung from him by that thought, and Constance had heard and guessed its import. She knew not at first what she said, but one thought, one feeling, one stern necessity was distinct upon her mind; all else was confused and painful, as if a dark cloud had folded up her brain, leaving nought clear but the letters of fire in which that one stern necessity was written.

"And dost thou indeed, in very deed, so love me, Luigi? Oh! then thou wilt grant my boon; thou wilt not let thy Constance plead to thee in vain," said she, after many, many minutes had rolled by, unheeded in that sad commune, and she lifted up her pale and mournful face, as the white rose that, bent by some heavy storm, droops its lovely head to earth, ere one leaf had lost its freshness.

"Boon—in vain. Constance, mine own sweet love, is there aught thou canst ask Luigi will deny?"

"Ah! thou knowest not the weight of that I crave; nor will I speak it on thy simple word. Thou must pledge it me, my love; aye, by solemn oath—by hallowed vow—I claim it on thy love, thy fealty, and how mayst thou refuse me?"

Playfully he besought her to speak it first, and then, dreaming not her object, unconscious even that the offered conditions were known to her, he knelt at her feet, and placing his hands between both hers, which felt strangely and fearfully cold, he solemnly swore to do her bidding, whatever it might be. The words were said, and Constance sank upon his bosom.

"Saved! saved! oh, I have saved thee, Luigi; thou wilt live—be free—thou shalt not die!"

He started to his feet; the whole truth bursting on his mind, and yet, if so, why did she so cling to him, as if he were spared to *her?* no, no, it could not be. "Live, Constance, my blessed one, what canst thou mean? my life is forfeited!"

"No, no, no!" she reiterated, "it is granted to thee, and on conditions easy to accept. Luigi! thou hast sworn to grant my boon—to do my bidding; and I bid thee live! live, to be happy, glorious, as I know thou wilt be! Speak not; hear me. Frederic is no longer a king; Naples no longer a kingdom; she is parcelled out to others; she hath no sons—no name—one hour acknowledging the rights of France, the next bowed to the arms of Spain. To one or other of these mighty potentates she must belong. My poor, poor father can never claim her more. Luigi, my own Luigi, banish the vain hope of her freedom—her future influence. Were Frederic here, thou knowest he would say to thee, as he did to all when he departed, 'My children, 'tis vain to struggle; make peace with whom ye will; Frederic absolves you of your allegiance. No oath of fealty restrains you.' Hast thou forgotten this? no, no; then wherefore shouldst thou pause; many have bowed to Louis, why not to Ferdinand? Luigi, my own Luigi, thou shalt live!"

"Constance," he answered, and he drew her closer to his bosom, while his whole frame shook, "Constance, were this the sole condition, for thy sake, beloved, I had not paused—even thus I would have lived; for this poor, unhappy country, I feel, will never rise again; such oath reflects no shame upon her sons. Constance, was this all they told thee?"

"Luigi, no; there is another—we must part—for ever! Yet—yet, I bid thee live." Slowly every word fell; but so distinctly, so expressively, that despite that low gasping tone, he heard them all, and not he alone.

"Ha! thou knowest this. Part, Constance! and thou bidst me live! I choose death instead. I will not lose thee; I will not wed another."

"Thou wilt—thou shalt! Luigi, Luigi, 'twill be but a brief, brief pang, followed by years of bliss. Oh! do not think this moment's agony will never, never pass away. The hero's glory,—the warrior's fame,—the statesman's pride—all, all, shall be thine own. Ambition, with her hundred paths to immortality, shall lure thee to forgetfulness, and then to peace; and she—she, who will be thy bride,—oh, if she love thee, as they say she does, even she at length will woo thee into joy. Luigi, my own, my own, why dost thou turn from me? Speak, oh, speak; tell me thou wilt live!" She sunk on her knees before him, as if that action should continue the entreaty for which voice for the moment had utterly failed.

"Constance, Constance! Dost thou urge me? Thou—wilt *thou* give me to another? Is it *thou* who bidst me thus be happy? No, no; thou knowest not how much I love thee!"

"Do I not love thee, Luigi?—Oh! it is only thus that I can save thee,—only thus they will grant thy life—and what care I for my happiness? Luigi, if thou diest, how mayst thou love me—guard me as thou wouldst? Oh, live, live! —in my lonely convent cell let me think of thee as I know thou wilt be,—honoured, loved—aye, and in time so blessed! Let the bright thought be mine,—that I, even I, poor, simple Constance, have saved thee. Luigi, deny me not this, turn not away. Thou canst not refuse me,—thou DAREST not—thou art SWORN!"

The countenance of Vincenzio became more and more terribly agitated,—he struggled to break from her hold; but the grasp of agony was upon his cloak, and either held him with a giant strength, or his every limb had lost its power, and chained him there. He sought to speak; but only unintelligible murmurs came, and again that voice of impassioned appeal came upon his heart, crushing it almost to madness. It bade him live; she might need his friendship, though denied his love, when time permitted such intercourse innocently to both. That tall form bowed, as stricken by a mighty wind: a moment, and he had caught her to his bosom, had murmured some inarticulate words, and a burst of passionate weeping convulsed his frame. Ere the paroxysm passed, he was alone; soldiers, officers, Constance, all were gone.

V.

It was noon; the brilliant sun of Italy poured its golden flood through the high pointed casements of a small private chapel, in the citadel of Barletta, which had been set apart for the sole use of Gonzalvo de Cordova, his family, and personal attendants. It was lavishly decorated, seeming in all points well suited to the establishment of the great captain. Heavy brocades, worked in gold and silver, hung from the walls, shading many a shrine, of the same precious metals, where saints, Virgin, and Saviour were all blazing in gems. A cloth of gold covered the altar, which stood just beneath a gorgeously-painted window, that when lighted up, as now, with the sun of noon, flung down the most brilliant colouring on floor and wall. This day a rich carpet of superb Genoa velvet covered the mosaic pavement at the foot of the altar, and decorated cushions seemed to denote that some unusual ceremony was then to be performed; while the number of sumptuously-attired nobles, Spanish, French, and Neapolitan, already assembled, and the private chaplain of Gonzalvo, missal in hand, behind the altar, with his priestly attendants, proclaimed the hour at hand. The great captain himself was present, magnificently attired, leaning on his jewel-hilted sword, wrapt, it seemed, by the fixed repose of his countenance, in deep meditation, which none present chose to interrupt.

The interest increased tenfold when, attended, or rather guarded—few could tell which—Luigi Vincenzio, attired with some care, but deadly pale, bearing an expression of fearful internal agony on his countenance, slowly advanced up the choir to the altar. The gaze of Gonzalvo moved not from him; serious it was, yet scarcely stern, and the tone was calm in which he said, "We have heard, Signor Vincenzio, you accept the conditions proposed!—have we heard aright?" Luigi simply bowed his head in answer, imagining the oath of fealty to Ferdinand, and denial of Frederic, would next be administered; but it came not, silence reigned again uninterrupted as before. Then came sounds along the corridor; the folding doors at the base of the chapel were flung wide open, and the

Lady Elvira, more than usually majestic in mien and carriage, entered, followed by several attendants; her resplendent beauty was heightened by an expression of countenance none could define, save that it affected the most indifferent spectator then present with a species of awe, of veneration, that could have bowed every knee in unfeigned homage. Stars of diamonds glittered in her raven hair, and sparkled down the bodice and front of her dark velvet robe. The first glance of all rested immovably, seemingly fascinated, on her; the next turned on the slight figure she led forward; but every curious effort to discover the stranger's identity, was rendered vain by the thick shrouding veil which completely enveloped her; permitting nothing but the tiny foot and exquisitely-turned ankle to be visible.

A strong shudder had convulsed the form of Vincenzio; he tried to step forward, to speak, but all power appeared to forsake him, till a voice, sweet, clear, and silvery, uttered the simple words "I will," the customary rejoinder to the priest's demand, "wilt thou accept this man as thy wedded lord," and its attendant vows to "love, honour, and obey." The voice thrilled through him, awakening him to consciousness, he knew not how or why; and he saw he was kneeling before the altar, beside that veiled and shrouded form by whom Gonzalvo and his daughter were both standing, as if from their hands he received her. Gradually everything became distinct; La Palice was at his side, his hand upon his shoulder, as if rousing him from that deadening stupor. He recognised his friends amidst that noble group standing around. Had the marriage vow been administered to him? If so he must have replied, or the ceremony could not have continued, but he knew not that he had spoken; and what had in fact aroused him?—a voice!—whose voice?—to whom was he irrevocably joined? Not that one whom his fevered fancy had so wildly pictured, for she stood there looking on the ceremony, as calm and motionless as the most indifferent spectator.

It was over. Vincenzio and his nameless bride rose from their knees, and then it was the hands of Gonzalvo removed the veil and led her forward, that the eyes of all might rest with admiration on the loveliness disclosed. A cry of astonishment burst simultaneously from the French prisoners and Neapolitans around, and the latter rushed forward and prostrated themselves before her, clasping her robe, her feet, 'mid sobs and tears calling on heaven to bless the daughter of their king, the being whom from her cradle they had well-nigh worshipped—the Princess Constance! but one alone stood speechless; one alone had no power to go forward, for all seemed to him a dream, whose bewildering light and bliss would be for ever lost in darkness. But as those eyes turned on him, that radiant glance sought his, there was one sob, one choking cry, and Luigi had bounded forward, had clasped her to his heart. And then he would have flung himself at Gonzalvo's feet, to pour out the burdening load of gratitude that almost crushed him with its magnitude, but Gonzalvo, grasping his hand in the friendly pressure of sympathy, forbade all speech till he had been heard.

"It has been said," he exclaimed, "that to the King of Naples and his ill-fated family Gonzalvo de Cordova is incapable of generosity, or even of humanity; because the stern mandate of his sovereign demanded the sacrifice of his own private sentiments of generosity and honour, and compelled the captivity of Frederic's heir. My friends, I plead no excuse, no defence for this dark deed; but now that nought but Gonzalvo's own heart may dictate, I bid ye absolve me of all undue severity, all unjust dishonour. The Princess Constance offered her liberty for that of the Signor Vincenzio; but, nobles of Naples, Gonzalvo scorned it. She is free, as is her husband. His ransom, five thousand marks, is discharged from my private coffers, and settled as a marriage dowry on his bride. Both, then, are free, unshackled by condition, free as the winds of heaven to travel where they list. We heard of a noble of France hostile to this union, and on account of his birth approved of by King Frederic; and therefore is it we have been thus secret, and would counsel Signor Vincenzio to accept the vessel lying at anchor, ready for his use, and convey his gentle bride to the court of her father without delay. We will take all blame; for the union, as ye have all witnessed, hath been without consent of the bridegroom. For thee, Signor Vincenzio, thy fault is unconditionally pardoned, a grace won for thee by the truth and glorious heroism of thy gentle bride. No thanks—to us they are *not* due; we had been terrible in wrath, resolute to demand the forfeit of rebellion, even to the last, save for one whose earnest pleadings we had no power to resist. In your love, your happiness, think on Gonzalvo's daughter, for to *her* ye owe it all."

It needed not the name: ere that rich voice ceased, Vincenzio and his bride were kneeling at the feet of the Lady

Elvira; the former pouring forth with passionate eloquence his gratitude, his veneration; in words burning, thrilling, known only to Italy's impassioned clime. She heard, and a faint quivering smile was on those lips; one hand she yielded to his respectful homage, and laid the other caressingly, fondly, on the beautiful head of Constance, whose face was lifted up to hers beaming in all the blissful confidence of love, of joy, of devotion, conscious that to her she owed all that made life dear.

"Bid Constance tell thee how much Elvira owes to her, Signor Vincenzio, and thou wilt learn I have yet more cause of gratitude than thou hast," she said, and not one word quivered. "To thee she has given a life; to me—what is far more valuable—Elvira to herself, unstained, unscathed; her soul of honour cloudless, true, when all methought had failed. Farewell! be happy, and may good angels guard ye both!"

She raised the Princess, and folded her to her heart. "There was an eye thou knewest not upon thee in his prison," she whispered, ere she released her. "Constance, hadst thou failed, we had both been lost, for I had seen no stronger spirit than my own. Thou hast saved us both, and must be blessed." She printed a long kiss on that beautiful brow, and placed her in her husband's arms. A brief interval of congratulation, of joyful conference followed, and then all within that chapel was silent and deserted. Hours passed. The chieftain of Spain had returned from accompanying Vincenzio and his bride to their vessel, though he had tarried to watch them weigh anchor and disappear in the distance. He inquired for his daughter, sought her in all her haunts, and lastly, with a strange foreboding, re-entered the chapel. No voice, and at first no figure met his eye or ear; he rushed forwards, a beautiful form lay either lifeless or in a deep swoon at the altar's foot, her rich and luxuriant hair falling heavily and darkly around her. It was the Lady Elvira.

* * * * * *

The remainder of the Lady Elvira's career is a matter of history: with it the romancer interfereth no further.

The Authoress.

I.

"You surely do not intend acting such a fool's part, Dudley, as that our little world assigns you?" was the address of one friend to another, as they drew their chairs more cosily together, in the little *sanctum* to which they had retreated, after a *tête-à-tête* dinner.

"And what may that be, my good fellow?"

"Why, throw away yourself and your comfortable property on a person little likely to value either one or the other, and certainly worthy of neither—Clara Stanley."

Granville Dudley coloured highly. "Oblige me, at least, by speaking of that young lady with respect," he said; "however you and your companions may mistake my intentions concerning her."

"Mistake, my good fellow; your face and tone are confirmation strong. I am sorry for it though, for I would rather see you happy than any man I know."

"I believe you, Charles; but what is there so terribly opposed to my happiness in an union with Miss Stanley, granting for the moment that I desire it?" Charles Heyward sat silent, and stirred the fire. "Because she is not rich? nay, I believe, rather the contrary."

"I do not think you worldly, Granville."

"Thank you, for doing me but justice. I am perfectly indifferent as to wealth or poverty in a woman. But what is your objection then? She is not superlatively beautiful nor seemingly first-rate in accomplishment; but what then? She is pleasing, unaffected, full of feeling, very domestic, for I seldom meet her out."

Again were the poker and the blazing coals at variance, and more noisily than before.

"My good friend, you have roused that fire and my curiosity to a most unbearable state of heat. Do speak out. What is the matter with Miss Stanley, that when I mention the words 'feeling' and 'domestic,' you look unbelieving as a heretic? Can you say 'Nay' to any one thing I have said?"

"Nay to them all, Granville Dudley," exclaimed Heyward, with vehemence. "It is because you need a most domestic woman for your happiness, I tell you do not marry Clara Stanley: she is a determined blue—light, dark, every imaginable shade—a poet, a philosopher, a preacher—writes for every periodical—lays down the law on all subjects of literature, from a fairy tale to a philosophical treatise or ministerial sermon. For heaven's sake! have nothing to do with her. A literary woman is the very antipodes to domestic happiness. Fly, before your peace is seriously at stake."

Granville Dudley looked, and evidently felt disturbed. At first, startled and incredulous, he compelled his friend to reiterate his charge and its proofs. Nothing loath, Charles Heyward brought forward so many particulars, so many facts, concerning the lady in question, which, from his near relationship to the family with whom she lived, he had been enabled easily to collect, that Granville, unable to disprove or even contradict one of them, sank back on his chair, almost with a groan.

"Why, my dear sober-minded philosophic friend, you cannot surely have permitted your heart to escape your wise keeping so effectually in so short a space of time, that you cannot call it back again with a word? Cheer up, and be a man. Thank the fates that such a melancholy truth was discovered before it was too late. I have heard you forswear literary women so often that I could not stand calmly by, and see you run your head blindfold into such a noose; she is a nice girl enough, and if she were not so confoundedly clever, might be very bearable."

"But how is it I never discovered that she is so clever? If it be displayed so broadly, how can she hide it so completely before strangers?"

"She does not display it, Granville. No one would imagine she was a whit cleverer than other people; she has no pretension, nor airs of superiority; but she writes, she writes, 'there's the rub,' and she loves it too—which is worse still—and a public literary character cannot be a domestic wife; one who is ever pining for and receiving fame can never be content with the praise of one; and one who is always creating imaginary feelings can have none for realities. To speak more plainly, those who love a thousand times in idea can never love once in reality; and so I say, Clara Stanley cannot value you sufficiently ever to possess the rich honour of being chosen as your wife. Do not be angry with my bluntness, Granville; I only speak because I love you."

Granville Dudley was not angry; perhaps it had been better for his happiness if he had been, as then he would not have been so easily convinced by the specious reasoning of his friend. The conversation lasted all that evening, and when Dudley retired to rest, it was with a firm determination to watch Clara Stanley a few weeks longer, and if it really were as Heyward stated, to dismiss her from his thoughts at once, and even quit England for a time, rather than permit a momentary fancy to make him miserable for life.

Now, though Charles Heyward had spoken in the language of the world, he was not by any means a worldly man; nor Granville Dudley, though he had listened and been convinced, unjust or capricious. Unfortunately for Miss Stanley's happiness, Granville's mother had been one of those shallow pretenders to literature which throw such odium upon all its female professors. From his earliest childhood Dudley had been accustomed to regard literature and authorship as synonymous with domestic discord, conjugal disputes, and a complete neglect of all duties, social or domestic. As he grew older, the excessive weakness of his mother's character, her want of judgment and common sense, and—it appeared to his ardent disposition—even of common feelings, struck him more and more; her descriptions of conjugal and maternal love were voted by her set of admirers as perfect; but he could never remember that the practice was equal to the theory. Nay, it did reach his ears, though he banished the thought with horror, that his father's early death might have been averted, had he received more judicious care and tender watchfulness from his literary wife.

Mrs. Dudley, however, died before her son's strong affections had been entirely blunted through her apparent indifference; and he therefore only permitted himself to remember her faults as being the necessary consequence of literature and genius encouraged in a woman. He was neither old nor experienced enough, at the time of her death, to distinguish between real genius and true literary aspirings, and their shallow representatives, superficial knowledge and overbearing conceit.

As this was the case, it was not in the least surprising that he should be so easily convinced of the truth and plausibility of Heyward's reasoning, or that Charles Heyward, aware of all which Dudley's youth had endured from literature and authorship in a mother, should be so very eager to save him from their repetition in the closer relationship of a wife.

But Clara Stanley was no mere pretender to genius; the wise and judicious training of affectionate parents had saved her from all the irregularities of temper, indecision of purpose, and inconstancy of pursuit which, because they have characterised some wayward ones, are regarded as peculiar to genius. Her earliest childhood had displayed more than common intellect, and its constant companions, keen sensibility and thoughtfulness; a vivid imagination, an intuitive perception of the beautiful, the holy, and the good; an extraordinary memory, and rapid comprehension of every variety of literature, alike prose and poetry, unfolded with her youth, combined with the most persevering efforts after improvement in every study which could assist her natural gifts. It was impossible for her parents not to regard her with pride, but it was pride mingled with trembling; for *they* knew, though *she* did not, that even as she was set apart in the capability of *mind* from her fellows, so she was in the capability of *suffering*. Knowing this, their every wish, their every effort, was directed to providing her with a haven of refuge, where that ever-throbbing heart might find its only perfect rest. Taught to regard mental powers, however varied, as subordinate to her duties as a woman, and an English and religious woman, modesty, gentleness, and love marked every word and every action. Few there were, except her own immediate circle and friends, who knew the extent of her mental powers, or the real energy and strength of her character; but countless was the number of those that loved her.

It was not, however, till after her father's death she saw and felt the necessity of making her talents a source of usefulness as well as of pleasure. She was then little more than seventeen, but under the fostering care of an influential literary friend, she was introduced to the periodicals of the day, her productions accepted, and more requested from the same hand.

Though a few years after Mr. Stanley's death, however, their pecuniary affairs were so advantageously settled that Clara had no longer any necessity to make literature a profession. Their income was moderate, but it rendered them happily independent.

"Now, now," was Clara's ardent exclamation, as she clasped her arms about her mother's neck, "I may concentrate my energies to a better and holier purpose than the mere literature of the day; now I may indulge the dream of effecting *good*, more than the mere amusement of the hour; now I am no longer *bound*. Oh, who in this world is happier or more blessed than I am?"

And as long as she resided under her mother's roof, in the pretty little village which had so long been her home, she was truly happy. Encouraged by the popularity which, through her literary friend, she learned that she had acquired; satisfied that he thought her capable of the work she had attempted, and blessed with a mother for whose sake alone Clara valued fame; for she knew how sweet to maternal affection were the praises of a child.

But this might not last. Before she was one-and-twenty Clara was an orphan, and long, long it was ere she could resume the employments she had so loved, or look forward to anything but loneliness and misery. Every thought, every task was associated with the departed, and could filial love have preserved the vital spark the mother had yet been spared; and had Granville Dudley known Clara in that sad time he would have been compelled to abjure his belief in the incompatibility of literature with woman's duties and affections.

But of such a trial both Granville and Heyward knew nothing; nor, when the latter said that she *loved* her profession, did he imagine the struggle it had been for her to resume it—how completely at first it had been the voice of duty, not of love. Fame had never been to her either incentive or further reward than the mere gratification of the moment, and as a source of pleasure to her mother; and how vain and hollow did fame seem now! But hers was not a spirit to be conquered by deep sorrow. She resumed her employments when health returned, with a bursting heart, indeed, but they brought reward. They drew her from herself for the time being, and energy in seeking to accomplish good gradually followed. The severity of her trial was, however, if possible, heightened by the great change in her mode of life. Her only near relation was an uncle, who lived and moved in one of those circles of high pretension and false merit with which the metropolis abounds. His wife, an ultra-fashionist, lived herself and educated her daughters for the world and its follies alone, inculcating the necessity of *attracting* and *gaining* husbands, but not of keeping them. Exterior accomplishment, superficial conversation, graceful carriage, and fashionable manners were all that were considered needful—and all of feeling or of sentiment rubbed off, as romance much too dreadful to be avowed.

To this family, at the request of her uncle, who actually made the exertion of fetching her himself, Clara removed eight months after her mother's death. Yearning for affection, and knowing little of her relatives, Clara had given imagination vent, and hoped happiness might again be dawning for her. How greatly she was disappointed our readers may judge by the sketch we have given. In their vocabulary, authorship and learning were synonymous with romance and folly; and worse still, as dooming their possessors, unavoidably, to a state of single blessedness, and therefore to be shunned as they would the plague itself. That Clara devoted to her literary pursuits but the same number of hours that one Miss Barclay did to music (that is its mechanical not its mental part), another to oriental or mezzotinting, or another to the creation of wax-work, Berlin wool, etc., was not of the least consequence; their horror of blueism was such, that to prevent all supposition of their approval of Clara's mode of life, they never lost an opportunity of bewailing her unfortunate propensity—and of so impressing all who visited at the house with the idea of her great learning and obtrusive wisdom, that the gentle, unpretending manners of the authoress could not weigh against it; and she found herself universally shunned as something too terrible to be defined.

"With all this, I write on, hope on," she once wrote to an intimate friend; "struggling to feel that if indeed I accomplish *good*, I shall not live in vain; and my own personal loneliness and sorrow will be of little consequence. But, oh! how different it is to write merely for the good of others, to the same efforts, to the same goal, pursued under the influence of sympathy and affection! Because a woman has *mind*, she is supposed to have no *heart*, and has no occasion therefore for the sweet charities of life; when by her, if possible more than any other, they are imperatively needed. Others may find pleasure or satisfaction in foreign excitement; to her, home is all in all. If there be one to love her there—be it parent, husband, or friend—she heeds no more; the yearnings of her heart are stilled, the mind provides her with unfading flowers, and her lot is as inexpressibly happy as without such domestic ties it is inexpressibly sad. Do not wish me, as you have sometimes done, dear Mary, to love, for it would be unreturned; simply, because it is the general belief that an authoress can have no time, no capability of any emotion save for the creations of her own mind."

So wrote Clara; though, at the time, she knew not how soon her words would be verified. As soon as the term of mourning had expired, though little inclined for the exertion, she conquered her own shrinking repugnance to asserting and adopting her own rights; and, to the astonishment of Mr. and Mrs. Barclay, she accepted some of the invitations which courtesy had sent her. Though entered into merely as a duty, society gradually became a source of pleasure, in the discovery that all her aunt's circle were not of the same frivolous kind; and then slowly, but surely, the pleasure deepened into intense enjoyment from the conversation and attentions of Granville Dudley, whom she met constantly, though he did not visit her uncle. Clara was so very unlike her cousins, whose endeavours to gain husbands were somewhat too broadly marked, that Dudley had been irresistibly attracted towards her; a fancy which every interview so strengthened, that he began very seriously to question his own heart as to whether he really was in love.

As Miss Stanley's name was not generally known to the literary world, and the lady, at whose house Granville mostly met her, was herself scarcely aware that she was anything more than an amiable, sensible, and strongly feeling girl, Granville Dudley knew nothing of her claims to literature and authorship till his conversation with Charles Heyward, near the close of the season, revealed them as we have said. The very next time they met, Dudley, half fearfully, half resolutely, led the subject to literature and literati, and drew from Clara's own lips the avowal he dreaded. In the happy state of feeling which his presence always created, she at first imagined he thus spoke from interest and sympathy in all she did; and enthusiastic, as was her wont in conversation with those who she thought understood her, she said more on the subject, its enjoyment and resources, than she had ever done in London. Granville said nothing in reply, which could have chilled her at the time. Yet when the evening was over, Clara's heart sunk within her; she knew not wherefore, save that a secret foreboding whispered within her *that* conversation had sealed her fate. Dudley would not trust his happiness with her.

At one other party she was to meet him, ere the season closed, and the veriest devotee to balls and *soirées* could not have longed for it more than poor Clara; who looked forward to it as the confirmer or dispenser of her fears. The morning of the day on which it was to take place, little Emily, the youngest of the family, was seized with a violent attack of fever, which increased as evening advanced. It so happened that all the Barclay family who were "out" were engaged that evening; Mr. and Mrs Barclay, and their two elder daughters, at a card and musical *soirée;* the other two, and their brothers, under the *chaperonage* of Mrs. Smith, the *gouvernante*, at the ball to which Clara looked forward with so much eagerness. What is to be done? The child could not be left; and without Mrs. Smith, what was to become of her sisters? It was impossible for them to go alone, and equally impossible for mother, father, or either sister of the little sufferer, to give up a fashionable party for the dreadful doom of sitting by a sick bed.

Looks and hints of every variety were levelled at Clara; who, with her usual benevolence, had stationed herself close by her little cousin, ever ready to administer kindness or relief. At any other time, she would not have hesitated a moment; but with the restless craving to see Granville Dudley again, the giving up her only chance, for a time at least, was so exquisitely painful, that she could not offer to remain. Mrs. Barclay, however, seeing hints of no avail, at length directly entreated that, as she was less fond of going out than any one else, she might be glad of the excuse, to give the time to her books and writing, and it would really be doing her (Mrs. Barclay) an especial favour if she would stay and nurse Emily. Clara's high spirit, and strong sense of selfish injustice, obtained such unusual dominion, that she had well-nigh proudly refused; but the little sufferer looked in her face so piteously, and entreated her so pleadingly to remain, that, ever awake to the impulse of affection, Miss Stanley consented.

The disappointment was a bitter one, though Clara's strong sense of rectitude caused her to reproach herself for its keenness, as uncalled for. What did Granville Dudley care for her, that she should so think of him? but vain the question. Every backward glance on their intercourse convinced her that he had thought of her, had singled her out, to pay her those attentions, that gentle and winning deference, which, from a man of honour, such as the world designated him, could not be misconstrued. There was one comfort, however, in her not meeting him; if he knew what kept her at home, he would scarcely continue to believe that her only thoughts were of literature and authorship.

Little did she know that, before they departed on their several ways, it was settled in the Barclay parliament that nothing whatever was to be said of little Emily's illness, lest people should fancy it contagious, and send them no more invitations, so closing their chances of matrimony for that season, before it was quite time.

"If Clara is asked for, my dears—which is not at all likely—you can say you know that she could not leave her writing, or correcting a proof, or some such literary business. I leave it to you, Matilda; you are sharp enough, particularly in framing excuses for a rival, whom I know you are glad to get out of your way. Folks say Granville Dudley had a literary mother; he is not likely to wish for a literary wife."

The young lady answered with a knowing nod; and performed her mission so admirably, that after that evening Granville Dudley disappeared. Power she certainly had to separate him from Clara, but to attach him to herself was not quite so easy. The answer she had given to Granville's inquiries after her cousin was so carelessly natural—that Clara, as an authoress, a literary character, had so many superior claims, that parties and everything else must be secondary, and this followed up by a high encomium on her great talent, she should say genius; but it was, she thought, almost a pity to be so gifted, as it incapacitated her from common sympathies and duties—that it confirmed Granville's previous fears. And while it made him almost turn sick with disappointment and anguish, for it seemed only then he felt how completely she had become a part of himself, he vowed to tear himself from her influence ere it was too late, and the very next morning left London.

"You were right, Heyward. I suppose I shall be a happy man again some day or other, but not now; so do not try to philosophise me into being so."

"But, my good fellow, perhaps after all we have been frightened at shadows; and, hang it! but I am sorry I said so much at first. That Emily Barclay has been very ill, and was so that eventful night, are facts; and, in my opinion, Clara stayed to nurse her, because the others were all too selfish."

"A sentimental excuse to obtain time for dear, delightful, solitary musings, or some such thing. It is too late, Howward; she *is* literary, and so she cannot be domestic. I will not think of her any more."

This was not quite so easy to do as to say; but Granville Dudley was a man of the world, far too proud and resolute to bow, or seem to bow, beneath feeling, particularly when he believed himself on the point of loving one who was utterly incapacitated from giving him any heart in return. He went abroad, travelled during the remainder of the summer, joined the first Parisian circles in the autumn, and before the year closed was a married man.

II.

Eight years have passed, and Clara Stanley is still unmarried; yet she is happy and contented, for she is once more amid the scenes of her childhood; once more the centre of a domestic circle, who vie with each other who can love her best. Two years after she heard of Granville Dudley's marriage, finding a London life less and less suited to her tastes, and not conceiving any actual duty bound her to reside with her uncle's family, she resolved on making her home with an intimate friend of her mother's, who was associated with all the happy memories of her own childhood and youth. Reduced circumstances had lately compelled Mrs. Langley to take pupils; a fact which had instantly determined Clara's plans. She was the more desirous for retirement and domestic ties, from the very notoriety which the constant success of her literary efforts had flung around her. She did not disdain or undervalue fame; but all of expressed admiration, all public homage, was so very much more pain than pleasure, that she shrunk from it; longing yet more for some kindly heart on which to rest her own. Let us not be mistaken: it was not for love, in the world's adaptation of the word, she needed; it was a parent's fostering care—a brother's supporting friendship—a sister's sympathy, or one friend to love her for herself, for the qualities of *heart*, not for the labours and capabilities of *mind*. From the time she heard of Dudley's marriage, all thought of individual happiness as a wife faded from her imagination. Her only efforts were to rouse every energy to supply objects of interest and affection, and so prevent the listlessness and despondency too often the fate of disappointed women. This had, at first, been indeed a painfully difficult task; for her heart had whispered it was because she was different from her fellows, because she was what the world termed literary and learned, Granville had shunned her; and a few words, undesignedly and carelessly spoken by Charles Heyward, relative to Dudley's dislike to female literature, from its effect on his mother, confirmed the idea, and made her shrink from her former favourite pursuits. But she, too, had a character to sustain; and once more she compelled herself to work, believing that her talents were lent her to be instruments of good, not to lie unused. And yet, to a character of strong affections and active energies, mental resources, however varied, were not quite sufficient for happiness; and therefore was it she formed and executed the plan we have named.

So seven years had sped, and there was little variation in the life of our heroine for her biographer to record. Her constant prayer was heard. Her name had become a household word, coupled with love, from the pure high feelings and ennobling sympathies which her writings had called forth. Her works had made her beloved and revered, though her person, nay, her very place of residence and all concerning her were, as she desired, utterly unknown. This in itself was happiness, inexpressibly heightened by her present domestic duties, lightening Mrs. Langley's household cares; giving part of every day to that lady's pupils; teaching them not only to be accomplished and domestic, but to be *thinkers;* training the *heart*, even more than the mind; making nature alike a temple and a school: all the sweet charities of home were now hers, and her heart was indeed happy and once more at rest.

And was Granville Dudley, then, forgotten? When we say that Clara might have married more than once, and most happily, but that she had refused, simply because she could not permit an unloved reality to usurp the place of a still loved shadow—all doubts, we think, are answered.

Of Granville Dudley she could never hear; all trace of him seemed lost. Within the last few years the newspapers had indeed often teemed with the praises and speeches of a Sir Dudley Granville; but though the conjunction of names had at first rivetted her eye and made her heart turn strangely sick, she banished the thought as folly. It was a Granville

Dudley, not a Dudley Granville, whom she had so fondly loved.

Miss Stanley had resided about seven years with Mrs. Langley, when application was made to the latter lady to receive the only child of Sir Dudley Granville as her pupil. The child was motherless, and in such very precarious health, that the milder climate of Devonshire had been advised, as, combined with extreme care, the only chance of rearing her to womanhood. Mrs. Langley's establishment was full, six being her allotted number, which no persuasion had as yet ever induced her to increase. There was something, however, in the appearance of the little Laura which so unconsciously wore upon Clara, that she could not resist pleading in the child's behalf; and as one of the pupils was to leave the next half year, Mrs. Langley acceded. Clara's name, however, had not been mentioned in this transaction. The lady who had the charge of Laura had indeed conversed with her, and had been charmed with her manner; but little imagined she was enjoying the often-coveted honour of conversing with an authoress, and one so popular as Clara Stanley. She said that Laura, though eight years old, literally knew nothing. Lady Granville had been the belle of her time, but one who had the greatest horror of all learning in woman, and in consequence possessing nothing of herself but showy accomplishment, which told in society. She had neglected the poor child, wasted alike her own health and her husband's income in the sole pursuit of pleasure, and hurried herself to an early grave. Laura's health had been so delicate since then, that her father feared to commence her studies, even while he was most anxious she should become a sensible and accomplished woman, with resources for happiness within herself.

"And she shall be, if I can make her so," was Clara's inward thought, as she looked on the sweet face of the child, and a new chord in her heart was touched she knew not wherefore. It was impossible to analyse the feeling, even to one long accustomed to analysing hearts, and Clara gave it up in despair; but affection and interest alike clung round the child, who gave back all she received. Her weak health prevented her entering into all the routine of the schoolroom, and she became Clara's constant companion and pupil. Repeatedly the artless letters of the child to her doating father teemed with the goodness, the gentleness, the tenderness of Miss Stanley; soon convincing Sir Dudley how quick and ready were her powers of comprehension, and filling his heart with gratitude towards that kind friend, whom he knew not, guessed not was the authoress of the same name whose gentle eloquence in her sex's cause had even now his admiration.

Laura Granville had been with Mrs. Langley about eight months, when she became extremely ill, from an epidemic that had suddenly broken out in the village; all Mrs. Langley's household were attacked by it in a greater or less degree, but in Laura alone did it threaten to be fatal. Careless of her own fatigue, Clara devoted herself, day and night, to the young sufferer. Her affections had never before been so warmly enlisted; not one of her young friends had ever become so completely part of herself, and as she watched and tended her morning prayers for her recovery, it seemed as if the child must be something nearer to her than in reality she was.

An express had been sent off for Sir Dudley Granville; but, from his having gone unexpectedly to visit a friend in Germany, it was unavoidably delayed on its way, and nearly three weeks elapsed ere the baronet reached Ashford. From the haste with which he had travelled, no account of her progress could reach him; and it was in a state of agony and suspense no words can describe that the father flung himself from his carriage at Mrs. Langley's gate, and rushed into her presence.

"Your child lives; is rapidly recovering—may be stronger than she has been yet," were the first words he heard, for his look and manner were all-sufficient introduction; and the benevolent physician, who had that instant quitted his little patient, grasped Sir Dudley's hand with reassuring pressure. The baronet tried to return it with a smile, but his quivering lip could only gasp forth an ejaculation of thankfulness, and, sinking on a chair, he covered his face with his hand.

"Let me see this incomparable young woman, the preserver of my child!" he passionately exclaimed, as Dr. Bernard and Mrs. Langley, after describing the progress and crisis of Laura's illness, attributed her unexpected recovery, under Providence, to the incessant care and watchfulness of Miss Stanley, the physician declaring his utmost skill had been, without it, of no avail whatever. Being assured his appearance would not injure Laura, who was, in truth, daily expecting him, he eagerly followed Mrs. Langley to the room, and paused a moment on the threshold unobserved.

Laura was sitting up in her little bed, supported by pillows, looking pale and delicate, indeed, but smiling with that joyous animation which, in childhood, is so sure a sign of returning health; and dressing, with the greatest zest, a beautiful doll, which, with its plentifully-supplied wardrobe, lay beside her. Near the bed, and seated by a small table, covered with books and writings, was Clara, who, by the rapid movement of her pen, and her immovable attention, was evidently deeply engrossed in her employment. Sir Dudley could not see her face, for it was bent down, and even its profile turned from him, but a strange thrill shot through him as he gazed.

"Oh! look, Miss Stanley, how beautiful your work shows, now she is dressed. How kind you were to make her all these pretty things. I can do it all but these buttons, will you do them for me?"

Clara laid down her pen with a smile, to comply with the child's request; and, as she did so, Laura laid her little head caressingly on her bosom, saying, fondly, "Dear, dear Miss Stanley, I wish papa would come; he would thank you for all your goodness much better than I can."

"I wish he would come, for your sake and his own, dearest—not to thank me, though I shall not love you the less for being so grateful, Laura," was the reply, in a voice, whose low, musical tones brought back, as by a flash of light, to Sir Dudley's heart, feelings, thoughts, memories, of past years, which he thought were hushed for ever.

"Miss Stanley! Clara!—inscrutable Providence!—is it to you I owe my child?" he exclaimed, springing suddenly forward, and clasping his little child to his heart—one moment covering Laura's upturned face with kisses, the next turning his earnest, grateful gaze on the astonished Clara.

For an instant her heart grew faint, for the fatigue of long-continued nursing had weakened her; nor could she realize in that agitating moment the lapse of ten years, since she had last looked on his face, or listened to his richly expressive voice. Time had passed over her heart, leaving its early dream unchanged, and vainly she strove to feel how long a period had flown. All seemed a thick and traceless mist; but when she succeeded in shaking off that prostrating weakness, forcing herself to remember it was Sir Dudley Granville, not Granville Dudley, who had thus addressed her, still one fact was certain, the object of her first, her only affection was at her side once more—it was *his* child her care had saved.

Day after day did Clara Stanley and Sir Dudley Granville pass hours together by the couch of Laura. Though conscious her secret was still her own, and grateful that, after the first burst of natural feeling, Granville's manner to her was only that of an obliged and appreciating friend, Clara's peculiarly delicate feelings would have kept her from Laura's room during the visits of her father; but the child was restless and uncomfortable whenever she was absent, and Granville so evidently entreated her continued presence, that to keep away was impossible. It was during these pleasant interviews Sir Dudley related the cause of his change of name. He had become, most unexpectedly, the heir to his godfather, Sir William Granville, who had left him all his estates, on the sole condition of his adopting, for himself and his heirs, the name of Granville—Sir Granville Granville, he added, with a smile, was not sufficiently euphonious, and so he had placed the Dudley first, instead of last. He alluded in terms of the warmest admiration to her works, and wondered at his own stupidity in never connecting the Miss Stanley of his Laura's letters with the authoress he had once known. A very peculiar smile beamed on the lips of Clara as he thus spoke, but she did not say its meaning.

One day, some six or seven weeks after Granville's appearance at Ashford, Clara had just comfortably seated herself at her desk, after seeing Laura ensconced in her little pony chaise, when she was startled by hearing Sir Dudley's voice, in accents of unusual seriousness, close beside her.

"Will you tell me, Miss Stanley, how you can possibly contrive to unite so perfectly the literary with the domestic characters? I have watched, but cannot find you fail in either—how is this?"

"Simply, Sir Dudley, because, in my opinion, it is impossible to divide them. Perfect in them, indeed, I am not; but though I know it is possible for woman to be domestic without being literary—as we are all not equally endowed by Providence—to my feelings, it is *not* possible to be more than usually gifted without being domestic. The appeal to the heart must come from the heart; and the quick sensibility of the imaginative woman must make her *feel* for others, and *act* for them, more particularly for the loved of home. To *write*, we must *think*, and if we think of duty, we, of all others, must not fail in the performance, or our own words are bitter with reproach. It is from want of thought most failings spring, alike in duty as in feeling, From this want the literary and imaginative woman must be free."

Granville's eyes never moved from the fair, expressive face of the gentle woman who thus spoke, till she ceased, and then he paced the room in silence; till, seating himself beside her, he besought her to listen to him, and pity and forgive him, and *prove* that she forgave him; and, ere she could reply, he poured forth the tale of his earlier love—how truly he loved her, even when his idle prejudices against literary women caused him to fly from her influence, and enter into a hurried engagement with one, beautiful indeed, but, from having no resources within herself, the mere votaress of pleasure and outward excitement. How bitterly he had repented through seven weary years the misery he had brought upon himself—how constantly he had yearned for a companion of his home and of his mind—and how repeatedly, as he glanced over her pages, where pure fresh feeling breathed in every line, and the love of home and its sacred ties were so forcibly inculcated, he had cursed his own folly. How he had sought to drown thought in a public career, but had still felt desolate; and now that he looked on her again, not only in her own character, but as the preserver of his child, how completely he felt that happiness was gone from him for ever, unless she would give it in herself!

Clara's face was turned from him as he spoke, but ere he concluded, the quick, bright tears were falling in her lap; and when she tried to meet his glance and speak, her lip so quivered that no words came. It was an effort ere she could tell her tale; but it was told at length, though Granville's ardent gratitude was for the moment checked by her serious rejoinder.

"It is no shame now, dear Granville, to confess how deeply and constantly I have returned your affection; but listen to me, ere you proceed further. I do not doubt what you say, that your prejudices are all removed; but are you certain, quite certain, that a woman who has *resources of mind* as well as of heart can make you happy, as you believe? At one-and-twenty you could have moulded me to what you pleased. I doubt whether I should have written another line, had you not approved of my doing it. At one-and-thirty this cannot be. My character—my habits are formed. I cannot draw back from my literary path, for I feel it accomplishes good. Can I indeed make your happiness as I am? Dearest Granville, do not let feeling alone decide."

"Feeling! sense! reason! Clara—my own Clara—all speak and have spoken long. Make my child but like yourself, and with two such blessings I dare not picture what life would be—too, too much joy."

* * * * * *

And joy it was. Joy as it seemed. Granville has felt that for once imagination fell short of reality, for his path is indeed one of sunshine; and as Lady Granville, the authoress, continues her path of literary and domestic usefulness, proving to the full how very possible it is for woman to unite the two, and that our great poet* is right when, in contradiction to Moore's shallow theory of the unfitness of genius to domestic happiness, he answered—"It is not because they possess genius that they make unhappy homes, but because they do not possess genius enough. A higher order of mind would enable them to see and feel all the beauty of domestic ties."

* Wordsworth.

Helon.

A FRAGMENT FROM JEWISH HISTORY.

"Joy! joy! Spring hath come!
Bounding o'er the earth,
Laughing in the insect's hum,
In the flow'ret's birth.
Ere his spirit springs above,
Summer's wreath to twine,
Oh, what joy for me, my love!
Then thou wilt be mine!

"Joy! joy! though awhile,
Dearest, we must part,
Warmly will thy sunny smile
Rest upon my heart.
Spring the earth is greeting, love,
With a crown of flowers;
For the hour of meeting, love,
Sweeter hopes are ours."

So sung, in a rich, mellow, though somewhat subdued voice, a young man, as he stood beneath the window of a grim old mansion. The sun had but just risen, and sky and earth seemed still bathed in his soft rosy glow. Flowers of delicate form and many a brilliant tint were gemming the greensward, which looked fresh and bright as emerald. Fringed with hoary rocks and thick dark woods, lay the deep blue waters of the lovely Rhine, seeming as if the spirits of the early morning had flung on them a rich robe of golden sheen. Even the black forest in the far distance, and the old, apparently half-ruinous mansion itself, all but laughed in the glowing light; hailing, as they did, the new birth of nature, as well as that of the day. Spring had, within the last few days, leaped from the arms of winter; and flowers and birds, and earth and sky, welcomed his birth, as with a very jubilee of gladness.

The deep seclusion of the scene, however, was remarkable: castles and towns, convents and monasteries, generally studded the banks of the Rhine, even as early as the close of the eleventh century, the period of our narrative; but here there was not a habitation of any kind visible, save this one old house and its out-door offices.

It was a Hebrew school or college, the origin of which was so far removed into the past as to be involved in mystery. From its extreme seclusion, it had remained undisturbed, when elsewhere every trace of Israel's locality had been washed out in blood. Century after century beheld it occupied by a succession of venerable teachers, learned in all the mysteries of their law, and faithful to its every ordinance; by some few Hebrew families who, from being pupils, loved its peaceful seclusion too well to exchange it for the dangers of towns; and by some youths, brought there by anxious parents, or their own will, to learn such lessons as would bid them live to glorify their faith, or die to seal its truth with blood.

The young minstrel, whose song we have given, had been one of these pupils since the age of ten, and was about returning to Worms, his native city, to see his widowed mother, from whom he had been parted fourteen years, obtain her blessing on his choice (the daughter of one of his teachers), and then return for his betrothed, either to dwell in this safe retreat or elsewhere, as circumstances might be.

A knapsack was on his shoulder, and in his eager look upward as he sung, his cap had fallen off, and one of those countenances which, once seen, rivet themselves upon the heart, was fully displayed. It was purely spiritually noble; expressive of every emotion which can elevate and rejoice, and utterly devoid of that abject mien and fearful glance, the brand which persecution laid on the Israelites of towns.

A sweet face appeared for a minute at the window as the song ceased; a smile whose sunny warmth the poet had not too glowingly described, a fond wave of the hand, and then the window was tenantless again, and the young man turned away, still humming—

"For the hour of meeting, love,
Sweeter hopes are ours;"

when he was joined by the companion for whom he had waited: a man some ten years his senior, dark and stern in aspect, as if every human emotion had been battled with and conquered.

"Joy—hope! Have such words meaning for an Israelite?" he said, bitterly. "Art thou of the doomed and outcast race, and canst yet sing in the vain dream of joy? Knowest thou not the fate of Israel, when once looked on by man? The rack, cord, death! Hast thou not heard, that in this new war of the accursed Nazarene, their holy war, the signal for marching is the death-shriek of the slaughtered Jews? Spires, Metz, Cologne, Treves, Presbourg, Prague, ask them the fate of Israel, and sing if thou canst. Ask yonder river, from whose kindly waters those who had sought their calm repose, rather than wait the cruelty of man, were drawn forth and butchered on the blood-reeking land. Ask yon river the fate of the hundreds who threw themselves within it—and then sing of joy!"

"I do know these things, Arodi," was the calm reply, though the flushed cheek denoted some feeling of pain. "I know that for Israel there is only such joy as may be resigned at a moment's call; only such hope as looks beyond this world for perfection and fulfilment. Think you because, with a grateful heart and joyful song, I breathed forth a dream of earthly happiness, that I am less fitted than yourself to give up all of joy, hope, and love, if such be the will of God?"

"It cannot be. You love, you are joyful. You have woven sweet dreams, whose destruction will bow you to the dust. Human affections fetter your soul to earth. How can it give itself to God?"

"Through the blessings He has given; blessings which so fill my heart with love for Him, that without one murmur I would resign them at His call."

"You think so now; beware lest this, too, prove a dream. For me, hope and joy are as far from me as yon blue arch from the cold earth on which I see but my brethren's blood."

"Look beyond it, then," answered Helon, fervently. "Why should there not be joy for Israel? Dark as is his present, so bright will be his future. As both have been prophesied, so both will be fulfilled."

He spoke in vain; as well might he have striven to pour forth sunshine on the dark bosom of night, as infuse his spirit in the heart of his companion.

Their way being long, and travelling tedious, from the trackless forests and mountain torrents which they were repeatedly compelled to cross, they found they had miscalculated their time, and that the solemn festival of the Passover, which they had hoped to celebrate in Worms, would fall some few days before they reached it. Remembering that a kind of hostelry, kept by one of their brethren, lay but a few roods out of their way, they determined on abiding there till the festival was over.

It was on the fourth day that a man rushed into the court, covered with dust and mud, and so exhausted as barely to be able to tell his horrible tale. Massacre and outrage again menaced the hapless Jews. He stated that, on the first day of Passover, as the procession of the Host had passed down the Jewish quarter of Worms, a cry arose that it had been insulted by two Jews, who had vanished directly afterwards. That, were not the real criminals given up, the whole Jewish population should be exterminated, without regard to age, sex, or rank. Seven days were allowed them to determine their own fate; a useless delay, for when all were innocent, who could avow guilt? The city gates were closed; not a Jew allowed egress from the town, and, at the imminent risk of his own life, the bearer of these horrible tidings had alone escaped.

Darker and sterner grew the countenance of Arodi, as he heard. He had neither relative nor friend amid the doomed, but once more the curse had fallen on his people, and he burst forth in fearful execration.

"Ye sang of joy," he exclaimed, turning fiercely towards Helon, on whose face, though pale as marble, a strange yet beautiful light had fallen. "Sing on! a joyous song to greet a mouldering home and murdered parent. Ye dared hope—ye dared be joyful—'tis the wrathful voice of the avenger!"

"Peace, Arodi; they shall yet be saved."

"Saved! bid the ravening wolf release the lamb, the hungry lion his fought-for prey." Helon's sole answer was so thrilling in its low brief words, that Arodi started several paces back, gazing on him, as if he had doubted or understood not the meaning of his words. "Canst thou—wouldst thou—what! resign all?" he rather permitted to fall from his lips than said.

"I do not resign them—'tis but their exchange for bliss which is unfading."

"And Admah—Helon, hast thou thought of *her?*"

"Thought of her!" and the strong convulsion passing over Helon's face and frame was indeed sufficient answer. Yet he added calmly, after some minutes' pause, "For this she, too, would resign me. Her spirit speaks within me, bidding me do what my full soul prompts. What is the happiness of one compared with the lives of hundreds?"

The soul of the dark, stern man shook within him. He battled with emotion for the first time in vain. Falling on Helon's neck, these words broke forth in sobs: "Forgive me, oh, forgive me, brother! I despised, contemned thee; yet from thee I learn my duty. 'Whither thou goest, I will go.' What thou doest, I will do. Brother, make me as thyself."

But one night intervened, and the wretched Jews of Worms, in the stern stillness of utter despair, awaited their fearful doom. The festive rejoicing which, even in the darkest era of persecution, ever attended the Passover, was changed into deepest mourning. Not one ray of human hope illumined this horrible darkness. The similar fate of hundreds, aye, thousands, even millions, yet rung in their ears. He who alone could save had turned His face in wrath from his afflicted people. They had but one consolation, and mothers clasped closer their unconscious babes, and husbands their trembling wives, in the one glad thought that none would be left to lament the other—they should die together.

Night fell, calmly and softly; oh, who that looked up on those radiant heavens, losing all of earth in the thoughts of the hundreds and hundreds of unknown worlds filling the vast courts of trackless space, can imagine without a shudder, the mighty mass of human passion and human suffering which one little corner of the globe contains? Who that feels for one brief minute the pressure of infinity upon his soul, speaking, as it will, in the solemn stillness of spiritual night, can come back to earthly things, without shuddering at the awful amount of countless cruelties worked by insect man, without feeling that we have indeed

"Need of patient faith below
To clear away the mysteries of such woe?"

There was one lone watcher of the silent night, but he thought not of these things. For above an hour a tall muffled figure had been standing without the window of a lowly Jewish dwelling, gazing within, and wrapt up in the strong emotions which the gaze called forth. A lamp was burning on a table, round which a mother and her children sat. Years had passed, long years, since the lone watcher had been among those loved ones, save in dreams; and now, while his whole heart yearned to fling himself upon that mother's neck, and feel her kiss, and claim her blessing—to clasp hands once more with those loved companions of his childhood, now sprung into sweet blooming youth—he dared not follow feeling's impulse. Better his own heartsick yearning, the agonized throb of human love and human fear, than the momentary bliss of meeting, to part again for ever.

He had seen the burst of terror, of the wild clinging to life, even such life as theirs, natural to youth, soothed by a mother's prayer. He had seen them twine hand in hand with hers, and lift their bright heads to heaven in that meek, enduring constancy, the undying attribute of persecuted Israel; and then the mother was alone, and the watcher beheld the calm a brief while give way, and natural anguish take its place.

"My God! thou wilt spare one," fell on the hushed air, "my first-born, first-loved, my beautiful Helon! I had thought to look on him again, but I bless thee that thou hast refused my prayer. Bless him, oh, bless him, Father! my own bright boy!"

Was it her own low sob she heard, or its echo, that she so started even from so much grief, and looked fearfully round? There seemed a shadow between the window and the faint moonlight, but ere she could trace it to a human form it had gone.

The morning was clothed in dull, leaden clouds; and, flocking from their dwellings, as was their wont, on the seventh day of Passover, in holiday attire, and with composed appearance, every Jewish family sought the synagogue. Divine service commenced, proceeded, and was concluded without interruption. Scarcely, however, had they reached the outer court to return to their homes, than fearful shouts smote the ear, waxing louder, hoarser, more terrible with every passing moment. On came the infuriated crowd, a dark impenetrable phalanx, increasing in every street, and fearfully illumined with blazing torches held aloft; blades gleaming in the red flame; clubs, axes, pitchforks, every weapon that first came to hand. On they came, wrought into yet wilder frenzy, yet deeper thirst for human blood, by their own mad shouts, and the lurid flames that, as they rushed down the Jewish quarter, marked their progress. And how stood their victims? So firm, so motionless in the shadow of their house of prayer, that even the wild mob, when they first beheld them, fell back a moment powerless. Formed in a compact square, women, children, and tottering age in the centre, youth and manhood stood around, with arms folded and head erect; not a limb, not a muscle moved; not a sound broke forth, even when their fiendish foes poured down and faced them. It was an awful pause; lasting not a minute, yet seeming to be hours; and then, with brandished arms and wilder cries, they rushed on to the work of death.

"Back!" exclaimed a voice not loud nor stern, but so thrillingly distinct and sweet, that it was heard by every individual of both parties, and involuntarily compelled obedience. "Back!—touch not the innocent. Ye have demanded the criminals, BEHOLD THEM! Ye have sworn their lives shall suffice—take them, torture them as ye list; but touch not, on your peril, touch not these!"

Two strangers stood suddenly between the murderers and the victims, as the unknown voice spake, the one in the loveliest bloom of youth, the other in manhood's prime. With an appalling yell of disappointed malice, hate, and aggravated wrath, the fierce crowd rushed forwards, and closed round the voluntary martyrs. And here we pause, for how may the pen linger on the horrible tortures, the agonizing death inflicted on these noble men; or the horror of the stunned yet liberated Israelites, in being forced by their tormentors to witness the fate of their preservers? Yet no groan escaped the victims, to glut the long pent up fury of their foes; no word to reveal to their brethren whence they came or who they were, or that they had spoken but to save.

The poet's prophecy was fulfilled: "Ere spring had changed to summer," Helon and his faithful Admah had met again, where hope was lost in fulfilment, temporal joy in an eternity of bliss. The summer flowers had twined their clinging tendrils round a lowly tomb of pure white marble in the graveyard of that old mansion, Helon's home so long, and half hiding the single word "Admah" with their radiant clusters, whispered in sweet breath to the passing breeze the bliss of a pure spirit, so early freed from the detaining fetters of a broken heart.

To this day the names of the martyrs rest unknown; but the two lamps still kept burning to their memory, in the synagogue of Worms, testify the truth of this fearful tale, and bear witness to a faith, a self-devotedness in scorned and hated Israel, unsurpassed in the annals of the world!

Lucy.

AN AUTUMN WALK.

It was a lovely afternoon, in the fall of the year; that season by many deemed the most melancholy of them all. The fallen leaves, the decay of vegetation, the absence of flowers, the trees shorn of their summer glory, are to some such painful emblems of man's estate, that they shrink in strange and melancholy trembling from the calm and pensive aspect of autumn, as if the death of Nature whispered of their own. Yet it is not so. Autumn, even in its sadness, looks beyond the grave, and breathes of immortality. The shorn tree will put on its gala dress again; the withered hedge will send forth the loveliest flowers. Earth, burdened now in seeming with its emblems of decay, in reality derives thence her nourishment and strength, and will spring up again, bright and beautiful, strong and smiling in her reawakened joy. And shall man alone, amid the creation of Omnific love, pass hence for ever? No, oh, no! As a flower to bloom and be cut down, so as a flower will he burst forth again in a lovelier world and never-ending spring.

The day was well suited for such consoling musing; there was a balmy freshness in the air, a clearness in the atmosphere, in the cloudless expanse of azure, stretching above and around; a warmth and glow in the sun, even as he approached the west, unusual to the season. And there was beauty, too, in the landscape; or the fountain of enjoyment which Nature had unsealed in our hearts, bathed the scene in its own bright colouring, as in those exquisite lines of Coleridge:—

. . . "We receive but what we give,
And in our hearts alone does Nature live;
Ours her wedding garment, and ours her shroud,
And would we aught receive of higher worth,
Than that inanimate, cold world allow'd
To the poor, loveless, ever-anxious crowd?
Ah! from the soul itself must issue forth
A light, a glory, a fair luminous cloud,
Enveloping the earth."

The trees lifted up their graceful heads to the circling heaven; every branch and every spray clearly defined against the blue; so still, so moveless, they looked like pencil-sketches of exquisite delicacy and softness. Then often, as in beautiful relief, started up a gigantic holly, every leaf green and glossy as in the richness of summer, with clusters of its bright scarlet berries standing out against the dark leaf, like sprays of coral. Ever and anon, a break in the hedge displayed towering hills and far-stretching meadows, green and glistening from the late rains; while bold crags, chained by the gray lichen and golden stonecrop, and patches of gloomy firs, frowning like grim shadows in the sunshine, proclaimed the mountainous district to which we were approaching, and heightened, by contrast, the beauty all around. There was something in the whole aspect of Nature so calm, so cheerful, bereft as she was of every flower and leaf, and all her rich summer hoards, that made us compare her to one on whom affliction has fallen with a heavy hand, whose flowers of life are withered, but who can yet lift up heart and brow, with serene and placid faith, to that heaven where the vanished flowers wait her smile again.

The very sounds, too, were in unison with the scene. The sweet note of many an English bird, not in full chorus of melody, as in the warmth and luxury of summer, but one or two together, answered by others as they floated to and fro in the field of azure, or paused a moment on the quivering spray. Then came the twinkling gush of a silvery stream, seeming, by its blithesome voice, to rejoice in its increase of waters from previous heavy rains. Then, sparkling and leaping in the glittering rays, like a shower of silver, a rustic watermill became visible through the trees; the music of its splash and foam bringing forth the voice of memory yet more thrillingly than before, for it was a sound of home We paused; when suddenly another sound floated on the air, of more mournful meaning. It was the solemn toll of a church bell, distinct though distant, possessing all that simple sanctity peculiar to the country—that voice of wailing which comes upon the heart as if the departed, whom it mourns, had had its dwelling there, claiming kindred alike with our sorrows and our joys. We hurried on, and just as we neared the ivy-mantled church, the solemn chanting of a psalm by several young and most sweet voices sounded in the dim distance, and, becoming nearer and more near, proclaimed the approach of the funeral train. The peculiar mode of tolling the bell, as is customary in those primitive districts of the north of England, had already betrayed the sex of the departed, and with foreboding spirits we listened for the age. We counted twenty-one of those mournful chimes, and then they sunk in silence solemn as their sound.

The church was situated midway on the ascent of a hill, or rather mount, guarded by a thick grove of yews and firs, their sad and pensive foliage assimilating well with the olden shrine. The ivy had clambered over the slender buttress, clustering round the old square belfry, decking age with beauty, and moss and lichen pressed forth in fantastic patches on the roof. The green earth was filled with lowly graves, thickly twined with evergreen shrubs and hardy flowering plants. Headstones and marble tombs there were; some so crusted over by the cold finger of Time, that even the briefest record of those who slept beneath was lost for ever; and others gleaming pure and white in the declining sun, seeming to whisper hope and faith in the very midst of desolation and death.

The clergyman stood at the churchyard gate, waiting the arrival of the corpse. He was leaning against the stone pillar which held the hinges of the gate, his head buried in his hands, and his bowed and drooping aspect breathing a more than common love. His figure was so peculiarly youthful, we wondered at his full canonical costume.

The psalm continued; now low, as mourning the departed —now in solemn rejoicing that a ransomed soul was free. The snow-white pall which covered the coffin, the white dresses and hoods of the bearers and the young girls, who, to the number of eight or ten, headed the train, confirmed the mournful tale which the bell had already told. A young girl of one-and-twenty summers was passing to her last long home. There were but few chief mourners, and these seemed struggling to subdue their grief to the composed and holy stillness meet for such an hour. As the train entered the last winding path of the ascent, the bell began again to toll, and the sound seemed to rouse the young minister from his all-absorbing grief. He started, with a visible shudder, and the expression of agony that his face revealed haunted us for many a long day. There was a strong effort at control: and he turned to meet the corpse, repeating, as he did so, in low impressive tones, part of the burial service. He walked at the head of the train to the place appointed—the centre of a little cluster of yews; and there, in silent awe, we watched the ceremony of the interment.

An aged minister had been among the train of mourners, and, as they entered the churchyard, had approached the officiating clergyman, evidently entreating to perform the melancholy office in his stead. The reply was merely a strong grasp of the hand and a mournful shake of the head; and the old man fell back to his place, his eyes still fixed on his young brother, and gradually they filled with large tears, which fell unconsciously, and seemed more for the living than the dead. Once only the service was wholly inarticulate, and the old man drew near hurriedly, as fearing the calm of mental torture must at length give way; but still he struggled on, though the tone in which the awful words—"earth to earth, and dust to dust," now at length pronounced, was as if the very spirit had been wrung to give them voice. Never did the sound of filling in the grave fall with such cold and heavy weight on our hearts as at that moment, yet still, spell-bound, we lingered.

The early twilight of autumn had deepened the beautiful blue of the heavens, as the service concluded, and with low, subdued chant the mourning train departed. The slender forms of the young girls, in their snowy robes, gleaming strangely and fitfully through the darkening shadows of the winding paths; their sweet, young voices sounding almost like spirit music, as they faded, fainter and more faint in the far distance.

Still the young clergyman remained, pale, rigid, moveless, gazing on the newly-turned-earth, till he fancied he was alone with the homes of the dead; and then, with a low, smothered groan of anguish, he flung himself on the damp grave, clasping it with his outstretched arms, pressing his cold lips upon it, his whole frame quivering with the effort to restrain his bursting sobs. The old man hurried forwards and laid his trembling hand on his arm, the tears streaming down his furrowed face the while, and with faltering accents conjured him to take comfort, for his poor mother's sake.

"I will, I will," was the agonized reply. "Leave me, leave me to my God. He will bring peace. I see but the cold grave now; but faith will come again. She is free, rejoicing. She will know now how much, how faithfully—but leave me, leave me now." And the old man turned sorrowingly away: and softly and sadly, for such grief might not bear a witness, we departed also—our last lingering glance revealing the youthful mourner kneeling in voiceless supplication on the sod.

To the aged minister so often mentioned we were indebted for that true English hospitality still so warmly proffered in these "nooks of the world;" and in listening to the following sad and simple story, the evening hours sped on.

Lucy Lethvyn was the daughter of a rich merchant, in one of our large commercial cities of the north of England. The village of Elmsford had been the site alike of her childhood and happy schooldays; and so associated was it with hours of peace and joyance, far removed from the strife and confusion around her city home, that her wonted summer visit to its shades and flowers was ever welcomed with delight.

At the vicarage of Elmsford, then occupied by our venerable host, Mr. Evelyn, Mrs. Lethvyn and her daughters were constant visitors; and there it was that Nevil Herbert, the young clergyman who had so deeply interested us, again met Lucy after a lapse of seven years. Formerly they had been frequent companions, from the near relationship of their parents; and Nevil had been accustomed to think of Lucy as the gentle, artless, affectionate little girl of ten summers, he had last beheld her. Her occasional letters, breathing the same fresh, childlike spirit, increased this illusion. She had called him brother, and often wished he had indeed been such; and he had laughingly acknowledged and promised to value the relationship. In those seven years of separation, however, Nevil's lot had changed. At eighteen he lost his father, and the same stroke cast him and his mother penniless on the cold world. A rich relation promised to give him a collegiate education, preparatory to his taking orders, a living being in his gift. The offer, benevolently made as it was, might not be rejected; though to Nevil, the parting with his mother, for her also to endure the miseries of dependence, was fraught with such anguish, that he would willingly have worked for her in the meanest capacity, so that she might still feel free.

Mrs. Herbert was, however, much too unselfish to permit this: she soothed, urged, and in part comforted him, by the anticipation of the time when they might be once again together, assuring him that to contribute to that joyful end, much more painful alternatives could not be borne than the one that she had chosen.

On all that Nevil Herbert had to endure in college we

have no space to linger. Suffice it he was poor—he was dependent; and however lavish may be the kindness and benevolence bestowed, it will not take away the sting contained in these two words, or permit the taking that station in the world for which such spirits pine. It is strange how often poverty will change to reserve, and bitterness, and pride, dispositions which in affluence would have been humble, and loving, and open as the day. And sad, oh! how bitterly sad it is that the cold, heartless world should fling such scorn and contempt upon that word, and shrink, from the children of poverty, noble-gifted though they be, as they would from crime, and, by a thousand nameless slights and petty provocations, add a hundred-fold to the misery already theirs. Philosophy may preach, and religion soothe; but while such things are, poverty must ever be regarded as a doom of horror and of dread.

Nevil Herbert's peculiarly sensitive nature caused him to feel these evils even more keenly than the multitude so situated; and therefore the rest and peace of the vicarage of Elmsford was, indeed, to him almost heaven upon earth. There nothing ever galled him, but all around breathed the balm of that true sympathy and appreciation, which, raising the drooping spirit to its proper level, restores its self-esteem, and consequently its happiness.

Nevil was just two-and-twenty when his ideal of female loveliness and innocence burst upon him in most exquisite reality, through the childlike loveliness and artlessness of Lucy. Alike the favourites of the vicar, he rejoiced to see them together, and never dreamed that to his petted Nevil danger might thence accrue. To him Lucy was still a child, as so she was to herself and to all around her, but to one, and that one, unhappily, was Nevil. He guessed not her influence till he returned to his solitary studies, and then he felt, too keenly, that, despite his every resolution, he loved—and loved in vain; not only from their different stations, but that it was still only as a brother she regarded him.

The next recess found them again together, more closely than before, for Lucy was the old man's guest equally with himself; but a change had come upon her—not towards Nevil, but in herself. The child had sprung into the woman—the incipient germs of thought and feeling burst into the full-blossomed flowers. There was a deeper tone in her sweet voice, a more intense light in her radiant eye, a fuller sentiment in her bright smile. Yet to Nevil's eye alone these things were visible. None other, even of those who loved her best, saw the change; but Nevil read by the light of his own feelings, and they told him she, too, loved—and loved another.

It was even so, and from her own lips the artless tale was poured into his ear. She called and felt him brother, and claimed his sympathy as such; feeling that, did she conceal anything which concerned her happiness from one so true, and kind, and good as Nevil Herbert, she wronged him, and deserved to lose his friendship altogether; and even at such a moment Nevil's martyr spirit did not forsake him. The hand, indeed, was cold and damp which pressed the fairy one held out to him, as she spoke, but the lip did not quiver, nor the voice falter, in which he assured her that her confidence was not misplaced—that her happiness and interest were dear to him as his own.

A few weeks brought Mr. and Mrs. Lethvyn and Mordaunt Lyndsey to the vicarage. Handsome, intelligent, and animated, there was much in the latter to possess and win. He had been Lucy's partner at her first ball, and by the magic charm of his varied conversation, the magnetic power which fascinates at a first interview, and calling forth the yearning to know more, gradually changes into earnest and lasting love, fixed that evening indelibly on her mind and heart.

It is in vain to argue either on the birth, the nature, or the duration of love. It may spring into existence unconsciously; becoming so completely part of our being, that it remains unknown until some sudden shock of joy or grief awakens us from our rest, and dooms us to an almost overpowering sense of joy or an equal intensity of grief; or one little hour may reveal depths within the human heart, whose existence was never known before—will awaken restless, baseless imaginings, that linger, strengthening with every interview, till the earthly fate is fixed for ever. And how may we argue on this, how seek its explanation? Yet who, that hath once opened the wide, mysterious volume of the human heart, will deny that so it is?

It was so with Lucy. She who had remained free and childlike in her intercourse with Nevil Herbert (though her character assimilated with his far more than with Lyndsey's), was chained and bound for ever beneath the magic of Mordaunt Lyndsey's voice and smile. The spell of their first interview lingered to the second, and each day, each week strengthened Lucy's love.

Mordaunt Lyndsey was an orphan, and not rich enough to wed a portionless bride; but, unlike Nevil, as he knew not the privation and bitterness of dependence, so was he utterly ignorant of those finely organized feelings which could debar his association with the wealthier than himself. He made his way in the world, for he had good connections, well-sounding friends, and so was courted and received. It was some little time before Mr. Lethvyn could give his consent to their union, his ambition looking higher for his Lucy, but his paternal affection was stronger than his ambition; and perceiving how completely her happiness was bound up with Mordaunt's, for whom he himself felt prepossessed, he not only gave unqualified approval, but settled on his darling a portion almost startling in its profuseness, and promised his influence to get Mordaunt entered as partner in the firm. Lucy was still so young, that her parents prevailed on Lyndsey, though very much against his inclination, to wait six months, and celebrate their nuptials with the completion of her eighteenth year.

It had been with perfect sincerity that Nevil Herbert had promised Lucy to comply with her artless entreaty; and, like Mordaunt, not only for her dear sake, but from the same honourable and religious principles which actuated all his conduct. Why, he asked himself, should he hate and shun a fellow-creature because he was happier than himself? and could he have esteemed as he wished, and hoped to do, young Lyndsey, this principle would have been followed by a friendship as disinterested as was felt by man.

But this could not be. Rendered watchful and penetrative by his pure and most unselfish affection, a very, very brief interval of intimate association convinced him that Mordaunt was not a character worthy of one like Lucy. She would need, as a wife, tenderness as unvarying as it was exclusive, sympathy in all her high, pure feelings, as in detestation of all worldliness and art; encouragement in her simple duties and tastes; in a word, love as faithful, as clinging, as constant as her own, and this Nevil saw Mordaunt could not give. Even now, Lucy was not the world to him as he was to her, and Herbert could not argue that such difference was but in nature, that man could not love as woman; for his own aching spirit told him the creed was false.

Time passed. The Lethvyns and Mordaunt returned to their city homes, and Nevil to his solitary studies. Weeks sped on to months, the eventful day was near at hand, and Lucy's bridal attire nearing its completion. The nuptials were to be on a scale almost princely; for as princes did Lethvyn's ambitious spirit regard the merchants of England, forgetting, in his vast schemes and golden visions, that the wealth of yesterday may be poverty the morrow. The expected bridal was the talk of the city; anxiety for her child's happiness the only thought of the mother; love for Mordaunt the sole existence of Lucy; and therefore it was not very strange that, by these severally interested parties, Lethvyn's unusually harassed countenance and excited manner were unnoticed. Ten days before that appointed for the bridal, however, the blow fell—the firm failed. Lethvyn was utterly and irretrievably ruined; unable, by the dishonest conduct of one of the partners, even to pay one shilling in the pound.

The usual excitement which such events in provincial cities always create, was heightened by the universal sympathy for the principal sufferers. Lethvyn's profuse benevolence and affability having made him generally beloved, many pressed forward eager to prove what they felt; but the unfortunate man turned from them with a heart-sickness, a loathing of himself and the whole world, which no human consolation could remove.

That her father should be so prostrated by his failure was a matter of grief, but scarcely of surprise, to Lucy; but that it could in any way affect Mordaunt, was a mystery she could not solve. Loving him, and him alone, with such love that she cared not how lowly was their dwelling—nay, rejoicing that she could now prove her love in a hundred little caressing ways, which in a wealthier and more influential station would be denied her—how could the thought enter her pure mind, that in *his* affection her wealth had equal resting with herself?—that his ardent desire for the speedy celebration of their marriage originated as much to possess her dowry as herself? the insecure tenure of merchants' wealth never having for one instant faded from his mind.

To Elmsford, at the earnest entreaty of Mr. Evelyn, the ruined family retired; but vain were all exertions of his friends to rouse Mr. Lethvyn from his despondency; he drooped and drooped, and there were times when he would fix his eyes on his Lucy with such an expression of intense suffering, of foreboding misery, that she would fly to him fold her arms about his neck, and weep, and then conjure him to tell her what he feared ; and then he would fold her closer and closer, the big tears rolling down cheeks on which the furrows of age had been hollowed in a single week, but the cause of such emotion never found a voice.

Too soon, however, did the cause reveal itself. With every manifestation of strong feeling and real affection, Mordaunt Lyndsey confessed that to give Lucy the home and comforts which he felt she so deserved and needed, he had not the adequate means. They were both still young, and he would go abroad, seek his fortune in India, where a lucrative situation had been offered him; and if, indeed, his Lucy would love him still, through absence, and distance, and time, he would in a few brief years either send for her to join him, or return for her himself, as circumstances would permit.

Pale, rigid, almost breathless, Lucy sat while her lover spoke, her hands pressed tightly one over the other, and every feature still almost to sternness ; but as he fixed the full glance of his eyes on hers—and they seemed to glisten in tears as he called her name in that accent of love which ever thrilled through her heart and frame—she fell upon his bosom, and, with a passionate burst of weeping, besought him not to leave her. Were there not some sweet spots in England—oh! surely there were—where they might live, even with his moderate means, in comparative affluence? Solitude, privation—all more welcome, rather than part with him.

"And so sacrifice your first bloom, your glowing youth, my Lucy, and struggle on through life, wasting your best years, buried in a wild, amid rude boors, who could neither understand nor love you."

"What care I for others? Have I not you, dearset Mordaunt? Do I seek, ask for, need aught else?"

"For that very love I would not so sacrifice you, sweet one; and—oh! Lucy, forgive me—man is different to woman. My spirit is restless and ambitious. I could not live in the retirement of an English cottage, and restlessness might seem like irritability; and then—then, Lucy, you would—you must cease to love me!"

She lifted up her sweet face, and, oh! the expression of unutterable sadness upon it. A chill had fallen on her yearning heart, stagnating its every bounding pulse—a sicknes and dread, more agonizing than parting's self; for, for the first time, she felt "he does not love as I love;" but she spoke no word, she uttered no sigh—it was but the shadow on that lovely face which betrayed the cloud that had buried the sunshine of her heart; and when with words of repentant agony, almost in tears, Mordaunt flung himself on his knees before her, covering her cold hand with kisses, and imploring her not to doubt his love, his truth, because he had thus spoken, she tried to smile, to forget herself for him, drawing from him with such sweet gentleness his plans and wishes, that his spirits returned, and he forgot even the fancy that he had given her pain, or that the word of a moment could break the fond dream of months.

Mordaunt Lyndsey went to India. We may not linger on that bitter parting, or on the feelings of either, save to say, that with Mordaunt sorrow was so transient, that ere the long voyage was completed, new scenes, new hopes, new wishes had obtained such dominion there was scarcely a void remaining. With Lucy could this be? Alas! she was a young and loving woman; and in those words we have our answer. Nor was she one who had ever so sought outward excitement and enjoyments, as to find in them relief from anxiety, or rest from sorrow. The simple, trusting religion of her own heart—the refreshing and soothing influences of nature—the calm repose of seeking the happiness of others, of devotion to all who gave her the sweet meed of affection; these were her consolations, and enabled her to meet her heart's deep loneliness with cheerfulness and smiles. And when Mr. Lethvyn sunk gradually away, it seemed not only with individual and present sorrows, but with the dim forebodings of his child's future, it was Lucy who soothed and comforted her mother, and, by her meek and gentle influence, restored peace and serenity to their lowly cottage, and robbed even the memory of death of its lingering sting.

And towards Mordaunt what were her feelings? Though the conviction that his love was not as hers never left her mind, her affection was too pure and true to know the shadow of a change. She thought it was but the diverse nature of man and woman; that the varied pursuits, the very strength of the one prevented the exclusiveness, the devotedness of the other, and her gentle spirit turned longingly to the time when she should be all his own; and when, perhaps, tired of excitement and ambition, his heart would turn to his home and to herself for rest and peace, and she would be to him, indeed, almost as he had ever been to her.

His truth she never doubted. Deception, fickleness or caprice, unkindness or neglect, were things unknown to her; and how then could she associate them with the earthly idol her soul enshrined? She had carried the guilelessness, the innocence, the freshness of the child into the deeper feelings, the clinging devotedness of the woman. Her being was wrapt in the beautiful halo her fancy had flung round another, and did a storm disperse that halo, it would have crushed her in the same destroying blast.

It was this childlike confiding spirit, the rays of her own heart, which shed such warmth and glow over Mordaunt's letters; for, by spirits more exacting and suspicious, the vital spark from the heart, giving life to the words of the head, would have been found wanting.

In the second year of their separation, Mr. Evelyn was raised to a deanery in one of the adjoining counties, and his former living became the property of Nevil Herbert, who had just received his ordination. Again, therefore, was this noble-hearted young man thrown into the closest intimacy with the gentle object of his ill-fated attachment, and in circumstances which could not fail to strengthen its endurance and its force. The barrier between wealth and poverty had been shivered—Lucy was now but his equal; nay, circumstances had rather placed him above her. An unexpected legacy, and some recovered debts of his late father, had given him not only independence, but competence; and he could now have offered her the home, the simple comforts and enjoyments which the more he knew her, the more he felt were all she needed for her happiness. Her friendship, the regard of her poor widowed mother, the delight with which ever the young Margaret welcomed his visits, the consciousness that he was of use to them, all prevented his keeping aloof, as perhaps would have been better for his peace: besides, how could he do so without some cause?—he, whose adversity their prosperity had soothed and blessed! No, better the torture of lingering in her presence, feeling she was the property of another, and that other, one who loved not, valued not as he did, than be, even in seeming, one of the butterfly crowd, who sport in the sunshine to fly from the storm. And though repeatedly alone together, though thrown in constant association, intimate and affectionate, in very truth as a brother with a sister, never once in those eighteen months did Nevil Herbert, by sign or word, betray to Lucy, or to any other, even to his much-loved mother, the dread secret which bowed his heart and paled his cheek, and dashed his youth with the calm seriousness—the quiet hush of age.

It was three years after Mordaunt Lyndsey's departure that the longed-for summons came. He could not return for her himself, his situation would not permit his absence for so long a time; but if, indeed, she loved him still sufficiently to encounter the miseries of a long voyage, of a life in India, the banishment from mother, sister, friends—all for him alone, the sooner their term of suffering and separation closed, the happier for them both; but if time had cooled the enthusiasm of her love—if one feeling of regret, however faint, bound her to England—one emotion of dread accompanied the idea of the voyage, or the thought of dwelling in a strange and dangerous land—he released her from her engagement. She was free. He besought her to think well ere she decided; that he could not, dared not, urge her to make such a weighty sacrifice for him. He did not dilate on his own feelings, but if Lucy marked the omission, she believed he had done so purposely, that no thought of him should bias her decision. Yet even what appeared to her guileless spirit his unselfish resignation of personal happiness for her sake, could not remove the bitter anguish it was to feel, that even now, tried as she had been through absence and time, he did not, could not, understand the might, the devotedness of her love.

"I will go to him—he shall learn how much I love him, if he know it not now," was her inward ejaculation; and at that moment Nevil Herbert entered the room. She welcomed him gladly, for she needed him even more than usual; and in agitated accents entered at once on the subject which engrossed her, pausing, in sudden fear, as she beheld Nevil's very lips grow white, and the damp drops standing like beads on his high forehead.

"Nevil, dear—dear Nevil, you are ill; and I, selfish as I am, prevent your going home to rest. You are more than tired. Pray let me get something for you."

She laid both hands on his arms as she spoke, looking up in his agitated face with an expression of such anxious affection, that it was with difficulty Nevil could restrain himself from snatching her to his bosom, and pouring forth the agony which at that moment well-nigh prostrated mind and frame;

but he did not. Even at that moment religion and virtue were triumphant; he conquered the wild impulse of passion, assured her it was but passing faintness, which a glass of water would remove; and when she flew to fetch it, he bowed his head upon his hands in prayer, and, on her return, received it with his own meek, soul-felt smile.

With all the artless confidence of her nature, Lucy imparted every feeling which that letter caused, except its pain, for that would seem reproach on Mordaunt. She would depart herself for answer—to write first would be but waste of time. The term of parting known, it was better for her mother as for herself to be spared the suffering of anticipation; besides, her uncle only waited for her to set sail for India;—his wife went with him, and such an opportunity might not occur again.

And what could Nevil Herbert answer? Could he reiterate Mordaunt's own counsel, and beseech her to ponder well ere her final decision? A chill for her had fallen on his heart. He bade her repeat again and again that part of Lyndsey's letter which she had confided to him; and each time confirmed the dread conviction, that it was in no spirit of self-sacrifice Mordaunt had written, but that the engagement hung upon him as a weight and chain, from which he longed to be released, yet shrunk from the dishonour of breaking it himself In vain Nevil struggled with the idea; it would force itself upon his mind, regard it which way he would. Could he but have believed she was going to happiness, he would not have paused till all in his power was done to forward it; but, as it was, the chaos of that fond and faithful heart no words are adequate to describe. He felt she was going to misery, which he was denied all power, all possibility of averting—nay, which he was compelled, by a stern peremptory destiny, to advise and forward.

A few words must suffice to narrate Lucy's departure from her native shores, and uneventful voyage. Doting as she did upon her mother, yet so strong, so omnipotent, was that young girl's love for her betrothed, that even this pang was assuaged by the intense delight which even to think of gazing on his face, of listening to his voice again, never, never more on the earth to be divided, emanated over her whole being. The long weary months of the voyage were beguiled by such fond visions; they told of dangers, of hovering storms, and she smiled, as if love could guard her even from these; and the fond fancy was realized, for she reached India in safety.

To Mrs. Lethvyn and Margaret, Lucy's departure was indeed desolation; and as Nevil tried to soothe and comfort by the anticipation of her happiness—oh! what a storm of contending feelings crushed his very heart. He heard her mother bewail that love had not sprung up between her Lucy and himself; that two beings, each so fitted to form the happiness of the other, fate had so divided; and, though his very spirit trembled, he smiled, and with gentle monition, soothed the momentary irritability by a reference to that wiser, kinder Providence, from whom all things, even the darkest, have their source in love.

From a return ship, which had met the Syren about two hundred miles from her destined port, the anxious friends of Lucy received intelligence of her safety thus far; and Nevil nerved his heart and frame to receive, without any visible emotion, the intelligence expected in her next—her arrival and her marriage.

The time seemed unusually long before the Indian mail came in; and when he saw by the papers that it had, and the postman passed the vicarage, evidently on his way to the widow's cottage, Nevil felt as if all physical power had departed from him. How long he thus sat he knew not;—the papers on which he had been writing notes for his next sermon were before him, and his mother fancied he was still busied with them. A hurried step aroused him, and Margaret Lethvyn rushed into the parlour, every feature betraying agitation.

"Oh! Mr. Herbert, come—pray come with me to poor mamma. Lucy—our own, dear, injured Lucy! That wretch—that villain, Mordaunt! Oh! that I were but a man, that I could but seek revenge!"

"Margaret!" exclaimed Nevil, springing from his seat, and convulsively grasping her arm, his face livid as death, while that of the young, high-spirited Margaret glowed like crimson; "revenge! for what? on whom?—What of—of—speak, for God's sake!"

"He has deceived, has dealt falsely and foully with her—our own Lucy; who left friends, home—all, all for him; and loved him with such love! Oh! Mr. Herbert, do not chide me for the sinful feelings, but I must hate him—must pray for vengeance on him. He has deceived her. Even when he sent for her, he was MARRIED—MARRIED to another!"

Nevil Herbert sunk back on his seat with a groan so deep, a shudder so convulsive, that his mother and Margaret flew to his side in terror. It was long ere he could rouse himself; his forebodings all were realized; the blow had fallen; and for Lucy—who may tell the agony of Nevil's heart, when he thought of its effect on her?

It was but too true. Incapable of any strong or enduring emotion, still seeking and loving worldly aggrandizement above all other consideration, Mordaunt Lyndsey had not been a year in India before he felt his engagement with Lucy as a heavy chain, which he longed to cast aside. He found himself courted and followed; and could he but have stifled the voice of conscience, would have married before the termination of eighteen months. A nature heartless as his own could neither appreciate nor understand the depth of Lucy's. He purposely became colder and colder in his letters, but the warmth and trust of her own heart prevented her perceiving it. He magnified the miseries, the dangers of an Indian life, particularly to a female so thoroughly English as Lucy; but all was in vain;—every post brought him letters full of love and confidence, as at first. His feeble affections had been transferred to a wealthy heiress, caught by the diamonds which had sparkled in her ball costume. Dazzled into forgetfulness of all the past, conscience became drowned in the mad excitement and hilarity with which he pursued his advantage, and not till he was irretrievably engaged, did he remember he was the betrothed of another.

In one part of her statement Margaret was wrong. Mordaunt was not actually married when he last wrote to Lucy. In vain even his heartless nature struggled to write those words which could separate her from him for ever. For the first time the full extent of her love seemed to rush upon him, and he started up, and cursed his evil stars for making him such a wretch. For a moment, the idea of dissolving his present engagement entered his mind; but ere he reached the door, a vision of gold and gems, of untold wealth, came upon him, and the demon triumphed. His better angel fled; and he wrote to Lucy, as we have seen, believing, with pertinacious self-delusion, that his meaning would be so evident that she would break off the engagement herself—she *must* read that he was changed. At least she would write again ere she decided on leaving England, and then it would be easy for him to prevent it; and confiding in this, not a month after his letter had been despatched, the heiress became Mordaunt Lyndsey's wife.

Our tale is well-nigh done, for to breathe one word of Lucy's feelings would be profanation. In vain her aunt and uncle conjured her to remain with them in India, and prove how little Mordaunt's baseness had affected her, by a speedy marriage with another, above him alike in birth, wealth, and station; for such unions in India were easily accomplished. By some, perhaps, the proposal would have been seized with avidity, and a broken heart effectually concealed beneath an outward show of prosperity and pride. With Lucy this could not be. The storm had burst, the halo was dissipated; its beauty and its sunshine, its purity and truth, vanished like falling stars in the dark abyss of fathomless space; and the gentle spirit, folded in the glowing halo, lay shrined 'neath the shock. Her yearnings were now for home, for a mother's tenderness, a sister's caressing love, a brother's supporting friendship, which would lead her failing heart up to the only fount of peace. And, after a long and weary interval—a voyage, whose many dangers, delays, and all but shipwreck, were, it seemed, as unfelt as unnoticed—those yearnings were at length fulfilled.

Again was Lucy Lethvyn an inmate of her mother's lowly roof; but, oh! how unspeakably changed, yet still so exquisitely, so radiantly lovely, that the eye turned again and again upon her, first in delight, and then with such a strange quivering of the lip and eyelid, betraying that tears were nigh. The smile—oh! what a history gleamed from it, of a woman's heart broken, yet even from its every shivered fragment reflecting the quickness and confidence—aye, and deep heavenly love, which had descended on it from above. Not a bitter word, not an unkind reflection, not a selfish murmur ever escaped those lips. Those who loved and tended her alone occupied her thoughts and deeds. There were times, indeed, when a paroxysm of mental agony came upon her, bowing her fragile frame even to the dust; but of these intervals no earthly eye was witness. They were only marked by a rapid increase of exhaustion, and all the fatal evidences of decline and death; and so months passed. And Nevil, may we write of him, as day by day he watched over the fading form of one so long, so secretly, so unchangeably beloved? Alas! for him, even as for Lucy, silence is the most eloquent. We do not give such feelings words.

Autumn had come with a mildness and beauty unusual and most soothing. Lucy's couch had been drawn to the window at her own request, and her eye wandered over the landscape with a pleased and quiet smile. Nevil Herbert was alone beside her; he had been reading from that blessed book which had given comfort and strength to both, but had paused, seeing her inclined to speak.

"Yes!" she exclaimed, the fervour of her spirit flushing her cheek with sudden crimson, "yes! His words and works alike proclaim him Love! Oh, Nevil! God has heard my prayer. He has spared me till I could realize the beauty and goodness, and the glory of this world. There was a time when, outward and inward—all was dark. Not a ray illumined the sluggish depths of misery and despair. Beauty had vanished with truth. I prayed for death; and once, as I stood alone upon the deck, the dread temptation was upon me to end misery and life together. It was but one plunge, one little moment's resolution, and all would be over. All! Oh, what a flash of bewildering and awful light burst upon my mental darkness, sent as an angel of mercy to my soul! I had loved a mortal, and not God! The world was beautiful with human love—not with His, from whom it sprang;—and the light of human love was quenched, to teach me other things: and then it was I prayed, in the deep agony of remorse, my God would spare me, even in suffering, till even this world were lovely to my heart once more; till I could feel His love more deep, more precious, than the love of man. And he has done this. Nevil, dearest Nevil. A few, a very few hours, and I shall be with Him whose all is joy, and loveliness, and love, for ever and ever."

There was no answer, and Lucy turned with difficulty towards him. His face was buried in his hands and his whole frame shaken as with convulsion.

"Nevil," she said, softly, "dearest Nevil, you are in sorrow, and I can do nothing to relieve it; I—to whom you have been such a true consoling friend. I have long feared you had some secret grief; not in the selfishness of my joy, but since—since I have returned. Oh, that I could be to you what you have been to me!"

It was too much for Nevil. In the passionate emotion of

that moment, he flung himself on his knees beside the couch, poured forth the torrent of that overwhelming love—how it had lingered with him through years of hopelessness and misery; and he besought her, in agony, to say that she would live—live to bless him yet; and, as he spoke, the pious, the strong-hearted Nevil Herbert wept, till, as an infant, his very soul seemed powerless within him.

"And you have loved me thus!—you, the good, the noble, the exalted! Oh! I thought human love was all an idle dream—a vain delusion; but it is not—it is not. Even this may be beautiful and true," murmured Lucy, raising herself with difficulty till her head rested on the bosom of Nevil. "Do not—do not weep, Nevil! Our Father will bring peace and love. And oh! if the pure and ransomed spirits may hover beside those still lingering on this earth, be it mine the blessed task of bringing you the comfort I would give you now. I was never worthy of such love—and from you, dearest Nevil!—how much less worthy now, that even, were life granted, I could give but a broken heart, whose all of life and energy had been devoted to another. You must not weep for me, Nevil! You must not let my memory blight your path of holiness and good. Think of all you have been to me, have done for me; and—and if that will comfort you, oh! believe all—all of love this aching heart may yet give to earth, Nevil, dearest Nevil! is your own!"

She raised that sweet face, which had become suddenly pale and dim, as if a shadow had stolen over it. Nevil clasped her convulsively to his heart, and struggled vainly to speak; his white and quivering lips pressed hers with a long, lingering kiss, and she shrunk not from them. It was his first and last; for sleep stole upon her, and bowed her head more heavily, more caressingly upon his bosom. And Nevil stilled his heart's full beating, and hushed his very breath, lest that calm slumber should be broken. He yearned to look once more in those lovely eyes, to drink in once, but once again, the gushing music of that thrilling voice; but vain those mortal yearnings. Human love, the purest, mightiest, has no power to chain the heaven-born spirit from its soaring flight. She never woke again!

And Mordaunt Lyndsey—was there no vengeance, no retribution for him? Did justice indeed so slumber? Long years rolled on ere aught could be distinguished to mark his prosperous path from that of his fellows; but some twenty years after our "Autumn Walks" in the lovely vales of Westmoreland, we learned that the hand of Heaven had dashed his lot with poison. A blooming family had sprung up around him; but each more or less touched by the malady of their mother. He had wedded madness!

The Spirit's Entreaty.

FOUNDED ON A HEBREW APOLOGUE.

THERE was a pause in the courts of heaven. Seven times had the voice of the Eternal resounded through the vast realms of space, and from the very centre of chaotic darkness a world of beauty had sprung forth. Thousands of angelic spirits floated round and round the new-born globe, tending the innumerable sources of loveliness and life, which had burst at once into perfected being at the all-creating word. With every new creation, an increased effulgence flashed over the angelic hosts; and richer tones of mighty harmony proclaimed the power, and the glory, and the mercy of their God.

Deep in the unfathomable abyss of formless space hung the new-formed world, suspended from its parent heaven by chains of diamond light, visible only to the pure spirits, who on them ascended and descended, in performance of their newly-assigned employments.

Myriads of celestial beings stood in dazzling files without the veil, which in unapproachable and indescribable splendour concealed the throne of the Creator; whence issued that Eternal voice which spake, and creation was! None, not even the highest and the purest, the most etherealized amidst those spiritual ranks, could gaze on the ineffable glory piercing through the effulgent veil; nor dared approach it, without covering his face with his glittering pinions, and falling low in prostrate adoration. In their several ranks they stood, the glorious archangels to whom the ways, clearly as the works of the Eternal, were revealed. Hierarchs, who had penetrated deeper and deeper the mysteries of infinity, and by long-tried obedience, and faithfulness, and love, had won the glorious privilege of commune with the Ineffable Majesty of the Supreme. Even to the young seraph, commencing his heavenly career, satisfied to labour and to love, till he should pass through the intermediate ranks, and rising higher and higher in angelic intellect, and the beatified nature of his tasks, at length attain the arch-angelic goal.

Seven times had gone forth the Omnific Word, and seven times had the Eternal pronounced it good; and each time of that approving Word, had the resplendent pinions of the hosts of heaven fluttered in irrepressible rejoicing, till space itself seemed lost in one vast flood of glistening and iris-coloured light, and music, soft, spiritual, and thrilling, marked every movement of the radiant wings, and filled up each pause of song.

And then, midst the deep stillness which succeeded, again spake the Eternal voice: "Let us make man!" and the mandate with the velocity of light rushed through the angelic-peopled courts; and every spirit of every rank, and every host, caught up the Omnific Word, and, in the full song of adoration, testified their joy. But suddenly a hush sunk on the rejoicing myriads; for, darting at the same instant from their respective ranks nearest the Eternal's throne, three glorious spirits met together before the resplendent veil, and prostrated themselves in supplication.

They were of the highest order of the archangels, each intrusted with an attribute of his Creator to uphold its glory and its beauty amidst the celestial and spiritual worlds. And one spake, and his wings of sapphire, his dazzling brow, his radiant eye, before whose single look the mists of error passed; his crystal spear, before whose slightest touch, falsehood fled trembling and self-abhorred; alike proclaimed the gift of which he was the guardian. The spirit of TRUTH implored—

"Father, create him not—life will be overshadowed by deceit!" and the spirit bowed his effulgent brow upon his wings in grief.

And then the second spirit spake,—akin to Truth but sterner. His glorious brow was shaded by a glittering helm, and his right hand grasped an unsheathed sword; a raiment, resembling an hauberk of golden light, clothed his graceful limbs, and the rich full voice, in its entreaty, breathed his name.

"Father and Lord, create him not! He will destroy yon beautiful world by his unrighteousness; and I, unto whom thou hast intrusted thine attribute of Justice, will seem to him, in his darkened light, as the avenger. Father, create him not!"

And then spake the third archangel,—his pure white pinions fluttered tremulously around him, and the exquisite beauty of his youthful face seemed disturbed by the intense ardour of his supplication; a wreath of amaranths bound back his flowing hair from a brow of such transcendent loveliness, that one look upon it filled the soul with balm; he held a bough of emerald resembling the olive-leaf, but radiant with a liquid lustre unknown to the plants of earth.

"Create him not, oh, Father!" implored the spirit, and the brightness of his meekly expressive orbs was dimmed; "create him not! he will chase me from the earth. PEACE will be but a name amidst the awful scenes of internal and external war, with which man's passions will devastate yon beautiful world. Father, create him not!"

The spirit ceased; and, hushed to a solemn stillness, the listening myriads waited the answering Word. The effulgence piercing through the veil appeared slightly shadowed, as if the Almighty presence had withdrawn his immediate glory, and the entreaty of his favoured angels would be granted. But far, far, in the unfathomable distance, a resplendent star seemed floating towards the veil, and faint yet thrilling melody proclaimed the rapid advance of angel wings. On, on—and the semblance of a star gave place to the form of a beatified spirit, whose dazzling loveliness irradiated space itself, and heightened the glory all around; and every rank he passed hailed him, even in that awful hour, with an irrepressible burst of song, and drew closer and closer round; and watched him with such love as only angels feel; and he smiled on them, but paused not in his rapid course, and the smile kindled hope anew, and confidence and joy banished the momentary shade.

It was the Spirit of LOVE; the best beloved of the Eternal; the guardian essence of the whole angelic hosts; angels and archangels, hierarchs and seraphs, alike acknowledged him, and bowed before his sway, as the representative of the Supreme. And on he floated in his indescribable beauty, and every court of heaven sent forth increased effulgence as he passed. He neared the veil, and bowed down before it, and then he spake, and his low soft tone penetrated the farthest limit of that immeasurable space.

"Create him, oh, Father!" he prayed; "create him to love, and be beloved! What if he err? what if he sin? Thou wilt pardon him; for thy love is greater than his sin!"

A burst of bewildering glory flashed through the veil

upon him, as he knelt, and darted its dazzling rays through the thousand ranks of heaven at the same moment. It was the assenting sign of the Eternal; and again the Omnific Word went forth: "Let us make man!" and millions and millions of voices swelled the glad chorus, that another and yet mightier creation should bear witness to the loving mercy of their God. And TRUTH and JUSTICE, and PEACE joined in the thrilling strain, for the Spirit of LOVE had touched them with his quivering breath, and they felt his words were true. Man might still err, but created in love, the immortal spirit breathed into the shell of clay; the angelic hosts gave vent to the full song of rejoicing; for the Spirit of LOVE hovered over the new-born world, as over theirs, endowed by the measureless compassion of the Eternal to purify and pardon.

Idalie.

THE STORY OF A PICTURE.

No place is more calculated to call forth all the vagaries of the imagination than an old half-ruined castle, surrounded by wood and mount, hoar from many centuries, and lying in such deep seclusion, as to be unseen by the more casual traveller. On such a spot, completely circled by a branch of the Cevennès, in the ancient district of Auvergne, it was once my hap to light. Trees of such gigantic growth, that they appeared bending beneath the weight of ages, frowning rocks, and overgrown brushwood formed so close a fortification, that the building might have been passed and repassed within a mile of its vicinity undiscovered.

It was a gothic chateau of the olden time, just sufficiently ruinous to give it the interest of age, yet containing costly tapestried chambers, pannelled halls, long rambling galleries, secret rooms, and those deep dark dungeons, where many a brave man has languished and died unknown, save by his ruthless captor, all still in sufficient preservation to fill the mind with visions of the past as with the breathing realities of the present. There was a small chapel in the building, which had once been evidently richly adorned, but whose shrines and hangings were now all crumbling to decay. It was a melancholy visionary place, yet infused with a charm impossible to be resisted, and day after day my wanderings turned to the chateau; contented at first with rambling over chamber, hall, and gallery, imagination feasting on the thoughts of what had been the life, the stir, the pageantry, where all was now the solitude of silence and neglect. There were still some pictures hanging from the walls, but seemingly so resigned to the cobweb and the dust that I had heeded them little, till one day the sun gleaming upon an antique frame, unobserved before, attracted me to the picture it enshrined, and in a moment heart, mind, and fancy were irresistibly enchained.

To attempt description of that face, to say why it haunted me for days and nights, as something almost unearthly, would be a hopeless task; yet, turn from it as I would, or seek amusement in other objects, still it rose before me, pale, shadowy, yet so lovely, baffling every effort to dismiss it from my mind. Stars and braids of diamonds seemed still literally to glisten in the long jetty tresses, falling as a veil around her. Hands small, thin, and delicately white were crossed upon her bosom; the large dark eyes were raised, and the pale lips parted as in prayer; she seemed standing near an ancient altar; but every other object in the picture time had rendered wholly indistinct.

That I could obtain any information from the half blind, wholly deaf guardian of the chateau was little probable; but the old man, to my astonishment, volunteered the tradition of the portrait, even before I had sufficiently rallied from its effect to look into its past. This tale, when separated from the garrulous annotations of his age and office, was simple and brief enough, yet to resist its spell was impossible. The beings of whom I heard seemed to breathe and move around me, the old castle to resume the state and order which had characterised it nearly three centuries ago, the very woods to lose their wild appearance, and blending in beautiful keeping with mount and rock, and richly cultured lands, seemed to teem with the innumerable retainers of the proud nobles to whom they had once belonged. Under the influence of such dreamy visions the following papers were hastily written. Pretensions to a connected romance they have none; they tell but the story of a picture, which I would fain bring before the mind's eye of the reader, even as its remembrance still so vividly lingers on my own.

I.

It was the third day of the brilliant show, yet was there no relaxation of chivalric ardour, nor semblance that lords and gentles were wearied with martial sports, or that the galaxy of beauty which the ornamented galleries presented had in aught diminished of loveliness and grace. Never had the fair sun of Paris looked down on a scene of more spirit-stirring interest, never had the blue arch of heaven re-echoed more martial sounds than on the day which witnessed the last tournament of France. The lists extending through the most central parts of Paris, flanked on one side by the terrific towers of the Bastile, were adorned by pavilions and tents of every variety of colouring and material. Heavy brocades, velvets, and silks, adorned with the devices of their owners betrayed the names and bearings of well-nigh all the nobility of France. Over one, whose silver covering glittered so resplendently in the July sun that the aching eye turned from its lustre, hung the heavy folds of France's banner, the *fleur de lis*, which, combined with the splendid accoutrements of esquires and pages lingering around, proved that majesty itself was amongst the combatants. The light breeze sporting with the many standards, at times gave their devices to view, at others, laid them idly by their staves. Streamers and pennons in gay relief stood forth against the clear blue sky; while the brilliant armour, the glittering spears, and stainless blades so multiplied the dazzling rays, there seemed a hundred suns.

France and Scotland, Spain and Savoy, in the honour of which last these jousts were given, were all marshalled in the lists, for none chose to remain mere spectators of games in which their chivalric spirits so heartily sympathised. The princes of the lordly house of Guise vying, in richness of apparel and number of retinue, with royalty itself. Montmorenci, Coligny, Andelot, Condé, Nemours—names bearing with them such undying memories, their mention is sufficient —all were this day present; for the blood-red standard of intolerance and persecution as yet remained unfurled. The very sounds that stirred the air added to the excitement of the scene. There were the proud neighings, the hurried snort of eager chargers impatient for the onset; the pealing shouts of welcome as each knight was recognised, marching at the head of well-trained bands to his pavilion; the answering cheers of the men-at-arms; the trampling of many steeds; the frequent clash of steel, as the knights passed and repassed in the lists ere they formed into bands; now and then the loud voice of the herald, or the shrill prolonged blast of the trumpet, and ever and anon a thrilling burst of martial music, lingering awhile in its own rude tones, then subsiding gently into the softer song of minstrelsy and love, more fitted to the ears of beauty than the wilder notes of war.

And beauty was indeed assembled in the many galleries erected round the lists. Even had there been no Catherine de Medicis, whose character was not yet fully known, and who now, as the queen consort, claimed and received universal homage; no fair and gentle Elizabeth, the youthful bride of Spain, whose child-like form and diminutive though most expressive features accorded little with the heavy gorgeousness of her jewelled robes; no retiring yet much-loved Margaret, the sister of Henri and bride of Savoy; no Anne of Este, whose regal beauty and majestic mien would have done honour to a diadem—had there been none of these, there was yet one in the royal group who, though girlhood had barely reached its prime, fascinated the gaze of every eye and fixed the homage of every heart. The diamond coronet of *fleur de lis* entwining the sterner thistle, that lightly wreathed her noble brow, betrayed her rank; and the simple mention of Mary of Scotland, the queen dauphine, is all-sufficient to bring before the reader a fair, bright vision of loveliness and grace, that imagination only can portray. She sate the centre of a fair bevy of young girls, indiscriminately of France and Scotland, all bearing on the smooth brow, the smiling lip, the unpaled cheek true tokens of those fresh unsullied feelings found only in early youth.

The trumpets breathed forth a prolonged flourish, echoed on every side by the silver clarion and rolling drum, and Henri himself entered the lists. Clothed in the richest armour, mounted on a beautiful Arabian, and still wearing across his breast the black and white scarf in homage to Diana, the chivalric monarch challenged one by one the bravest warriors and the first nobles of his kingdom. Excited by the presence of his distinguished guests, he appeared this day urged on by an ardour and impetuosity which, while it endeared him to his subjects, caused many a female heart to tremble.

"Has thy knight turned truant, Idalie, or is he so wearied from the exertions of the last two days he has no strength or will for more?" asked the queen dauphine of one beside her, whose large dark eye and soul-speaking beauty betrayed a birth more southern than Scotia's colder shores.

"He enters not the lists, royal madam," she answered, in a lowered voice, "for he fears the challenge of the king—fears not defeat, but conquest. The king has skill as yet unrivalled, courage none dare question; but the practice of a soldier brings these things to greater perfection than monarchs ever may obtain. Our gracious sovereign challenges the bravest knights to-day, and therefore does the count avoid the lists."

"Perhaps he does well. But see how gallantly thy father bears himself; disease hath worked him but little, or rusted his sword within its scabbard. I would trust myself to the men of Montemar, Idalie, with better faith than to many of those more courtly-seeming bands. And who is yon gallant, bearing thy colours? Is the young esquire of thy father a rival to the goodly count?"

"Not so, gracious lady. Louis de Montemar and I are cousins in kindred, friends in affection, and playfellows from infancy. I broidered him the scarf he wears as token of my love, when he doffed the page's garb and donned the squire's. When he hath won his spur, perchance my scarf will be of little value."

"Thinkest thou so? Methought the lowly homage that he tendered spoke humbler greeting than that of a brother. But there is some stir below; the trumpets sound the king again as challenger."

A long flourish of trumpets again riveted the attention of the spectators, and the heralds in set phrase, challenged, on the part of their liege lord and gracious sovereign Henri of France, Gabriel de Lorges, Comte de Montgomeri, to run three courses with the lance or spear, and do battle with the same. Thrice was the count challenged according to form, but there was no answer.

A deadly pallor spread over the flushed cheek of Idalie de Montemar, and, clinging to the dauphine's seat, she exclaimed, "Lady, dearest lady, oh, do not let this be! in mercy speak to her grace the queen, implore her to avert this combat!"

"Thou silly trembler, what evil can accrue? Nay, an thou lookest thus, I must do thy bidding," and Mary hastily approached the seat of Catherine de Medicis, whom, however, she found already agitated and alarmed, and in the very act of despatching an esquire to implore the king to leave the lists. Somewhat infected with the terror she witnessed, yet unable to define it, the dauphine returned to her seat, seeking to reassure the trembling Idalie, and watch with her the effect of the queen's solicitation.

At the moment of the esquire's joining the knightly ring, the Comte de Montgomeri, unarmed and bareheaded, had flung himself at the king's feet, imploring him in earnest accents to withdraw his challenge, and not expose him to the misery and danger of meeting his sovereign even in a friendly joust. It was no common fear, no casual emotion impressed on the striking countenance of Montgomeri; he was not one to bend his knee in entreaty, even to his sovereign, for a mere trivial cause. The princes and nobles round were themselves struck by his earnestness, knowing too well his great valour and extraordinary skill in every martial deed to doubt them now. The king alone remained unmoved.

"Tush, man!" he said, joyously; "what more harm will your good lance do our sacred person, than those whose blows yet tingle on our flesh? we have run many a gallant course to-day, and how shall we be the worse for a tilt with thee? Marry, thou art over bold, sir knight, we will not do thy courage such dishonour as to tax it now; yet, by our Lady, such presumption needs a check. Come, rouse thee from this folly, and don thine armour, as thou wouldst were our foes in Paris; my chaplet is not perfect till it hath a leaf from thee."

"It may not be, my liege. I do beseech your grace to pardon me, and seek some opponent more worthy of this honour."

"I know of none," replied the king, so frankly and feelingly, that the warrior's head bent even to the ground; "and Montgomeri will obey his sovereign, if he will not oblige his friend. Sir Count, we COMMAND your acceptance of our challenge."

Sadly and slowly the count rose from his knee, and was reluctantly withdrawing, when the king again spoke—

"We would not, good my lord, that you should prepare to accept our challenge even as a criminal for execution; therefore, mark ye, lords and gentles, and bear witness to our words—whatever ill or scathe may chance to us in our intended course, we hold and pronounce Gabriel de Lorges, Comte de Montgomeri, guiltless of all malice, absolving him from all intentional evil, even if he work us harm. How now, sir squire, what would our royal consort, that ye seek us thus rudely?"

The esquire bent his knee, and delivered his message.

The king laughed long and lightly.

"By our lady, this is good," he said. "Heard ye ever the like of this, my lords? What spell doth our brave Montgomeri bear about him, that we may not meet him even as others in friendly combat? Back to your royal mistress

Conrad; commend us in all love and duty to her grace, and say we will break this lance unto her honour. Would she have our noble guests proclaim Montgomeri so brave and skilful that Henri dared not meet him even after his challenge had gone forth? Shame, shame on such advisers!"

The esquire withdrew, and the king taking a new lance, and mounting a fresh charger, slowly proceeded round the lists, attended by pages and esquires, and managing his fiery steed so gracefully as to rivet on him many admiring glances. He paused beneath the queen's gallery, doffing his deep-plumed helmet a moment in the respectful greeting of a faithful chevalier; then looking up, he smiled proudly and undauntedly. At that moment the trumpets proclaimed the entrance of the challenged, and the king hastily replacing his helmet, clasped it but slightly, and galloped to his post.

A loud shout of welcome greeted the appearance of Montgomeri, and as the spectators marked the pink and white scarf across his shoulder, and the opal clasp that secured the deep plumes of his helmet, all eyes involuntarily turned to see the fair being to whom those colours proclaimed him vowed; nor when they traced the bandeau of opals on the pale high brow of Idalie de Montemar, her flowing robes secured by a girdle of the same precious stones, and discovered it was to her service the knight was pledged, did they marvel that at length the cold, stern, unbending Gabriel de Lorges had bowed beneath the spell of love.

The lists were cleared, and deep silence reigned amidst the assembled thousands. The combatants, ere the signal sounded, slowly traversed the lists, meeting at both extremities, and greeting each other in all solemn and chivalric fashion. Montgomeri's lance sank as he saluted the queen's pavilion, but it was to Idalie his lowest homage was tendered. She sought to smile in answer; but her lip only quivered, for her eye, awakened by love, could trace his deep reluctance to accept the challenge.

The signal was given, and with a shock and sound as of thunder the knights met in the centre of the course. The lances of both shivered. A loud and ringing shout echoed far and wide, forming a deep bass to the military music bursting forth at the same moment; but then the sound changed, and so suddenly, that the shout of triumph seemed turned, by the very breeze which bore it along, to the cries of wailing and despair. The horses of both combatants were seen careering wildly, and with empty saddles, round the lists. Princes, nobles, and knights crowded so swiftly and in such numbers to the spot where the combatants had met, that the eager populace could trace nothing but that one warrior was down and seemingly senseless, the which no one could assert. Order and restraint gave place to the wildest tumult; the people, *en masse*, rushed indiscriminately into the lists, heedless of the efforts of the men-at-arms to keep them back, and scarcely restrained even by the rapid and agitated approach of the queen consort and the princesses towards the principal group. Words of terrific import were whispered one to another, till the whisper grew loud and rumour became certainty. The music ceased, save the solitary flourish of trumpets proclaiming the warlike sports concluded. As if by magic the lists were cleared, the tents struck, and every trace of the tournament removed. But even then the popular ferment continued; there were men hurrying to and fro, little knots of persons assembling in the streets, speaking in anxious whispers, or hastening in silence to their homes. Ever and anon the muffled tone of heavy bells came borne on the air, and then the dead silence, ever the shapeless herald of some dread calamity. Ere night all traces of the morning's glittering splendour and animated life had disappeared, and Paris seemed changed into a very desert of solitude and gloom.

II.

Eleven days had passed since the sudden termination of the fatal tournament, and Henri of France still lay speechless and insensible as he had fallen in the lists, when, from the insecure fastening of his helmet, it had given way before the lance of Montgomeri, and caused him to receive the full force of the blow on his eyebrow, thence fatally injuring the brain. Still life was not extinct, and, though against all reason, hopes were still entertained by many for his eventual recovery. In one of the apartments of the Louvre, forming the suite of the queen dauphine, sat the unfortunate Comte de Montgomeri and his betrothed bride. Sometimes sanguine that Henri would, nay, must recover; at others plunged in the depth of despair—had been the alternate moods of the count during these eleven days. His friends conjured him to lose no time in retiring from France, at least for a time; and Idalie herself, though she shrunk from the idea of parting, with an indefinable feeling of foreboding dread, yet so trembled for his safety if he remained, as to add her solicitations to those of others. Still the count lingered. The very thought of his having been the ill-fated hand to give the death-blow to the monarch he revered, and the friend he loved, was too horrible to be realized. He could not believe that such would be; yet so dark was his despair, so agonizing his self accusations, that even his interviews with Idalie had lost their soothing sweetness, and he did but deplore that her pure love had been given to one so darkly fated as himself.

It was after one of these bursts of misery that the Comte de Montemar, who had been engaged with papers at the further end of the apartment, approached and sought to comfort him by an appeal to those holier feelings, which Montgomeri possessed in a much higher degree than most of his countrymen.

"It is not well, my friend," De Montemar said, "to poison thus the brief moments we may yet pass together. Remember, thou wert no willing agent of that higher power, by whose mandate alone it was that our monarch fell. All may seem dark, yet even out of darkness He brought forth light—out of a very chaos the most unwavering order; and does he not do so still? Abide by the advice of those who urge thee to quit France till order is restored, and our gracious sovereign's last words remembered and acted upon. Italian blood is hot and eager to avenge; but fear not, we shall meet again in happier days, and oh, embitter not thus the few moments still left my poor child!"

Softened and subdued more than he had been yet, Montgomeri folded his arm round the weeping Idalie, kissed the tears from her pale cheek, conjured her forgiveness, and promised to battle with the despondency that almost crushed him.

"And thou wilt indeed do this?" she rejoined, imploringly. "Oh, bless thee for such promise! Yet I fear thee, Montgomeri. And when apart from me, these troubled thoughts regain ascendency, thou wilt rush on danger, on death, to escape them. Think, then, dearest, that it is not your own life alone which you risk; that one is bound up in it which cannot rest alone. Will the ivy blossom and smile when the oak has fallen? And as the oak is to the lowly yet clinging ivy, so art thou to me."

Folding her still closer, Montgomeri in his turn sought to

reassure and soothe, but with less success than usual. Every look and tone of Idalie betrayed that heavy weight which had increased with each day that brought the hour of parting nearer. Breathed to none, and battled with as it had been, still it seemed to hold every faculty chained, and at length caused her head to sink on the bosom of De Lorges with such a burst of irrepressible anguish as to excite his alarm, and tenderly he conjured her to reveal its cause.

"I know it is a weakness, a folly, Gabriel, unworthy of the woman whom thou lovest; but scorn it not, upbraid it not, bid it go from me! Is there not woe enough in parting, that before the hope of meeting ever rises a dim and shapeless darkness impossible to be defined, yet so folding round my future as to bury all of hope, of trust, of every feeling, save that *we shall not meet as we have parted?*"

"Is it change in me thou fearest, love? No. Then heed it not; 'tis but a baseless fancy, which will come when the frame is weakened by the anguish of the mind. Believe me—"

He was interrupted. The hangings over the door leading by a private passage to the dauphine's own rooms were suddenly drawn aside, and, closely muffled, Mary of Scotland stood before them, with anxiety and haste visibly imprinted on her features.

"This is no time for ceremony, my lord, or we would apologize for our intrusion," she said, turning towards the Count de Montemar; "our business is too weighty for an indifferent messenger. Count de Lorges," she added, addressing him abruptly, and pausing not for Montemar's courtly words, "tarry not another night in Paris; you have been unwise to loiter here so long. Pause for no thought, no marvel. Fly at once; put the broad seas between you and France, and there may be happiness in store for you yet. Dearest Idalie, for thy sake, even as for Montgomeri's, I am here; do not look upon me thus."

"*Now* must we part—now? Your highness means not now!" exclaimed Idalie, as her cold hands convulsively closed round the count's arm. "What has he done that he should fly?"

"Nothing to call the blush of shame to his cheek or thine, dear child. The words I have heard may mean nothing, may be but wrung from woman's agony, for the grief of Catherine de Medicis is of no softening nature; yet ought Montgomeri to leave Paris without delay, for there may be some to act on broken words, even as on an imperial mandate. Detain him not, Idalie; we shall visit Scotland perchance ere long; and there no grief shall damp a bridal."

"Stay but one moment more, royal lady," entreated De Lorges, as the dauphine turned to go; "one word, for mercy! How fares the king? Is there no more hope? Does he still lie as he has done ever since that fatal stroke?"

Mary looked at him somewhat surprised, and very sorrowfully.

"No, Montgomeri, no!" she said, after a pause of much feeling; "the soul has escaped the shattered prison, and Henri is at rest."

Montgomeri staggered back with a heavy, almost convulsive groan. He knew not till that moment how powerfully hope had sustained him. The shock was almost as fearful as if he had never thought of death; and yet the horrible conviction that he was a regicide had scarcely for one instant left his mind.

"Montemar, let not this be, for the sake of thy poor child, of both. Part them ere long," whispered the queen (dauphine no more), as the count knelt before her in involuntary homage; "think not of us now. Would to God we were still Dauphine of France and not her queen. Montgomeri's danger, I fear, is imminent; let him not linger, and may our Lady guard him still."

She departed as she spoke; and Montemar, infected with her evident anxiety, hesitated not to obey.

"Rouse thee, Montgomeri," he said, earnestly; "fly, for the sake of this poor, drooping flower; let not our Idalie weep for a darker doom than even this sad parting. Come to thy father's heart awhile, my child. Have I no claim upon thy love?"

Gently he drew her from Montgomeri's still detaining arms, almost relieved to find her insensible to any further suffering. His beseeching words to fly ere Idalie again awoke to consciousness, moved the count to action. Still he lingered to kiss again and again the pale cheek and lips of his beloved: then convulsively wringing the count's hand, rushed from the room and from the palace at the very moment that voices shouted, "Long live Francis the Second! God preserve the king!"

III.

Eighteen months had passed, and still was the Count de Montgomeri an exile from his country; and so virulent was Catherine against him, so determinately forgetful of Henri's last words, absolving the count of all intentional evil, whatever might ensue, that even his best friends dared not wish him back. For Idalie, this interval was indeed heavy with anxiety and sorrow, and all the bitter sickness of hope deferred. No doubt of his affection ever entered her heart; she knew him fond and faithful as herself; but there seemed no end, no term to the long, long interval of absence. Her future was bounded by the hour of meeting, and a very void of interest, and hope and pleasure seemed the space which stretched between. Yet, for her father's sake, her ever unselfish nature struggled with the stagnating gloom. The court was loathsome to them both, for even the friendship of the young queen could not remove from Idalie the horror which Catherine de Medicis inspired. In the Chateau de Montemar, then, these eighteen months had mostly been passed, and Idalie compelled herself to seek and feel interest in the families of her father's vassals, and in the many lessons of feudal government and policy which, as the heiress of all his large estates and of his proud, unsullied name, her father delighted to pour into her ear.

One other subject engrossed the Count de Montemar, and of which he spoke so often and so solemnly to his daughter, that his feelings on the subject became hers; it was the wide-spreading over France of the new religion, deemed by all orthodox Catholics as a heresy, which if not checked, would entirely subvert and destroy their ancient faith, and in consequence bring incalculable mischief to the country, both temporarily and spiritually. De Montemar was no bigot, looking only to violent measures for the extermination of this far-spreading evil; but it grieved and affected him in no common degree. He spent hours and hours with his confessor and his daughter in commune on this one engrossing subject; and from the sincere and earnest lessons of the priest, a true and zealous though humble follower of his own church, he became more and more convinced of the truth of the olden creed, and what he deemed the foul and awful apostasy of the new.

Yet no violence of party spirit mingled in these discussions, and therefore it was that Idalie felt the conviction of the truth and beauty of her long cherished religion sink into her soul like balm. Saddened by her individual sorrow, shrinking in consequence from all the exciting amusements then reigning in France, her father's favorite subject became equally a resource and comfort to her, thus unconsciously fitting her for the martyr part which she was only too soon called upon to play.

The Count de Montemar had been a soldier from his youth, and was still suffering from the serious wounds received in his last campaign. Within the last three months he had gradually become weaker and weaker, till at length Idalie watched beside the couch, from which she had been told that her beloved and loving parent would never rise again. She had heard it with an agony of sorrow, which it was long ere the kindly sympathy of the benevolent priest and of her cousin Louis could in any degree assuage. Motherless from early childhood, a more than common tie bound her to her father; and so deep was the darkness which those cruel tidings seemed to gather round her, that even love itself succumbed beneath it, and the strange, wild yearning rose, that she, too, might "flee away, and be at rest."

Unable to endure any longer these sad thoughts, Idalie arose from the seat where she had kept vigil for many weary nights and days, and looked forth upon the night. The moon was at the full, and shed such clear and silvery light around, that even the rugged crags and stunted pines seemed softened into beauty. The vale beneath slumbered in shadow, save where, here and there, a solitary tree stood forth, seemingly bathed in liquid silver. Sweet odours from the flowers of the night lingered on the breeze, and the rippling gush of a streamlet, reflecting every star and ray upon its bosom, was the only sound that broke the silence. The holy calm of Nature touched a responding chord in the heart of the watcher, and even grief felt for the moment stilled. A few minutes afterwards the voice of the count recalled her to his side.

"Is it fancy, or was Louis here but now, my child?" he asked feebly. "Is he from the court? and did he not bring news? Wherefore came he?"

"Because he heard that I was in sorrow, my dear father; and he sought, as he ever does, to soothe, or at least to share it."

"Bless him for his faithful love! He has in truth been to me a son, and will be to thee a brother, mine own love; but tell me, is it indeed truth, or have my thoughts again wandered, has my young sovereign gone before me to the grave?"

"Alas! my father, 'tis even so."

An expression of deep sorrow escaped the lips of the dying man, and for several minutes he was silent. When again he spoke, his voice was firmer.

"Idalie, my child, I shall soon follow my royal master; and it is well, for the regency of Catherine de Medicis can bring with it but misery. Listen to me, beloved one! I leave thee sole heiress of our olden heritage, of a glorious name, which from age to age hath descended in a line so pure, so stainless, that the name of De Montemar hath become a very proverb for all honourable and knightly deeds. There have been times when daughters, not sons, succeeded; and yet did its lusture not diminish nor its power decrease. Thou knowest this, my child. I know not wherefore I recall it now."

"Dost thou doubt me, father?" replied Idalie, sadly, and somewhat reproachfully. "Thinkest thou my heart is so engrossed with selfish sorrows that I feel no pride, no love for mine ancient race, that its glory and its power shall decrease with me?"

"No, no, my noble child. Forgive me, I have pained thee, yet I meant it not." Pausing a moment, he continued hurriedly, "Idalie, our faith, our blessed faith is tottering, falling in this land. Each month, each week the heretics gain ground; nor will all the bloody acts of Catherine and the princes of Guise arrest their progress. Were health and life renewed, I would neither raise sword nor kindle brand for their destruction; but my whole soul trembles for my native land. Idalie, my child, I know thy heart beats true as mine to our ancient creed. I know thou wilt never turn aside thyself from the one true path; but oh, for thy dead father's sake, let not a heretic be master of these fair lands, and tempt thy vassals to embrace his soul-destroying creed. Thou wilt not wed with heresy, my child?"

"Never, my father! I can pity and pray for these misguided ones; but never shall my hand be given to one unfaithful to his God. Yet wherefore this fear? Am I not the plighted bride of one who would rather die than lead me astray, or turn aside himself?"

The fading eyes of the dying lit suddenly up with feverish radiance, his cheek burned, and his mind evidently so far wandered as to prevent either his hearing or understanding his daughter's last words.

"And thou wilt promise this?" he said, in a voice at once alarmingly hollow, yet strangely excited; "thou wilt solemnly promise never to give thyself and thy fair heritage to the heretic; thou wilt not let the foul spot blacken our noble line? Promise me this, my child."

Alarmed at the change in his appearance, and convinced that Montgomeri, who, when he left her, had been as true and zealous a Catholic as herself, was not of a nature to change, Idalie knelt down beside the couch, and in distinct and solemn accents made the vow required.

The Count de Montemar raised himself with sudden strength, and laid both his hands on the bent head of his child. "Now blessings, blessings on thee for this, my sainted one!" he said, distinctly; "thou hast removed all doubt, all fear; death has no terror now, no sting. God's blessing be upon thee, love, and give—"

His voice sunk, but his lips still warmly pressed her brow, and minutes thus passed. A cloud had come before the moon, and when her light broke forth again, Idalie knelt by the couch of the dead.

IV.

Idalie de Montemar was not long permitted to indulge her grief in solitude. Scarcely two months after her loss, an express arrived from Paris, and she was compelled to prepare her chateau and vassals for the reception of the young king, the queen mother, and court, who in their progress to the south passed through Auvergne. Idalie roused herself from the sorrow which weighed so heavily on her spirits. Although chivalry had lost much of the enthusiasm and warmth which had characterised it not half a century previous, its memory still lingered in the minds of men; and something of this feeling actuated the men of Montemar as they looked on their youthful countess. Shrinking and timid as she had been while her parent lived, a new spirit now seemed her own; and it was with all the proud consciousness that she was now sole representative of one of the most ancient and most noble families of

France that Idalie de Montemar, at the head of her loyal vassals, received her royal guests, and knelt in homage to the youthful Charles.

But amid all that royal group only one had power over the heart of Idalie, and she grieved to see the saddened brow and anxious glance, which had usurped the place of the radiant smiles and sparkling eye, which had never before failed to beam forth from the lovely countenance of Mary Queen of Scots. Robed so completely in white (the costume of royal widows) as to receive the designation of La Reine blanche, her beauty rather increased than diminished by its softened tone; she was to many an object of still deeper interest now than she had been hitherto; but it was very soon evident to Idalie that the petty mortifications springing from rooted envy and dislike, to which she was daily, almost hourly subjected by Catherine, were poisoning all youthful enjoyment, and that even while she clave with her whole soul to France, she felt it must not be her home much longer.

Feeling deeply, as she did, that it was to Mary's faithful friendship her betrothed husband owed his life, Idalie's high spirit rose indignant at this treatment. That the marked respect with which she treated her, the constant deference to her wishes, during the royal sojourn, exposed her to Catherine's fatal malice, she cared not for. Soothed by her affection, roused to a sense of her own dignity as sovereign of Scotland, if no longer of France, it was during her sojourn at the Chateau de Montemar, Mary resolved on her return to her native land, and by earnest persuasions prevailed on the young countess to sue for the royal permission to accompany her. It was granted, ungraciously enough; for her engagement with the Count de Montgomeri was known, and the hatred borne by Catherine de Medicis towards that unfortunate nobleman, had in no way diminished by time.

"Will the good Count Gabriel de Lorges accompany his young bride on her return? Know ye, my lords, if so, we will give him welcome," the queen mother soon after inquired, in the hearing of Idalie, and in a voice so peculiarly sweet and gracious as to cause the countess's heart, for the moment, to bound up with sudden hope of his permitted, even welcomed return, and then as suddenly sink down, she knew not wherefore, save that Catherine's deadliest purposes ever breathed through smiles.

A few months after her visit to the chateau Mary quitted

France, attended by Idalie de Montemar, and some other youthful friends, to whom she clung, as the sole memories left her of that beautiful and happy land, which her foreboding spirit whispered she should never look on more. Intent on soothing the grief of her royal friend, Idalie had but little time to think of her own feelings; but when she did seek to define them, she became conscious that they were not all joy. Again did the same dim shadow envelope every thought, every hope directed towards the hour of meeting. Every day that brought it nearer seemed to throw a chilling weight on her heart's ecstatic bound. Her very love felt too intense, too twined with her being, to find rest, even in the thought of looking on him, listening to him again. She strove with the baseless shadow, but it clung pertinaciously to every mental image, and weighed upon her spirits like lead.

Scotland was reached at last; the heavy pomp and ceremony attending the sovereign's landing and progress to Holyrood at length at an end, and Idalie had retired to the chamber appointed for the use of herself and suite, seeking calmness and rest from the opposing emotions at one and the same time engrossing her.

Why should she not be joyful? the morrow Montgomeri would be at her side once more, and all unchanged to her; not a doubt had stolen on the bright vision of his love, not a shade darkened the pure thoughts of his constancy—what then did she dread?

A summons to the chamber of the queen startled her, for she had been dismissed, she thought, for the night. Hastily obeying, she ran lightly along the private gallery pointed out as her nearest way, and without pausing drew aside the arras and entered. A cry of astonishment, of bliss at the same moment escaped her lips, and, clasped to the heart of the Count de Montgomeri, all darkness and dread faded for the time in a burst of happy tears upon his bosom.

V.

"Nay, chide me not, that my cheek is paler than when we parted, dearest," said Idalie, after long and earnest commune, as they sat together the following day in an olden chamber of Holyrood, far removed from the sovereign and the court. "Thou too art changed; and if in thee, a soldier and a man.

absence can have wrought furrows on thy brow, pallor on thy cheek, and even touched thy hair with grey, is it strange that I, a poor weak girl, should suffer too? I scarce had loved thee, Gabriel, had there been no change."

"I would not have taxed thy love, even had it left less touching impress on thy cheek," replied the count; "but for me, harsh storms and ruffled thoughts have joined with the yearning thoughts for thee to make me as thou seest. Why look upon me thus? canst doubt me, dearest?"

"Oh, no, no! thy love is not changed, save that it may be dearer still; but thine eyes looked not thus the day we parted. There are deeper, sterner feelings in thy soul than heretofore; the change is *there*. The storms of which thou speakest have not been outward only—glory, ambition, love, are not the sole occupants of thy spirit now."

"And what if thou hast read aright, sweet one, wilt thou not love thy soldier still?"

"Oh, yes! for nought could enter the heart of De Lorges his Idalie may not revere. But tell me these inward storms—why is thy look, save when it is turned on me, so strangely stern? It was not always thus?"

"Call it not stern, my love: 'tis but the shadow of my spirit's change. I did not think thou wouldst so soon have marked it; yet 'tis not sternness, or if it be, 'tis only towards myself. When we parted, dearest, I lived for earth and earthly things; but with sorrow came thoughts of that higher world, which must banish the idle smile and idler jest; 'tis thus that I am changed."

"And is this all?" faltered Idalie, looking fearfully in his face; "is this enough to cause the struggle, of which thy cheek and brow bear such true witness? The thought of heaven brings with it but balm and rest—not strife and pain. Gabriel, this is *not* all."

"It *is* not all, my own! I would not have a thought concealed from thee; and yet I pause, fearing to give thee pain. Listen to me, beloved one! and oh, believe, Montgomeri would not lightly turn aside from the path his fathers trod; yet hast thou seen, as I have, the gross crimes, the awful passions, which have crept into the bosom of our holy church; the fearful darkness of ignorance and bigotry overspreading the pure light marking the path of Jesus, thou wouldst feel with me, and acknowledge that I could not think of God and heaven, and yet be other than I am. Idalie, speak to me! wherefore art thou thus?"

He ceased in terror; her features had become contracted, his lip and cheek blanched almost as death. Her large eyes distended in their terrible gaze upon himself, and the hands which had convulsively closed on his, were cold and rigid as stone.

"It cannot, *cannot* be," she murmured, in a low shuddering tone. "Montgomeri could not be other than true; no, no. Why will you speak thus, love?" she added, somewhat less unnaturally. "What can such strange words mean, save that thy sword, like my father's, will never be unsheathed in persecuting wars—answer me, Gabriel, is it not so?"

"Alas! my love, I may not rest in quiet when the weapon of every true man is needed to protect the creed which conviction has embraced. In these dark times this badge of Protestantism and the sword of defence must ever be raised together. Idalie, the world may term me heretic; but thou—"

"Thou art *no* heretic; no, no—it cannot be!" burst from the wrung heart of Idalie, as she wildly sprung from his embrace. Montgomeri, thou art deceiving me—thou wouldst try the love I bear thee! Oh, not thus, not thus! Say thou art no heretic; thou art still the man my father loved, trusted, blessed; him to whom he gave his child. Speak to me; answer me—but one word!"

"I will, I will, mine own! let me but see thee calm. Am I not thine own? Art thou not mine? Come to my heart, sweet one; thou wilt find no change towards thee!"

"Answer me," she reiterated; "Gabriel, thou hast not answered! By the love thou bearest me, by the vow unto my father—to love and cherish me till death—by thine own truth—I charge thee answer me, thou art no heretic?"

"If to raise my voice against the gross abuses fostered by the Pope and his pampered minions in every land, to deny to them all allegiance, to refuse all belief in the intervention of saints and martyrs, or that absolution, bought and sold, can bring pardon and peace; if to read and believe the Holy Scriptures, and follow as they teach—if this is to be a heretic, Idalie, even for thy dear sake, I may not deny it Yes, dearest, I am a heretic in all, save love for thee!"

A low, despairing cry broke from those blanched lips, and Idalie fell forward at his feet. It seemed long ere Montgomeri could restore her to life, though he used a tenderness and skill strange in a rough warrior like himself; but no fond look returned his anxious gaze. She struggled to withdraw herself from his embrace, but the tone of reproachful agony with which he pronounced her name rendered the struggle vain; and, clinging to him, she sobbed, "I thought not of this, dreamed not of this; even in the dark foreboding haze clinging round the hour of meeting. Gabriel, in mercy leave me, or I shall forget my vow, and hurl down on me the wrath of the dead."

"Leave thee!—vow!—wrath of the dead!" he repeated. "Oh, do not talk so wildly, love; reproach, upbraid me, as thou wilt; but tell me not to leave thee. Wherefore should we part?"

"Gabriel, it *must* be! I have no strength when I gaze on thee. Let not perjury darken this deep misery; leave me!"

"Perjury! what hast thou sworn?" demanded Montgomeri, hoarse, and choked with strong emotion.

"Never to wed with heresy! To retain the faith of my ancestors pure and unsullied as I received it. My father, from his bed of death, demanded this vow, and I pledged it unhesitatingly; for could I doubt *thee?*"

She had spoken with unnatural composure, but there was such a sudden and agonized change on the features of the count, that it not only banished calmness, but reawakened hope.

"Oh, say thou wert deceiving me, Gabriel. Dearest Gabriel, have I not judged thee wrongly that still we may pray together as we have prayed? Thou hast not turned aside from our old and sainted creed. Say but this grief is causeless; that I may still love thee without sin; that there is no need to part!"

"Part!" he passionately exclaimed, "and from thee? Oh, no, no!"

"Then thou art, in truth, no heretic? It has all been a dark and terrible dream, and we shall be happy yet, love!" she answered, in a voice of such trusting joyance, that Montgomeri started from her side, and hurriedly paced the room.

She laid her hand gently on his arm, and looked up confidingly in his face; but its expression was enough. Shrinking from him, she implored, "Gabriel, Gabriel, look not on me thus, or that fearful dream will come again!"

"Would, would to God it were a dream!" he exclaimed, and his hands clasped both hers with convulsive pressure. "Idalie, I am no Catholic; I dare not again kneel as I have knelt, or pray as I have prayed. No, not even to retain thy precious love, to claim thee mine—thee, dearer than life, than happiness, than all, save eternity—I dare not deny my faith. But, oh, is there no other way? Can it be, that for this, a firm conviction of truth, an honest avowal of that which my soul believes, for this that we must part? Idalie, canst thou sentence me to *this?*"

"I have sworn," she said, her white lips quivering with the effort. "My vow is registered in heaven—sworn unto the dead; by death only to be absolved."

"To retain the line of Montemar unsullied in its ancient faith. Idalie, oh, hear me; let me plead now! Give to Louis de Montemar the government of thine ancestral lands, the control of thy vassals. Thou shalt seek them when thou wilt, unaccompanied by thy husband, unshackled by his counsels. I ask but for thee; and here, far removed from the blood and misery deluging unhappy France, we may live for each other still. May not this be, love, and yet thy vow remain unbroken?"

"Montgomeri, it may not be," she said, in a low yet collected tone, for it seemed as if the noble spirit of her race returned to give her strength for that harrowing hour.

"Tempt me not by such words as these—the love I bear thee is trial all-sufficient. My oath was pledged that I would never wed with heresy—never give my hand to one unfaithful to our old and sainted creed. Perchance that oath alone may save me from a like perdition, and if so, then is it well."

"And dost thou scorn me for this—despise and loathe me? Oh, Idalie, thou knowest not all I have endured. In mercy add not to the anguish of this hour, by scorn of the change which imperious conscience alone had power to impel."

"Scorn thee, Montgomeri! No; if thou, the good, the wise, can thus decide, and so find peace, is it for me to judge thee harshly? No, Idalie can never *blame* thee, Gabriel."

He caught her to his heart, and she resisted not the impassioned kisses he pressed on cheek and brow. She felt his hot tears fall fast upon her face, for in that suffering hour it was the iron-souled warrior that wept, not the pale, slight girl he held.

"This must not be, beloved," she whispered, in low soothing tones. "Montgomeri, my noble love—for in this last hour I may still call thee so—oh, rouse thee from this woman's weakness; this is no mood for thee. Thou must forget me, Gabriel; or so think of me as to be once again the brave, the high-souled warrior thou hast ever been. For my sake, rouse thee, love! The God we part to serve will hear my prayers, and bless thee."

"And thou!" burst passionately from the lips of the count. "Oh, what shall comfort thee, and fill for thee the void of everlasting absence? In the rush of battle the warrior may find forgetfulness in death; but—"

"No, no, not death; Gabriel, for my sake, live, though not for me; add not this pang to a heart already tried enough. Promise me to live, and for me! Leave me to my God, Montgomeri, and He will give me peace."

He could not answer, and minutes—many minutes—rolled away, and neither moved from the detaining arms of the other. Fortunately perhaps for both, a page entered with a summons to the count from the queen. Idalie lifted up her head, and while her very blood seemed turned to ice a smile circled that pale lip.

"Thou must leave me, dearest. Mary loves not to wait, indulgent as she is."

"But we shall meet again, sweet love?"

There was no answer; but Montgomeri would not understand that silence. He strained her once more to his heart, and turned away: another minute the arras fell, and he was gone. Idalie made one bound forward, as if to detain him, and, with a low shuddering cry, dropped senseless on the ground.

VI

It was in a lordly chamber of the Chateau de Montemar, about three months after the event narrated in our last chapter, that the only remaining scions of that noble house were seated in earnest and evidently sorrowful converse. The beams of the sun, rendered gorgeous by the richly-stained glass of the antique windows through which they passed, fantastically tinged the oaken floor and walls. The furniture was of ebony, inlaid with silver, interspersed with couches and cushions of tapestry, ancient as the days of Matilda of Flanders, which, though somewhat heavy in themselves, accorded well with the aspect of solemn grandeur prevading the whole apartment.

"Do not refuse me, Louis," pleaded Idalie, after a long

and painful discussion relative to her papers and parchments, which strewed the table, had passed between them; "do not thus entreat me to retain mine heritage. Is a broken heart, a sinking frame fit chief for Montemar? I have borne much, suffered much, sought even the court of Charles, which my whole soul loathes, to obtain the transferment to thee of all my earthly possessions, and now do not refuse to relieve me of their heavy charge."

"But only wait awhile, sweet cousin," he replied; "sorrow has had as yet no time to expend its force. Do not act so soon on the resolution of a moment's agony; wait but one brief year, and think well on all you would resign. Has earth no spell to fright away thy purpose?"

"None; it is but the casket, whence the jewel has departed. Nay more, it is filled with hopes I dare not hope, and thoughts I dare not think. I would fly from these."

"And will a convent aid thee so to do?"

"I know not; yet there at least temptation, which I have no strength to meet, will not assail me more.,"

"No strength to meet! Dearest Idalie, the martyr at the stake might envy thee thy strength."

"Not now, Louis, it has all gone from me," and for the first time her voice quivered, and she buried her face in her clasped hands. A fierce malediction on Montgomeri was bursting from the lips of Louis, as he looked on the faded form, and seemed to feel for the first time the full extent of his cousin's agony. Young, buoyant, and ever joyous himself, Idalie's perfect calmness since her return had deceived him; but the tone in which those few words were said strangely and suddenly revealed the whole, and the young man's whole heart spoke in his half-uttered curse.

"No, no; curse him not, Louis!" passionately implored Idalie. "Promise me, by the sweet memories of our childhood, still to be his friend. In these awful times, when the poisoned draught and midnight dagger are ever near these persecuted men, be near him to warn, shield, save."

"I will, I will, for thy sweet sake," he replied earnestly. "Yet why fear such danger for him? he never will be rash enough to return to France."

"Louis, he is even now in France, and therefore is it I so conjure you to be his friend. He is here, may be near me still, even as he hovered close beside me in my passage home. He thought to be unknown, even to me; me, whom he was there to guard, protect to the last, speaking not one word to betray himself, or give me again the torture of farewell. I knew him close beside me; I heard the disguised accents of his voice, and yet we were as if the grave had parted us. Oh, Louis, Louis! the strength which then upheld me has departed from me; I dare not look upon his face and listen to his voice again. Only the convent walls can shield me from a broken vow, a dead father's curse; and wilt thou keep me from their refuge? No, no; relieve me from this fearful heritage, *and let me be at peace.*"

* * * * * *

One week after Louis de Montemar had been acknowledged by all the vassals of his cousin as their suzerain or feudal lord, to whom and to his heirs they had sworn undying allegiance, Idalie stood within the convent church of our Lady of Montemar, preparing to take those awful vows which severed her from earth, and all its cares and joys, and hopes and woes, for ever. It was midnight, but the large waxen tapers burning on the high altar and many shrines completely illuminated the main body of the church, while the deep shadows of the aisles and more distinct arches of the nave heightened the effect of light, and rendered the building larger in appearance than in reality. Clouds of incense floated on the air, from the rich silver censers held by six beautiful boys, clothed in white, standing on either side the altar. Behind, and exquisitely illuminated by a peculiarly softened light falling full upon it, hung a picture of the Saviour kneeling in the garden of Gethsemane, his countenance powerfully expressive of the words, "Nevertheless, not what I will, but what Thou wilt."

The church was crowded in the nave and aisles, the choir and chancel being left for the relations of the novice and those of higher rank. As Idalie had but few of the former, and had particularly wished the ceremony to be as private as possible, these parts of the building were comparatively unoccupied, except by monks and priests.

Clothed with unwonted gorgeousness, Idalie stood beside the altar. A rich robe of grey Genoa velvet descended to her feet, sweeping the marble ground in heavy folds, girded round the waist with a broad belt of large rubies and opals; glittering stars of the same clasped down the stomacher, and looped the wide sleeves of richest lace, and braids of diamonds glistened in the dark tresses of her hair, and sparkled on the high, pure brow, which, marble pale, seemed all unfitted for their weight. Her eyes were raised, her lips slightly parted, her thin white hands crossed upon her bosom, as in the heartfelt utterance of voiceless prayer. Silence, deep as the grave, had succeeded the priest's prayer, lasting but a moment, for Idalie sinking noiselessly on the ground, the black pall was thrown over her, and the distant discharge of cannon, mingled with the muffled toll of the convent bell, proclaimed far and near that Idalie de Montemar was now an inmate of the tomb. A groan so deep and hollow at that instant reverberated through the building, that all present started, and shudderingly drew nearer each other, unable to trace whence or from whom it came, until a tall shrouded figure was discovered leaning against one of the pillars supporting the arched roof of the choir; his face was buried in his cloak, but he was seen to shiver, as by some rudely-passing wind. The organ swelled forth in thrilling tones the requiem for the dead, sweet childish voices prolonged the solemn strain, till it faded softer and softer in the distance, swelling, falling, then dying all away. Removing the pall, the priests waited for Idalie to rise and kneel before the altar, that the ceremony might continue. They waited, but there was no movement. She lay even as she had fallen. A cry of terror burst from the aged priest, and at the same instant, heedless of the personal danger inseparable from discovery, bareheaded and unshrouded—heedless of all save one agonizing fear—Gabriel de Lorges rushed forwards, and knelt beside her.

"Idalie! loveliest! dearest! speak to me, answer me; say that I have not murdered thee! Answer me, in mercy, but one word!"

He spoke in vain. Louis de Montemar, priests, and many others crowded round him. They sought to withdraw her from Montgomeri's convulsive hold, to wake her from the seeming trance. But all was useless; she had passed to heaven in that music swell. The broken-hearted was at rest.*

*The after-fate of the unfortunate but guiltless regicide belongs to history.

Lady Gresham's Fete.

A TALE OF THE DAY.

It was near the end of May, beautiful May, that month of strange contrarieties in our lovely land. In the haunts of Nature, robed with such gorgeous beauty, bringing such a lavish garniture of tree and shrub, and flowers; such fresh and dewy mornings; such glorious sunsets; and those soft sweet hours of twilight, so fraught with spiritual musings; and those lovely nights, when the mind loses itself in the infinitude of thought, in the vain yearning to grasp something beyond our present being, in itself evidence of Immortality! In the city, in the proud metropolis, seat of empire and wealth, fashion and beauty, luxury and pleasure, crime and famine, misery and desolation, clothed as May still is with her natural beauty, we know her not, save as the "Season!" and in that word what a host of thoughts spring up—enjoyment, luxury, fêtes, balls, dinners! These were *once*, and but few years back, its sole association; but now a mighty spirit is abroad, and over the festal halls a dim cloud is hovering, breathing of oppression born in that very thoughtless joyance. Through the gay music, the silvery laugh, the murmur of glad voices—aye, through every tone that tells of luxurious pleasure only—a thrilling cry is sounding! the voice of suffering thousands, claiming brotherhood with Joy; demanding a portion of that which a beneficent Father ordained for ALL—rest, recreation, homes.

In the drawing-room of one of the smaller mansions of the aristocratic west, a young lady was sitting near an open window, inhaling the delicious scent of the beautiful flowers, which filled the balcony in such profusion that, shaded in the background as they were by the magnificent trees of the park, they looked as if the goddess May had brought a garden from her most sylvan haunts, to mark her presence even there.

Lucy Neville, the sole inmate of this pleasant room, was neither very young nor very beautiful, yet she had charms enough to occasion some degree of wonderment that she should have passed through four London seasons and attained the venerable age of three-and-twenty, and was Lucy Neville still. She had the advantage of mingling with some of the most highly-gifted and most learned patriots of the age; for her brother, Lord Valery, of whose house she was the sole mistress, was one of the most influential men of his day. She went into society also continually; and, altogether, it was a constant marvel to all those who had nothing to do but to talk of their neighbours, why she had never married. Lucy Neville might not have had regular beauty, but she had something better—she had MIND, and a heart so full of good and kindly feeling, that she was an exception to the general idea, that we must know sorrow ourselves before we can feel for others. She was, indeed, only just putting off mourning for a young and darling brother; but she had begun to think years before that, and the six months of quietude had only deepened, not created, the principles on which she acted.

"Visitors so late! why, it is just six o'clock!" passed through her mind, as a loud, impetuous ring announced a carriage; and a party of young ladies, of ultra-fashionable exterior, hurried into the drawing-room, all talking at once, and of something so very delightful, that Miss Neville had great difficulty in comprehending their meaning.

"Now, Lucy, don't look so bewildered. You are quick enough at comprehension sometimes, and I really want you to understand me with a word now, for I am in a terrible hurry. I ought to have come to you by eleven this morning, but really this short invitation has given me so many things to think about, I could not."

"But what am I to understand, Charlotte?" replied Miss Neville, laughing so good humouredly, that it was difficult to discover why those of her own age and standing so often kept aloof from her, as having so little in common. "Laura—Mary—have pity on my obtuseness."

"Why, Lady Gresham's long-talked-of fête is fixed at last; and of course you will go. Your invitation was enclosed in mamma's last night. Absolutely her ladyship condescends to entreat her to introduce you. I cannot imagine the reason of this sudden *empressement*—she could have visited you long ago, had she wished it."

"She did wish it individually, I believe; but an unfortunate misunderstanding between her brother and mine prevented it. Edward has long wished the estrangement to cease, so

I shall be very happy to meet her half way, and accept the invitation. When is it?"

"Next Monday."

"Monday! Why, to-day is Friday! You must mean Monday week!"

"Indeed I do not. How she will manage I cannot tell, except that when people have more wealth than they know what to do with, they can do what they please. Her villa at Richmond, too, is just the place for a *fête champêtre;* and the novel shortness of the invitation, and being the day before a drawing-room, will crowd her rooms, depend upon it. It is something unusually exciting, the very bustle of the thing."

"But I thought it was not to be until—"

"Until Herbert Gresham returned. Nor will it. He arrives to-morrow night, or some time on Sunday, quite suddenly, not having been expected for several weeks yet. What with his foreign honours, his promised baronetcy, and last, not least, his distinguished appearance, he will be sought and fêted by all the money-loving mammas and husband-seeking daughters for the remainder of the season."

"The worst of its being a *fête champêtre* is, that we must have complete new dresses," rejoined Laura. "And how to coax papa for the necessary help, I know not; my last quarter was all gone before I received it, and my debts actually frighten me. But what is to be done? go I must."

"And then the shortness of the notice!" continued Mary; "really Lady Gresham might have given us more time. Who can decide what to wear, or even what colour, in three days?"

"Come, Lucy, decide! But of course you will go!" exclaimed Charlotte, impatiently. "It will be your first appearance in public this season, and so you can have nothing to think about in the way of expense. Nothing but the trouble of seeing about a new dress."

"Which will prevent my going, much as I might wish it," replied Miss Neville, very quietly, though the faint tinge rising to her cheek, and the quiver of the lip, might have betrayed some degree of internal emotion.

"Prevent your going! What can you possibly mean?" exclaimed all her guests together.

"That as it is now six o'clock on Friday, and you tell me Lady Gresham's fête is three o'clock on Monday, I have not sufficient time to procure all I want (for having been so long in mourning, I have literally nothing that will do) without breaking a resolution, and sacrificing a principle, which I do not feel at all inclined to do."

"Sacrificing a principle! Lucy, you are perfectly ridiculous! What has principle to do with a *fête champêtre?* Your head is turned with the stupid cant of oppressing, and the people, as if we had not annoyances, and vexations, and pressure too, when we want more money than we happen to have! And as for time, what is to prevent your sending to Mrs. Smith to-night, (by-the-bye, how *can* you employ an English *artiste?*) and get all you want by ten o'clock on Monday morning? Why, I cannot even give an order till after the post comes in to-morrow. I must wait to know what was worn at the Duchesse de Nemours' *fête champêtre* the other day. One feels just out of the ark, in England."

"And I am sure I cannot decide what to wear till then," languidly remarked Mary.

"And as for me, I am in a worse predicament than either of you," laughed Laura, but her laugh was not a gay one. "Raise the wind I must, but it requires time to think how."

We have no space to follow this conversation further. Persuasions, reproaches, and taunts assailed Miss Neville on all sides, but she did not waver. Charlotte left her in high dudgeon; Mary marvelled at her unfortunate delusion, quite convinced that she was on the verge of insanity; and Laura wishing that she could but be as firm. Not that she comprehended or allowed the necessity of the principle on which she acted, but only as it would save her the disagreeable task of thinking how to get the necessary costume, when both *modiste* and jeweller had refused to trust her any more.

For nearly half an hour Lucy remained sitting where her visitors had left her, her hands pressed on her eyes, and her whole posture denoting a painful intensity of thought. Herbert Gresham returning! His mother's unexpected and pressing invitation! Could it be that the bar between the families was indeed so entirely removed, that she might hope as she had never dared hope before? Sir Sydney's hatred to her brother, from some political opposition, had been such, it was whispered at the time, that he had obtained his nephew some honourable appointment abroad, only because he feared that he not only loved Lucy, but leaned towards Lord Valery's political opinions. Four years had passed since then, and Herbert Gresham was no longer a cipher in another's hands. He had formed his own principles, marked out his own course;

and Lucy heard his name so often and so admiringly from her brother's lips, that the dream of her first season could not pass away, strive against it as she might, for she knew not whether she claimed more than a passing thought from him who held her being so enchained. And now he was returning; and to the fête to welcome him she was invited, with such an evident desire for her presence, that her heart bounded beneath the thronging fancies that would come, seeming to whisper it was at *his* instigation. And why could she not go? Was it not, indeed, a quixotic and uncalled-for sacrifice? How could the resolution of one feeble individual aid in removing the heavy pressure of over-work from the thousands of her fellow-creatures? There was time, full time, for all she required, if she saw about it at once. It was but adding an atom to the weight of oppression, which, whether added or withheld, could be of no moment; and surely, surely, for such a temptation there was enough excuse. How would Herbert construe her absence, if, indeed, it was at his wish the invitation came? Why might she not——

"Lucy, seven o'clock and not ready for dinner! Why, what are you so engrossed about?" exclaimed her brother, half-jestingly, half-anxiously, the latter feeling prevailing, as she hastily looked up. A few, a very few words, and he understood it all.

"And yet I know, even under such circumstance, you will not fail," he said; and how powerful is the voice of affectionate confidence in the dangerous moment of hesitation between right and wrong! "You may, indeed, be but one where there needs the aid of hundreds; but if all hold back because they are but one, how shall we gain the necessary muster? To check this thoughtless waste of human life, this (in many) unconscious crushing of all that makes existence, is WOMAN'S work. Man may legislate, may theorise, but he looks to his female relatives for its *practical* fulfilment. Dearest, do you choose the right, and trust me, useless as the sacrifice now seems, you will yet thank God that it was made.

Lady Gresham's fête was brilliant, *recherché*—crowded as anticipated. The weather was lovely, the gardens magnificent, the arrangements in the best state that an ultra-fashionist of some thirty years' experience could devise. Youth, beauty, rank, wealth, all were there, and the female portion set off to the best advantage by an elegance of costume and an extreme carefulness of attire, without which all knew an entrance into Lady Gresham's select coterie could never be obtained. A despot in the empire of dress and appearance, she little knew, and still less cared, for all the petty miseries (alas, that such a word should be spoken in the same breath with dress!) which her invitations usually excited. The resolve to outvie—the utter carelessness of expenditure while the excitement lasted—the depression, almost despair, at the accumulated debts which followed—the rivalry of a first fashion—the petty manœuvres not to give a hint of the intended costume, and the equally petty manœuvres to discover it—the mortification when, after all the lavish expense, all the mysteries, others appeared more fashionable, more *recherché*—the disgust with which, in consequence, the previously considered perfect dress was henceforth regarded—these, and a hundred other similar emotions had been, during the "season," called forth again and again; and in beings destined for immortality! was it marvel they had no thought for other than themselves?

That this fête was in commemoration of Herbert Gresham's return, and that he was present, the hero of the day, not a little increased its excitement and importance. But he moved amongst his mother's guests with native and winning courtesy indeed, but as if his mind were engrossed with other and deeper things. In the four years of his absence many changes, powerful in themselves, but still only invisibly working, had taken place in the political aspect of his country. By means of private correspondence with the most influential men of the day, and through the public journals, he had felt the deepest interest in these changes; and from the very fact of his looking on from a distance, and not mingling with the contending waves of party, he had formed clearer views concerning them than many on the spot. He had returned, determined to devote the whole energies of his powerful mind to removing *invisible* oppression, so lessening labour that MIND might resume her supremacy, and create for every position its own immortal joys. He was no leveller of ranks; no believer in that vain dream, equality. He had travelled and thought much, and felt to his heart's core the superiority of England as a nation, both for constitution and morality; but this conviction, instead of blinding him to her faults, quickened his perceptions, not only regarding the evils, but their causes, and increased the intensity of his desire to remove them.

It was not, however, only the habitude of thought which, on this occasion, had given him a look of abstraction. He was disappointed. His mother had told him that, in compliance with his desire, all foolish coolness between his family and that of Lord Valery should cease—she had condescended to make advances to Miss Neville, which were coldly rejected. She did not tell him that these advances had been merely an invitation to her fête (of whose sudden arrangement Herbert was himself unconscious), and did not know herself, and certainly would never have imagined the real reason of Lucy's refusal. Before the day closed, however, her son was destined to be enlightened.

He was standing near a group of very gay young ladies and gentlemen, conversing at first on grave topics with a friend, when his quick ear was irresistibly attracted by the mention of Miss Neville's name, coupled with much satirical laughter.

"She will become a second Mrs. Fry, depend upon it," was the observation of one. "I should not be at all suprised that at last we shall find her making pilgrimages through the streets of London, to see if all the shops are closed at a certain hour, and the released apprentices properly employed. She should set up an evening school for drapers' assistants and milliners' apprentices. Why don't you propose it to her, Miss Balfour?"

Charlotte, whose superb Parisian costume gave her the triumph of being almost universally envied, laughed, and declared it was too much trouble.

"You stand in rather too much awe of both her and Lord Valery," was her brother's rejoinder. "It is a pity, though, that Miss Neville has imbibed such *outré* notions, otherwise she would be a nice girl enough."

"And did she really refuse to come only because the notice was too short for her to get a proper costume without injuring or oppressing—as the cant of the day has it—the poor milliners? How perfectly ridiculous! I am sure the *artistes* who come for our orders are in the finest condition both as to health and wealth."

"And the shopmen—they are sleek, gay, care-nothing looking follows. As for their needing greater rest, more recreation, opportunities to cultivate the mind, one has only to look at them to feel the pure romance of the thing. What are some people born for but to work?"

"And just imagine how dull London would be if all the shops are closed by seven or eight o'clock! I should lose half my enjoyment in walking to my club."

"I should like to know what good Miss Neville and her party of philanthropists think they will accomplish by giving so much liberty and leisure. We shall have to build double the number of taverns, for such will be their only resort. What can such people know of intellectual amusement?"

"And if they did, what do they want with it? We should have a cessation of all labour, and then what is to become of us, or the country either?"

"It is pure folly. Some people must have a hobby to make a noise about; and so now nothing is heard but oppression, internal slavery, broken-hearted milliners' apprentices, and maimed drapers' assistants! Really, for so much eloquence, it is a pity they do not choose a higher subject!"

"And I wish the present *subject* may never drop till the *work* is done," interposed Herbert Gresham, joining the conversation with a suddenness, and speaking with such startling eloquence, that it caused a *general* retreat of *individual* opinion. He would have been amused had he felt less interested, to see the effect on both sexes of his unexpected interference. He spoke very briefly, for he was too disgusted with the littleness, the selfishness, of all he had heard to attempt anything like argument. And the effort to excuse former sentiments—to dare say he was right, but they had not reflected much about it—thought it a pity to alter things which had been going on so long—could not understand, even granting there was a good deal of misery, how it could be helped, but if Herbert Gresham thought it might be, no doubt there was more in it than they believed, and very many other similar speeches, only excited his contempt.

We must change the scene, for our space will not allow us more than a slight sketch: a momentary glance, as it were, on things passing daily, hourly around, and yet seen, known of, by how few! Four or five days after Lady Gresham's fête, Miss Neville might have been seen entering one of those small, close, back streets, found even in the aristocratic west, and whose dilapidated dwellings present almost as great a contrast with the proud mansions which surround and conceal them as the inhabitants themselves.

It was a poor old needlewoman whom Lucy was visiting, and, surprised at finding her usual sitting-room empty, and fearing she was ill—for there was no sign of work about, and Mrs. Miller was infirm and ailing—she gently entered her sleeping apartment. The rough bed was occupied indeed, but not by its usual inmate, who was sitting by its side, tears rolling down her withered cheeks, and her attention so fixed that she did not perceive Miss Neville's entrance. She was watching the painful, restless movements of a girl, who, in a high state of delirium and fever, was lying on the pallet; she was very young, and had been beautiful, but suffering had scarcely left any trace but its own. Earnestly and pityingly, Lucy entered into the sad, but only too common tale, her inquiries elicited; but the old woman's narration being garrulous and unfinished, we will give it in our own words.

Fanny Roberts and Harry Merton, born and nurtured in the same village, had been playmates, schoolfellows, friends, and at last lovers—not only faithful and affectionate, but prudent and thoughtful. The parents of both were poor, even in their humble village, but the wishes and interests of their children were their first object, and to see them somewhat higher in the world than themselves their sole ambition. To set up an establishment in the neighbouring town, combining linen-draper, dressmaker, and milliner, had been their day-dream from the time they had conned their school lessons and taken long walks together, instead of joining their playmates on the green; and to fulfil this earnest wish, their parents, by many sacrifices, which, measured by their love, seemed absolutely nothing, gathered together sufficient to send them to London, and apprentice them there. Harry was then nineteen and Fanny two years younger. Hope was bright for both. Their only drawback seemed the impossibility of meeting more than once a week; and six days of entire separation was a weary interval to those accustomed to exchange affection's kindly words and looks each day. Only too soon, however, did the oppressive reality of the present absorb the rosy hues of the future. On the daily routine of unmitigated work, the exhausting labour, the deadened energies, the absorption of every faculty in the depressing weariness, we need not touch. It was no distaste for work, for both had set to their respective duties with hearts burning to conquer every difficulty—to do even more than was required of them, the sooner to gain the longed-for goal; and had it not been for the fearful burden of over-work, the absence of sufficient rest, of all wholesome recreation, how brightly and nobly might these young loving beings have walked the path of life, by mutual exertion creating a HOME, and all the joys, which, in England, that one word speaks! Alas! ere eighteen months elapsed, every thought of buoyancy and joy seemed strangely to have deserted Fanny. She could not tell why, for outward things seemed exactly the same as they had been at first. Harry was still faithful, still fond. Her heart intuitively felt that he was altered. Why, she would often ask herself, could she no longer feel happy? Why should every thought of her own dear home cause such a sickly longing for fresh air and green fields, that the hysteric sob would often rise choking in her throat, and more than once, nothing but a timely burst of incomprehensible tears had saved her from fainting as she sat. She could not satisfy herself; but in reality it was the silent workings of insidious disease, seeming mental, because impossible to be traced as physical, save by the constant sensation of weariness, which she attributed merely to sitting so long in close and crowded rooms; but though happiness seemed gone, she retained the power of *endurance;* woman can and will endure, but in nine cases out of ten, man cannot. In the one, suffering often purifies; in the other, it but too often deteriorates.

Harry Merton had entered on his work joyfully and buoyantly, determined to make the best of everything, and be good friends with everybody. Naturally lively, with the power of very quick acquirement, and a restless activity of mind as well as body, a very few months' trial convinced him that if he had not entirely mistaken his vocation, he certainly must do something to make it more endurable. He had heard of institutions for the people in London, of amusements open even to the most economical; he had pictured enjoying them with his Fanny, and gaining improvement likewise. He found it all a dream. There were, indeed, such things, but not for him or her. The hour of his release found not only every wholesome amusement closed, but himself so weary, that mental recreation was impossible, and yet with the yearning for some pleasure, some relief from wearisome work, so natural in youth, stronger than ever. His convivial, unsuspecting disposition led him to join the most seemingly attractive, but in reality the most dangerous, of his companions. The consequences need scarcely be narrated. He became intemperate, gay, reckless, looking back on the pure, fresh feelings of his early youth with wonder, and retaining but one of their memories, his love for Fanny; but even that was no longer the glad, hopeful feeling which it had been. He was constantly told, and he saw, that it must be years before they could marry. He was laughed at for imagining that either he or she would retain their early feelings. He heard her beauty admired, and then pitied as a most dangerous gift, which must eventually and most fearfully separate her from him; and the most furious but most unfounded jealousy took possession of him, and so darkened every hour of meeting, that poor Fanny at length anticipated them with more dread than pleasure. It was long, indeed, nearly three years, before things came to such a crisis; but the gradual conviction of the deterioration of her lover's character was to Fanny the heaviest suffering of all: that she still loved him, surely we need not say. She saw the *circumstances* of this miserable change, not the change itself. Her woman heart clung to him the more, from the very anxiety he inspired. So intensely did she mourn for his long, wearisome hours of joyless toil, that she scarcely felt her own; though, when he was released at ten or eleven, she was often working unceasingly till two in the morning. The choking cough, the shortened breath, the aching spine, she scarcely felt, in the one absorbing thought of him.

Whenever she could be spared, which in the "season" was very seldom, it was Fanny's custom to go to Mrs. Miller (her only friend in London) Saturday night and remain till Sunday evening. Two or three days before the invitations were out for Lady Gresham's fête, a note was given to her from Harry, the perusal of which occasioned deeper suffering than anything she had yet endured. Snatching half an hour from the scanty time allowed for sleep, the following was her reply:—

"Harry! Harry! this from you! when you so fondly promised you would never doubt me more! Yes, he did seek me that Saturday night, or rather Sunday morning, for it was one o'clock; and I would not have gone there, had you not made me promise that I would not disappoint you, and that you would take me home. Why were you not there? Why did you leave me to the chance of such a meeting? And then upbraid me with putting myself in that bad man's way! Oh, Harry! Harry! by the memories of our early home, our early love, spare me such unjust suspicion! You tell me writing will not satisfy you, you must see me, hear from my own lips my version of this cruel and most false tale. How can I see you till Saturday night, the earliest, if then? Sunday, if I can only crawl to Mrs. Miller's, indeed I will come, pain as it is now to move. Only trust me till then, dearest, dearest Harry. Do not add to your burden and mine by thoughts like these. You know that I am innocent; that I never have loved, never can love, any one but you."

The Sunday came, but Fanny was unable to keep her engagement Madame Malin was so overwhelmed with orders for Lady Gresham's fête, that even the Sabbath-day was compelled to be sacrificed. The peculiar trimmings which it was absolutely necessary for Miss Balfour to have to complete the Parisian costume (the details of which never arrived till eleven o'clock, Saturday, and then all the materials had to be purchased) were Fanny's work; and, from her delicate taste, she, of all the assistants, could the least be spared. In fact, extra hands were hired; for to complete twenty or thirty full dresses from the noon of Saturday to ten o'clock Monday, in addition to those already in hand for the drawing-room the following day, was an unusual undertaking, even for the indefatigable Madame Malin. Hour after hour those poor girls worked,—through Saturday night, the yearned-for Sabbath, again late into the night, till many fainted on their seats, and the miserable toil was continued in a recumbent posture by those unable to sit upright. A dead weight was on poor Fanny's heart, a foreboding misery; but the sufferings of the *frame* were such as almost to deaden the agony of mind. The hour of release came at length, inasmuch that, ill as she was, she craved permission to take home some of the dresses, that she might call at Mrs. Miller's on her way back, and learn some news of Harry, and beseech her old friend to seek him, and tell him the reason of her forced absence. Exhausted and most wretched as she was, she had to wait till the dresses were tried on—the capricious humour of the young ladies proved, by altering, realtering, and final arrangement as they were originally—to bear with petty fault-finding—until her whole frame seemed one mass of nerve; and so detained, that she only entered the street leading to her old friend's abode, as the carriages whirled off their elegantly-attired inmates to Lady Gresham's fête.

What a tale awaited her! Harry, restless, miserable,—almost maddened by the false reports against her,—and from the great pressure of business in his master's shop, from the innumerable visits of *modistes'* assistants to procure the necessary materials so needed for the costumes of Mrs. Gresham's fête, not released till past one o'clock Sunday morning, had perambulated the streets all night, in the vain hope of meeting Fanny, encountering one of his jovial companions, who, half-intoxicated, swore he had seen her entering a coach with—Merton knew whom—and when collared and shaken by the infuriated lover till he recovered his more sober senses, declared he could not tell exactly, but he thought it was her: at all events, Harry would know to-morrow, if she had gone as usual to Mrs. Miller's.

There she was not. Never before had six o'clock on Sunday evening come without her presence; and really anxious, Mrs. Miller (though not believing a syllable against her) conjured the unhappy young man to call himself at Madame Malin's, and inquire if she were ill or detained. He did so. The well-instructed lacquey declared the family were all at evening service, and if the apprentices were not with their friends, he supposed they were there also; he knew nothing about them; but he was quite sure his mistress never permitted them to work on Sundays. Harry was in no state coolly to consider his words. He rushed back like a madman to Mrs. Miller, uttered a few incoherent sentences, and darted away before she had time or thought even to reply. That very evening he enlisted, and the Monday found him marching to Southampton with other troops about to embark for India. A few lines to Mrs. Miller told her this, and accompanied a parcel directed to Fanny, in case she should ever see or hear of her again. The poor girl had just strength to tear it open, to discover all her letters and formerly treasured gifts, even to some withered flowers, returned with a few words of stinging reproach, bidding her farewell for ever, and dropped lifeless at the old woman's feet. One or two intervals of coherency enabled her, by a few broken phrases, to explain the reason of her absence; but brain-fever followed, and even when Miss Neville saw her, all hope was over. Vain was the skill of the gifted and benevolent physician Lucy called in. Disease had been too long and too deeply rooted for resistance to a shock which, in its agony, would have prostrated even a healthy constitution. A few, a very few days of intense suffering, and the crushed heart ceased to beat, the blighted frame to feel, and misery for her was over. But for poor Harry—for the parents of both—what might comfort them? We have seen the deterioration of Harry's character. There were many to mark and condemn the *faults*, but none to perceive their *cause*. And when he absconded from his apprenticeship, it did but bring conviction as to his determined depravity. Who may tell the agony in those two humble English homes, when the post brought the miserable news of death to the one, and of sin and utter separation to the other? They had not even the poor comfort of knowing the cause of their son's change; their own, bold, free, happy, loving Harry,—how could his parents associate him with sin?—or Fanny, the healthy, rosy, graceful Fanny, with suffering and death? And what caused these fearful evils, amongst which our tale is but one amongst ten thousand? Lucy Neville buried her face in hèr hands as she sat by the lowly pallet, where lay the faded form whence life had only half an hour before departed, and thanked God that the temptation had been indeed resisted, and that she had not made one at Lady Gresham's fête. It had not, indeed, been the primary or even the secondary cause. It did but strike the last blow and shiver to atoms the last lingering dream of hope and joy which, despite of oppression, misery, despair, *will* rest invisibly in the youthful heart, till driven thence by death.

"Lucy!" exclaimed Lord Valery that same day, stopping the carriage unexpectedly as it was about to drive off from that part of St. James's where it usually waited for her (she shrunk from the notice which a nobleman's carriage, seen in such localities as Mrs. Miller's, would inevitably produce),—"Lucy, an old friend wishes to recall himself to your memory; will you give him a seat in your carriage, and take me on the box? We both pine for fresh air, and a drive in the Park will revive us for dinner, which, whether he will or no, I intend this gentleman to partake."

The words were the lightest, but the tone which spoke them betrayed the truth at once. It was Herbert Gresham by his side. Herbert Gresham, whose earnest eyes were fixed on hers, with an expression in their dark depths needing no words to tell her that his early dream, even as her own, was unchanged—that the first action of his now unshackled will was to seek her, requiring no renewal of acquaintance, again to love and trust her. And though the suddenness of the meeting, the rapid transition from sorrowing sympathy to individual joy, did so flush and pale her cheek, that her brother looked at her with some alarm, there was neither hesitation nor idle reserve. Her hand was extended at once, and the pressure which clasped it was sufficient response. Whether they continued so silent, when Herbert did spring into the carriage, and took his seat by her side, indeed we know not. Certain it is that, had it not been for Lord Valery, the footman might have waited long enough for orders to drive "home;" and equally certain that no day had ever seemed so short to Lucy,—short in its fulness of *present* enjoyment; in its *retrospect*, could it have been but one brief day?

"And that poor girl is really gone?" inquired Lord Valery, just as Herbert Gresham was about taking his departure, most reluctantly warned to do so by a neighbouring clock striking midnight. "Another victim to that hateful system, desecrating our lovely and most noble land!"

"Dear Edward, hush!" interposed Lucy, gently, as her eye rested on her lover.

"Do not check him, dearest, though I prize that fond thought for me. I know the whole tale—that the fête welcoming my return, by misdirected zeal and thoughtless folly, has added incalculably to the *general* burden, and to *individuals* brought death and a life-long despair. The past, alas! we cannot remedy—the future——" and his arm was fondly thrown round Lucy, and his lip pressed her brow—"dearest, let us hope next season there will be another Lady Gresham's Fête fraught with happiness for all."

The Group of Sculpture.

"I have no hope in loving thee,
I only ask to love;
I brood upon my silent heart,
As on its nest the dove;

But little have I been beloved—
Sad, silent, and alone;
And yet I feel, in loving thee,
The wide world is my own.

Thine is the name I breathe to heaven—
Thy face is on my sleep;
I only ask that love like this
May pray for thee and weep."

L. E. L.

"We know not love till those we love depart."

L. E. L.

"Why will you sing that old-fashioned song, dear Annie, when you have so many much better suited to your voice?" expostulated Reginald de Vere, as he led the young songstress from her harp to a more retired seat. "I do not like your throwing away so much power and sweetness on a song which, of all others, I hate the most."

"Do not say so, Reginald. You are not usually fastidious, or I would say, had that sweet melody Italian words instead of English, you would acknowledge its beauty, and feel it too."

"Perhaps so, as it is not the melody, but the words I quarrel with—'Home, sweet home!' What charm has home ever had for me? Change the words, dear Annie, English or Italian, I care not, only remove all association of home, and I will learn to love it more."

"Nay, Reginald; to banish such association would be to banish its greatest charm. One day you, too, may feel its truth."

"Never, never!" he answered, passionately; there is a

blighting curse around me, which it were worse than folly to resist. I must toil on, lonely, and unblessed by one sweet tie of home—seeking for no love, and receiving none—isolated in a world! There are many others whose destiny is the same. Bound by the iron chain of fate, he is but a madman who would seek to break it."

"Destiny—fate! I thought you had long ere this banished their baneful influence," said Annie, in a tone of mild reproach.

"From your ear, my gentle friend, because I saw you loved not their expression; but not from my own heart. Yet you, too, believe all things to be pre ordained; that not a sparrow falls to the ground unmarked. Then, why so start at me—is not our creed the same?"

"It cannot be, Reginald. I am not wise enough to know wherein the difference lies, I can only judge from effects; and when they are so opposed, I fancy the cause must be so also. I do believe that all things are ordained, but yet I am no fatalist."

"Will you try and explain the distinction, for your words seem somewhat contradictory."

"I fear they do," she replied, simply; "and I am over bold to speak on this weighty subject at all. Your creed appears to me to consist in this; that before your birth, your path was laid down—your destiny fixed; that you are, in consequence, bound in chains, enclosed in walls, from which no effort of your own will can enable you to escape; that you must stand the bursting of the thunder-cloud—for you have no force or energy to seek shelter, no free will to choose—swayed by an irresistible impulse, and, consequently, not a responsible being. Such seems to me the creed of a fatalist."

"And you are right. Now, then, for yours; less difficult, I should imagine, to explain, than that in which you have no interest."

"I differ from you, Reginald. It is comparatively easy to define the subject of a passing thought or an hour's study; but that which we feel, feel to our inmost soul, is not so easily clothed in words. I believe that an eye of love is ever watching over me—a guiding arm is ever round me; that nothing can happen to me, unless willed for my good by my Father in heaven; but I do *not* believe my lot in life marked out before I saw the light. Such a creed at once changes the law of love into a dark and iron-bound necessity, from which my whole soul revolts. Where would be the comfort of prayer in such a case—the blessedness of pouring forth one's whole soul in the hour of affliction? for how could prayer avail us were our lot marked out?"

"And do you think prayer ever does? Do you believe that you are answered?"

"I do, indeed, dear Reginald; not always as our own will would dictate, but as a loving Father knows it best. I was not answered as my heart implored when my only parent was taken from me; but I was answered in the strength that was granted me to feel that he was happy, and God's will kinder and better than my own. I am not here because it is my destiny, but because it is better for me than the calm and quiet life I have hitherto enjoyed."

"Your creed is indeed that of a gentle, loving woman, Annie," said her companion, more playfully; but he smiled not, for he knew how chillingly a smile will fall on young enthusiasm. "But it is too visionary, too ethereal, for cold-hearted man; perhaps not for some, but for me there are no such dreams. My heart was once full of hope and faith, and all things bright, and fond, and beautiful; but now, crushed, blighted, trampled on, how may it dream again? But this is folly," and with a strong effort he subdued emotion, and spoke more calmly. "Let us talk of something else. You alluded but now to your change of life, and I thought, sadly. Are you not happy?"

"I shall be in time, Reginald," answered Annie, on whose fair sweet face a shade had flitted at her companion's bitter words. "All are kind to me. My mother was Lord Ennerdale's favourite niece, and he loves me for her sake, and so pets me that I cannot but love him most dearly."

"And Lady Emily?"

"I shall learn to love as soon as she will let me. I fancy she thinks me but a simple romantic girl, and I have not courage to undeceive her—that I can love and reverence other things beside poetry; but it is the change of circumstances that sometimes makes me sad. Clair Abbey is so far removed from Luscombe Cottage, that time has not yet reconciled me to the great change."

"Time is slow in effecting changes in you, Annie; yet ere we meet again, trust me, you will have learned to love Clair Abbey, or changed it for another home as high in sounding, and yet more dear."

"Changed it ere we meet again! What can you mean, Reginald?" said Annie, startled yet more by his tone than by his words, but she was not answered; for Reginald turned away directly he had spoken, his attention called by Lord Ennerdale; and another quadrille being formed, her hand was claimed, and she was led off almost unconsciously—so strangely was she preoccupied—to join it.

There had been nothing in the quiet yet earnest conversation of Reginald de Vere and Annie Grey to cause remark amongst the light-hearted group who were that night assembled in Lord Ennerdale's hospitable halls. They had been intimate from childhood, and as Annie was almost a stranger to all present, and merely regarded as a simple country girl hardly emerged from childhood, no one was surprised that she should prefer Reginald's society; though there were some young men who, attracted by the timid yet intelligent style of her beauty, half envied De Vere the privileges of intimacy which he so evidently enjoyed. Annie's place seemed not amidst the followers of fashion; the long, rich, chestnut hair owned no law but that of nature, and flowed at will from her pale, high brow over a neck and shoulders, whose exquisite form and whiteness were displayed to advantage by the simple fashion of her plain black dress; the eye so "darkly, deeply, beautifully blue," the fair soft cheek ever varying in colour, revealed every thought and feeling that stirred within. The world's lesson of concealment and reserve she had not yet learned, for living in perfect retirement with a kind and judicious father, of whom she was the idol, her enthusiasm had been regulated not chilled, and every high and poetic sentiment raised up to and purified in the only rest for such minds—the religion of the Bible and of Nature. Her life had passed in a small cottage on the banks of Windermere, diversified only by occasional visits to an old relation in Scotland; where, in fact, the first six months of her mourning had been passed. And there, had it not been for one cogent reason, she would have preferred remaining, as more congenial to her taste and feelings, than the form and grandeur which she imagined must surround the dwelling of an earl.

Lord Ennerdale and his family had often sought to draw Sir Edward Grey from his seclusion, anxious to notice his child; but fearing to disturb Annie's tranquil happiness by an introduction to a mode of life and pleasures which her very limited fortune must prohibit her enjoying, he had invariably declined these solicitations. Yet when Lord Ennerdale, notwithstanding his age and infirmities, made a rapid journey from London to Luscombe Cottage, purposely to soothe his dying hours by the assurance that his Annie was amply, even richly provided for, and therefore there could be no objection to her making Clair Abbey her future home, Sir Edward placed his weeping child in the arms of her aged uncle, and died with a prayer for both upon his lips.

But much as Annie loved and venerated her father, it was scarcely so much his last wish as the restlessness of her own heart, which, even while she preferred the simple mode of living at Kelmuir, yet reconciled her to a residence at Clair Abbey. She was restless because her quondam playmate and chosen friend, Reginald de Vere, was far away in his own most wretched home, with none to sing or smile him into peace, or cautiously and gently argue away his fits of morbid sensitiveness or overwhelming gloom. That Lord Ennerdale not only sympathised in the young man's causes of depression, but loved his better qualities, admired his talents, and regretted his failings, was sufficient to excite the warm affections of his great-niece towards him. No spell is so powerful in opening the heart as sympathy, with regard to the character of those we love.

Clair Abbey's great attraction, then, to Annie Grey was, that there she should constantly see Reginald; his concluding words, therefore, had both startled and pained her; but she vainly waited for their solution. She looked earnestly for Reginald to return to her; but he was constantly engaged in apparently earnest conversation with one or another of Lord Ennerdale's guests. She was too guileless to believe he shunned her merely because he failed in courage to tell her more.

The evening closed at length; and passing along the corridor leading from the library to the stairs, a well-known step suddenly sounded behind her, and the voice of Reginald de Vere called her by name.

"I thought you intended to retire without even wishing me good night," she said, playfully, her spirit rallying with his appearance. "What do you mean, sir, by such treatment? Be better behaved to-morrow, and I will be merciful and forgive."

"You must forgive me to-night, dearest Annie; for to-morrow will see me many miles on the road to Portsmouth, thence, speedily to embark for Spain."

"Portsmouth—Spain!" repeated the bewildered girl; and her hand so trembled, that the lamp she held dropped from it, and was instantly extinguished.

"Yes, Annie, to Spain!" he answered, struggling for calmness. "I am of age now; poor, but not so utterly dependent as I have been. My father's house I will never enter more. You start, Annie, but do not—do not condemn me. Judge me by no reasoning but that of your own kind, gentle heart. I can bear no more than that which I have borne. Boyhood must submit to a parent's tyranny; but manhood owns no such law. You know how I would have loved my father, and how he has spurned me. Still I lingered, vainly striving to elicit one softer feeling, hoping—idiot that I was—that he would yet love me. But the dream is over! He drew the reins still tighter, and so snapped them; there is a measure to endurance even in a son. Do not weep thus, Annie," he continued, conquering his own emotion to soothe hers, and passing his arm round her, as he had so often done in earlier years, when, as a brother, he had soothed her griefs and shared her joys. "I will not burden you with the final cause of my present resolution. I have neither means nor influence to tread the path to which my inmost soul aspires; and to toil for lingering years behind a merchant's desk or tradesman's counter my spirit will not bear. I have obtained a commission amongst the brave fellows now about to join General Mina in his gallant defence of the young queen; and with him these restless yearnings may be stilled in the activity of martial service, or the quiet of the grave. And who will mourn for me?" he continued, rapidly and bitterly; "who, in the wide world, will think of me, or shed one tear for me, save thine own sweet self? Oh, Annie, speak to me! Tell me you will think of me sometimes. I know there will be many, very many, to supply my place to you; but, oh, who will ever be to me as you have been?"

"And yet you have decided on this plan, endured more than ever, and told me not a word. Reginald, was this kind?" she said, struggling with the tears that nearly suffocated her.

"You were in grief already, Annie; how might I ask your sympathy in mine? I know it never was refused me. I know it would not be, even in your own sorrow; but oh, Annie, I felt if I waited to look on you again, I should fail in courage to leave England. Yet why should I linger?

Changed as your prospects are, loved as you will be by those so much more deserving, what could I be to you?"

"Reginald!" murmured poor Annie, wholly unconscious of the nature of her own feelings, yet unable to utter another word.

"I know you will not forget me Annie, dearest Annie, your nature is too good, too kind, too truthful for such change; but, fated as I am, how dare I ask for, hope for more than a sister's love? Say you will sometimes think of me, love me as—as a brother, Annie, darling! and life will not be so wholly desolate."

Her reply was almost inarticulate, and passionate words rose to Reginald's lips, but they were not spoken. He led her to the door of her apartment without another word, wrung both her hands in his, bade "God bless her!" and was gone. Annie stood for a few minutes as if stunned; mechanically she loosed the wreath of white rosebuds from her hair, the fastening of her dress, which seemed to stifle her very breath, and then she sunk on her knees beside the bed, and the hot tears gushed forth; and long, long she wept, as that young guileless girl had never wept before.

Reginald De Vere was the youngest son of a private gentleman of moderate fortune, residing in a populous city in the north of Yorkshire. It is not necessary to dilate on feelings which Reginald's own words but too painfully portrayed; the "iron rule" of tyranny is best described in the effect which it produces. The Calvinistic principles of the elder De Vere found no softening of their natural austerity in the acidity and moroseness of his temper; the evil had been increased by his union with a young Spaniard—lively, frivolous, and a Roman Catholic. How this marriage had ever come about, nobody succeeded in discovering. Strange unions there are, but seldom between such antipodes in character and feeling as were Mr. and Mrs. De Vere. Their large family grew up amidst all the evils of domestic dissension, and its subsequent misery—a father's unjustifiable tyranny, and a mother's as blamable weakness. Basil De Vere sought to instil his peculiarly stern doctrines in the minds of his children; his wife prayed, in their hearing, that they might be saved from such cold, comfortless belief; they shrunk from the one, and learned no religion from the other. To shield them from the father's tyranny, the mother taught them deceit, lavished on them weak indulgences, which were to be forfeited if ever revealed. Ever witnessing and suffering the effects of dissension, what affection, what harmony could exist between themselves? The ill effects of this training were more discernible in some of their matured characters than in others; some pursued an honest course, as soon as their departure from their father's house permitted the influence of their better qualities, but these were mostly dwelling in foreign lands; some had married with, some without his consent; and in his old age Basil De Vere found himself master of a deserted hearth, with none of his once blooming family beside him but one, and that one was Reginald. The weak indulgence of his mother had never softened for Reginald the tyranny of his father. She died in giving him birth, and he had to battle through his unhappy childhood alone. Shrinking almost in agony from his father's voice, yearning, with all the clinging confidence of childhood, for love, but finding none, he turned in loathing from the continued scenes of discord which characterised his home. He spurned with contemptuous indignation offers of indulgence and concealment, to act as he saw others do, and thus constantly drew down upon himself the enmity of his more wily brothers and sisters. He shrunk, in consequence, more and more within himself, striving to keep peace with his father, but in vain; for De Vere often raged at his children without knowing wherefore, and the calm, dignified bearing of his youngest son would chafe him into greater fury than palpable offence. But there were seeds of virtue, aye, of the "nobility of genius," in the disposition of Reginald, that bloomed and flourished despite the unhealthy soil and blighting atmosphere in which he moved; perhaps the kindly notice of Sir Edward Grey assisted their development. The pale, silent, suffering boy had appealed irresistibly to his kind heart, and for Reginald's sake he condescended to make acquaintance with his father.

As long as they remained in Yorkshire, Sir Edward permitted Reginald to share much of the instruction which he himself bestowed upon his Annie; a kindness so delicately and feelingly bestowed, that Reginald by slow degrees permitted his whole character to display itself to Sir Edward, and allowed himself to feel that, with so kind a friend and so sweet a companion, he was not utterly alone. Even when Sir Edward removed to Windermere their intercourse continued; for there was ever a room prepared and a warm welcome for Reginald, who turned to that cottage as a very Eden of peace and love.

As Reginald increased in years, felt more fully his own powers, and through Sir Edward's friendly introductions associated with other families, his morbid feelings did not, as the baronet had fondly hoped, decrease, but rather strengthened, in the supposition that his fate alone was desolate. He saw happy homes and kindly hearts; no exertion, no effort, no sacrifice could make such his, and he believed an iron chain of fate was round him, dooming him to misery. The kindness of Sir Edward, of Lord Ennerdale, and others, only deepened the vain, wild yearnings for home affections—the peace, the confidence of home. A peculiarly fine organization of mind, an acute perception of character caused him to shrink with pain from general notice. The talented and gifted he admired at a distance, feeling intuitively that such would be his chosen friends; yet, from a sense of inferiority, refusing to come forward and permit his fine talents to be known; at the same time shrinking from the common herd, convinced that amongst them he should meet with neither sympathy nor appreciation. A happy home would have been all in all for Reginald; there the incipient stirrings of genius would have been fostered into bloom, and the morbid feelings too often their accompaniment regulated into peace.

The death of Sir Edward Grey and the future destination of his daughter were, however, the final cause of his determination to leave England. He knew it not himself; and if a light did flash upon the darkness, it only deepened the gloom around him, by the conviction that his doom was ever to love alone. More and more earnestly he sought to soften his father's temper, even to conquer his own repugnance to the path of life his parent might assign him; but in vain. To enumerate all the petty miseries this struggle cost him would be impossible. The mind rises purified and spiritualized from great sorrows; but there is no relief from the trial of an unhappy home, no cure for the *wounds of words.* If domestic love and peace be ours, we can go forth with a firm heart and serene mind to meet the trials of the world; alas! alas! for those who have no such haven, no such stay!

Never did Reginald De Vere make a greater mistake than in the supposition that a military life would bring him the happiness for which his parched soul so thirsted. He could not associate the favourite pastime of his childhood, carving in wood, stone, or whatever material came first to hand, with the feverish yearning for exertion and excitement, which possessed his whole being. He could not feel that the one sprung from the other, or rather that the power which urged the former was secretly working in his mind, and causing an utter distaste for all mechanical employment. He was too unhappy to examine the source of his restlessness, and knew no one who could explain it for him.

Lord Ennerdale and his sons were all men of worth and talent, and firm encouragers of art and literature: but not themselves children of genius, they failed in the subtle penetration which could discover its embryo existence. Had Sir Edward lived he would have seen further; but still all his friends had dissuaded Reginald from entering on a military career, but he was firm; and in less than a week after his agitated parting with Annie, a fair wind was rapidly bearing him to the shores of Spain.

Days and weeks passed, and Annie Grey sought with persevering effort to regain her former calm and happy temperament; and she succeeded so far as to conceal from her relatives the secret of her heart. The agony of that parting moment had transformed her, as by some incomprehensible spell, from the child to the woman; and so sudden had been the transition, that she felt for days a stranger to herself. Reginald had always been dear to her, but she knew not, imagined not how dear, until that never-to-be-forgotten evening; his words returned to her again and again, and sad, desponding as they were, she would not have lost one of them. She who had been so constantly active, flitting like a spirit from one favourite employment to another, now seemed to live but on one feeling; but her mind was too well regulated to permit its unrestrained indulgence. Young as she was, dependent on herself alone for guidance in this new and absorbing state of being, thrown in quite a new position for luxury and wealth, as a cherished member of her uncle's family, yet her character, instead of deteriorating, matured, uniting all the outward playfulness of the child with the inward graces of the woman.

Lord Ennerdale's domestic circle formed a happy contrast to that of the ascetic Basil De Vere. His children were all married except his eldest son, Lord St. Clair, and eldest daughter, Lady Emily; but the ties of family had never been broken, and happy youth and blooming childhood were almost always round the earl. With all these Annie was speedily a favourite; and easily susceptible of kindness and affection, Clair Abbey soon became endeared to her as home.

By a strange contradiction, Annie's interest and affection were, however, excited the strongest towards the only member of Lord Ennerdale's family who retained reserve towards her. What there was in Lady Emily St. Clair to attract a young and lively girl, Annie herself might have found it difficult to define; for not only her appearance, but her manners were against her. Stiff, cold, even severe, she usually appeared: and when she would at times relax, and seem about to enter with warmth and kindness into Annie's studies or pursuits, she would suddenly relapse into coldness and reserve. Sometimes, when eagerly conversing with Lord St. Clair, on the exquisite beauty of nature, or of some favourite poem, when the spirit of poetry breathed alike from her eyes and from her lips, Annie would catch the eye of Lady Emily fixed upon her sadly and pityingly; or if she smiled, the smile was peculiar, it might be even satirical; yet she was never satirical in words, nor did it seem in character—too feelingly alive to the dictates of kindness ever willingly to inflict a wound. To discover her real character was difficult; Annie judged more by her habits than her words. Lady Emily never said that her love of flowers amounted to a passion, that to have them around her in their freshness, to seek them alike from the garden and the wild, to collect, dry, and arrange them in such tasteful groups and such brilliancy of colouring, that the choicest paintings looked dim beside them, was her favourite pleasure, but Annie was ever ready with some newly discovered plant, or the moss and weed she needed—ever the first to remove the dying buds, and supply their place around her boudoir with the freshest and fairest she could select. Lady Emily never spoke of poetry, never acknowledged that she could either admire or enter into it; but there were extracts in her writing, attached sometimes to drawings, sometimes to her books of flowers, that betrayed such a refinement of taste, and acute perception of the pure, the beautiful, and the spiritual, in nature and in man, that Annie suspected she was herself a poet; but yet how could she reconcile the unimpassioned coldness of her usual mood with the light and life of poetry? Yet though fairly puzzled, Annie so judiciously assisted her researches, that Lady Emily often wondered how a mark could come so exactly in the place she wished, when the thought, for whose echo she looked, had been breathed to none; but even had these attentions escaped her notice, it must indeed have been an icy heart to withstand the sweetness of Annie's manner;

whenever her cousin's mood was irritable, her temper somewhat ruffled, there seemed a magic around Annie not only to bear with irritation, but to reconcile the subject of that irritation to herself and all around her; and when so languid and weak as really to be ill, though she would never allow it, who so active as Annie to prevent all annoyance to the invalid, or interfere with the only pursuit she could enjoy? Yet no show of affection acknowledged these attentions: but by very slow degrees the Miss Grey changed into Anne, and finally into the pretty denomination by which she was always addressed: and the smile and tone with which she spoke to her, satisfied the orphan that she had not worked in vain.

Even if Annie's conduct had failed to rivet the notice of Lady Emily, it had gained for her the interest and sincere affection of another. Lord St. Clair was devotedly attached to his sister, and all who had the good sense to appreciate her were sure to obtain his esteem; then in the prime of life, he foresaw no danger in his intimate association with and admiration of his young cousin, a girl but just seventeen; and it was a pleasure to him to draw her out, and repay by every kindness on his part her attention to his sister. A disappointment when very young had caused him to remain single. "I do not say I shall never marry," he often said, in answer to his father's solicitations on the subject; "for then I should consider myself bound not to do so, however my heart might dictate; but it is unlikely."

Annie Grey had not, however, been domiciled many months in Clair Abbey, before Lord St. Clair's sentiments on this subject underwent some change.

From the time of Reginald's departure the public journals became suddenly endowed with an interest to Annie, equal to that of the most ardent politician. The disturbed state of Spain, the constant marchings and counter-marchings of General Mina's army, prevented any regular communication from Reginald; once or twice she had heard from him direct, and treasured indeed were those letters, honourably as the young man kept to his resolution, never by one word to draw Annie into an engagement, or even an avowal that she returned his love. In the papers she often read his name amongst the bravest and most daring of the British soldiers. One anecdote, officially reported and communicated to Lord Ennerdale, afforded her still dearer food for fancy. The service in which he was engaged was exposed to all the horrors of civil warfare; slaughter and desolation followed in the train of both armies. Young De Vere, at the head of a picked band, had thrown himself into the very midst of a *mêlée*, determined on saving the unoffending women and children, and aged peasants of the opposing party, all of whom were about to be sacrificed to the misguided rage of the royal troops; the village was in flames, and the peasants, neutral before, swore to be avenged. The exertions of the young Englishman, however, worked on both parties; he calmed the excited spirits of his own men and promised protection and safety to the oppressed. One group particularly attracted him; a young mother, clasping an infant tightly to her breast, and two fine boys, twining their arms around her, as to protect her with their own lives. Reginald did not know that it was her infant he had saved from a brutal death, but his look was arrested by the intense feeling glistening in her large dark eyes, and by the impotent passion of her eldest boy, who, clenching a huge stick, vowed he would join his father, who was a Carlist soldier, and revenge the insults offered to his mother. De Vere jestingly laid his hand on the stripling's shoulder, declaring he was a young rebel and his prisoner. The agonized scream of the poor mother changing on the instant into the wildest accents of gratitude, as she recognised in Reginald her babe's preserver, and to the earnest supplication that he would send them on in safety, removed all feelings of mere jest. Reginald soothed her fears, and selecting a guard of his own countrymen, on whom he could depend, sent her and her children under their care to the outposts of the Carlist camp. General Mina smiled sadly when this anecdote was told him. "The age of chivalry is over, my young friend," he said, mournfully. "Your act was kind and generous, but I fear of little service. The Carlists are not likely to check their career of devastating warfare because we have spared one insignificant village; nor will you have any demand upon their favour should you unfortunately fall into their hands."

"Chivalry and its romance may be over," thought Annie, as again and again her mind reverted to its one fond theme. "But my father once told me 'a deed can never die;' and, even if indeed it were to do no good, surely his motives will meet with the appreciation and admiration they deserve; there must be some among the good and noble to do him justice."

How the young heart revels in every proof, however trifling, of the worth of him it loves. The restlessness of a scarcely acknowledged passion merged into a species of glowing happiness, the basis of which Annie might have found it difficult to define. In its indulgence she forgot the distance between them, the darkening aspect of his future, the despondency breathing in his last farewell—forgot all but the passionate words, "Who will be to me as you have been?" And what will so elevate the character and purify the heart, and shed such sweet rosy flowers over every thought, and act, and feeling, as the first fresh feelings of all-hoping, all-believing love! Annie's beauty, matured beneath the magic of such dreams, excited universal admiration: but the young girl knew it not.

"No breakfast for loiterers!" exclaimed Lord St. Clair, playfully holding up his hands, as Annie sprang through an open French window into the breakfast-room one lovely summer morning, her cottage bonnet thrown back, her luxuriant hair somewhat disordered, her cheek and eye bright with health and animation, and laughing gaily at Lord St. Clair's threat.

"Here has Emily been looking starch and prim for the last half-hour, thinking unutterable things of the folly and romance which can be the only reason of young ladies' early wanderings in the lonely districts about Keswick Lake. Ah, you little fox, prepared with a bribe to ward off the weight of her displeasure," he said, as Annie laid the fruit of her researches, a rare and exquisite plant, on the table by her cousin, and Lady Emily half smiled.

"And there is my father in a complete fever, fearing that his blooming little niece had been carried off, or eaten up by one of the wild men or monsters of the mountains, and threatening to search for her himself, directly after breakfast."

"Thank you, my dear, kind uncle," replied Annie gaily, bending over Lord Ennerdale to kiss his forehead. "Never be anxious about me. I have suffered no further inconvenience than extreme hunger, which I satisfied at Nanny's cottage, by a slice of her brown bread and a cup of warm milk. No romance in that, Lord St. Clair, at least."

"A fortunate occurrence for you, as it may save you from a lecture on the impropriety of indulging love-lorn dreams in solitude. Why, Annie, you are actually blushing; if it were not an utter impossibility for romantic young ladies to feel hungry, I should say your very looks pleaded guilty. Look at her, Emily—you had better begin."

"No, I thank you, Henry; I never give lectures, even when deserved, in public," was his sister's quiet reply.

"Well, the offence brings with it its own punishment, for here come the contents of the postman's bag, and so a truce to our sage converse; and you, Miss Annie, must eat your breakfast in meditative silence."

"Or in perusing what she likes better. Here, my little politician; your eyes are pleading, though your lips are silent," said Lord Ennerdale, gaily throwing to her a packet of newspapers without opening them.

"You are much too young to be a politician; besides, I hate women to dabble in politics, so give me a better reason for being the first reader of all the papers, or you shall not have them," interposed Lord St. Clair, keeping firm hold of the packet, which he had caught.

"On my honour, I never read a word of politics," replied Annie, half playfully, half eagerly, but blushing deeply as she met Lord St. Clair's penetrative glance. He relinquished them with a half sigh, and bent over his despatches. Silence ensued for several minutes, each seemingly engrossed with his occupation. Lady Emily was the first to move, and after carefully sorting and arranging the flowers Annie had brought her, was about to leave the room.

"Annie, my dear child! what is the matter?" she exclaimed, in a tone which electrified her father and brother, so utterly was it unlike her usually measured accents; and startled out of all stiffness and dignity, she was at the poor girl's side in an instant. Annie's cheek, lips, and brow were cold and colourless as marble, and there was such rigid agony imprinted on every feature, that Lady Emily well-nigh shuddered as she gazed. "Speak to me, Annie, love! What is it? Try and speak, dearest; do not look at me with such a gaze," she continued, as Annie slowly raised her eyes, which were bloodshot and distended, and fixed them on her face; she evidently tried to speak, but only a gasping cry escaped, and that terrible agony was lost for a time in an unconsciousness so deep that it almost seemed of death.

Lord St. Clair stood paralyzed, but then he snatched up the fatal paper, and one glance sufficed to tell him all, all that he had suspected, all that for his own happiness he had feared; but he could only think of Annie then, and perceiving how ineffectual were all the usual efforts to restore animation, he threw himself on horseback, and never rested till he had found and dragged back with him the medical attendant of the family, whose skill was finally successful. Annie woke from that blessed relief of insensibility to a consciousness of such fearful suffering, that as she lay in the perfect stillness enjoined by the physician, she felt as if her brain must reel, and fail beneath it. It was not alone the death of him she loved, that the idol of her young affections was lost to her for ever, but it was the horrid nature of his fate which had so appalled her. In the gallant defence of a royal fort he had been left almost alone, all his companions falling around him; severely wounded, and overpowered by numbers, he was taken by the Carlists, dragged to their camp, and twenty-four hours afterwards shot, with other ill-fated men, literally murdered in cold blood. Three times Annie's eyes had glared on the paragraph, reading again and again the list of the unfortunate men who had thus perished, as if Reginald's name could not be amongst them; alas! it was there, pre-eminent, from the courage, the youth, and the official rank of the bearer. And in that dreadful stillness the whole scene rose before her, vivid as reality—ghastly figures flitted before her; and then she saw Reginald as they parted; and then full of life and excitement in the field; and then covered with blood and wounds. She seemed to see him bound and kneeling for the fatal stroke, and the shot rung in her ears, clear, sharp, and strangely loud, till she could have shrieked from the bewildering agony: she tried to banish the vision, to escape its influence, but it gained strength, and force, and colouring, and before midnight Lady Emily watched in grief and awe beside the couch where her young cousin lay, and raved in the fearful delirium of a brain fever.

Many weeks elapsed ere Annie could again take her place amongst her family; alternate fever and exhaustion had so prostrated her that her life was more than once despaired of. Had she been aware who it was so constantly and gently tending her, teaching her voice to forget its coldness, her manner its reserve, to soothe and comfort those hours of agony, she would have felt that some simple "deeds indeed could never die;" and that to her own sweetness of temper, and forbearing and active kindness, she owed the blessings of a sympathy and tenderness almost equalling a mother's. But it was long before she was conscious of any thing, or even capable of rousing herself from the lethargic stupor which still lingered even when sense and strength returned. That she sought earnestly to appear the same as usual—to evince how gratefully she felt the kindness lavished on her—to return to her employments, was very evident; but it seemed as if bodily weakness prevented all mental exertion. She shrunk in anguish from the thought that she had betrayed her love, though by neither word nor hint did her companions ever allude to the immediate occasion of her illness.

"Would she but shed tears—but speak her grief," exclaimed Lord St. Clair to his sister, one day, after vainly endeavouring to excite a smile, "she would suffer less then; but she has never wept since; and before, the most trifling emotion, even of pleasure, would draw tears. Could you but draw forth her confidence—but make her weep. Is there no possible way?"

"I fear none: she shrinks from the slightest approach to the subject. I feel as if I dared not speak poor Reginald's name."

Chance, however, did that for which even Lady Emily's courage failed. Annie was reclining, one morning, in a favourite boudoir, her eyes languidly wandering over the beautiful landscape, which stretched from the window. When last she had noticed it, the trees were bending beneath the weight of their glorious summer dress, and the gayest and brightest flowers were flinging their lavish beauties on the banks of the small but picturesque lake. The scene was still lovely, but it had changed; the trees which still retained foliage were all in the "sere and yellow leaf," the ground was strewed with fallen leaves, the flowers were all gone, and Nature herself seemed emblematical of the change in Annie's heart. Lady Emily watched her some time in silence, and then gently drew her attention to some beautiful groups of flowers which she had lately arranged. Annie turned from the window with a heavy sigh, and bent over the flowers; while Lady Emily continued her employments without further notice. She forgot that amongst those groups there was the plant, to find which Annie had rambled over hill and dale that fatal morning. From its extreme rarity and beauty she had placed it alone upon the page: and as Annie gazed upon it, a rush of feeling of the bright, sweet memories which had thronged her mind during that solitary ramble came back upon her—the dreams of hope, and joy, and love—with the force, the intensity of actual presence; as if they might still be realized, and the intervening time had been but a dark and troubled blank. She pushed the flower from her. and her head sunk on her clasped hands.

"My poor child, I forgot that flower was amongst them!" exclaimed Lady Emily, in a tone at once of such self-reproach and earnest sympathy, that Annie, with an uncontrollable impulse, suddenly sprung up, and folding her arms round her neck, burst into a passion of tears. All her cousin's previous kindness she had attributed to pity for bodily suffering. That she could sympathize in her mental affliction, she had fancied—as the young are too prone to do of the colder and more experienced—was impossible; but the tone, the allusion to that little flower, betrayed that she, too, could believe in and understand the association of the material with the immaterial world; and Annie now wept upon her bosom, in the consoling consciousness that, cold as that heart seemed, it could yet feel and weep for her.

Lady Emily trembled; for the deep emotion she beheld recalled passages of equal suffering in her own life, which she had thought buried and at rest for ever. She trembled, lest in this appeal to her inmost soul her long striven-for calmness should fail, and her weakness should increase rather than soothe Annie's anguish. Her hand shook, and her lip so quivered, that it was some minutes ere she could speak. We need not linger on the words which followed. The ice, which had seemed to close round Annie's heart, dissolved—Reginald's name was spoken—the fond secret of her life revealed; and from that day she found more strength to struggle with depression—to leave no effort untried to regain serenity, and conquer that worst foe to happiness, indifference, which the human heart contains. Once convinced, by the representations of affection and experience, that it was her duty *actively to do*, as well as passively to endure—to prove her resignation to the blow, which, though heavy, was still dealt by a Father's hand, she did not fail. A yet more earnest desire to seek the happiness of others, and complete disregard of self—a calm and still serenity of word and look, were now her outward characteristics; while, within, though her spirit had gained new strength in its upward flight—new clinging love for that world where all is peace, the thought of the departed yet remained, gaining, it seemed, increase of power with every passing month. It had lost its absorbing anguish; but not its memories. Too truly did she feel, with that sweet chronicler of woman's heart—

"We dream not of Love's might,
Till Death has robed, with soft and solemn light,
The image we enshrine. Before *that* hour
We have but glimpses of the overmastering power
Within us laid."

There were times when the thought would come, and so vividly she could scarcely believe it only a thought, that Reginald might yet live, the public records be deceivers. But Lady Emily's assurances that her father and brothers had made every inquiry, but that all the information obtained only confirmed the statement, proved the utter fallacy of the dream.

II.

"Ah! let the heart that worships thee
By ev'ry change be proved."

L. E. L.

"I could forgive the miserable hours
His falsehood, and his only, taught my heart;
But I can not forgive that for his sake
My faith in good is shaken, and my hopes
Are pale and cold, for they have looked on death.
Why should I love him? he no longer is
That which I loved."

L. E. L.

"Thou livest! thou livest!
I knew thou couldst not die!"

De Chatillon—Mrs. Hemans.

Nearly two years had elapsed since the death of Reginald De Vere, ere any event of sufficient importance occurred in Annie's life for us to resume the thread of our narrative. A shock like that, and on such a disposition, could never be forgotten, though time, the softener of all ills, had restored her to some degree of her wonted animation, and though the elastic spirits of the young girl had given way, the woman had become yet more attractive and loveable. The first London season after Reginald's death she had not accompanied her uncle's family to the great metropolis, but spent the period of their absence quietly in Scotland. The second she did not refuse to join them; but scenes of festivity were so evidently distasteful, that her friends did not urge her entering more into society than her own inclinations prompted. But in her uncle's house she was seen and known only to be admired and loved, receiving, to her extreme astonishment, an unexceptionable offer of marriage before she had been two months in London. It was declined gratefully, but so decidedly as to give no hope. Some weeks afterwards, Lord St. Clair one morning entered Annie's room. She was alone, so intently engaged in drawing as not to observe the very peculiar expression of countenance with which he regarded her some minutes without speaking.

"I would give something to read your thoughts, cousin mine," she said, playfully, at length raising her eyes to his face, which instantly resumed its usual kind and open expression. "I could hardly believe you were in the room, you were so silent."

"I was thinking how very wise the world is, Annie. It knows and vouches for so many things concerning individuals, of which they are utterly ignorant themselves."

"Why, what is the report now?"

"Only—" he paused for a second, then rallied so quickly, that the huskiness of his first word was unperceived, "that you and I are engaged in marriage, and that I only wait till you are of age, that the disparity of years may seem less."

"The world must think much too highly of me for such a report to gain credence," replied Annie, simply, yet gravely, though she did start at the intelligence.

"What can you mean?"

"That they must hold me in much greater respect than I deserve, to unite my name, even in thought, with yours."

"My dear Annie, can you mean that you are undeserving of the regard of any man, however high his worth? How little do you know yourself! Believe me, it is I who should feel proud that the world should believe this so strongly that not even the disparity of years between us is considered an objection."

"Do not talk so, dear Henry, or I shall fear I am losing one of the truest friends I have. You have always treated me with such regard as never to flatter me; pray do not begin now."

"Indeed you do me injustice, Annie; might I not return the charge, and accuse you of flattering me?"

"No, dear cousin. How can I do otherwise than look up to, and venerate your worth, associating with you at home, as I have done for nearly three years, and receiving such constant kindness, that had I been your own young sister you could not have shown more? Do I not see you as a son and brother? and if I did not venerate you, should I not be the only one, either at home or in the world, who did not do you the justice you deserve?"

"And may I not equally have learnt to know and love you?"

"Yes, as a child, a sister, but not as the wife you need."

"Is the disparity of years, then, in your mind so great an obstacle? Do you think it quite impossible a man of eight-and-thirty can love a girl of twenty?"

"No, not impossible."

"But impossible that a girl of twenty could love a man of eight-and-thirty; is that it?

"Far less unlikely than the other case," replied Annie, half smiling, for her complete unconsciousness caused her to be amused at her companion's pertinacity.

"Then why should the world's report be so utterly without foundation, dearest Annie?" inquired Lord St. Clair, with such a sudden change of countenance and tone that it startled her almost into consciousness. The arch and playful look vanished, her cheek paled, and the tears started to her eyes, and laying her hand confidingly on his arm, she said, with quivering lip—

"Dearest Henry, do not let me lose the kind brother, the true friend I have so long believed you."

"You shall not, Annie," he answered fervently, "even if to retain such appellatives makes me more miserable than you imagine."

"Do not, do not say so! my thoughts are all memories, and were the world's report indeed true, would be faithless every hour; could this make your happiness?"

"But must this always be? Is devotion to the departed a higher duty than giving happiness to the living? So purely unselfish as you are, would you not in time better secure your own peace by giving inexpressible happiness as the beloved and cherished wife of the living, who would never expect you to love as you have loved, than by indulging in the luxury of memory and devotedness to one who is in heaven? Is not this a question worth considering, Annie?"

"Not now, now now! oh, do not urge me now!" she implored, bursting into tears; and her companion on the instant banished every word and thought of self to soothe and calm her.

A month or two afterwards, Lord St. Clair, to the astonishment of his friends, by whom he was regarded as a particularly quiet, stay-at-home sort of person, accepted a diplomatic embassy to the courts of Germany and Russia, likely to detain him twelve or eighteen months. He had besought and received Annie's permission to correspond with her. Letters from a mind and heart like his could not be otherwise than interesting. His words returned repeatedly to her thoughts; she loved him sufficiently to feel a degree of pleasure in the idea of adding to his happiness, and six months after he had left England, her answer to a letter from him, in which generalities had merged into personalities, contained the following words:—

"If, dearest Henry, the gratitude and reverence of one whose best affections still linger with the dead are indeed of sufficient worth to give you the happiness which you tell me rests with me, I will not refuse to become yours, if a twelvemonth hence you still desire it. Give me that time. The painful feelings with which I now look to marriage, as almost faithlessness to one who, though the actual words never passed his lips, I do believe loved me most truly, will then perhaps, in some degree at least, have subsided, and I may be able to give you all that your wife should bestow. I know and feel that time is the comforter as well as the destroyer, and that though it is actual agony to think that my heart will ever so change as to feel less acutely the loss I have sustained, I know it will and must, and that it is right and best it should do so. Give me but time, then, dearest Henry—let the memories of the dead be so softened that I may do my duty lovingly as well as faithfully to the living; and till that may be, let us continue as we have been to the world and to each other."

Lord St. Clair did not hesitate to accede to this request. Even his letters did not change their tone; he was still the friend more than the lover; but he contrived to shorten the period of his voluntary banishment, and eleven months after he had quitted England beheld his return.

There was a change in Annie, however, which alarmed and pained him; she was pale and thin, and strangely and feverishly restless. Lady Emily, from being constantly with her, had not remarked the great alteration, but acknowledged, in answer to St. Clair's anxious queries, that she had seemed more unhappy the last four months, that the calm and tranquil cheerfulness which had characterised her had given place to alternations of fitful gayety and more frequent depression; but what had occasioned it she could not tell; she thought it might be physical, as she had had a slight cough hanging about her for weeks, which nothing she took seemed to remove. Four months previous! was it possible that she might regret the promises she had so ingenuously given? Lord St. Clair more than once caught her glance fixed with a degree of pleading earnestness upon him, as if she failed in courage to speak; and as he was not one to encourage painful doubts where a word might solve them, he took an opportunity of kindly and affectionately inquiring why she was so changed.

The cause was soon revealed. About ten days after she had written to him, as we related, she had seen, amongst other despatches directed to Lord St. Clair, which were lying on the library table waiting to be arranged and forwarded, a single letter, the writing of the direction of which had caused such a sudden thrill and subsequent faintness, that it had been with difficulty she refrained from involuntarily tearing it open, to know from whom it came. She said that she had endeavoured to conquer the strange fancy; to reason with herself, that the resemblance to a writing she but too well remembered was mere accident. Yet so powerful had been its effect, that even when she recalled the superscription, the same feelings of heart-sickness returned as had overpowered her when it first met her eye. It had been put up with other public despatches—the family having before its arrival closed and sent more private letters; that as he had never alluded to it, she had struggled to believe it could have been nothing of interest to her, and yet the subject would not leave her mind, allowing her neither sleep at night nor rest by day. She knew it folly, she said, but conquer it she could not.

And that fearful state of internal restlessness was fated to continue; for, most unfortunately, the packet of despatches in which that was had been lost, in the overflow of a river which the messenger who bore it had to ford, and Lord St. Clair had never alluded to it, for his letters to Annie had been shorter than he liked, from the annoyance and increase of trouble which the loss of this very packet had occasioned him in his political employment. That the post-mark seemed Italian was all she could tell him, and his anxiety became as great as hers, though that it could really be what it was easy to discover Annie really imagined it, he believed impossible.

Meanwhile, the poor girl's health—under a suspicion which,

however imaginary, was very fearful—did not improve, and her relatives rested not till a skilful physician had been consulted; his opinion instantly decided them, and, despite of Annie's resistance, a tour on the Continent was resolved on, Lord Ennerdale desiring her not to let him see her again, till she could bring back her own rosy smiling self.

The party consisted of only Lord St. Clair, Lady Emily and Annie; and, making only a brief stay at Paris, they proceeded in a south-easterly direction, crossed the Jura, and fixed their residence for some weeks in the vicinity of Geneva. The complete change of air and scene seemed so to renovate Annie, that physical strength gradually returned, and with it more apparent calm of mind. Congeniality of taste in our companions is indispensable for the real enjoyment of travelling, and this Annie fully possessed; those three years of intimate association with the apparently cold and passionless Lady Emily had deepened Annie's regard, but not altered her cousin's chilling manner. But this delicious commune with nature, uninterrupted by intercourse with the world, caused her more than once so to relax as to excite even Annie's surprise, and convince her more than ever that Lady Emily had not always been what she then was.

They were sitting one evening under the projecting roof of a jutting gallery belonging to a cottage in the beautiful valley of Chamouni; Lord St. Clair had that day left them to join a party of excursionists, in an expedition somewhat too fatiguing for his companions. The cottage, situated on a projecting mount or cliff, commanded a more extensive view than the parish of Prieuré itself permits. The rich luxuriance of the vale stretched beneath them, intersected with cliffs covered with foliage and large patches of emerald moss, and variously-tinted lichen clothing the gray stones. Here and there a true Alpine cottage peeped through dark woods of fir and larch, and the blue and sparkling Arve glided noiselessly along, still more lovely in the evening hour, as the glowing rays of sunset are contrasted with the deep shadows falling all around. Above them towered mountains of every form, blending their separate charms in a whole so sublime and extensive that height and breadth were lost in distance; misty vapours, or light fleecy clouds, were ever wreathing their snow-capped brows, while Mont Blanc itself stood alone in its sublime grandeur, and in the unsullied purity of its snowy robe. The sun itself was invisible, but its glowing rays were shed upon the mountain, dyeing it with a deep, rosy flood of light peculiar to that locality, and only to be described by its thrilling resemblance to that fearfully brilliant flush sometimes traced on the countenance of mortal beauty, when life is fading imperceptibly away, and the strange yet perfect loveliness rivets not alone the eye but the imagination with a species of fascination which we have no power to resist. The period of its continuance might have been from fifteen to twenty minutes, when it suddenly changed into a pale grayish tinge, of a shade and appearance so peculiar, that it affected the heart and mind with the same species of awe as that with which we regard the sudden change from brilliant life to the ashy hues of death.

An exclamation of admiration, even of delight, broke so naturally from the lips of Lady Emily St. Clair, that her young companion looked up in her face with astonishment.

"Have I so surprised you, Annie?" she said, with a quiet smile. "Are you still amongst those who believe that one so cold and silent as I am now can have no feeling for enjoyment, can see no beauty in nature, no poetry in the universe?"

"No," replied Annie, earnestly; "I know so much of you that mere superficial observers can never know, that I can well believe there is still more which my inexperienced eye can never reach. I wish," she added, after a short pause, and with some hesitation, "that I were worthy to know you as you are, that you loved me sufficiently to unveil sometimes that which is so studiously concealed."

"Do not do me such wrong, dearest Annie, as to doubt that I love you, because I am to you, in general, as to indifferent persons. I cannot change the manner acquired by months, nay, whole years of suffering, even to those whose affections I would do much to win. There is little of interest and much of suffering in my past life; but you shall hear it if you will."

"Not if it give you pain, my kind friend," said Annie; but she looked inquiringly as she seated herself on a cushion at her companion's feet, and rested her arm on her knee. Lady Emily paused, as if collecting firmness for the task, then briefly spoke as follows.

"Few, who have only known me the last fifteen or sixteen years, would believe that I was once, Annie, far more enthusiastic and dreamy, and what the world calls romantic, than you were when I first knew you. An ardent love for the exalted and the beautiful, alike in man and nature; a restless craving for the pure and spiritual; an almost loathing for all that was mean and earthly: these were the elements of my romance, but carried to an excess, that instead of being beneficial, as they might have been, became indeed the height of folly, which is the world's meaning for such feelings. I was a poet, a visionary, an enthusiastic, feeding a naturally vivid imagination on the burning dreams of minds whose wings soared even higher than my own. By my family I was regarded with admiration and love, as one whose talents would raise me far higher than my rank. I had the advantage of association with the genius and the student; and their opinion of my powers, their sympathy, urged me on till I was astonished at myself. But there was a blank in the midst of pleasure; I soared too high in the moments of excitement. My mind, unable to sustain itself in the airy realms of an ill-regulated imagination, was fraught, on its return to earth, with a gloom and void even more exquisitely painful than its previous mood had been joyful. Yet had poetry been my only gift, its pains and pleasures might have been confined to my own breast; but the powers of satire, mine in no ordinary degree, were far more dangerous to myself in their baleful influence upon others. I indulged in the most cutting irony, careless whom I might wound, regardless of any feeling but my own pleasure; I knew religion only as a name, whose every ordinance was fulfilled by attending public service once a week. I heard and read that, to some minds, poetry vitalizes religion, for every throb unanswered upon earth lifted up the whole soul to that world where all was love and all was joy. I laughed at such romance, as I termed it, for I could not understand it. In the gloom and void occasionally felt, pride and triumph at my own superiority to my fellows were the constant occupants of my heart, urging me but too often to level the dart of venomed satire on those whose more worldly sentiments and coarser minds excited my contempt; even the young and gentle often bled beneath that cruel lash, if in the merest trifle of word or manner they differed from my idea of excellence. My own family loved me too indulgently to be aware of the dreadful extent of this vice; Henry, the only one whose noble nature and judicious feeling would have guided me aright, was a student in Germany, and I had no one whose counsels might have spared me, in some measure at least, the bitter self-reproach which heightened the chastisement preparing for me.

"But I am lingering. Amongst the numerous guests at

my father's was one, combining noble birth, genius, light and ready wit, with all the fascination of sparkling features, graceful form, and a manner whose elegance I have never yet seen equalled. He courted my society; he did not *flatter*, for that I ever scorned, but he *appreciated.* His manner always evinced respect for me, and pleasure at having found one to whom he could converse on nobler subjects than the mere chit-chat of a fashionable world. It needs not to enlarge upon our intimacy, or the means he took to make me believe, without in the least committing himself, that I was to him the object not of esteem or admiration alone.

Why should I hesitate to speak that which is now as if it had never been? I loved him, Annie, how deeply and passionately! till my whole soul was wrapped in his image, and my very nature so changed, that I looked on this world with gentler feelings, and believe that the earth which contained him could not be as little worth as I had deemed it. All this would be useless to repeat; the blank in my heart was filled up; my woman soul, which neither fame nor talent could satisfy, was at rest; the actual words had not passed his lips indeed, but yet I did not, could not doubt him. That is not love in which a doubt can enter. I was visiting a mutual friend, and daily in expectation of his arrival; to relieve the yearning restlessness of anticipation, I had taken my tablets to a concealed nook in the garden, and was pouring out my whole soul in burning words, when his voice arrested me. The remark preceding his words I had not heard, but all which followed is written on my brain.

"'Propose to Emily St. Clair!' he said, in a tone which, while it retained its beautiful harmony, was so changed in expression that I only knew it his by the agony thrilling through my whole being at the words, 'Percy, you are mocking me! Marry a blue—a wit! worse still, a poet! Pray procure me admission into a lunatic asylum the very hour I make the proposal; for, at least, were I sufficiently mad to say, Will you have me? certain as I am of being accepted, I should escape being rendered more so. No, my good fellow, the lady is agreeable enough as long as I am unchained; but once fettered, her folly and romance would send me to heaven much sooner than I have the least inclination for. Why, were I in such a predicament as marriage with her, how do you suppose I could live for ever the actor I am now, when conversing with her, drawing her out as it were, to afford me amusement afterwards? The very idea is exhaustion!'

"'It is well her brothers have not seen the progress of your attentions,' was the reply. 'You might have to answer for such species of amusement.'

"'Nonsense, man! Were the Courts of Love in vogue as they were once, she could allege nothing against me to make me her prisoner for life. Why, it was the very effort to keep up the *liaison*, and yet not say one word which her romantic fancy could construe into an offer, that was so fatiguing. Her delight in my society was so evident, that I was obliged to be on my guard; words meaningless to others would have been seized upon by her, and then *misericordia!*'

"'Out upon your consummate self-conceit; she never forgot her self-respect,' was the reply, and the voices faded in the distance."

"And you heard this!" exclaimed Annie, indignation compelling the interruption. "Gracious heaven! can there be such men?"

"Be thankful you can still ask such a question, dearest Annie. I did hear—and more, remained outwardly calm; at that moment I believe I was conscious but of one feeling, not indignation; no, he might have spoken yet more cruelly, more contemptuously. I heard but one, felt but one truth—that he did not love me—that the deep whelming passion he had excited was unreturned—that he scorned those gifts which I had lately only valued as I believed them valued by him. My brain reeled for the moment; but sense and energy returned, as gradually, but with fearful distinctness, his every word and tone resounded in my ear. Anguish, which had been the first feeling, was as nothing, literally nothing, to that chaos of misery which followed—to disrobe the idol my heart had so madly worshipped of the bright colouring of honour and worth, to teach myself he was *unworthy*, had deceived, wilfully deceived. What was the suffering of unrequited love compared with this? He had said, too, that my preference was so evident, I would have grasped the faintest whisper of an offer. I knew the charge was false as himself; but that he should have believed it, added its bitter pang. How was I to act? My brow was burning, my pulses throbbing, yet return to my own home I would not; I would not feign illness, though God knows it would have been little feigned. I would meet him, pass in his company the period I had promised to my friend, and then I cared not."

"And you did this?" asked Annie, clasping Lady Emily's

hand in both hers, and almost startled at its coldness—the only proof that the narrator told not her tale unmoved.

"I did more, my child. Though poetry and satire were now to me but fearful spectres, from which a tortured spirit shrank—though that very hour I burned every fragment of composition once so precious, yet, during three long weary weeks, I was to him and to all around me as I had always been; perhaps even more sparkling, more animated, and far more joyous. Without any visible effort, I so far changed in bearing towards him, that instead of finding in his conversation as before an echo to my own, I questioned, I doubted, and more than once I saw him quail beneath my glance or tone, compelled, ere we parted, to doubt the influence which he had boasted he possessed. But what availed all this? It did not, could not quench the burning fever within; and when I returned to the quiet of my father's roof, the tight-strung cord was snapped, and overwrought energies so gave way, that for months, nay, years, the effects of that struggle were visible in a state of health so precarious, so exhausted, that I have seen my poor father pace my chamber hour by hour in silent agony, without the power to address him. For many months all was to me a blank; yet I believe I was not wholly insensible nor always under the influence of fever. Ere I recovered sufficiently again to mingle with the world, he who had so deceived me became the husband of another; and that other, one who had been my dearest friend, and who has shunned me since as if she too had deceived, and had courted me from policy, not love. I have had no proof that this really was the case, but my faith in all that was good, and beautiful, and true was so shaken, I believed it as a thing that must be, for such was human nature. This marriage sufficiently accounted to my family for my mysterious illness. Indignation was so generally felt, that had I been awake to outward things, my mind might have been perfectly at rest that I had given him no undue encouragement: and his manner had indeed been such as to give, not alone to myself, but to all who had observed, no doubt of his apparent meaning; but I knew nothing of all this. While chained to my couch by bodily exhaustion, memories of my past life rose to appal me, and to add the bitter agony of unmitigated self-reproach to that of unrequited affection. Precious gifts had been intrusted to me, and what account could I render of them at that awful throne, before which daily, almost hourly, I expected to be summoned?

They had estranged me from my God, and from his creatures. I learned to feel his words were true. Unguided by either religion or reason, what could I have been but the idle follower of folly and romance? No throb of kindness or of gentle feeling had interfered to check the attempt I felt for, and breathed in cutting satire upon, others. I had wilfully trampled on many a young kind heart, and it was but just that I should have been thus trampled on myself. Presumption and self-conceit caused me to smile, to scorn the censure of the world, and in all probability my manner had been too unguarded. This bitter self-humiliation only increased the struggle to forget that I had loved. In reproaching myself I ceased to reproach him; the pride that had supported me was gone. These thoughts continually pressing on heart and brain were, I am well aware, the sole sources of my long and incurable disease, but I had no power to shake them off; and, fearfully as I suffered, I have never ceased to bless the gracious hand that sent the chastening, and recalled me, ere it was too late, unto himself."

Lady Emily paused; the quivering of her voice and lip betraying emotion which she evidently struggled to suppress. Annie's tears were falling on her hand, and ere she spoke again, she bent down and kissed her forehead.

"You now know, dearest Annie, more of me than I ever breathed to mortal ear," she resumed, in her usual calm and quiet tone, "more than I ever thought could pass my lips. But do not weep for me, my child; I am happier, safer now, than I could have been had the wild, misguided feelings of earlier life continued. It was no small portion of my suffering so to control myself as never to give vent to the satirical bitterness that, when I rejoined the world, tinged my words and thoughts more darkly than ever. The determination never to use that dangerous gift, gave to my words and manner a stiffness and cold reserve which have banished from me all those whose regard I would have done much to win. Many young loving hearts have shrunk from me, perceiving no sympathy in their warm imaginations and glowing feelings; and I dared not undeceive them, for I felt no confidence in myself, and feared again to avow sentiments I had buried so deeply in my own heart. Others again shunned me, because terrified at a semblance of austerity, which they could not know was exercised only towards myself; and frequently have I wept in secret at the loneliness which seemed to characterise my path on earth. Even you, my Annie, gentle and forbearing as you were, till I could not but love you, have often checked your animated words beneath the cold, withering influence of my glance or smile."

"Do not call it cold and withering, my dear, kind friend," replied Annie, warmly. "I learned to love you long before I dared hope to win your regard; but could I doubt you in my hour of anguish? Though even then I did you wrong; for I thought I was alone in my misery—and you had suffered doubly more."

"You needed not such awful chastisement, my love; I brought it on myself. But you are right; fearful as is the death of a beloved one, it is happiness compared to the *death of love*, to the blasting of our belief in the good and true; the disrobing an idol, till we ask what it is we have loved. My dearest Annie, bless God that this you have been spared."

Annie was silent several minutes, and then raising her head, she abruptly and strangely asked, "Aye, this; but there are other trials. Oh, Lady Emily, what must be the agony of that heart, who, sacrificing for the sake of the living the memories of the supposed dead, finds too late, that circumstances, not death, have come between her and the object of her first affection; that they love each other still, yet must be strangers, parted more completely than by death? What must be her duty then?"

"You ask me a difficult question, my dear child. If the heart clings to such a thought, better never wed."

A bright gleam, as of relief, flitted over Annie's features; but, changing the subject as abruptly as she had entered upon it, she asked, with hesitation, "And that poetic talent to which you have alluded, do you never exercise it now?"

"Never," replied Lady Emily, taking her companion's arm, and entering the house. "On my first recovery I dared not, for my sinful abuse of the power had been too recent; though I do believe, that as my taste had completely changed in the poets which I read, so too would my writings have done. But year after year passed; gradually I destroyed every memorial of my past life, and found peace and happiness in the employment which you have seen and aided, until at length even the inclination to write passed away; and I forgot, even as you must, dear girl," she added, with a smile, "that I had been a poet, and one of no mean grade."

The silent pressure of Annie's hand was sufficient guarantee for Lady Emily that her confidence had not been misplaced; and she was happier, for she no longer feared that, misunderstanding, Annie would at length shrink from her.

We will not linger with our travellers while *en route.* They visited all of interest in Naples and Rome, and resolved on passing the winter at Florence. Many weeks had passed in their delightful tour; Annie's health was decidedly renovated; but there were still times when her spirits seemed to sink beneath a weight of depression for which neither of her relatives could account. Each month that passed diminished the time specified by Annie as the term of mourning, and yet Lord St. Clair vainly tried to rejoice; he saw that, instead of decreasing, the memory of Reginald became stronger—that the extraordinary impression made by the superscription of the letter would remain—and ardently he wished that Annie had followed her impulse, and opened it ere it was sent on. He never spoke of love, he never recalled her promise, and Annie so blessed him for his forbearance that, could she but have realized the universal belief in the death of Reginald, she would at once have given him her hand, glad to exchange the torturing doubts which engrossed her for the tranquil calm which must, she thought, attend devotion to one who so nobly proved the love he bore herself.

The many interesting works of ancient art in Florence, so riveted the attention and occupied the time of our English travellers, that the one subject engrossing the whole attention of the Florentines was for some little time unheeded. The town was full of the unrivalled success of a young sculptor, who had burst into fame, no one knew how or where. He had been studying the last two years, amidst the superb specimens of art, in the galleries of Florence, but so silently, so unassumingly, that he was only known as famous. His copies of Canova and other celebrated sculptors had been pronounced perfect by able judges; but it was not till he had completed an original group that he at all seemed to sue for notice, and when that did appear, the easily-excited Italians received it with such universal admiration, that the unknown artist was sought for on all sides, courted, flattered, and, better far, appreciated by those whose opinions were of value. Italy is indeed the country where talent may rise to eminence, fostered and cherished by the encouragement for which it so thirsts. In this case however, the interest excited originally by genius was heightened by the reserved manners of the young sculptor, who rather shrunk from than courted notice, except from the Italians themselves. It was rarely an English *soirée* could obtain the favour of his presence. His appearance and name declared him Spanish, a supposition which, as he never contradicted it, gained universal belief. That he spoke English, French, and Italian as fluently as Spanish, and was intimately acquainted with their literature, only proved that his mental capabilities were not confined merely to his art. How he found time to execute all the orders for busts, ornamental groups, &c., which he received was a mystery to the idler, and a wonder even to the brethren of his craft, greatly heightened when his first original group appeared. It was not alone the execution, but the daring boldness of his subject which had occasioned such universal notice. Boldly leaving the beaten path of classic subjects, his group, though consisting only of three figures, embodied a striking incident in the earliest stage of the French revolution. A young and beautiful girl had flung herself before an aged parent, clasping his neck with one hand, and by the attitude of the other, combined with the expression of the face, was evidently imploring life for him, even by the sacrifice of her own. On the touching and, to the Italian eye, somewhat peculiar beauty of the face, the matchless grace of the attitude, and exquisitely modelled limbs, the sculptor appeared to have lingered till he had outdone himself. The countenance of the father breathed but admiring love for the heroic being whom his arm encircled, as if every thought centred in her, to the total exclusion of all terror for himself. Before them, in a crouching attitude, as in the act of filling a goblet with the loathsome fluid which deluged the streets, was a half-naked form, whose ruffian features and muscular limbs contrasted well with the graceful beauty and nobleness of form in the other figures. The head was upraised, a withering sneer upon the lips, a combination of triumph and barbarity on the whole countenance, which so explained the tale it recorded, that, as an animated Italian told Lord St. Clair, the heart of the gazers throbbed, and the cheek paled, as if life itself were before them. It stood in an apartment of the Palazzo Vecchio, where he entreated his English friends to go and see it. "I will not only see this wonderful group, but make acquaintance with its artist," he replied; "for, after hearing all this, know him I will."

"That you will find some difficulty in doing," was the rejoinder. "He shrinks from all you English; besides, he is, I believe, now at Bologna, and his return is uncertain."

"Never mind; trust me for making acquaintance with this lion, shy though he be."

"There is but one fault in his female figure," observed a gentleman who had joined the group, and was greeted with much warmth by Lord St. Clair, "a fault which we English ought to consider a virtue, but yet is in contradiction to Signor Castellan's apparent reserve towards our countrymen. The beauty of the female is too English for a French incident and purely French characters. It is very lovely, I grant, but the loveliness is our own."

The observation naturally produced a warm discussion, which ended, as most discussions do, in each party retaining his own opinion; and Lord St. Clair taking his newly-found old friend home with him, introduced him to Lady Emily and Annie.

"And are you settled down at last, Kenrich, tired of wanderings and adventures? though last time I heard of you, you were actually enjoying the wars and cabals of Madrid."

"I am not very sober yet, St. Clair; but I was fool enough to join the Carlists three or four years ago, and their barbarity to my own countrymen so sickened me of war, that I threw up my commission, and have never drawn sword since."

"What barbarity?" asked Lord St. Clair, catching almost by instinct more than look the expression of Annie's face.

"Why, you must have heard—the English papers were full of it—that fine fellow, Captain De Vere, was amongst them. He and eight or ten others were taken prisoners, and were all murdered—for it was nothing else."

"But are you sure he was amongst them? We all knew and loved De Vere, and long hoped he might have escaped, and only been reported amongst the killed."

"Escaped, my dear fellow! how was that possible? Besides, he was so terribly wounded, that he could not have survived, even had they not so cruelly dealt with him. I could not save him, but I saw him decently interred, and from that moment loathed military service, and left Spain."

"It was full time, I think," quietly rejoined Lady Emily. "Annie, will you try if you can match this shade for me amongst the chenilles in my room? I cannot finish this leaf without it, and your eyes are better than mine."

Annie took the chenille designated from the frame, over which her cousin was bending so intently in seeming, that she did not even look up as she addressed her, and quietly left the room. The moment she did so, Edward Kenrich burst into lavish praises of her beauty, declaring that was the exact style of Castellan's figure, and therefore he was right, and it must be too English for perfect art, so running on in his usual wild strain, that Lord St. Clair had great difficulty in bringing him back to the point from which he had started, and gathering from him every particular of the death of Reginald De Vere.

Annie did not reappear, and Lady Emily's great desire to finish her leaf seemed to have subsided with her absence, for she made no effort to recall her. Just before dinner however, Lord St. Clair, noticing the flutter of her white dress between the orange trees, which almost concealed the balcony leading from the drawing-room, hastily rejoined her. She looked up in his face without a word, but he answered her thoughts, tenderly and gently repeating all the information he had gained. There could be no doubt, and for one brief moment the poor girl's head sunk on his arm, with a sudden burst of tears.

"I know it is all folly, Henry. I had no right to hope; forgive me, I do but distress you; and yet that writing—that strange writing, whom could it have been from?"

"Not from Reginald, dearest, or it would have been to you, not to me. Has that never struck you, Annie?"

It had not till that moment, and it convinced her. She remained alone that evening, in deep meditation and earnest prayer; and the result was a firm conviction that nothing but a new and solemn duty would restore her to the calm of mind for which she yearned—that devotion to another well worthy of it must draw her from herself. A sleepless night confirmed this resolution, and the very next day the promise passed her lips to be the wife of Lord St. Clair, within a week of their return to England. A few days afterwards they went to the celebrated church of Santa Croce during vesper service. The magnificent interior, heightened in its effect by the light and shadow flung by huge waxen tapers, the superb monuments, the white-stoled monks and dark dresses of the officiating priests, the kneeling and standing group, silent and motionless as the marble monuments around—the deep-toned organ, and swelling voices of the choristers, completely enchained the imaginations of our travellers. It was strange, excited almost to pain as she was, that Annie at length found her whole attention unconsciously fixed on a single figure, who was leaning against the tomb of Michael Angelo. His face was turned from her, but there was something in his bearing and his attitude which riveted her as by a spell, and the longing to look on his face became strangely and indefinably intense. The soft light of a taper burning over the tomb brought out in good relief the stranger's uncovered head, whose small and classic shape was shaded by clustering hair of glossy black.

"There he is! there is our sculptor, Renaud Castellan!" whispered one of the Italians who had accompanied them, directing Lord St. Clair's attention to the very figure on whom Annie's gaze was so strangely fixed; but even as he spoke, the young man moved his position, and disappeared in one of the aisles, leaving Annie's desire to see his face ungratified, and only permitting Lord St. Clair to catch the outline of his figure.

"Was not Mrs. De Vere's maiden name Castellan?" St. Clair asked of Annie, as they walked together from the church to the house of their Italian friend, who had claimed them for a *petit souper*, and some music. The answer was in the affirmative, and Lord St. Clair remarked it would be strange if this young Spaniard proved to be of the same family. "I must seek him out."

"See his group first," was the rejoinder of one of the party; while to Annie the words seemed to disperse the miserable doubts again thronging round her—being of the same family might account for a casual resemblance.

It was with some little difficulty Annie was prevailed upon to sing; but when once seated at her harp, timidity gave place to her real love of the art, and the simple purity, the touching pathos of her style charmed all who heard. The entrance of a guest had not interrupted her, nor disturbed the listeners. Lord St. Clair was amused at the look of admiring perplexity with which he regarded Annie, not himself perceiving that, where the Italian stood, the light fell upon her countenance, so as to give it a different appearance and expression to that which was generally perceivable.

Approaching her, as soon as the buzz of admiration had somewhat subsided, he engaged her in animated conversation; nor was Lord St. Clair's curiosity lessened by hearing him inquire "if the signorina were not acquainted with the young sculptor, of whom all Florence raved?" Much surprised, she answered in the negative.

"But surely you have been introduced to him, have you not?"

"No," replied Annie, smiling at his earnestness. "I never even heard of him till I came here; and he has been at Bologna, till this evening, ever since."

"Then he has seen you, signora, either in his sleeping or waking dreams," was the rejoinder, in so animated a tone that it arrested the attention of the whole party; "for never did marble and life resemble each other as the beauty of your face and of his creation. Surely you must all see it," he continued, turning to his friends with the sparkling vivacity peculiar to his countrymen when excited. "Why, it is not feature alone, but the character, the grace, the similarity is perfect!"

"I told you so, but you would not believe me," bluntly answered Kenrich. "I told you it was an English face and English character; but you all denied it. I am glad my lovely countrywoman has opened your eyes."

"Why this is better and better, Annie; do not blush so prettily about it," whispered Lord St. Clair, as, attention once aroused, the similarity was universally acknowledged. "If the resemblance be chance, it is something to marvel at; if intentional, why I shall be jealous of the sculptor."

"You need not, Henry," was the reply, in a tone so sad that it pained him.

"Well, well, we will go and see it at least, love, and judge of its merit with our own eyes."

The next day accordingly they went, and (the most convincing proof of the perfection of the work) were not disappointed. Neither its beauty nor its eloquence had been exaggerated, and the resemblance to Annie was so extraordinary that the eyes of all tbe spectators within the room were attracted towards her; but the expression of the countenance of the father iu the group riveted her attention far more than the female figure. It was with a heavy sigh she turned from it, and was pale and silent during their way home; but St. Clair was so engrossed by the beauty of the work, the strange resemblance, and his resolution to leave no stone unturned to gain the acquaintance of the young artist, that it passed unnoticed even by him.

"Why, what ails you, Annie? are you not well, dear?" kindly inquired Lady Emily, some hours later. Wondering why her young companion did not join her as usual, she had sought her in her own room, and found her with her face buried in her hands, and her whole attitude denoting suffering. "Henry has gone to seek out this Signor Castellan, to find out, if he can, in what this strange similarity originated and who and what he is."

"Shall I tell you?" answered Annie, in a tone so strange that it startled almost as much as the whiteness of her face. "Reginald Castellan de Vere! Was not his mother's name Castellan? and has he not often and often boasted his descent from Spanish heroes, and from this feeling fought for Spain in preference to any other country? Did he not always love the art of sculpture? Can it be chance that has marked the father and daughter of the group with the characteristics of the revered friend and favourite companion of his youth? No, no, no! Oh! Lady Emily, you bade me once thank God that I had never been deceived; teach me how to bear this."

"Bear what, my poor child?" replied her companion, soothingly, as Annie threw herself on her neck in fearful agitation. "If this be indeed as you say, what can there be but happiness for you? It is for another we must feel."

"Happiness for me! and he has never even so far thought of me as to tell me the report of his death was false, and he still lived—never recalled himself to one whom, when he departed, he so loved—loved! how know I that? he never said it; why should I believe him different to others?"

"My dearest Annie, this is not like yourself. Why, if he have ceased to love you, should the work of his hand—a work which must have employed his mind and heart long days and nights—bear the impress of your face and form?"

"Memory, association, mere casualty—the days of his boyhood may be dear to his mind; but now can affection, even a brother's, have inspired that group, when—when he has allowed me so long to believe him dead?"

"It is all a mystery, my dear child; but I feel convinced it will be solved, if we can really prove his identity. May he not have written, and the letter miscarried?" Annie wildly raised her head. "May he not have been deceived? perhaps—for we can never trace rumours—but may he not have heard that of you which, to a mind like his, would cause him to shrink from recalling himself? He left you such a child, how might he build on having so won your regard that you would remain single for his sake? Dearest Annie, if this indeed be not all imagination, and Reginald really lives, trust me you will be happy yet."

How will a few judicious words change the whole current of thought and feeling! Before Lady Emily ceased to speak, Annie was weeping such blessed tears. The proud, cold mood which, had her companion spoken as her own experience of man's nature must have dictated, might have been retained and made her miserable for life, dissolved before returning trust and hope. She dared not define what it was she hoped; but it was not till she heard Lord St. Clair's voice, and she tried to spring forwards to meet him and know the truth, that a sudden revulsion of feeling so completely overpowered her that she sunk back upon the couch. How dared she rejoice, even if Reginald lived? what could he be to her who was the promised bride of another?

"Emily!" exclaimed Lord St. Clair, in utter astonishment, as, on his entering the drawing-room, his cold and dignified sister hastily met him, and taking both his hands, tried to speak, but failed; and leaning her head against him, he felt that she was in tears. "What is the matter, love? something very dreadful, for you to weep."

She controlled herself with a strong effort, and entered at once into the recital of the scene between her and Annie. "Could it possibly be as she supposed?"

"It may be," was the reply, in a calm, firm tone; "there is nothing impossible in it. I went to his lodgings, but, as I supposed, he was either out or too much engaged to be seen; but I am to meet him to-night at the Contessa Corsini's, and this strange mystery will be unravelled."

"And you, dear Henry—" she could say no more, so holy seemed his feelings.

"And I, my dear sister, will act as that man should whose aim is not the gratification of his own desires, but the happiness of one far dearer than himself. I do not tell you I shall not feel, and deeply; but does the warrior shrink from the battle before him because he may be wounded? You may love me more, my Emily, if you will," he continued, fondly passing his arm round her, and kissing her cheek, "for affection is always balm; but I will have no tears—they are only for the unworthy. Where is Annie? poor child, she must be overwrought, from many causes; let me see her, she will be calmer then."

He was right. What passed between them it needs not to relate. Our readers can little enter into the high character of Lord St. Clair, if they cannot satisfy themselves as to the manner, as well as the nature and extent, of the sacrifice he made. He was not one to wring the gentle heart he so unselfishly resigned, by the betrayal of personal suffering; he coveted the continuance, nay, the increase of her regard, and nobly he earned it.

In was a brilliant scene on which, a few hours later, he entered, introduced by the same Italian, Signor Lanzi, who had been the first to trace the resemblance between Annie and the female figure of the group. But neither loveliness nor talent, both of which thronged the halls, had at that moment attraction for Lord St. Clair; his glance had singled out a tall, slight form, leaning against a marble pillar, and half shaded by the drapery of a curtain. His head was bent down; he seemed in the act of listening and replying to the smiling jests of the countess, who was sitting near him; the cheek and brow were very pale, and the mouth, when still, somewhat stern in expression; but it was a fine face, bearing the stamp of genius too visibly ever to be passed unremarked.

"You may smile, and look incredulous, signor," were the words that first met the ears of the English nobleman, from the young countess, in Italy's sweetest tone; "but since you deserted us for Bologna, a living likeness has appeared of your beautiful Amélie."

"Mademoiselle de Sombreuil herself, perhaps," he replied, half smiling. "Fancy would indeed have served me well, had such a chance occurred."

"You are quite wrong. I doubt whether Mademoiselle de Sombreuil would herself resemble your fancy statue, as much as la bella Inglese does."

"La bella Inglese! who may she be?" inquired the young sculptor, somewhat agitated.

"A lovely girl, who only appeared in Florence as you left it. Lanzi informed me the resemblance was so perfect, he imagined she must know you; but she had never even heard of you till she came here."

"And what may be her name?"

"As you seem so interested, I regret that I cannot tell you. It is so truly English that it will bear no Italian accent, therefore I cannot remember it: but find Lanzi, I expect him here to-night, and he will tell you all about her."

The arrival of new guests, and the attention of the countess called for from himself, the sculptor hastily turned, as in the act of seeking the individual she had named. He had not advanced many yards when he started violently, and with a sudden impulse retreated into a small withdrawing-room, near which he had stood.

"Why shun me, Signor Castellan?" inquired a frank, kind voice in English; and Lord St. Clair's hand was extended, and, after a moment's visible hesitation, accepted and almost convulsively pressed. "Why this long mysterious concealment, my young friend? were there none, think you, to rejoice that you were still amongst the living?"

"Was not your lordship aware of my existence, insignificant as it is, more than a twelvemonth since? My own hand and signature were surely sufficient guarantee," he answered, in a cold proud tone.

"Then you did write, and Annie was not deceived! Little did I know the precious intelligence contained in the packet, lost on its way to me in Russia, and the want of which, in a political view, caused me such annoyance. But why wait so long, my dear fellow, to give us tidings so many would have rejoiced to hear?"

"So many! There were more, then, to mourn me dead, than to love me living! But, forgive me," he continued, less bitterly; "your family would have been my friends, and therefore was it I wrote to tell you that I lived."

"But was there not one, Reginald, who deserved an earlier notice at your hands? why leave her so long to mourn you as dead, and then to learn such joyful tidings from others than yourself? The ties of early youth, of fond associations, I should have thought sufficient of themselves alone to prevent such wrong."

Reginald's very lip grew white as he replied, "Was not her husband the fittest person to give Lady St. Clair such tidings?"

"Her husband, Reginald? You speak enigmas."

"How!" gasped the young man, as he laid his cold and trembling hand on his companion's arm. "Is not Annie Grey your wife?"

"No!" replied Lord St. Clair, the peculiar expression clouding his noble countenance for the moment passing unnoticed; "her heart was with the dead!"

Reginald De Vere struggled with bursting emotion, but his trembling limbs refused to support him; and sinking powerlessly on a sofa, he covered his face with his hands, and wept such tears as only spring from manhood's unutterable joy.

It still wanted an hour to midnight, and Lady Emily was in vain endeavouring to prevail on Annie to retire to rest.

"You are feverish and worn out already, Annie. How will you be able to support the excitement of to-morrow without rest to-night?"

"It would be no rest if I lie down; I cannot sleep. Only let me know he lives!" and she twined her arms round Lady Emily's neck, and looked so appealingly, so mournfully, no heart could have urged more.

There was a pause of several minutes, and then Annie started up.

"It is Henry's step!" she exclaimed, and would have sprung forward, but her feet felt rooted to the ground; another moment Lord St. Clair was at her side.

"Promise me to bear the shock of joy better than you did the shock of grief, or I can tell you nothing," he said, gently; but there was no need for another word. Faint as she was, every object in the room seeming to swim before her eyes, every word to be indistinct, yet one figure was visible, one voice calling her his own, own Annie—beseeching her to forgive and bless him! reached her heart, and loosed its icy chains, till she could breathe again. She felt not that strength had entirely deserted her, for she was clasped to the heart of Reginald De Vere, and the deadly faintness passed in the gushing tears that fell upon his bosom.

* * * * * * *

Mysterious as was Reginald De Vere's silence, its causes may be summed up in a few words. To his own generous deed, recorded in the early part of our tale, he owed the preservation of his life. When bleeding and exhausted he was led a prisoner to the Carlist camp, he was instantly recognised by the poor woman whose child he had saved, and whom he had sent on to her husband. The tale of his kindness, his generosity, his bravery had been repeated again and again by the happy wife, and created amongst the common soldiery a complete sensation in his favour; so that very many were found eager and willing to aid Juan Pacheco in his resolution to return the good conferred and save his wife's benefactor at the hazard of his own life. He had already been disgusted with his life in the camp; the beauty of his young wife had exposed him and her to insults which, as he had no power to retaliate, urged him to seize the first opportunity to desert. One by one the prisoners had been led to executior and one by one had fallen. Reginald, unable to support himself from wounds and exhaustion, though quite conscious he was placed there to die, was loosely bound to a post, as a better mark to the soldiers who fronted him. They fired—the girthings which bound him gave way, and a dead faint succeeded; but they had fired with harmless weapons, and when Reginald awoke from what he fancied death, he found himself in a covered cart, carefully watched and tended by the young mother and her boy whom he recognised at once; his captain's uniform placed on the body of a young Spaniard who had fallen in battle, and whose features were not unlike those of De Vere, no doubt caused Edward Kenrich's belief in his being really Reginald, and his having been in consequence honourably interred. Juan Pachecò's knowledge of the wilds and intricate windings of his native country enabled him ably to elude the pursuit to which, as a deserter, he was liable; but De Vere suffered so dreadfully from alternate fever and exhaustion, during the journey, that many times his kind preservers feared their care would be in vain, and death would release him ere earthly rest and shelter were obtained. But at length the goal was gained—a small cottage belonging to a monastery of Saint Iago, situated in so retired a pass of the Pyrenees that none but mountaineers knew of its existence. Under the skilful medical aid of one of the fathers Reginald slowly regained health; but it was not till nearly a year after his supposed death that he regained the elasticity and entire use of his limbs, such as he had previously enjoyed. The severity of monastic discipline did not characterise the monks of Saint Iago. They were but few in number; old and respectable men, who had turned from the distracting turmoils of their unhappy country, and sought peace in study and deeds of kindness. In one of these aged men Reginald discovered an uncle of his mother—one who had always mourned her departure to another land, and union with a heretic, but who had loved her to the end, and was willing to receive with affection any of her children. The fearful sufferings and deep melancholy of the young Englishman had attracted him, even before the picture of his mother, which Reginald constantly wore, discovered the relationship between them. For nearly two years De Vere remained in this solitude; the fear of drawing down ruin and misery on his preservers prevented his writing to his commanding officer, to state his escape—Padre Felipo alleging the state of the country was such, that his letter might not only be seized and himself retaken, but Pacheco exposed to the danger of execution as a deserter and abettor of his escape. After the first year he made many attempts to communicate with his friends in England—Annie Grey amongst the number—but he never heard in return; therefore concluded, and with justice, that his letters had never reached a post.

But the two years of solitude, instead of being a mental blank, was the hinge of circumstances on which his whole after-career turned. To amuse his confinement and please the children, he resumed the favorite amusement of his boyhood, carving in wood and stone, and with such success as to astonish himself. He found an admirer and instructor where he little expected it, in one of the monks; and under his guidance, and emboldened by encouragement, made such rapid progress, that his whole soul became wrapt in the desire to visit Italy, and study there. His pantings for fame were now defined—a flash of light seemed to have irradiated his whole being, and to burst the chains of destiny, which still cramped energy and life. It was the consciousness of genius, the proud conviction that he might indeed win the object of his love; win, and be worthy of her, and give her a name proud as those of the men of genius whose lives they had read and venerated together.

The days when all the fortunes of the monks were devoted to their abbeys or to a patron saint were over, and Padre Felipo rejoiced at possessing the means effectually to aid his young relative. He settled on him a sum more than sufficient to gratify all his desires, and Reginald hesitated no longer to concentrate all his energies on this one pursuit. He went to Italy, adopting the name of his benefactor, which was also that of his mother; and the wish not to be known in England, until he had perfected himself in his art, caused him to retain it, even when no danger was attached to the acknowledgment of his existence.

But once in Italy, the yearning to hear of his family and friends became intense, while a strange feeling of dread withheld him from again addressing Annie. It was two years and a half since they had parted, two since he had been reported dead. What might not have occurred in that interval? He had left her free, and so childlike, so simple in character, that how could he, how dared he indulge the hope that she had so returned his love, as to remain single for his sake? He had never spoken of love to her; his affection was so pure and true, that it had withheld him from linking, by a too impetuous avowal, her fate with one so gloomy as his own. His genius seemed now to promise a fairer destiny, but his heart, still darkened by the fearful creed of fatalism, believed that this very promise would be dashed with gloom, and from the ascendency of this unhappy feeling, failing in courage to address Annie herself, he wrote to one of his sisters, beseeching a speedy reply, with information of his father, and all she could learn of Miss Grey. The reply was many weeks before it came, pleading the usual excuse for unjustifiable silence—stress of occupation and dislike to letter-writing. Basil De Vere was in America, and Miss Grey on the eve of marriage with Lord St. Clair; the whole London world was full of it, on account of the disparity of years between the parties, and because Lord St. Clair had never seemed a marrying man; but that it was a settled affair there was not the smallest doubt. She wrote as if it could concern Reginald but little; but the pang was such as to confirm his fearful creed of an inexorable fate, and plunge him into a despondency, that genius itself seemed unable to remove. At first he worked at his art mechanically; but gradually his mind became aroused, and he tried to forget the heart's anguish in such persevering labour, that though to mere observers its effects were marvellous in so speedy a perfection, it was, in fact, but the natural consequence of unceasing mental and manucipal work. He constantly reproached himself for the agony he felt; what right had he to suppose he had had any hold upon her? Why could he not rejoice in her happy prospects, and write to tell her so? But weeks merged into months ere he could do this, and then he could not address herself, but wrote to Lord St. Clair, revealing his escape, his concealment, and finally the promised success of his art, with a calm, affectionate message to Annie. The letter cost him a bitter struggle, and with feverish restlessness he awaited the reply; but when none came, bitter thoughts possessed him. He believed himself entirely forgotten and uncared for by his friends; and every energy cramped (save for his art) by his spiritless belief, he determined to remain so, and shun alike England and her sons. It was his fate, he inwardly declared, and he must bend to it; and thus, as is ever the case with these dark dreamers, he created for himself the lonely doom he imagined his destiny marked out. The death of his aged relative, in the monastery of St. Iago, placed a moderate fortune at his disposal, and enabled him still more successfully and earnestly to pursue his art. For a time the excitement attendant on the creation of his group roused him from himself, but the reaction was plunging him still deeper into the dark abyss of misanthropy and gloom when his discovery, through his own beautiful work, the sudden and almost overwhelming happiness bursting through the darkness of his spirit, in the consciousness that Annie was free, that she had ever loved him, completely changed the current of his thoughts, and permitted him a realization of joy, before which the dark creed of destiny fled for ever.

It is in a cheerful sitting-room of a picturesque dwelling on the banks of Keswick Lake, that our readers may once more look on Annie Grey, ere they bid her farewell—Annie Grey indeed she was not; but there was little change visible, save that her fair cheek bore the rose, and her beautiful form the roundness of more perfect health, than when we last beheld her. The large French windows opened on a small but beautiful garden, where the taste of England and Italy was so combined, as to render its flowers and statues the admiration of every beholder. The opposite window opened on a conservatory of beautiful exotics, and exquisite specimens of painting and sculpture adorned the room itself. An uncovered harp filled one corner, on which the evening sun, shining full from the stained glass of the western window, flung tints as bright and changing as those of the kaleidoscope. A *hortus siccus*, opened on a group half arranged, was on a table, at which Lady Emily St. Clair was seated, and Annie was standing at her side, with a volume of poems in her hand.

"You idle girl! you would have found what I wanted in five minutes a few years ago. What are you thinking about? Ah, Reginald, you are just in time, or Annie's restlessness would have invaded your sanctum, depend upon it."

"And had I not cause? A whole hour, nearly two, after your promised time; and your cheek pale, and your brow burning! Dearest, do not let your art be dearer than your wife!"

"What! jealous of all my marble figures, love? For shame!" replied her husband, playfully, twining his arm round her, and kissing her cheek; "but I will plead guilty to fatigue to-night, and you shall cure me by my favourite song."

Annie flew to her harp, and De Vere, flinging himself on an easy chair, drank in the sounds with an intensity of delight which he never believed *that* song could have had the power to produce. "Yes!" he exclaimed, as her sweet voice ceased, "what are palaces and their pleasures compared to an hour like this? There is, indeed, 'no place like home;' what, oh! what would the artist and the student be without it?"

"Why, how is this Signor Rinaldo? what extraordinary spell has been flung over you, so to change your opinion of a song that once you would not even hear?" laughingly exclaimed Lord St. Clair, springing from the balcony into the room. Good evening, Mrs. De Vere; I have some inclination to arrest you for using unlawful witchcraft on this gentleman, even as I once thought of seizing him for allowing you to die of grief for his loss, when he was all the time in life!"

"Guilty, guilty; we both plead guilty," replied Reginald, in the same tone; "but my guilt is of far deeper dye; my Annie's witchery has but thrown such a halo over my home, that all which speaks of its charm is as sweet to my ear as to my heart. I am changed, St. Clair, and not merely in loving a song I once despised," he added, with much feeling, "but in being enabled to trace a hand of love, where once I beheld but remorseless fate; and my wife has done this, so gently, so silently, that I guessed not her influence until I found myself joining her own lowly prayers, and believing in the same sustaining faith."

"And has she explained its mystery?" inquired Lady Emily, with earnest interest.

"No, dear friend; nor do I need it now. The belief that a God of infinite love and compassion ordains all things, yet leaves us the perfect exercise of our free will, and in that freedom, and the acts thence ensuing, works out his divine decrees, constraining no man, yet bringing our most adverse wills to work out his heavenly rule—this is a belief that must be *felt*, it cannot be explained, and thrice blessed are they on whom its unspeakable comfort is bestowed!"

The Spirit of Night.

FOUNDED ON A HEBREW APOLOGUE.

"Let there be light!" the Omnific Word had spoken, and light was. Over the newly-created world the pure element rushed from the spiritual courts of the High Empyrean, where it had reigned from everlasting. In its subtle essence, its ethereal exhalations, fit only for the atmosphere of those angelic spirits, who, at the word of the Highest, took their appointed stations in the new-formed world. Radiance too glorious, too resplendent for mortal view, filled the illimitable space, uniting earth with heaven as by a cloud of glory. Where had been Chaos, circled with shapeless darkness, now revolved, in its vast flood of irradiating lustre, the new work of the Eternal. Thousands of radiant spirits floated to and fro on the refulgent flood. The dazzling iris of their wings, the music of their movements, filling space with beauty and with sound; while up, up from the lowest Heaven to the High Empyrean—from the young seraph to the mighty spirits nighest the Invisible Throne, whose resplendent presence dazzled even the purified orbs of their angelic brethren—up, through every heaven and every rank, sounded the glad hallelujahs of love and praise.

At every word of the Highest, creation sprung. Darkness, borne back by the mighty torrent of effulgent light, would have passed annihilated from the face of the new-born world, but, shielded by angelic ministers, it lingered, in its new-appointed sphere, to do its destined bidding. A firmament of sapphire, stretched between the waters and the waters, veiling the glory of the spiritual heavens from the grosser earth. Land rose from the liquid deep. The rolling waters rushed impetuously to their destined boundaries, held there by the Omnific will. And over the land the creating Word went forth; and, at once, the mountains raised their stupendous forms, crowned with imperishable verdure; the valleys, and woods, and glens rose and sunk in their appointed rests; and flowers, and trees, and streams, and thousand other charms of sight, and sound, and sense, burst forth into perfected being. Myriads of angels hovered round, visible *then* in their beauty; but *now* heard only in the sweet breath of the gentle flowers; in the varied sounds of the forest trees as the wind floats by; in the summer breeze, or the wintry storm; in the musical gush of the silvery rill; aye, and in the deep hush and calm of the evening hour, when nature herself, as conscious of their ministering presence, sinks into deep and spiritual repose.

But not for the abode of angelic spirits was this lovely world. A new creation was to raise the voice of love and adoration! and for such, the spiritual light enveloping the infant globe was too ethereal, too resplendent. Nought but the purified orbs of the angelic and archangelic hosts could gaze on its refined effulgence; and, therefore, from the council of the Eternal went forth the decree :—

"Let there be two great lights to rule the earth, the one by day, and the one by night, and they shall rule times and seasons." And as He spake it was. Instantaneously the minute particles of the ethereal essence formed into an orb of splendour, fraught with such power and glory, that the lustrous flood rushed back into the Heavenly Fount—earth needing it no more;—circled by a diadem of many-coloured light, extending in resplendent rays over the new-born world, infusing its golden glory over the azure heavens; clouds, dyed with the brilliant tints of amethyst, and rose, and ruby, formed before him and faded into glory as He passed. Earth, through her ministering spirits of mount, and wood, and stream, and flower, sent up her thrilling song of thanksgiving, echoed and re-echoed by the myriads and myriads of angels peopling the spiritual courts. Heaven and Earth rejoiced. Increased and dazzling beauty enveloped the new creation. Luscious fragrance issued from the flowers; their petals, adorned by their guardian seraphs, expanded to the glorious orb, and shone in his rays like gems. The Spirit of Day, selected from the highest and purest order of angels, to renew and tend the beauteous work, ascended his throne in the burning centre, whence the effulgent rays emanate on earth, but on which no mortal eye can look; and proudly and rejoicingly as a bridegroom coming forth from his chamber, as a youthful hero from his victorious career, he guided the glorious luminary on its resplendent course, joining his voice to the hallelujahs pealing around.

And in varied but equal beauty rose the second light; but its guardian spirit, selected from the same pure and exalted ranks, looked on the effulgence of the Orb of Day, and beheld his brother spirit circled by glory more dazzling than his own. His invisible throne was within the silver radiance of his orb. Light, ethereal and pure as the heavenly essence of which both sun and moon had been formed, enriched him; less glittering, but equally resplendent. But a deep shadow stole over the exquisite colouring of the spirit's wings. His voice of music refused to join the pealing hallelujahs.

"Wherefore?" he exclaimed; and the troubled accents sounded through space, strangely and darkly falling on the full tide of song. "Wherefore do two monarchs occupy one throne? Wherefore to me is given less than to my brother? I have loved, I have served as faithfully as he. Why, then, should I be second, and he the first? Earth rejoices when he comes. Heaven greets him with songs of love. What need is there for me, unless to me the same is given?"

The hallelujahs ceased. A sudden silence, awful in its profoundness, sunk on the rejoicing myriads. The pure founts of ever-living light became obscured. Thunder rolled over the illimitable expanse. The superb radiance of the effulgent moon vanished, and, spreading far into the Empyrean, became the glorious host of stars, each with its attendant spirit as it formed. Darkness clothed the complaining angel; the beautiful luminary given to his charge, seemed quivering and fading into space; while, still strong and rejoicing, the Orb of Day held on his victorious career.

Prostrate and convulsed with remorseful anguish, the spirit sunk before the celestial hosts. He who had been of that favoured class to whom the ways as well as the works of the Highest were revealed, had fallen lower in intellect and love than the youthful seraph, whose task was only to worship and adore. Where could he hide himself from their searching orbs? Where fly from the flashing light that, as the thunder rolled, played round him, marking him disgraced and criminal? But Him whom he had offended, he loved as only angels love. And so he welcomed that remorseful agony, and prayed, "Have mercy, Father of all Beings! My Father, have mercy on me!" And out of that awful stillness issued a thrilling strain of gushing music—low, soft, spiritual—the murmured prayer, from countless myriads, for pardon for an erring brother. The dimness fled from the founts of light. The thunder ceased; the scorching lightnings blazed no longer. A mild effulgence circled the sorrowing spirit as he lay, burying his refulgent brow in the darkened iris of his wings.

From the invisible throne of the Highest, the mightiest, the best beloved, most favoured messenger of the Eternal, the Spirit of Love, winged his downward flight, and on the instant, space became irradiated. New lustre spread over the vast courts of Heaven; the richest harmonies attended every movement of his wings. Angels and archangels, seraphs and ministers, pressed forward as he passed, to bask in the wondrous beauty of his lustrous face, and raise anew the irrepressible burst of song.

"Spirit of Night, arise!" he said, and the repentant angel lifted up his brow once more in returning hope, so thrillingly that voice of liquid music fell; "arise, and list the irrevocable decree of the Eternal! Because thou has envied the resplendence of the Spirit of Day, the radiance of thine orb will henceforth be borrowed from His lustre; and when yonder earth passes thee thou wilt stand, as now thou dost, deprived of thy glory, and eclipsed, either wholly or in part. Thou hast dared arraign the wisdom and the goodness of the Highest; and though He pardons, yet must He chastise, lest others sin yet more. Yet weep not, repentant brother! thy repining is forgiven, and thou too shalt reign a monarch in thy radiance! Queen of the lovely night will thine orb be hailed; the tears of thy repentance shall be a reviving balm to all that languish; imparting consolation to the mourner, rest to the weary, soothing to the careworn, strength to the exhausted. Peace shall be thy whisper, and in thy kingdom of stillness and repose, breathe thrillingly the promise of Heaven, and its rest. Go forth, then, on thy mild and vivifying career. The Orb of Day will do his work, and be hailed with rejoicing mirth; but many a one shall turn to thee from him, and in the radiance of thy tears find consolation."

He spake: and behold! the pale but lovely lustre in which the Orb of Night still shines flowed round her. The Spirit of Night resumed his silvery throne, and in the profound submissiveness of most perfect love entered upon his silent and beautiful career, circled by the glittering radiance of the attendant stars. Soon was revealed the benignant mercy of His sentence. Even ere sin darkened the lovely earth, His beauteous orb was hailed by all creation with rejoicing; and when man fell, when labour and weariness, sickness and woe, obtained dominion, how soothing the consolation whispered by the Spirit of Night! Weeping oft at the remembrance of his own fault, the Spirit commiserates the tears of others, Floating over the earth, invisible, save through the exquisite beauty of his orb, and the thrilling thoughts of Heaven and immortality awakening in the soul, which, formed of kindred essence, becomes thus conscious of his presence, the Spirit sends his soft rays, formed from the liquid lustre of his tears, on all who need his pity and repose. By the couch of the sufferer—the side of the sorrowing—by the kneeling penitent—by the wakeful mourner—by the careworn and the weary—to the hut of the beggar as the palace of the king—he sends pity, and peace, and consolation. Nor does he sympathise with sorrow alone: the joy which, in the sunshine and midst the turmoil of the world, has agitated the soul even to pain, he softens into such deep calm, as to whisper of that Heaven whence alone the full bliss comes. Love, shrinking from the garish day, finds in his presence eloquence and voice. The poet, oppressed and suffering in the rich blaze of day, at night pours out his full soul in stirring words; for, conscious of a spirit's presence, the pressure of infinity is then less painful to be borne. The artist, does he dream of giving life to the vacant canvas, the senseless marble, or voice and sound to the rich harmonies for ever breathing in his ear—labours in toil, often in despondency, during the day, for Earth only is present then; but when alone with his own soul and the holy night; when the Spirit, visible either through his silvery tears, or in the rich beauty of his starry zone, penetrates his whole being with his heavenly presence, then life is strong once more! The dream of Immortality on Earth, even as in Heaven, dashes down all earthly fears. The spark of the Deity in every soul is rekindled by the touch of its kindred essence, and Hope, and Truth, and Beauty start into enduring glory beneath the vivifying flash.

Beautiful Spirit! such has been, and is, and will still be thy task. Over the earth thou floatest, and man, be he in gloom or gladness, aspiring or desponding, hails thee with rejoicing; and even as the pale flowers drooping beneath the noontide heat, and the parched and languishing earth, so does he turn to thee for coolness and repose. Beautiful Spirit! thou hast sinned and been forgiven—therefore we rest on thee!

Recollections of a Rambler.

It was on a beautiful morning, in quite the beginning of May, that, leaving the Globe Hotel, on the Beacon Hill, Exmouth, I strolled forth at a very early hour, determining to ramble wherever chance might lead. There was no fear of my missing any particularly lovely spot in following this determination. The very watering-places combine all the charms of sea and country to an extent peculiar to this lovely county. Ten minutes suffice to bear the wanderer to such seeming solitude of hill and dale, and glen and wood—will scatter around him such a profusion of ever varying yet ever beautiful scenery, that it is difficult to believe that all those artificial luxuries and pleasures necessary to the trifler and the fashionist, would we seek them, are close at hand.

Every season has its own charm in England. Even winter, in its stern, rude aspect, its brawling voice of winds and storms, has, in the deep, still haunts of nature, its own peculiar beauty. Spring, with its young fresh joyousness, its sparkling glory of earth and sky—its gushing atmosphere; for as the breeze comes laughing and dancing along, we can give it no other term. Summer, with its still deeper feeling, as if the dancing light and glittering love of the youthful year had sobered into a being deeper, stronger, more fervid and intense. Then autumn, decking decay with such bright beauty, shedding a parting halo on the fading year; concentrating all of loveliness in that sweet, dreamy pensiveness, which, while it lingers almost mournfully on earth's parting glories, looks through their passing light into their renovated being, reading in the death and resurrection of nature the spirit's immortality.

One charm, indeed, spring possesses beyond those of the other seasons; it is, that almost every hour of the day is equally delicious; in the morning, noon, afternoon, or evening, we may come forth and make acquaintance with her in every variety of aspect, each one as lovely as the other. Evening indeed is the hour of that delicious musing which, in the very blessedness of the PRESENT, unconsciously recalls the loveliest images of the PAST, and adumbrates the FUTURE, by the thrilling whisper of our immortal goal. It is then that, as Wordsworth says—

"We are laid asleep
In body, and become a living soul."

But these are not the sensations of the morning; then life is infused with the PRESENT alone. We can neither recall, nor think, nor hope; we do but believe, and love, and feel, conscious only of the blessing of Existence, of the omnipotence of Love!

It was with all the elastic joyousness of such sensations I hastened up the Beacon Hill, pausing involuntarily on the top to gaze beneath me. There lay Old Ocean, slumbering in the early sunshine as a lake of molten gold, tinged here and there with the shadow of overhanging rocks, and ever and anon fringed with a snowy crest, as a passing breeze rocked the waves into heavier swell. The broad and graceful river, rushing boldly and proudly into its parent sea; its undulating course visible for miles up the land; its shores skirted with towns half buried in foliage; churches, towers, and villages coming forth in the glowing light from their background of hills dark with verdure; headlands, bold, rugged, and broken into every diversity of form: Powderham's castellated mansion glancing through magnificent plantations, with their glades and lawns of emerald issuing from the deeper shadows as jewels of the sunshine. Mamhead, just visible through its dark, dense woods; and farther still in the distance, woody uplands and barren rocks towering above the broken summits of the headlands, taking every grotesque form from the clouds lingering above them, and at length fading into ether, changing like phantasmagoria beneath the magic influence of light and shade, and mist and sun.

My path now lay across one or two fields, inlaid with a perfect mosaic of gold, and white, and green, formed by the patches of grass, kingcup, and daisy, leading into those narrow, luxuriant lanes, with their gurgling streamlets and clustering flowers which mark at once the county of Devon.

The hedges rose high above my head, and from them sprung forth the oak, and elm, and beech, and ash, bearing the weight of centuries on their lofty trunks and far-spreading branches; the hawthorn, with its blossoms just tipping its rich green as with a shower of snow; and the holly standing forth, dark and stern, amid the more tender foliage of the early spring. Every field-gate or occasional break in the hedge disclosed a complete map of hill, and wood, and orchard; on one side bounded by sea and sky, on the other stretching farther and farther inland, till hills met the sky, and seemed to close around the landscape. Every shade of green, from the darkest to the lightest, was visible in the tender foliage—some as if already clothed in the intenser hues of summer; others so lightly, so delicately shaded, that their exquisite tracery was distinctly marked against the clear blue sky. The orchards already lay as patches of snow in their verdant dells, and primroses and violets by thousands clustered on the banks of the clear, trickling streamlet which skirted the deep green hedge as a fringe of silver.

I do so love the primrose; there is something so sad and pensive in her meek, pale flowers, gleaming forth as silent stars from their darkly-closing leaves, and bending over the laughing waters as if their very mirth were sad to her. And the deep purple violet, shrouding itself in silence, yet seeming in its very scent, to smile and whisper joy. And the speedwell, with its full blue petals and delicate stems, which literally bend beneath their weight of blossoms, light and fragile as they are; the deep red campion, with its gorgeous clusters, looking proudly down on its humbler brethren, rejoicing in its lofty home, that it may fade unplucked upon its stem; these and countless other flowers gemmed the hedge as a very garniture of love.

There was no sound save the delicious music of the fresh spring breeze, as it wantoned with the glistening leaves, or played with the gushing waters, inciting them to break in tiny waves against the hedge; and the rich thrilling melody of the happy birds, calling to each other from tree to tree, or sending forth such a gush of song, such a trilling flow of rapture, that their slender throats seemed quivering with the effort; then would come silence, as startled and hushed by their own joy; and then a low-twittering, with perhaps the distant call of the lonely cuckoo, and a burst of melody again.

After rambling amid such scenes and sounds for about two miles, a thick grove of lofty trees, interspersed with thatched roofs, ivy-clad and smoke-dyed walls, and chimneys of every architecture, marked its termination. The lane narrowed, and hastening onwards, a rustic gate opened into an old churchyard, surrounding a village church of such extreme old age, and so picturesque, that it sent me back in fancy centuries at once. There was the low, square belfry, indented and fractured, with lichen, and moss, and flowering weeds springing from every crevice; the long and rambling choir, roofed with copper; the slender buttresses; the small-paned windows, some of Saxon, some of Tudor architecture; the large square porch or entrance, with its grotesque carvings, that could only belong to the middle ages. The very trees, massive alike in root, and trunk, and branch; yews so dark and thick, they seemed in the distance more as solid masonry than trees—looked as if they had stood there grim guardians of the holy dead for centuries; and grassy graves and quaint old tombs, so battered with age and atmosphere as wholly to obliterate their inscriptions—though some bore date as far back as 1500—strewed the ground, so closely congregated that there was no space for a foot between.

The very birds seemed imbued with the spirit of the place, for they were silent, either flying noiselessly over the graves, or winging their way to less sacred groves. A sudden sound awoke me from my musing, and transported me at once from past to present; a joyous peal burst forth from the old belfry, and a kindly voice accosted me with—"Maybe you'd like to walk in, sir, and see the old place? You'll ha' time to look round ye afore the wedding party comes; and if not, there'll be time enow during the service."

The offer was accepted so eagerly as to delight my old guide; for if one place in the country be more interesting to me than any other, it is an old village church, so buried in its own beautiful site that the roar of the railroad can never reach it; where we can stand still and breathe, apart from the rush and the turmoil, and the haste, still pressing onward—onward, in the vain strife for man's intellect to keep pace with the giant he has raised, which is now the constant accompaniment of the neighbourhood of towns. The interior betrayed still greater age than the exterior; the windows were painted rudely but gaudily, throwing streams of coloured light where the early sunshine fell, and leaving the remainder of the interior in that dim twilight so in unison with holiness and age. An antique shrine, adorned with most grotesque, and to me incomprehensible carvings, ran between the nave and chancel. The nave, fitted up as a Protestant place of worship, with pews and seats, looked more modern than the chancel; though the very black oak of its furniture gave it a venerable appearance, and seemed to mark its date as among the earliest of the reformed churches, while the dilapidated pavement and crumbling seats of the chancel spoke of an age still farther back. The front was roughly hewn out of a single stone. I was intently engaged in endeavouring to decipher the inscriptions and dates on the stone flooring, which appeared entirely made up of graves, when the entreaty of the old clerk that I would withdraw into a pew, as the wedding party were approaching, most abruptly scared away all my antiquarian lore, and transported me very unwillingly, if the truth must be told, to the contemplation of that common everyday occurrence, a modern wedding.

But one glance at the group, consisting of only six or seven persons, riveted my interest. In my whole London career I had never seen such a face of intellect, and soul and beauty as that of the bride. Whether it was the contrast of such youthful grace and loveliness with the stern old shrine around, or the excessive agitation of the bridegroom, and the almost extraordinary self-possession of the bride, I know not; but no marriage ceremony ever affected me as this. Self-possessed as she was, there was no absence of feeling; her cheek was perfectly colourless, and at times there seemed a slight tremulous motion of the lips, as if the effort to retain her composure was too painful to be continued, and only persevered in for him. *His* responses were wholly inaudible; *hers* so distinct and thrilling, they affected me almost to tears. The clergyman himself, though young, and, by his gay careless face and manner, the only one who did not well assimilate with the scene, became gradually impressed with its unusual solemnity. The embrace with which, at the conclusion of the ceremony, the bridegroom folded the bride to his heart, was so full of passionate feeling, of such suppressed yet intense emotion, even I could scarcely witness it unmoved, and it completely checked the customary joyous greetings of their companions.

I followed them almost unconsciously from the church, saw them enter the two carriages waiting for them outside the little gate, and remained leaning on a tombstone overlooking the road, long after they had disappeared. My reverie was interrupted by a courteous address from the young clergyman, who, having noticed my attendance in the church, volunteered the information which I so much desired.

Pierre Laval, the only son of a very rich planter in Martinique, having received the best education which an alternate residence in France and England could bestow, returned to his father only to feel that a residence in Martinique was about the most miserable thing that could happen to him, and so again made his appearance in England. He sought no profession, because he had no need to do so, his father's possessions being immense. Joining in the very best society, in which a handsome face, elegant address, and highly-cultivated mind gave him many advantages, he became acquainted with the reigning beauty of the season, Helen Campbell. Now Pierre had a decided aversion to cried-up beauties, and so he resolved that, however she might conquer others, she should never obtain any power over him. It is one thing to make a wise resolution, and another to keep it. It so happened that Helen Campbell possessed none of the repulsive attributes of an acknowledged beauty. She was in truth much more lovely than he had anticipated, but it was the intellectuality of her sweet face which was its peculiar charm. She was frank, truthful, gay,—nay, almost wild in her joyousness; and, moreover, possessed the spell of one of the sweetest voices, either in speech or song, which he had ever heard. Pierre struggled a long time, but it would not do; he was fairly conquered: and then for the first time, he imagined himself wanting in every quality likely to make that love reciprocal, and, by sudden silence and reserve, was in a fair way of actually creating the evil he dreaded, had not a mutual friend opened his eyes, and with sudden desperation he urged his suit, and discovered, to his inexpressible happiness, that his love was returned.

For a brief period all was joy. Pierre had written to his father, and did not harbour a single doubt as to his residence being permanently fixed in England, although Helen had made no such condition to his acceptance. Anxiously the arrival of the packet was anticipated; but instead of the answer expected, it brought news so overwhelming, that the unfortunate Pierre was at first verging on distraction.

Monsieur Laval was almost irretrievably ruined; a revolt in the slave population of the island had taken place, and his extensive plantations were burnt to ashes. Other heavy losses had congregated round him; and what with these misfortunes, and having been severely wounded in the revolt, his health appeared rapidly failing. Panic and confusion still reigned; but the friend who wrote, expressed the hope that, when all was quiet again, the Laval losses might not involve such utter ruin as at present appeared. Nothing was so earnestly desired, in fact, so indispensable, as the immediate presence of Pierre.

For some time the young man strove in vain to reduce his thoughts to order; and at length, hardly knowing what he did, he sought his betrothed, told her all, and with a desperate effort, offered to resign all his pretensions to her hand; he was a ruined man—must labour for years in Martinique: how could he ask his Helen to leave her luxurious home, country, friends, all, to bear with poverty and misery in a distant colony for him? She heard him quietly to the end, and then clasping his hand, vowed nothing should part them. She was his by the most holy of all ties—mutual love and truth; and no persuasion, no effort, could turn her from his side. In vain her mother and all her friends seconded Laval's appeal, urging the madness of the sacrifice. Helen's only reply was, "Had the voice of man united us, would you thus persuade me? Would you not bid me follow my husband through weal and through woe? And shall I do less now, because freedom is in my power? I *could* desert him if I chose. No, no, mother, you have other children, who will be to you all I have been. Pierre has but me," and no subsequent persuasion had power to shake her resolution. It was, however, thought advisable that Pierre should seek Martinique alone; and that when affairs were a little quiet, he should either return for her, or she should go to him. But how could she join him, an unprotected girl, in a strange land? She saw that he hesitated to speak the only means, and so spoke them for him: "Give me the sanctity, the protection of your name, my Pierre, and then what tongue dare cast aspersions on a wife who joins her husband? If the day which unites us, must also bid us part, let it be so; but save me, as your wife, from attentions and notice, and persuasions which may be forced upon me."

Pierre's first answer was a wild passionate embrace; his next, as passionate a burst of sorrow, that it should be his doom to banish her to a home so little congenial to her taste, as the burning climate would be to her health. And it was long ere she could soothe or chide him into composure; for the more brightly shone forth her unselfish love, the more bitterly he felt the extent of sacrifice she made.

Helen had to endure a very tempest of opposition and

upbraiding as to her romantic far-fetched folly; but hers was not a mind to change or waver, when feeling and principle had alike dictated her resolution.

Pierre was to join his ship at Falmouth; and yearning for the quiet only found amid the repose of nature, Helen prevailed on her mother to reside for the next few months in Devonshire. Their bridal I had witnessed; and when I heard that the afternoon of that same day Pierre Laval was to part from his Helen for an indefinite period, that when united by the holiest of ties, made one for ever, but a few troubled hours were left them together, I no longer wondered at the emotion I had beheld.

Often and often has the vision of that morning haunted me with the vain longing to know if indeed that unworldly love has been blessed as it deserved, and when those loving and aching hearts did meet again. For years that olden shrine returned to me, as a dream of the far past in itself, blended with all the griefs and hopes of human hearts in the present; and never can I recall the old altar to my mind without beholding in fancy the sweet shadowy form of Helen Campbell, and the suppressed but terrible emotion of her Pierre.

"Cast thy Bread upon the Waters; thou shalt find it after many days."

"Why, Willie, what is the matter?" inquired Edward Langley, entering his father's office one evening after business hours, and finding its sole tenant, a boy of fourteen or fifteen, leaning both arms on one of the high desks, and hiding his face within them, whilst his slight figure shook with uncontrollable sobs. "And how came that drawer open?" he continued, more sternly, perceiving a bureau drawer half open, so as to display its glittering contents, which looked disturbed. "I hope you have not been doing anything wrong, Willie."

"Oh, sir, indeed—indeed I have not! Count the money, Mr. Edward; pray count it; see that it is all right, or I can never hold up my head again. The temptation was misery enough," returned the boy, as well as his sobs would permit, and displaying such a countenance of suffering, as to enlist all Edward's sympathy at once.

"But, my good boy, what could have tempted you? You seem so to feel the enormity of the sin, that I cannot imagine what thought came into your head."

"I only thought of my poor father, sir. Oh, Mr. Edward, he is in prison, and my mother is too ill to work; and she and my poor little sisters are starving," he replied, bursting again into tears. "I did not know what to do to help them; I give them all I earn, but that is so very little it only gives them a meal now and then; and then, when I saw that drawer accidentally left open, and remembered twelve pounds, only twelve pounds, would get my father out of prison, and he could work for us again, the horrid thought came into my head to take them; they would never be missed out of so many; and I had them in my hand. But then I thought what could I tell them at home? It would break my poor mother's heart to think her Willie was dishonest; she could better bear hunger and grief than that, sir; and I knew I could not hide it from her; and so I dashed them back! They seemed to scorch me! Oh, Mr. Edward, indeed, indeed I speak the truth!"

Edward did believe him, and he told him so. There was little need to speak harshly; the boy's own conscience had been his judge. To satisfy him, however, he counted the money, found it correct, and after talking to him a little while, kindly yet impressively, promised to do what he could for his father, and left him, indelibly impressing that evening upon Willie's mind, by never reverting to it again.

The tale, which his inquiries elicited, was a very common one. Willie's father had been an artificer in one of the manufacturing towns; but too eager for advancement, he imprudently threw up his situation and tried independent business. Matters grew worse and worse; his family increased and his means diminished. Hearing of an excellent opening at New-York, for an artificer like himself, he worked day and night to obtain sufficient means to transport himself and family across the Atlantic, and support them till a business could be established. His wife ably aided him, when unhappily he was tempted to embark all his little savings in one of the bubbles of the day, which he was confidently assured would be so successful as to permit his embarking for America at once, and so seize the opening offered. Few speculators had, perhaps, a better excuse; but fortune did not favour him more than others; it failed, and he was ruined. Three months afterwards he was thrown into prison for the only debt he had ever incurred, and though he had friends to persuade him to his ruin, he had none to liquidate his debt. His wife's health, already overworked, sunk under privation and sorrow; and though she toiled even from her fevered pallet, her feeble earnings were not sufficient to give her children bread.

Edward Langley was a creature of impulse; but in him impulse was the offspring of high principle, and, therefore, though the following it often caused him unlooked-for annoyance, it never led him wrong; and Willie's tale called forth sympathies impossible to be withstood.

"Edward," said one of his numerous sisters one evening, about three weeks afterwards, as they were sitting at tea—a meal which, bringing them all together, was universally enjoyed; "what have you done with grandpapa's birthday present? You were to do so many things with that money; and I have not heard you speak of it since my return."

"Because wonderful things have occurred since you left, Fanny," said another slily. "He is going to accompany Mr. Morison's family to Italy and Paris; and bring us such splendid presents. His fair Julia cannot go without him, and he has promised to join them."

"Wrong, Miss Ellen, I am not going," was the reply, with rather more *brusquerie* than usual.

"Why, have you quarrelled?"

"Not exactly."

"But she will be offended, Ned; I am sure I should be."

"No, you would not, Anne, if you knew my reasons.'

"What are they, Edward, dear? Do tell me, I am so curious."

"Of course, or you would not be a woman!"

Against this all his sisters expostulated at once; and even his mother expressed curiosity, adding, that he had talked of this continental trip so long, and with so much glee, it must be a disappointment to give it up.

"It is; but I do not regret it."

"But you must have a reason."

"The very best of all reasons; I cannot afford it."

"Come to me for the needful, Edward," said his father. "I cannot give you luxuries; but this is for your improvement."

"Thank you most heartily, my dear father, but I am, rather I was, richer than any of you know. I earned so much for my last engraving."

"And you never told us," said his mother and sisters, reproachfully.

"I did not, because it was already appropriated. I wanted exactly that sum to add to my grandfather's gift; and that was what I worked so hard for."

"To purchase some bridal gift," said Fanny, archly.

"No, Fan; I never mean to purchase love."

"But if the lady requires to be so conciliated?"

"Then she is not worth having."

"Of course not," rejoined Anne. "But come, Edward, you have never kept anything from us before. What is this mystery?"

"Out with it," laughingly pursued Ellen. "Julia Morison will not thank you for preferring anything to accompanying her, I can tell you; so, as Anne says, what is this mystery?"

"No mystery at all, girls. You will all be disappointed when I tell you; so you had better let it alone."

But beset on all sides, even by his father and mother,

Edward told the simple truth, which our readers no doubt have already guessed. His money had been applied in releasing Willie's father from prison; restoring his mother to health, by giving her and her children nourishing food; securing a passage for them all to New-York, and investing the trifling surplus for their use on their arrival. He told his tale hurriedly, as if he feared to be accused of folly, and his father did somewhat blame him. He was provoked that the little scheme of pleasure and improvement, which Edward had anticipated so many weeks, should be frustrated; and annoyed that he should be disappointed, though the disappointment was perfectly voluntary. How could he tell that the man's story was true? How was he sure the money would produce the good effect he hoped! He must say he thought it a pity, a very great pity; a visit to Paris would be so improving; Mr. Morison's family such a desirable connection—and other regrets, which, without being a very worldly parent, were not perhaps unnatural.

"My dear father," was Edward's earnest and affectionate rejoinder, "do not be vexed for my sake. A visit to the Continent would no doubt have been improving; but I will work doubly hard in dear old England, and that, though it may not be as much pleasure, will be just as serviceable. With regard to Miss Morison," his cheek slightly flushed, "if her affections are only to be secured by being constantly at her side, and always playing the lover, there could be no happiness in a nearer connection for either. A separation for three or four months can surely have no effect on real regard, and I am quite willing to subject both myself and Julia to the ordeal. As to not being sure of doing the good I hope—who can be? I do believe that poor fellow's story, I confess, and strongly believe he will do well; but I do not mean to give the subject another thought, except to work the harder. The money is as much gone as freely given, and I expect as little reward as if I had thrown it on the waters—"

"Where thou shalt find it after many days," continued his mother, so affectionately and approvingly, that Edward threw his arm round her and kissed her tenderly. "You have done right, my dear boy; and if Julia Morison does not think so, she is not worthy your love."

How quick is woman's, above all, a mother's penetration. From the first allusion to Miss Morison in the preceding conversation, she knew that something had occurred between them to annoy, if it did not wound her son; and the moment she heard the story she guessed the actual fact. Perhaps her penetration in this instance was aided by previous observation. She had never liked Miss Morison, desirable as from wordly motives the connection might be. Edward, youth-like, had been captivated by her beauty and vivacity, and gratified by her very marked preference for himself. His complete unconsciousness that he really was the handsomest and most engaging young man of the town of L——, by depriving him of all conceit, increased Miss Julia's fascination. Mr. Morison was member for the county, and had made himself universally popular; and certainly took marked notice of Edward. The good people of L——, were too simple-minded to discover that their member's attractions were merely graces of manner; and that he noticed Edward only because he was perfectly secure that his daughter would never do such a foolish thing as to promise her hand to the son of a country attorney, however agreeable he might be.

Edward's wish to accompany them to the Continent met with decided approval. Mr. Morison thought the young man would save him a great deal of trouble, as a kind of gentleman valet, without a salary; and Miss Julia was delighted at this unequivocal proof of his devotion, and at the amusement she promised herself in playing off her country beau on the Continent, his simplicity being the shield to cover her manœuvres; besides, he would be such an excellent *pis aller*, that she need never be without a worshipper.

That such a person could appreciate Edward's real character, or enter into his motives for, and his disappointment in, not accompanying her was impossible. For regret, even for anger, he had prepared himself, nay, might have been disappointed had she evinced no emotion; but for the cold sneer, first of doubt, then of unequivocal contempt, which was her sole rejoinder to his agitated confession, he was not prepared, and it chilled his very heart. Still he tried to deceive himself, and believe that all she said of benevolence, disinterestedness, and a long et-cetera was the sympathy he yearned for; but the tone and manner with which she informed her father in his presence of his change of purpose, and its praiseworthy cause, could not, even by a lover more infatuated than Edward, have been misunderstood; his spirit rose, and with it his self-respect. He said very little, but that little convinced both Julia and her father that he was not quite the simpleton which they had supposed him.

He left them, wounded to the core; to his warm, generous nature, worldliness was abhorrent even in a man, and in a woman it seemed to him something so unnatural, so revolting, that it dispersed at once the bright creation of his enthusiastic fancy, and displayed Miss Morison almost in her true character.

Still, notwithstanding all this pain and disappointment, Edward never once regretted the impulse he had followed; and when, about six or seven months afterwards, he received the most grateful letters from Willie and his father, informing him that the opening offered, though attended with many difficulties, promised fair, he felt the sacrifice was more than recompensed, and from that hour never thought of it himself again. But his assertion, that he would work the harder to make up for those continental advantages which he had lost, was no idle boast; he did so well, that even his father forgot his vexation; and his industry united with great personal economy, enabled him to give his sisters richer and more useful presents than the *bijouterie* which he had laughingly promised to bring them from France.

The marriage of Miss Julia Morison with some foreign Count, before six months elapsed, had happily no effect on Edward's equanimity; it might, nay, it did cause a transient pang, but he recovered it much sooner than his father did the loss of so desirable a connection.

"Never mind it, sir," was Edward's laughing entreaty; "I would rather earn my own independence, and make a connection through my own exertions than by the richest marriage I could make."

"That's just like your mother, boy," said his father, somewhat pettishly, "as if all depended on one's self."

"Thank you for the likeness, father. When I can bring you a daughter to be to me what my mother is to you, I shall have formed a desirable connection, though my wife be not set in gold."

And this even his father acknowledged, when two years afterwards, Edward married the daughter of their vicar, who proved in his own person that influence is not always inseparable from wealth, but may be found with worth as well. Time rolled on; twenty, thirty years. In the multitude of great and trifling events, which make up the sum of human life, during those years Edward Langley had so entirely forgotten the generous deed of his early youth, that he would have found it difficult to recall even the name of Willie's parents. His perseverance and talent had been crowned with such success, that when only eight-and-twenty he was taken into partnership by one of the first engravers of the metropolis. For twenty more years the business so flourished as to make all the principals very wealthy men; and Edward looked forward in two or three more years to resign in favour of his son, and retire himself from active business. He had never been ambitious, and a series of domestic trials in the loss of six children out of nine, all at that most interesting age when childhood is giving place to youth, caused him to turn with clinging love to those who remained, longing more to enjoy an Englishman's home than to continue amassing wealth.

Greatly against his wishes and advice, engagements and speculations had been entered into by the firm to an immense extent, more especially with establishments abroad. The dishonesty of distant agents, and the careless supineness, if not equal dishonour, of one of the principals at home, occasioned ruin to all, of course including Langley, though he had been most unjustifiably kept in ignorance of the real extent of their speculating schemes. Yet his high integrity enabled him to bear up against this sudden change of circumstances with more fortitude than any of his companions.

His wife's little property had never been touched, and he was therefore enabled to retire to a very small cottage in Cheshire, which soon displayed the refined taste and artistic skill of its gentle-minded inmates, to an extent that completely concealed their very humble means. Not that they were ashamed of their poverty; but the same self-respect that prompted their horror of all pretension, and resolution to live strictly within their means, threw a comfort and refinement around and within their lowly home, which the wealthiest might have envied.

For himself, Edward Langley would have been as happy as in the height of his prosperity; but he could not help feeling a very pardonable pang at this sad change in the prospects of his children. His son, emulating his firmness, sought and obtained an excellent situation in a thriving engraving establishment in Edinburgh, where his father's name and character spoke for him more forcibly than the highest premium. It was on Helen Langley the blow had fallen heaviest; the only one of his daughters who had reached the age of nineteen (for Fanny was still a child), frail, delicate in seeming as a beautiful flower. She had been nursed in luxury and affection, and guarded from even the approach of a storm; the deserved darling of all who knew her, rich and poor, her parents' love for her amounted almost to idolatry. Engaged to the son of one of her father's partners, then studying as a physician, a bright and happy future shone before them, when the thunderbolt fell before either had seen a cloud. George Ashley was summoned from Paris just as his diploma was obtained, and he was weaving fairy dreams of a speedy union with his Helen; recalled, not as he believed, still to study and gradually attain eminence, but to give up all ambitious dreams, and work as a general practitioner for actual subsistence. To marry before he had even the prospect of a connection and employment was absolute madness; to live any distance from Helen he felt was quite as impossible; so he settled himself in the old town of Chester, about three miles from her home, and for her sake exerted himself more than he had once believed was in his nature. At first, youth and excitement beheld only the brighter side; but after six months' trial, so endless and little remunerating seemed his toil, that he sunk into the deepest despondency, which neither Mr. and Mrs. Langley's kind advice, nor Helen's sweet counsels could remove.

Fearfully would Mr. Langley look on his darling, dreading that this constant pressure of anxiety and suspense would be as fatal to her as disease had been to her sisters; but though more serious than had been her disposition before, it was not the seriousness of gloom, but rather of a firm yet gentle spirit, forming internally some resolution which required thought and time for development. Her smile was as joyous, her voice as gleeful, as in happier years; her pursuits continued with the same zeal, if not with deeper earnestness. To persuade her to annul her engagement never entered either parent's mind, but the long vista of dreary years which they believed must intervene ere it could be fulfilled, was literally their only thought of anxious and unmitigated gloom.

"Give me up, Helen! I have no right to fetter your young life with an engagement which heaven only knows when we shall fulfil," passionately exclaimed young Ashley, about seven months after their misfortunes. "Your sweet face, and sweeter temper, and lovely mind must win you a position in life far higher than I can ever offer. You were only seen at the ball the other night to be admired."

"That unfortunate ball! I only went to gratify papa; and you are jealous, George, that your poor Helen was admired."

"No, Helen, no! I gloried in it; for I knew you were mine, mine in heart, faith, all but name. But then I thought how selfish, how utterly selfish I was still to claim you; to behold you wearing out your young life in all the sickness of hope deferred; when, by resigning you, you might be rich, admired, followed, occupy the station you deserve, and—"

"Be very happy, dearest George! This is a strange mood," said she, half reproachfully, half playfully. "Come, send it away, for it is not like you. I am very sorry I cannot oblige you; but as I consider myself as much yours as if the sacred words had actually been said, *you* may divorce me if you will, but *I* will never give you up."

"Helen, darling Helen! forgive me," he replied, his repentance as impetuous as all his other feelings. "Oh! if you would be but mine at once, I am sure I should succeed; with such a comforter, such a cheerer, work would be welcome. I would never despond again, dearest; loving as we do, why should we not wed at once? We must then do well."

"Must do well because we love, George? Yes, and so we shall, but not if we wed now. Ah, now you look reproachfully again. Dearest, you know I would not shrink from any hardship shared with you. I will work with you, work for you, if needed; but, young as we both are, is it not better to work apart a few years, that we may rest together? Think what five years may do for both, it may be less; I put it only to the extent. You are succeeding, and will succeed still more, the more you are known; but had you a wife and an establishment to support now, even with my very hardest exertions, we could not keep free from debt; and love, potent as it is, could not then guard sorrow from our dwelling. When wedded, if unlooked-for misfortunes come, we will bear them, and comfort and strengthen each other; but would it be right, would it be wise to invite them by a too early marriage? My own dear George, let us work while we have youth and hope, and trust me we shall be very happy yet."

It was scarcely possible to remain unconvinced by such fond reasoning; but still Ashley referred with deep despondency to the long, long interval which must elapse ere that happiness could be obtained.

"Not so long as you fancy, George. I never mean to be a rich man's wife, though you invited me to be so just now. I do not even intend to wait for comforts, but only just for that competency which will prevent those evil spirits, care and irritation to enter our home; and to forward this, listen to my plan, dearest George." And with some little tremor, for she dreaded his disapproval, she told him that she had accepted an engagement as governess, in a family at Manchester; a Dr. Murray, who was a widower, with four or five children; she had been mentioned by a mutual friend, and the Doctor was so pleased with Mrs. Norton's account, that he agreed even to give the high salary Helen required, without seing her. He had said that his mother, who lived with him, was too infirm to bear his children much with her, and he therefore wanted more from his governess than merely to teach; he was quite willing to pay for it, but a lady he must have."

"To bear with all his whims and fancies; to be tormented with spoiled children; put up with the old woman's infirmities; be insulted by pampered servants. Helen, you shall not go!" exclaimed George.

"Now, George, don't be foolish. I do not expect one of these evils; and if I meet with them I can bear them, with such a hope before me," she continued, fondly looking in his face.

"But governesses are so insulted, so degraded."

"Not insulted, if they respect themselves; not degraded, if those they love do not think so. But perhaps, George, you are too proud to marry a governess."

A passionate reproach was his reply.

"Well then, love, listen to me a little longer. Mamma still means to allow me enough for my quiet dress, so that I can put by every shilling that I earn; and only think what that may come to in a few years. Then I have a reason for choosing Manchester as a temporary home; you know I can draw, but you do not know that I can design—William took so much pleasure in teaching me—and, in a manufacturing town like Manchester, I may not only be able to use this knowledge, but perhaps gradually get introductions which will allow my successful pursuit of the art even as—as your wife, dearest George; and then, what with our mutual economy and mutual savings beforehand, and mutual work afterwards—oh, our future will shine as bright as it did before this storm!"

"God for ever bless you, Helen, my own darling! you are

indeed my best hope, my best comforter already," murmured George, half choked with strong emotion, which he tried to conceal by pressing her to his bosom, and kissing her cheek. "How can your parents part with you, and what will drive away my fits of gloom, when I cannot come to you for comfort?"

"Hope!" was her instant reply, in a tone so glad, so thrilling, that it pervaded his whole being ever afterwards like a spell. "Think, dearest George, of the hundreds who have to labour on, through lonely years, uncheered by either love or hope; who must work, wearily and unceasingly, only for means of existence. We have health and youth and love, and, above all, mutual faith to sustain us; and therefore we must be happy. You do not know how powerful is a woman's will.'

"Not more so than man's," replied Ashley, more cheerfully than he had yet spoken. "Helen, you have shamed me. I will become more worthy of such love."

Helen looked very much as if she thought that was impossible, but she did not say so.

It was no light task this gentle girl had undertaken. Hopefully as she had spoken and felt, her resolution had neither been formed nor matured without suffering, nor had it been the least portion of the trial to win over her parents to her wishes; but the wisdom of her plan was so evident, that they conquered all selfish feeling for their child's sake, and tried to be comforted by Mrs. Norton's assurance, that in Dr. Murray's family Helen would be as comfortable as she could be away from home.

And so she was. In fact so kindly was she welcomed and treated, that she could scarcely understand it. Dr. Murray was a man in reality under fifty, but looking much older, from a life of some hardships and much labour, the fruits of which he now enjoyed in the possession of a comfortable income. His manner, in general blunt and rough, always softened towards Helen, whom he ever addressed with such respect, as well as kindness, that all George's terror of her encountering insolence very speedily dispersed. Mrs. Murray had evidently not been born a lady, but her regard for Helen was shown in such a multiplicity of little kindnesses, that no feeling could be excited towards her but gratitude and love. Constantly as she was occupied with her pupils, Helen's careful economy of time yet enabled her actually to accomplish the purpose she had in her mind when she chose Manchester for her residence.

The idle, nay even the less energetic, would have declared it was impossible for any one person to do what she did; but not even the Doctor or his mother knew how her moments of made leisure were employed.

So nearly three years glided by; Helen's health, instead of failing, as her friends had feared, actually improved; and George declared there must have been some spell in her words or her example, for his prospects were brightening every year. Helen only smiled, and told him that the spell was simply in his own more hopeful exertions.

Dr. Murray's house was the frequent resort not only of men of talent from the higher ranks, but frequently of clever manufacturers and artificers, in whose works the Doctor and his mother were always particularly interested. It happened that Helen was present one evening when one of these gentlemen was regretting his inability to procure an appropriate design for some window curtains, of a new material, which he had invented; being no artist himself, he could not perhaps define his wishes with sufficient technicality, but all which he had seen were either so small as to have no effect, or so large as to look coarse and common. Before he departed the conversation changed, and Dr. Murray thought no more about it, until at a very early hour the next morning Helen entered his study with a roll of paper, which she asked him to examine, and tell her if he thought it the kind of thing Mr. Grey required. His astonishment that she should remember anything about it was only equalled by his admiration of her work. So great was his delight, that he declared he would convey it to Mr. Grey himself, and get her something handsome for it. He was not disappointed. Mr. Grey seized it with rapture, declared it was the very thing he meant; offered to pay any sum for it, and was struck dumb with astonishment, when told it was designed by the elegant young lady to whom he had been introduced the previous night, and whom he had scarcely deigned to notice, believing her the same as most young ladies—a very pretty but a very useless piece of goods. One of his young men, who had been eagerly examining it, said he was sure it was by the same hand as several other elegant designs which they had been in the habit of purchasing the last two years, but the name of whose inventor they had never been able to discover. He brought some, and compared them; and even the Doctor's unpractised eye could discern the same hand throughout. But how could Miss

Langley have accomplished all this, and yet so done her duty to his children? It was incomprehensible; and the good Doctor hurried home to have the mystery solved. Helen speedily explained it, adding ingenuosly, that she had worked in secret, only because she feared the Doctor or his friends might think she must neglect her duty to her charge to pursue this employment; but since he had expressed such perfect satisfaction, she had resolved on taking the first opportunity to tell him all.

"But my good young lady, you must have some very strong incentive for all this exertion." Blushing deeply, Helen acknowledged that she had. "Is it a secret, my dear child?"

For a minute she hesitated, then frankly told her story. The Doctor was so much affected by it as to surprise her, and expressed the most unfeigned regret that he had not known it before.

Not a fortnight afterwards, Mr. Grey sought an interview with Miss Langley; he wished, he said, to monopolize her talents, and offered, in consequence, with sufficient liberality as to tempt her to adhere to his employment, instead of taking the chance of larger remuneration for occasional designs. It was for this Ellen had worked and prayed and hoped—this which she had looked to, to follow even as a wife, and in her husband's house; and therefore we leave to our reader's imagination the gratitude with which it was accepted, the joy with which she wrote to her parents, to George, to whom her woman's heart so yearned in that moment of rejoicing, that for the first time since she had loved him she could scarcely write for tears. But the letters she received in reply sadly alloyed this dawning happiness. Her sister Fanny was dangerously ill; the same age, the same disease which had been so fatal to her family. All George's skill, and it was great, had been ineffectual; nothing could save her, the distracted father wrote; she was doomed like all the rest. But to Helen there was no such word as doom. She flew to the Doctor, repeated to him as well as she could the symptoms, and the remedies applied, conjuring him to think of something which would alleviate, if it could not cure. What should she write?

"Write, my dear child! that will be of little use: we will go together." And though there were no railroads in that direction, man's omnipotent will carried Helen and the Doctor to Mr. Langley's cottage in so short a space, that it seemed to Helen like the transfigurations of a dream.

For four days fearful were the alternations of hope and dread; the fifth, hope predominated, and by the end of the week, promptness and skill in the adoption of an entirely new mode of treatment were so successful, that Dr. Murray was blessed again and again by the enraptured parents as, under heaven, the preserver of their child. But, though all danger was over, the Doctor did not offer to quit the cottage for another week, which time he spent mostly in his patient's room, and in earnest conversation with young Ashley. Helen had intended to remain in his family till he could meet with some one to supply her place; but this he now declared should not be. She must be wanted at home, at least till she could finish her preparations for entering another; for, if he were George, he would not wait another month; she had had her own will too long already, and the future was bright enough now to permit him to have his. Helen's hand was clasped in her young sister's as the good Doctor spoke, but George's arm was round her, and her reply seemed to satisfy all parties.

All Mr. Langley's attempts to obtain a private interview with his guest were ineffectual until the day of his intended departure, when, with trembling hands and swimming eyes, he tried to press a pocket-book into the Doctor's hand. "It is inadequate, wholly inadequate," he said with emotion. "You have saved my child; so restored her, that she is better than she has been since her birth. You have given us your time, your skill, and you shrink even from my thanks. Were I a rich man, I should feel as I do now, that a fortune could not repay you; but, as a poor man, do not insult me by refusing the fee I can bestow."

"Mr. Langley," was the reply, "I tell you truth, when I assure you that you owe me nothing. I am in your debt far more, far more than my professional skill ever could repay."

"In my debt, Doctor? Ah, you mean my Helen's services; but those you have so liberally remunerated, and treated her with such kindness, that you have made me your debtor even there. No, no, I cannot allow Helen, precious as she is, to come between me and justice."

"I do not allude to Miss Langley, sir," and the Doctor spoke as if addressing a superior. "Her inestimable services to me and mine indeed nothing can repay; but it was not for her sake I came to you. The debt I allude to is of more than thirty years' standing, and it is due to you alone. On my first return to England, your position was higher, your fortune far superior to mine; and had I then sought you, it might still have been to receive benefits at your hand. In your noble endurance of misfortune, it would have been an insult to have discharged my debt, and therefore I waited and prayed for some opportunity not only to do justice, but to evince gratitude. If I have made your child happy, and shortened the term of her heroic exertions, you owe it to yourself. I could not take from you even the full amount of this visit, regarding it merely as professional, for I owe you in actual money more than that." Mr. Langley looked and expressed bewilderment; the Doctor's manner was too earnest to permit a doubt; but he tried in vain to recall to what he could allude.

"Have you so completely forgotten Willie Murray, Mr. Edward?" continued his companion, much agitated. "Willie Murray, the poor boy you not only saved from sin, but made so happy by your generous kindness to his family. Mr. Langley, I am that boy; my character, my success I owe to you. How can such a debt ever be repaid?"

Mr. Langley's astonishment was so great, as literally to deprive him for the moment of words. He only remembered Willie Murray as a pale, thin, intellectual boy of fifteen. To recognise him in the tall, stout, somewhat aged-looking man before him, required more imagination than he chanced to possess; but to doubt the identity was impossible. He grasped his hand warmly, and insisted on his giving him that very hour the history of his life. Our readers, however, must be contented with a very brief sketch of these details. Suffice it, that neither Willie nor his father rose to independence without constant toil and unwearying perseverance. Profiting by the trials of earlier years, the elder Murray laboured with an energy and skill which, until his timely release from prison, had appeared foreign to his character. Many difficulties he had to encounter; but once the manufactory established, competence was secured; and as his labour rather increased than slackened, fortune followed. His son's marked preference for the medical profession grieved him at first, but he lived long enough to see that he had chosen wisely, and at his death left all his children comfortably provided for, each possessing a share in the manufactory which his energy had established. Willie had always yearned to return to England, and did so directly he became a widower, his mother gladly accompanying him. He had finished his medical education in France, had a large practice in America, and, from his general intelligence, proved skill, and wide-handed benevolence, very speedily became popular in England. But amid all the chances and changes of his busy life, neither the fearful temptation of his boyhood nor Edward Langley's generous kindness had ever been forgotten.

Joyous indeed, and full of hope, was Helen Langley's bridal morn, though neither pomp nor fashion attended it, such as might have been the case some few years before. On retiring to change her dress, Helen found a heavy packet, directed to Mrs. George Ashley, on her table. It was a purse, containing three hundred sovereigns, with the following brief lines :—

"This is your father's gift, though it comes through me. I do but return a sum lent by him to me and mine, with the accumulated interest of three-and-thirty years. It is now added to the store earned by Helen Langley's meritorious exertions. WILLIAM MURRAY."

"Mother!" exclaimed Mr. Langley, after perusing this note, and turning to his now aged parent with some emotion, "do you remember your words, when I told you the money was as freely given, and I expected as little reward as if I had thrown it on the waters, 'that I should find it after many days?' You were right: I have found it indeed!"

The Triumph of Love.

> Millions of spiritual creatures walk the earth,
> Unseen, both when we sleep, and when we wake!
>
> MILTON.

I.

It was a scene of unrivalled beauty; yet might some marvel wherefore it was thus created, so far removed from mortal ken, so severed from the habitations of sin and death, that foot of man had never sullied the pure fresh green of the velvet grass; mortal hand had never culled the brilliant flowers, gemming each silvery stream; corporeal sense had never been regaled by their fragrant breath, or lulled by the sweet music of the waters. The leafy branches of the ancient trees stretched forth their deep green shadows, and hill, and stream, and valley, each clothed in its own peculiar beauty, derived fresh charms, as the seasons softly and silently sped by, leaving bright tokens as they sped. The stars still smiled at their own sparkling rays gleaming up from the gushing water; the pensive moon still touched the glossy leaves with her diamond pencil, still lingered on the verdant mount, leaving rich shadows on the luxuriant vales; the sun still sent forth his bright beams, to revive and cherish the glistening flowers, to whisper of his unfailing love; still did he bid them drink up the dewdrops, which, trembling beneath his earnest gaze, yet sprung up from their homes at his first call, eager to lose themselves in him. Day, in his mirth and light, gave place to silent and shadowy night; and night again to day. Yet man was not there, and wherefore had such loveliness birth?—wherefore was it so continually renewed?

Man would joy in the contemplation of beauty, such as this scene presented; yet his imperfect vision would see no further than mount and vale, and trees and shrubs, and streams and flowers; he would hear nought but the rustle of the leaf, the murmur of the breeze, the music of the brook, the luscious scents floating on the breeze, would be but indistinctly distinguished, and his fancy perchance yearn towards them, and long for perfume more defined, even as we sometimes seek to unite into sweet melody the thrilling notes, which, one by one, at dreamy intervals, linger on the distant air; and these things he would hear, and feel, and see, and dream not there were sights and sounds hovering around him too pure, too spiritual for earthly sense.

There were glorious spirits—angelic beings floating on the ambient air, and lingering beside the waters, and sporting with the jewelled buds. There were rich tones lingering on the breeze—sweet thrilling voices mingling with golden harps and silvery flutes; there were luscious scents ascending to the arching heaven; even as if, guided by ministering spirits, each floweret sent up her grateful incense to the throne of her Creator. As the dazzling flash of the diamond, the softer gleam of the emerald, the radiant beam of the sapphire, the intense rays of the ruby, so shone these beautiful beings, as they fleeted to and fro on their respective tasks. Some replenishing the brooks with living waters from vases which seemed moulded from precious gems. Some tending the flowers, inhaling and bestowing fragrance, or whispering those sweet memories, with which man ever finds the flowers of the desert filled. Some lingering in groups upon the mount, crowning its flowery brow as with a circlet of living rays. Some flying downwards, agitating the valley with soft delicious winds, and others freshening the rich tints of the far-spreading foliage; and far and near their voices sounded in one rich hymn of praise, whose theme was love; and the golden harps prolonged the hallelujahs, sounding up through the blue realms of space, till they mingled with the deeper, mightier harmonies around the Eternal's throne, bearing along its thrilling echo, joined by innumerable voices, till the whole air seemed filled with song, and still that song was Love!

Beautiful as were these celestial spirits—beautiful and blessed above all conception of finite man—yet they were not of the highest class of angels.

Incapable of sin, unconscious of pain or sorrow, but not yet admitted to hover over the dwelling of man, to minister unto the afflicted, to tend the couch of the dying, to whisper of rest to the weary, hope to the desponding, joy to the mourner.

Sensible of the Eternal's presence, their bliss made perfect in His glory, their task was to watch and tend inanimate creation;—to sing His praises amidst the glorious shrines of nature, till His works proclaimed him unto man.

Activity and obedience were the sole virtues demanded of these celestial beings in the tasks above enumerated, and when these had been sufficiently exercised, they graduated to a higher order of angels, nearer the Eternal's throne, who were permitted to receive His will and make it known to man. The desire to obtain this privilege was lively in all, but far removed from that grosser passion known to man as ambition. In them it did but add zest to enjoyment; give energy to love, inspiration to obedience. Faith they needed not; for to them the Eternal was revealed. Anticipation was lost in fulfilment—hope in completion. Their nature was *not* susceptible of a deeper sense of bliss; but as they ascended higher and higher in the scale of angels, the deeper, fuller, more glorious blessedness was met by a nature yet more purified, spiritualized, exalted, fitted for its reception, and strengthened to retain it.

II.

Reposing on a sunbeam lingering on the brow of a hill, a spirit lay, apart from his fellows. His brow was wreathed with the opal, emerald, and ruby; so blending their several rays that they seemed but as a circlet of ever-changing light. His long flowing hair shone as if each clustering ringlet had been bathed in the liquid diamond. His downy wings, woven of every shade, gently waved in air, wafting the richest perfume, and dyeing the sunbeam on which he lay in every brilliant tint. A light mist enveloped his angelic form—softening, not lessening, his resplendent loveliness. His eye shone as the midnight star; a bloom, softer, lovelier, purer than the earliest rose, played on his cheek; sparkling smiles wreathed his lips. He spoke, and his voice was music, though his golden harp lay silent by his side.

"Love! love!" he murmured. "Hallelujah to the Lord of love! Let the full choirs of heaven chant forth the immortal theme; proclaim, proclaim Him Love! Earth!

air! ocean! shout with your hundred tongues, send up your echo to the voice of heaven! Man art thou insensible?—Hearest thou not these living tones? Can doubt be thine, as I have heard whispered in the celestial courts? Created by Love—placed in a world of love—distant as thou art, yet cherished and beloved by Love, destined for immortal union with the Love that gave thee being!—canst thou be faithless, canst thou be senseless?—when above, below, around, within, soundeth the deep eternal voice of Love! Oh, insensates, if such things be! Immortal glory, bliss unfading, can it be for ye?"

Awhile he paused. A slight shadow passed athwart the brilliant rays with which he was encircled. He folded his wings around him, and laid his brow upon them.

"My thought has been rebuked," he said; "I have done ill. Enough for me the consciousness of love. Wherefore should I condemn, as yet unworthy to look on man? Let the hallelujahs sound forth again. Glory to the Eternal!—His works are wisdom. His thoughts are love!"

He swept his hand across his harp—the shadow had departed from his wings;—his chaplet shot forth again its living light. Celestial music flowed forth from his voice and hand:—the spirit smiled once more. Suddenly the hallelujahs ceased. To the eye of man twilight had descended; the stars began to light up the dark blue heavens. Mortal vision might trace the semblance of a falling meteor of unwonted brilliance dropping into space. The purified orbs of the seraph crowd knew that one of the highest class of angels was departing from his replendent seat, and winging his flight towards them. Instantly they rose up from their several resting-places, forming in files of unutterable brilliance. Increased happiness shed a new lustre on their brows, and heightened the glowing iris of their wings. One alone felt penetrated with an awe, which slightly lessened the feelings of joy which the visit of an angel ever caused. He feared it was to him the celestial mission came: that his condemnation of beings, whose nature and whose trials he knew not, had exposed him to censure, perhaps to a longer banishment from the higher spheres of glory; and while his brothers thronged round the favoured minister, to bask in the resplendent brightness of his smiles, to list to the words of melody flowing from his lips, to gaze on the mild yet thrilling softness of his celestial features, Zephon stood aloof, for the first time shrinking from the glance and voice he loved.

He saw not that the glittering helm and dazzling sword were laid aside, that his brow was wreathed with the softly gleaming pearl, his shining wings glistening through silvery radiance, bespeaking tenderness and mercy, and not now the wrath and chastisement of which, at his Maker's will, he was at times the minister.

His voice, melodious and thrilling as the silver trumpets of the empyreal heavens, sounded through space, as it called "Zephon!" The seraph paused not a moment, but darting through the incensed air, prostrated himself at the archangel's feet.

"Arise! and fear not, youthful brother," spake the messenger of the Eternal, departing not from the grave majesty of his demeanour, but smiling with such ineffable sweetness, the seraph felt its reviving influence, and spread forth his silken pinions rejoicingly again. "I come, the harbinger of peace and love. Thine impassioned zeal was checked ere it became a fault—checked ere it led thee to desire forbidden knowledge. Charged with a message of love and mercy from the Most High, I have besought and obtained permission to take thee as my companion. To thine imperfect vision, it seemeth strange that man, so especially the beloved, the cherished of the Eternal, framed to display, to uphold His stupendous power, to proclaim His might—His love—should ever fail either in obedience or adoration. Thou hast heard that such has been; for where sin hath so fearfully prevailed, that an immortal spirit has been excluded from these glorious realms, a dim shadow hath spread over Heaven's resplendent courts, and the celestial spirits of every rank have prostrated themselves before the invisible yet terrible Presence, adoring justice, while they supplicated mercy. Zephon! not yet may be revealed to thee the glorious mystery of the Eternal's secret ways. Thou mayst gaze with me on the earthly beings I have charge to tend; but it is forbidden thee to ask or seek the wherefore of what thou seest. Thou wilt behold even in this limited glance, enough to prove, that even if the human heart refuseth to send up its thrilling echo to the theme of Love, which thy zeal demandeth, the unfathomable love of its benignant Creator will receive and bless its faintest sigh; for to Him, and to Him alone, is known the *extent* of its trial—the bitterness of its grief—the difficulty of its belief in an ever-acting love. Zephon! if still thou wilt, thou shalt look on the human heart: yet pause awhile;—is thy love sufficiently strong to uphold thee in the contemplation of decrees, whose motives thou art not yet permitted to conceive? In thy blissful dwelling, thou hast no need of Faith; thou knowest not even its name; but if with me thou goest, Faith must be thy safeguard. Here thine eye seeth, thine ear heareth nought but love; there it may be darkly hidden from thee. Yet if thy faith or thy love should fail, if thou demandest the wherefore of what thou seest, it is our Father's will, that thou shalt be banished unto earth—banished from this glorious abode, condemned to struggle with the ills and sorrows of mortality, till pure and perfect faith shine forth, and fit thee once again for heaven. Speak, then, my brother; wilt thou depart with me, or still linger here? The choice is now thine own."

Awhile the seraph paused; the face of the archangel beamed on him with compassionating tenderness and redoubled love. The looks of his brother spirits, the soft fluttering of their wings, seemed to woo him to remain, to entreat him not to tempt the fate threatened if his love should fail, and therefore did he pause.

"No, no! wherefore should I fear?" he cried; "I will go with thee, minister of love. I will look upon my Father's dearest work, and despite of mystery and gloom—of sorrow—of pain, I will love and bless him still!"

A fuller, richer burst of melody filled the realms of air; thousands and thousands of voices swelled forth in triumphant harmony. A starry cloud descended, and, folded in its spangled robe, the departing spirits vanished into space.

III.

"Thy wish is fulfilled; the peculiar treasure of our Father is revealed. Zephon, behold!" the angel spake, as the shrouding cloud rolled away towards the fields of ether, and the celestial spirits hovered over the abode of man. A sudden, an indescribable consciousness of increased powers, of heightened intellect, shot from the starry eyes of the youthful seraph. Man in his majesty, his beauty—bearing in his every movement, his exquisitely-formed frame, his complicated economy of being, yet more impressive, more startling evidence of the might, the wisdom, the benevolence of his glorious Maker, than even the source of the river, the structure of the flower, the growth of the tree, over which the seraph had presided, finding even in such things ample scope for the soaring intellect which characterised his race. Man, proceeding from, destined for, immortality—the beloved, the peculiar care and treasure of the Eternal—man, beautiful man, stood revealed before him. Yet amidst the thronging multitude on which he gazed, but *one* HEART, in all its varied impulses, its hidden throbs and incongruous thoughts and ever-changing fancies—but one beautiful intellect, in all its secret powers and extent, was open to his inspection; and lovely, even to the eyes of a spirit, was the being in whom such glorious things were shrined.

She was a young and noble maiden, perfect in form and face; her virtues scarce sullied by a stain of earth, although, from the spirit of Poetry, the living fount of Genius, dwelling within, open to grief and trial, even from the faintest breath too rudely jarring on the heavenly-strung chords with which her heart was filled. A deep, lowly, clinging piety was ever ready to check the first impulse of impatience, to turn to the sweet joys of sympathy and universal love the too vivid sense of sorrow either for herself or others. Humility was there, to lift up that young spirit in thankfulness to its Creator, and to devote that powerful intellect, ever seeming to bear all difficulties before it, to His service in the good of her fellow-creatures.

Zephon saw that the praise of man was a source of pure, inspiring pleasure; but instead of filling her soul with pride, it ever bore it up in increased devotion to its God. He marked her graceful form, sporting to and fro amid the stately domains of her lordly ancestors. He marked the love of parents, brothers, friends, that ever thronged around her, and the fulness of joy that love bestowed. He saw, too, the impassioned longings for yet stronger love, the yearnings for fame; appreciation, not alone from the noble and the gay, but from the gifted and the good; the desire to awake, by the magic touch of genius, the same thrilling chords in other hearts, as the spell of others had revealed in hers.

The seraph looked long and earnestly. Suddenly he saw her standing in the centre of a lordly room, and loving and admiring friends around her; her lip, her eye, her heart breathed joy, well-nigh as full and shadowless as the blessedness of heaven. After awhile the angel spake.

"There is nought here to call for Faith," he said. "Yon favoured child of genius but awakens deeper yet more adoring love. Her lot *is* blessedness; her heart so pure, earth hath scarce power to stain that bliss. But now look yonder, Zephon. Seest thou amidst the multitude a being equally, though differently lovely—equally powerful in intellect, equally the child of genius, as richly gifted, alike in wisdom as in virtue, as fully susceptible of joy and sorrow; the same feelings, the same desires, the same deep yearnings for love on which to rest, for appreciation, fame; the same strung heart, thrilling to melody as keenly as to neglect. Mark well, young brother, and thou wilt trace these things."

Anxiously the seraph gazed, and again he was conscious of sufficient power to read the human heart. Again, amidst the multitude, one gentle being stood unveiled before him; and, save for the difference in form and face, he had thought perchance it was the same on whom he had gazed before, so similar were their virtues, powers, temperament, and genius;—similar in all things, save that the sense of bliss in the one already appeared more chastened, more timid than in the other. He looked, then turned inquiringly towards his companion.

"The will of the Eternal," he said, in answer, "produced at the same instant these lovely beings, and breathed into both the spirit which thou seest. Their souls are TWIN-BORN—twin-born in sensation, in power, in beauty, formed of the highest, most ethereal essence, and thus creating that which earth terms genius; destined at the same moment to animate the beautiful habitation formed for each, and at the same moment depart from it. Until now, their fate hath been, with little variation, the same, differing only according to their station; the one standing amidst the highest and noblest of her land, findeth fit companions for that nobleness and refinement indivisible from genius; the other already feeleth there is that within her incomprehensible to those around her; yet is the consciousness of little moment, for freely and joyously she roams amid the varied scenes of nature. She mingles but with those eager and anxious to enhance her innocent pleasures—to give to her exalted mind and gentle virtues the homage naturally their due. She looks on the world from a distance, and hath peopled it with all things fond, and bright, and beautiful, which take their exquisite colouring from her own lovely and loving mind. She yearns for appreciation, as thou seest—for the praise of the multitude won by her talents, but she asks not to mingle with them. She seeks but the love of one, and the proud consciousness of doing good to many. She demands not a statelier home, a prouder station. Thus, then, thou seest the earthly fate of these twin-born spirits hath rolled on the same; but now it is the will of the All-wise, All-merciful, All-just, that a shadowy change should pass over the one, and bliss, fuller, dearer, perfect as earth may feel, be dawning for the other. Thou hast marked the quick throb of joy now playing on the heart of the noble child of genius. She beholds her first triumph in the book she clasps. The thoughts that breathe, the words that burn, have found their echo in the multitude, and loving friends throng around to proclaim her dawning fame. There are tears in those lovely eyes; but 'tis a mother's voice of love, of tenderness, that calls them there. See, clasped to a parent's bosom, the swelling fulness of the spirit finds vent in tears, for joy, that pure, stainless joy, which is sent as the dim whisperings of heaven, ever turns to pain on earth, and had it not relief in tears, would bear the soul away to that world of which it speaks. She hath flown from the detaining throng, and hark!—hearest thou not the hymn of thanksgiving ascending up on high, till the tumultuous joy subsides, and peace is gained once more?"

He ceased; a brighter radiance passed over his benignant brow, and the voice of the seraph spontaneously flowed forth in kindred harmony with the hymn of earth, bearing it on the wings of melody to the realms of song. 'Twas hushed, and the Hierarch again spake.

"Behold!" he said, the music of his voice subdued and softened, "behold, yet murmur not! It is the will of the Eternal, and therefore it is well."

The seraph gazed on a changed and darkened scene. As deep, as full as was the bliss from which his eye had that moment turned, so deep, so intense was the anguish he now beheld. The gentle being in whom that twin-born spirit breathed, knelt beside the couch of the dead. He marked the wrung and bleeding heart; he read its utter loneliness, its agonized despair; he read it was a mother's loss she mourned—a more than mother, for by her, by her alone, her child's ethereal soul, her fond imaginings, her strong affections, had been known, and loved, and fostered; to her, her beautiful had ever come, to seek and find that sympathy which she found not in another—and she was gone, and the dark troubled strivings of that desolate heart not yet could deem it love.

"She weeps, and shall we condemn, young brother, that not yet her voice may join in the universal hymn? She weeps, yet knows not all her woe. The stability, the honour, the strength of her father were derived from the mild counsels, the gentle unobtrusive virtues of her mother; in him they have no stay. That moral evil, too darkly prevalent on earth, once more will gain dominion, and the joys of the innocent, the helpless, are blighted 'neath its poison. On earth she stands alone—yet hark! What means that burst of triumph in the skies?"

Ineffably brilliant was the smile on the countenance of the angel; and Zephon, startled, yet entranced, looked again on that bleeding heart. The dark and troubled waves within were stilled; there was no voice—no sign; but the lamp of faith was lit; her soul had murmured Love; and bowed, adoring and resigned.

IV.

Again did the youthful spirit gaze down on earthly joy, chastened in its fulness, yet ecstatic in its nature. Love, pure, perfect, faithful love, had twined around that fair and gifted child of earth, and filled the blank which yet remained; though fame, appreciation, triumph, sympathy, affection, all were hers. She had found a kindred soul, round which to weave the clinging tendrils of her own; virtues to revere, piety to support, uphold, and cherish the soarings of her own. She had found one whose praise might still those passionate yearnings, the which to satisfy she had vainly looked to fame; one, from whose lips how sweet became the praise of the world;—one to give new zest to her exalted genius; for by him it was most valued, most beloved. Zephon looked on the beautiful blossoming of genius, the expansion of intellect, the flowering of every budding hope; and he saw, too, the chastened humility, the unwavering love, which traced these rich gifts to their source, and lifted up her heart in universal love and grateful adoration; and again his voice joined hers in thanksgiving.

Once more, at the voice of the archangel, he sought and found the kindred essence, and love was on that heart, deep, mighty, whelming love, bearing before it for awhile even the sere and withered leaves, with which its depths were strewed.

He looked on the wreck of that which he had seen so lovely —the wreck of all save the gentle virtues, the meek submission which had characterised her youth; the rosy dreams, the glowing visions presented but a crushed and broken mass; their bright fragments seeking ever to unite, but ever rudely severed. Genius, in its deep wild burnings, its impassioned breathing, feeding as a smothered fire upon her own young heart, seeking ever to find a vent, an echo—to be known, acknowledged, loved; but falling back with every effort, till even genius seemed increase of sorrow—and hope yet glimmered there, pale, sickly, shadowy, in its faint rays emitting but increase of light, to be immersed in deeper gloom. And love was there, intense, all-mighty, yet it brought no joy.

"She loves—she was beloved," again spake the angelic voice; "but the sin of the father is visited upon the child. A little while he appeared devoted unto her, and to the memory of the departed; and though he led her from the scenes she loved, to mingle more closely with the world, his affection soothed, his hopes inspired; but he knew not the ethereal nature of that soul, and the scenes which earth terms gay and joyous touched no answering chord in *her*, and led *him* once again astray. Yet, for a brief while, happiness was hers, banishing those vain yearnings, ever proceeding from a soul too sensitive for earth; but the same hour which awoke her to a consciousness of love, given and returned, turned back that fountain of bliss upon her seared and withered heart, and changed it into gall. The child of a dishonoured parent was no fit mate for nobleness and honour, and earth is lone once more."

Tears, the sweet bright tears that angels weep, bedewed the eyes of the seraph; yet riveted their gaze on that one sad child of earth, as if in its dark and troubled chaos there were yet more to read. He saw, too, the slight and beautiful shell in which that spirit was enshrined quivering beneath the tempest, till at length it lay prostrate and unhinged, and intense bodily suffering heightened mental ill.

"'Tis the struggle for submission and resignation that hath done this," continued the angel. "Seest thou no dream of unbelief, no murmur of complaint hath entered that heart; anguish may wither up the swelling hymn, may check the voice of love, but faith is *there!* And mark! though, in His unquestionable wisdom, the Eternal's will is to afflict, though in impenetrable darkness, save to those beside His throne, He hideth the secret wherefore of that will, invisibly His ministers are charged to hover round His favoured child, to comfort and sustain, though lone and desolate on earth. Behold!"

Bright, beautiful spirits, robed in light and glory, hovered round the couch of sorrow; yet earth hid them from their kindred essence. She saw them not; felt not the mild reviving influence of their spiritual presence, save that gradually and slowly the chains which bound those beautiful limbs were loosed. The whirlwind sweeping over that heart subsided into partial calm; and strength was given her to struggle on and live.

Zephon looked on the child of sorrow, and a faint shadow stole over the brilliant iris of his wings; the living rays on his brow grew dim.

V.

Again did the seraph look down on earth, again did he gaze on the favoured child of joy. The ecstatic sense of bliss he had marked before had subsided into happiness as full, as pure, as thrilling, yet chastened in its fulness. There were young and lovely forms around her; a mother's love had added its unutterable sweetness to her lot. He looked on her heart, and marked how sweetly and beautifully its every dream, its every hope, had bloomed to full maturity. How softly its light cares were soothed by sympathy and love on earth, and trust and hope in heaven; how earnestly it sought to pour back its every gift into the gracious hand from which it sprung, and lead her children as herself, to the threshold of Eternal joy. He looked on that unveiled heart, as, wandering with those she loved amid the glorious shrines of nature, she found in every leaf, and stream, and bird, and flower somewhat to bid her children love, and add to the inexhaustible spring of poesie and genius which rested still within, and gave new zest, new brightness to her simplest joy.

He gazed on her alone, amidst the books she loved, the studies her genius craved; he read the deep, pure, shadowless joy it was to feel that gift had done its work, and sent its pure and lucid flame amidst the unthinking crowd, and carried blessings with it; that its rich music had left its impression on many a thoughtless heart: had shed sweet balm over hours of sad, lonely sickness; had spoken its soft sympathy to the diseased and sorrowing mind, and sent new, brighter, purer joyance to the young. eager, and imaginative soul. It had done these things, and was it marvel she rejoiced ?

Zephon gazed ; but the shadow passed not from his wings, and hastily and silently he turned once more to seek the kindred essence. The whelming woe had given place to a strangely complicated mass of cross and twisted strings, which tightly fettered down each glorious gift, each cherished hope, each fond aspiring, yet gave them space to throb, and live, and whisper still. The bright undying flame of genius never seemed to burn with more o'er-sweeping power ; yet the flashes that it sent but scorched the heart that held them. Hope still was there, sending forth her lovely blossoms ; but to be nipped and blighted 'neath the close and icy strings that stretched above them. There were chains upon that spirit, binding it to earth, when most it longed to spring on high ; and the shell, the lovely shell which held it was dwindling 'neath its withering spell. The seraph marked the tension of each vein and nerve, and pulse, till it seemed as if the very next breath of emotion, however faint, would snap them in twain ; the painful effort to restrain the irritation of bodily and mental suffering, the agony of remorse which the slightest ebullition of impatience caused.

He beheld her hour by hour, the centre of a noisy group of children, possessing not one attribute to call forth that torrent of love and tenderness with which her soul was filled. He marked the starting of each nerve, the bounding of each pulse, at every shout of rude and noisy revelry, the inward fever attending every effort to restrain and instruct. He saw her, when midnight enwrapt the earth, alone for a brief space, in a poor and comfortless room ; the bright visions of genius thronging tumultuously on mind and brain ; incongruous and wild, from their having been so long pent up in darkness, and woe. He beheld the effort to give the burning fancies vent ; the utter failing of the mortal frame ; the prostration of all power, save that which yet would lift up heart and hands in the low cry : "Father, it is thy will ; I know not wherefore ; yet, oh ! yet, if Thou willest it, it is, it must be well !" and he heard unnumbered harps bear up that voice of Faith, in melody overpowering in its deep rich tones. He marked the spirits of light and loveliness still hovering around, moulding those burning tears into precious gems, changing each quivering sigh to songs of glory ; yet still his sight seemed strangely dim, the shadow passed not from his wings.

"And man, her brother man, hath he no love, no tenderness, no thoughts for sorrow such as hers?" the seraph asked; "knows he not of the precious gifts, the gentle virtues that frail shell enfolds? Wherefore is she thus lone?—hath man no answering chord?"

"Man sees not the interior of that heart, as thou dost," rejoined the Hierarch. "When through disobedience sin entered yon beautiful world, man's eyes became darkened towards his fellows, and but too often his rebellious and perverted mind wilfully refuses knowledge of his brother, lest sympathy should bid him share the grief of others. In some envy, foul envy, the base passion which first darkened earth with death, wilfully blinds, lest the genius and the virtue of the *poor* should be exhalted above the rich; in others it is ignorance, contempt, neglect, springing from that rank poison selfishness, or the loathsome weed indifference, which flings a thick veil over others' woe, and so confines the gaze—it sees no farther than itself. To mortal vision yon gentle being is composed and calm. Man marks but the outward frame; love alone might trace the decline of strength, the failing of bodily power; but there is none near to love. Poverty hath flung those chains upon the heart, confining the ethereal spirit, dragging it down to earth, yet deadening not its power. Poverty, privation, have thrown her amongst those whose grosser, more material natures are incapable of appreciating the heavenly rays of genius; of comprehending its effect upon the temperament and the frame. They deem her lot a happy one, for they cannot know how much more she needs—what cause she has for sorrow. They would laugh in bitter scorn at those griefs which have their birth in *feeling*, whose intensity, whose depth of suffering are to them utterly unknown. No! man may not alleviate woes like hers. In the dark circle her fate is fixed; earth, mortal fading earth, is all; they have no time for dreams and thoughts of heaven. A spirit like to hers, bearing on its brow a stamp of glory not its own. Alas! my brother, man will not mark such things. Sin, foul sin, hath dimmed its gaze"

The seraph folded his beautiful wings around him. There was a strange dim sense of pain upon him, undefined yet sad, as the first clouding of mortal vision unto man, ere sight departs for ever. When he looked forth again, the scene was changed, and it was bright and beautiful, though death was there.

The blessed, the loved, the cherished!—she lay there, calm, yet rejoicing,—though the loved around her wept. Recalled to its native home, ere age or sorrow dimmed the spirit's glory; joyfully, willingly, she heard the call, for death had no pang for her. She knew she parted from her beloved to meet again, "where never sounds farewell." She knew she was departing to that blissful bourne, whose glorious light had beamed so softly and beautifully on her earthly course, gilding MORTAL happiness with IMMORTAL glory; to that goal, where each bright gift would be made perfect, her finite wisdom find completion in infinity. Still, still the comfort of her voice consoled the hearts that wept around; her lip yet sent forth gentle words to soothe and bless when she was gone; the mind, the beautiful mind, yet shone in all its living light—death had no power to dim its lustre. Brighter and brighter gleamed the departing soul; and thoughts, sweet thoughts, came thronging on that heart, of duties done, of life that sought but good, of universal love, benevolence, and peace; and blessings of the poor, the needy, and the sorrowing hovered round her as angels robed in light. Joy! joy! oh, still was that gentle spirit wreathed in joy, — the grave had lost its sting, and death was swallowed up in victory!

Irresistibly and rapidly the seraph sought the twin-born spirit,—which, at the same hour, was to wing her flight from earth. There were none to weep around her couch of loneliness and pain; but one, a kind and lowly hireling, was near to mark that spirit's parting pang, to smooth the pillow, and whisper of repose. No sign of luxury was there, no gentle hand, with luscious fruit or cooling draught, to tempt the fevered lip, the parched and tasteless tongue. Dark, close, confined, the chamber of the dying—but a few pale flowers, children of field and brook, alone stood beside her, to whisper 'twas a poet's dying home. Save that, perchance, the treasured volumes still around, disclosed that the mind was bright, and strong, and lovely still. Her thin hand still clasped a book, her eyes lit up as they gazed upon the page, and for a brief space her cheek shone with a bloom that scarce could seem of death. Zephon looked within the heart and started. Hope gleamed up amidst its crushed and broken chords; hope, aye, and one bright flash of joy darting forth as a sunbeam midst the shrouding mass of clouds, and momentary, coeval with that joy, the wish, fond wish to live.

"Start not, my brother!" the thrilling accents of the angel once more spake. "She gazes on her own fond dreams, her own pure visions; she clasps their record in the volume that she holds. Acknowledged, sought, appreciated; her genius has burst through the veil of obscurity and woe, and fame, undying fame, hath wreathed his laurels to adorn the dead. Man will weep upon her grave, will wreathe her name with glory, will reverence too late the genius that hath gone, —and therefore would she live. It is the last struggle, the last pang,—the spirit is too pure, too free, to fold too long the chain which earth holds forth, even though its links are joy. Behold!"

The seraph looked once more. There had been a struggle —a brief and anguished pang; joy and hope lay crushed for ever, beneath the sickening consciousness; 'twas all too late, and she must die! There came one murmuring doubt, one painful question—wherefore she was thus called away, when earth gave promise of such sweet reviving flowers? And darkness spread forth her pall, and shrouded up that heart, but speedily it passed; a soft and mellowed light gleamed up; the blackened shade rolled up and fled; the ruin and its chains were gone, and PEACE, and FAITH, and JOY twined hand in hand together.

VI.

Zephon looked not on the abodes of man. The Hierarch alone stood before him, surrounded by a blaze of glory. Ineffable brilliance shone forth from his brow and wings, yet softened into compassionating tenderness was his radiant look, his thrilling voice. A trembling awe spread over the seraph, and involuntarily he bowed before him.

"Thy will is accomplished, youthful brother, thou hast glanced on man," spake the angelic voice; "yet know, that which thou hast seen is but as a single grain amid the spreading sands of the boundless desert; as a single spark of earthly fire amid the countless stars and blazing suns of heaven, compared with the scenes of woe yon world of beauty holds. When Sin entered, Joy fled trembling up to the heaven whence he came. Twined as he was with purity and innocence, without them earth could have for him no stay, no resting; man reaps the fruit he sows,—for not in a guilty world may the Eternal mark the distinction between the righteous and the wicked. In that which thou hast seen there was no guilt, no sin. Twin-born in purity as in their high ethereal essence, yet, from the imperfection of earth, so widely severed their mortal fates, so strangely parted, if such things are, is't marvel that the hymn of love, of praise, from lips of man should be so faint and weak? Zephon, thou hast looked on earth; thou hast marked the dealings of our Father with His children. Speak then, my brother, oh, speak! will the song of joy, of adoration, still flow from thy lips—still, still canst thou proclaim Him Love?"

The harps of heaven were stilled. The invisible choirs hushed their full tide of song. Darker and darker, for a brief space, became the shadow around the youthful seraph, and his radiant brow was buried in its shrouding folds. Deep, awful was that momentary pause, for it seemed as if the hosts of heaven themselves were hushed in sympathy and dread.

A sudden flood of dazzling effulgence burst through the gloomy shade, dispersing it as a thin vapour on either side. Beams of living lustre illumined that glorious brow, and in liquid music his voice flowed forth.

"Shall I be less than mortal—I, who serve my Father amidst His chosen choirs, who knew Him, unobstructed by the veil of earth? Let the full song burst forth; let the bright seraphim strike the bold harps again; let the rich hymn swell out in deeper glory; hallelujah to our Father and our King! His ways are dark, but His will is love! Praise Him, ye myriads of angels; praise Him, ye heaven of heavens; proclaim, proclaim Him love! His ways are pleasantness, His paths are peace. Praise Him, ye glorious hosts—hallelujah, He is Love."

VII.

There was rejoicing amidst the heavenly choirs, rejoicing amidst the seraph band; for a bright and beautiful spirit, whose lot, even on earth, was joy, released from mortal chains, had joined their glittering files. Wafted from earth amidst strains of glory, lifting up her voice with theirs in thanksgiving, and consummating, in the centre of that glorious band, the hymn of beauty and of love commenced on earth.

There was rejoicing amid the angelic choirs, beside the shrouding veil, which softened even from their purified orbs the transcendant glory of their Father's throne—rejoicing amidst the archangelic choirs; for a bright and beautiful spirit, whose earthly doom had been shrouded in the impenetrable mists of darkness and woe, was wafted towards them on a golden cloud, amid a rich burst of glad triumphant harmony, rejoicing!—for mystery and gloom were removed from a child of God, and unsealed for her the secret of his ways.

There was rejoicing in the angelic hosts,—rejoicing through the central choirs,—for a youthful seraph, springing up on the bright wings of faith and love, had joined their glittering files, and songs of joy and melody encircled him, rejoicing!—above, below, within, till each resplendent court of heaven darted forth rays of inexpressible brilliance, and the whole universe of space, peopled with its myriads of angelic and archangelic spirits, sent forth its mighty depths of harmony, its thrilling voice of song; and still, oh still, its theme was Love!—Eternal, changeless, unfathomable Love!

THE END.

www.ingramcontent.com/pod-product-compliance
Lightning Source LLC
LaVergne TN
LVHW020104110826
845151LV00001B/60

* 9 7 8 1 4 2 5 5 4 4 6 4 5 *